THE ASSOCIATION FOR SCOTTISH LITERARY STUDIES

ALLAN CUNNINGHAM

TRADITIONAL TALES

*

THE ASSOCIATION FOR SCOTTISH LITERARY STUDIES

The Association for Scottish Literary Studies aims to promote the study, teaching and writing of Scottish literature, and to further the study of the languages of Scotland.

To these ends, the ASLS publishes works of Scottish literature (of which this volume is an example); literary criticism and in-depth reviews of Scottish books in *Scottish Literary Review*; short articles, features and news in *ScotLit*; and scholarly studies of language in *Scottish Language*. It also publishes *New Writing Scotland*, an annual anthology of new poetry, drama and short fiction, in Scots, English and Gaelic. ASLS has also prepared a range of teaching materials covering Scottish language and literature for use in schools.

All the above publications are available as a single 'package', in return for an annual subscription. Enquiries should be sent to:

ASLS, Scottish Literature, 7 University Gardens, University of Glasgow, Glasgow G12 8QH. Telephone/fax+44 (0)141 330 5309 or visit our website at **www.asls.org.uk**

A list of Annual Volumes published by ASLS can be found at the end of this book.

THE ASSOCIATION FOR SCOTTISH LITERARY STUDIES

ALLAN CUNNINGHAM

TRADITIONAL TALES OF THE ENGLISH AND SCOTTISH PEASANTRY

Edited by

TIM KILLICK

GLASGOW

2012

Published in Great Britain, 2012
by The Association for Scottish Literary Studies
Scottish Literature
University of Glasgow
7 University Gardens
Glasgow G12 8QH

ASLS is a registered charity no. SC006535

www.asls.org.uk

ISBN: 978-1-906841-08-9

A catalogue record for this book
is available from the British Library.

The Association for Scottish Literary Studies acknowledges
support from Creative Scotland towards
the publication of this book.

Typeset by AFS Image Setters Ltd, Glasgow
Printed and bound by Bell & Bain Ltd, Glasgow

Contents

Acknowledgements

I would like to thank the editors at ASLS for their help and support in the production of this volume. Particular thanks go to Duncan Jones, for his advice, professionalism and efficiency. I am also extremely grateful to folk musicians Geordie McIntyre and Alison McMorland, who very kindly provided the benefit of their exceptional knowledge of traditional Scottish songs and ballads to advise on the origins of the poetry contained in Cunningham's stories.

Editing *Traditional Tales of the English and Scottish Peasantry* would not have been possible without the support of my wife, Sonia, and this book is dedicated to her.

INTRODUCTION

Allan, true child of Scotland; thou who art
So oft in spirit on thy native hills,
And yonder Solway shores, a poet thou.

Robert Southey, 'Epistle to Allan Cunningham' (1828)

The Life and Works of Allan Cunningham

Allan Cunningham's origins were humble. He was born on the 7th of December, 1784, in the parish of Keir, Dumfries-shire, and like many of the poets and tale-tellers who began to produce printed literature based on Scottish popular ballads and folklore from the mid-eighteenth century, he came from a rural, agrarian background. At the time of his birth, Cunningham's father worked as factor (farm manager) for a Mr Cope-land of Blackwood, and for the first years of his life the family lived in a cottage in the grounds of Blackwood House. Cunningham's parents, John and Elizabeth, had nine children in all: five sons and two daughters. Allan was the fourth son, and his early childhood was spent moving between various farms and smallholdings in the Dumfriesshire region, as his father's work dictated.

Cunningham attended the village Dame-School at Quarrel-wood, where he quickly gained a reputation for skilfully improvising ballads, and for a streak of irreverence which often manifested itself in practical jokes. At the age of eleven, he was apprenticed as a stonemason with his elder brother, John, at the nearby village of Dalswinton. Cunningham worked as a mason until his mid-twenties, during which time he moved around Dumfriesshire. In 1809, while engaged on a job at Arbigland, on the Galloway side of the Solway Firth, he met and fell in love with Jean Walker, his future wife, for whom he wrote one of his best-known ballads, 'The Lass of Preston Mill'.

In his spare time, Cunningham indulged his passion for the songs and ballads of the region, committing many of them to memory. He also began composing his own poetry and reciting variants on traditional or popular airs. Encouraged by the success of his compositions at regional gatherings, and keen to become a published author, Cunningham sent some of his early poems to *Literary Recreations*, a London periodical. The editor, Eugenius Roche, responded enthusiastically to Cunningham's work and in total the magazine published twenty-three of his submissions between 1806 and 1808; under the pseudonym 'Hidallan' (one of the heroes of Ossian).[1]

As a keen student of Scottish literature, Cunningham was willing to go to great lengths to make connections with other writers. Along with another of his brothers, James, he once walked from Dalswinton to Mitchelslacks Farm, in Closeburn, to meet James Hogg, the Scottish poet and tale-writer, known colloquially as the Ettrick Shepherd. In his *Reminiscences of Former Days*, Hogg recalls the meeting with fondness: 'From that moment we were friends; for Allan has none of the proverbial Scottish caution about him; he is all heart together, without reserve either of expression or manner: you at once see the unaffected benevolence, warmth of feeling, and firm independence, of a man conscious of his own rectitude and mental energies.'[2]

On another occasion, after reading *Marmion*, Cunningham reportedly travelled the seventy-odd miles from Dalswinton to Edinburgh on foot to catch a glimpse of Walter Scott, after which feat he immediately commenced his long journey back. Yet another connection was made with Robert Burns, who spent some of his final years at Ellisland Farm, across the Nith from Sandbeds, where Cunningham was living. Cunningham, who was only a boy, claimed to have heard Burns recite 'Tam O'Shanter' in his father's cottage, and to have walked in Burns's funeral procession.

In 1809, Cunningham met R. H. Cromek—an antiquarian on a visit to Scotland from London to collect material for an edition of Scots songs. Cromek reportedly gave a lukewarm reception to some of Cunningham's poems, whereupon Allan hit upon the trick of passing some of his own work off as traditional material. Cromek was delighted and asked for more. Whether or not Cromek was aware of the duplicity is unknown, but the end result of the exchange was *Remains of Nithsdale and Galloway Song*, published by John Murray in 1810. Ostensibly, this was a volume of traditional ballads collected and edited by Cromek, with some assistance from

Cunningham. In fact, it contained several lengthy essays by Cunningham, as well as many of his own compositions. In later correspondence, Cunningham admitted to writing at least half the songs, and may have been responsible for expanding many more from scraps and fragments.[3] Despite the fact that Cromek's name appeared on the title-page, Cunningham felt that the *Remains* was largely his creation, and he enjoyed its success on publication. He wrote to his brother: 'The thing which pleases me in it, every article but two little scraps was contributed by me, both poetry and prose'.[4] Contemporary critics, including James Hogg, immediately cast doubt on the authenticity of some of the songs in the *Remains*, and the precise status of the collection remains unclear; however, Cunningham's part in the *Remains* controversy is certainly an early indicator of the predilection for blurring the boundaries between traditional material and original composition that he shows in *Traditional Tales* and other later works.

Cunningham moved to London in 1810, hoping to build on his early success and pursue a career as a writer. For the first few years he scraped a living. His masonry skills earned him a job assisting a sculptor, and he continued to write poetry for magazines including the *Day*, the *Scots Magazine* and the *Literary Gazette*, as well as working as a parliamentary reporter. During this time, Jean Walker joined Cunningham in London, and the couple were married in 1811. They settled permanently in London, where they brought up their six children.

A friendship with the sculptor Francis Chantrey led to the engagement of Cunningham as his secretary in 1814, a position which allowed Cunningham more time to write. The first collection of his own verse, *Songs: Chiefly in the Rural Language of Scotland*, was published at his own expense in 1813. Further contributions to the periodical press followed, beginning with a series of tales for *Blackwood's Edinburgh Magazine* in 1819, before moving to the *London Magazine*. Cunningham continued producing material for the *London* until 1824, during which time the materials that would go to make up *Traditional Tales of the English and Scottish Peasantry* were published.

The 1820s were Cunningham's most productive decade. *Traditional Tales* appeared in 1822, as did the drama *Sir Marmaduke Maxwell*, published in a volume along with twenty-two new poems. In 1825, Cunningham published *The Songs of Scotland, Ancient and Modern*. This four-volume collection brought together versions of traditional ballads with poems by eighteenth- and nineteenth-century writers, including Allan Ramsay, Burns and Cunningham himself. This ambitious editorial project had been a longstanding ambition, and Cunningham approached it with a degree of rigour that contrasts with the more cavalier attitude towards ballad-collecting he displayed in the production of the *Remains*. Nonetheless, he remained more than happy to leave his own mark on the traditional literature that passed through his hands.

Discussing the status of the poetry included in *Songs of Scotland*, Sigurd Bernhard Hustvedt summarises Cunningham's attitude:

> Cunningham was not the scholar, to distinguish painfully a narrative ballad from a lyric; to him they were all songs. Those which had a fixed form attached to some known poet he left pretty much unmolested; those that were not so circumstanced he treated as a sculptor treats modelling clay.[5]

For Cunningham, the act of re-composing oral material was never at odds with the desire for scholarly preservation. He saw himself always as both a writer and a collector, and his fascination with traditional literature fed into his original compositions.

Cunningham's last major poem, *The Maid of Elvar, a Poem, in Twelve Parts*, was published in 1832. As well as verse, drama and tales, Cunningham also attempted longer fictional forms, and produced a run of historical romances: *Paul Jones* (1826), *Sir Michael Scott* (1828) and *Lord Roldan* (1836). He was also the editor of *The Anniversary* for 1829, one of the popular miscellaneous gift-books published for the Christmas market. Cunningham continued to write songs and tales for the magazines throughout his life—as late as 1840 he began a series of nine stories for *Fraser's Magazine*, titled 'Rustic Controversies'. Towards the end of the 1820s, however, his primary focus shifted from poetry and fiction to biography, history and criticism.

Between 1830 and 1834, he produced a series of retrospective essays, 'Biographical and Critical History of the Literature of the Last Fifty Years', for the *Athenaeum*. He also published his *Lives of the Most Eminent British Painters, Sculptors, and Architects* in six volumes between 1829 and 1833. *Lives of the Painters* became one of Cunningham's most popular works, and was reproduced in various editions across the nineteenth century. He continued with biographical writing through the 1830s: his eight-volume *Works of Robert Burns; with his Life* came out in 1834, and his final major project was the unfinished *Life of Sir David Wilkie*, the Scottish painter. By the early 1840s, Cunningham's health had begun to fail, and the editing of the *Life of Wilkie* was completed by his son, Peter, and published posthumously, after Cunningham died of a stroke at his London home in 1842.[6]

The Publication of *Traditional Tales*

Traditional Tales of the English and Scottish Peasantry was the result of Allan Cunningham's long association with the periodical press. The book was a product not only of his fruitful relationship with the *London Magazine*, where these particular tales first appeared, but also his previous magazine contributions, stretching back to his earliest submissions to *Literary Recollections*, and the songs and ballads he published in a variety of periodicals during his years in London. Virtually all of Cunningham's magazine contributions, whether poems, tales or essays, were steeped in the traditions and popular literature of southern Scotland and northern England. In the ballads and legends of his native Dumfriesshire in particular, he found a seemingly inexhaustible vein of material—one that editors were always eager to publish, and in which he could combine his extensive knowledge of folkloric material with his desire to compose his own stories and songs.

His first major magazine breakthrough came in 1819, when he was commissioned to produce a series for *Blackwood's Edinburgh Magazine*. 'Recollections of Mark Macrabin, the Cameronian' appeared in twelve parts between November 1819 and January 1821. This series of anecdotal descriptions of Scottish provincial life had echoes of James Hogg's 'Tales and Anecdotes of the Pastoral Life', which had appeared in three parts in *Blackwood's* in 1817, and was Cunningham's first high-profile commission since his move to London. The Macrabin stories were popular enough to be considered for collection in book form, and their success helped to build

Cunningham a reputation as a writer of traditional-type tales.[7]

In 1820, Cunningham embarked on his long and fruitful tenure at the *London Magazine*. Over the following four years, he wrote regularly for the magazine, during which time the stories that would go on to make up *Traditional Tales* were published. Writing for the *London* not only gave Cunningham a regular outlet through which to develop the material and ideas that he had accumulated over the years, but also offered him an opportunity to theorise more widely about popular literature and the oral tradition. 'Traditional Literature. No. I', the first in the series, was published in the *London Magazine* for December 1820 (reproduced here, 307). In this essay, Cunningham presented his own version of the history of oral literature and laid out many of his concerns about the demise of orality, setting the tone for the tales which would follow.

The series is introduced by a narrator based in Cumbria (hence the 'Lammerlea, Cumberland' signature used by Cunningham). This elderly persona—not to be confused with Cunningham himself—describes three local characters from whom he had supposedly gleaned the traditions and legends that would follow: Richard Faulder (a Cumbrian mariner), Gilpin Macgowan (a Scottish shepherd), and Eleanor Selby (an elderly Jacobite dame). Over the course of the stories that follow, this tight unit of sources and locations is dissipated, and the main geographical focus shifts from Cumbria to Scotland. While Faulder and Selby do make several appearances, Cunningham seems to forget altogether about Macgowan (though similar Scottish tale-tellers do appear).

After establishing his thematic and geographical scope in this introduction to the series, Cunningham produced a piece under the banner of 'Traditional Literature' for most issues of the *London* up to December 1821 (for a full list of Cunningham's contributions to the magazine, see 333). In January 1822, he changed tack and began a new series titled 'The Twelve Tales of Lyddalcross'. This set of stories had its own elaborate framing narrative, which locates the tale-tellers as travellers who converge around the fireside of a mansion (reproduced here, 319). The Scottish setting of the 'Lyddalcross' series distanced Cunningham from the Cumbrian focus he had set up with 'Traditional Literature' and gave him an opportunity to introduce new narrators and settings.

Six stories from the 'Tales of Lyddalcross' were combined with ten from 'Traditional Literature' to make up the bulk of the collected version of *Traditional Tales*. The collection also included a narrative poem, 'The Seven Foresters of Chatsworth', which was published in the *London* for February 1822, but not affiliated to either series, as well as a new story composed specially for the book version, 'Ezra Peden'. The last magazine contribution to be included in *Traditional Tales* appeared in July 1822, though Cunningham continued to write for the *London* after the collection was published, producing essays, poems and tales up until December 1824.

The book version of *Traditional Tales* appeared in two volumes in August 1822, and consisted of eighteen separate pieces: seventeen tales and one long poem. The majority of the stories take place in the region that is now Dumfries and Galloway, but there are also narratives from the English side of the Solway Firth, and others which range down through Cumbria and Lancashire, reaching as far south as Derbyshire. The historical settings also vary, from the sixteenth to the nineteenth century, with the mid-to-late eighteenth century the most popular period.

With the exception of 'Death of the Laird of Warlsworm', each of the pieces in *Traditional Tales* also incorporates at least one song, ballad or poem. Some of this verse material has a folk basis or is attributed to other writers, but most, despite often being presented as having a traditional origin, was composed by Cunningham himself, or at least significantly reworked from oral sources. For example, the source for the motto to 'Richard Faulder, Mariner' (201) is given as '*Old Ballad*'; however, the song in questions appears in *Songs of Scotland* (IV, 271) under the title of 'The Mariner', with an attribution to Cunningham. Cunningham's own poetic style was more literary than oral, and the slightly flowery phraseology of his own compositions and reworkings is readily identifiable to experienced folk singers.[8]

Cunningham made some textual revisions in the process of transferring his magazine material into collected form (major instances of which are given in the notes to the text), but *Traditional Tales* as a book is not substantially different to the stories in the *London Magazine*. The changes are predominantly editorial refinements and modernisations; long paragraphs and conversations are broken up and the grammar is simplified and regularised. Antiquated spellings are also revised (chace/chase; chaunt/chant; cloaths/clothes; ladye/lady), and other updates are made: a 'hand-bow' in the *London Magazine* becomes a 'gun' in the book version (see 34n).

The older styling of the magazine pieces perhaps indicates a desire to communicate an impression of authenticity and oral origins, and the later shift away suggests Cunningham found the pseudo-medievalism too mannered for the more polished collected edition. He also removed the heavy italicisation from some of the magazine stories (notably 'The Last Lord of Helvellyn'), which again may be indicative of a desire to distance the book version from what with hindsight may have seemed a tendency toward melodramatic excess in the magazine stories.

For the most part, though, these changes are minor. Rather than a new work, the collected edition represents a way of bringing the tales together for a new audience, and rescuing them from the ephemeral pages of the periodical press. By the time that the collection appeared, Cunningham was pessimistic about its prospects and worried that the stories may have lost some of their appeal during the process of republication. In a letter to his brother, James, he wrote, 'I cannot anticipate what their success may be, but I shall be satisfied with little, as the fire-edge has been taken off them already, and they cannot have the charm of novelty'.[9]

Magazine publication, followed by a collected edition was (and often still is) the ideal objective for the writer of short fiction. It is a way of maximising profit and audience, and the process of transferring tales from magazine to book form was familiar to many writers of the period. A similar example from the period can be found in Hogg's 1820 collection, *Winter Evening Tales*, which was composed of material previously published in his own short-lived magazine, *The Spy*.[10] In Cunningham's case, the book version not only presented an additional source of revenue, but also offered him the potential to reach a different, wider readership than the predominantly metropolitan, male subscribers to the *London Magazine*.

The reception of *Traditional Tales* was largely positive, if slightly muted. Allan Cunningham's peers tended to view him as a writer whose primary merit lay in his natural, untutored abilities: a man who had raised himself to achieve a degree of literary success, despite his rustic origins and lack of formal education. With occasional condescension, he was categorised as a phenomenon of the peasant–poet variety. Walter Scott recalls a meal with Cunningham in London: 'We breakfasted at honest Allan Cunningham's—honest Allan—a leal and true Scotsman of the old cast. A man of genius, besides, who only requires the tact of knowing when and where to stop, to attain the universal praise which ought to follow it.'[11]

James Hogg, who was himself subjected to similarly patronising treatment at the hands of Scott and other educated commentators and acquaintances, also saw in Cunningham a powerful poetic ability, hampered by a lack of critical discrimination: 'I was astonished at the luxuriousness of his fancy. It was boundless; but it was the luxury of a rich garden over-run with rampant weeds.'[12] Cunningham himself seems to have been happy to play up his humble background. Thomas De Quincey, whose *Confessions of an English Opium-Eater* was serialised in the *London Magazine* in 1821, became friends with Cunningham and locates him in the 'class of rustic labourers and rustic poets, (a fact which I need not disguise, since he proclaims it himself upon every occasion with a well-directed pride).'[13]

Contemporary reviewers of *Traditional Tales* were happy to share the perception of Cunningham as an affable *Naturmensch*, who had contributed to the preservation of the heritage of Scotland with his tales and songs, whatever their provenance. The critical consensus was that Cunningham had produced a book in which any rough or unpolished qualities were mitigated by its spark and energy—'a mannerism and unchastised force which are the coinage of a vigorous mind'.[14] The *Monthly Review*'s assessment was indicative of the general tone:

> How far the legends contained in these pages may be the genuine relics of antiquity, we cannot determine: but we are sure that these tales are written in the spirit of that wild and simple romance, which is so characteristic of the ancient traditions and ballads of Scotland. In all probability, we owe many of them almost entirely to the fancy of Mr. C. himself; though he assures us that such as are not immediately copied from recitation are founded on traditions, or stories, prevalent in the north.[15]

Without ever creating a sensation, Cunningham's book achieved a position of respect and appreciation that encour-

aged him to persevere with his literary career. His series of
contributions to the *London Magazine* had elevated him from
rustic balladeer to quasi-scholarly authority on the songs and
legends of the Lowlands of Scotland, and the publication of
the collected edition of *Traditional Tales* was an achievement
that capped this phase of his career. As a prose writer, this
was Cunningham's high point. The novels that followed were
not as successful and generally less well received. Throughout
the remainder of the nineteenth century, his reputation gradually declined, and though many of his poems continued to be
anthologised and his artists' biographies remained in print, he
came to be regarded as something of a curiosity, and a relic
of the Georgian period's fascination with primitivism and
folklore.

Folklore in the Magazines

During the 1820s there was a rise in the popularity and status
of short fiction, both in the periodical press and in collected
form. Many of the authors and publishers of this new wave of
stories and collections sought to tap into the contemporary
vogue for traditional or folkloric material. The term 'folklore'
itself was not coined until the 1840s, and the folkloric material
that was published in books and magazines in the early nineteenth century was known variously as popular antiquities,
superstitions or simply as traditions.

The discipline, such as it was, was derived in part from
the interest in ballad-collecting that had developed during the
second half of the eighteenth century. The most famous collection from this period is probably Thomas Percy's *Reliques of
Ancient English Poetry* (1765), but a large number of others
were published from the 1760s onwards, by David Herd,
James Johnson, Joseph Ritson and others. Collecting and editing ballads remained popular amongst the subsequent generation of writers, with Walter Scott's *Minstrelsy of the Scottish
Border* (1802–03) and James Hogg's *Jacobite Relics of Scotland*
(1819–21) amongst the best-known Romantic-era examples.

As well as ballad collections, the late eighteenth and early
nineteenth centuries witnessed the emergence of the incipient
discipline of popular antiquities. Essentially the precursor of
folklore studies, which evolved over the course of the Victorian period, the contribution of scholarly collectors of popular

antiquities was to introduce an element of scientific scrupu-
lousness to the discipline: placing at its heart the concepts of
fieldwork, named sources and the indexing of variants. The
ballad revival and the new field of popular antiquities both
helped set up certain protocols which were highly influential
on those writers and collectors, like Cunningham, who followed the earliest practitioners. In essence, there evolved a
tension between practitioner and antiquarian, and a corresponding anxiety about how the process of collecting oral
material might serve to ossify traditions as much as preserve
them.

    One side of this conflict is occupied by the collector and/or
the editor (Percy, Joseph Ritson and R. H. Cromek, for
example). These were educated, professional men with
antiquarian interests. They also possessed, to a greater or
lesser degree, scholarly instincts and a desire for rigour and
accuracy in the material they collected. Ritson, for instance,
launched notoriously caustic attacks on the editorial standards
of other collectors, including Percy, in the prefaces to his
anthologies. Collections of traditional material were expected
to be the results of academic investigation, not of invention: as
the controversy over Macpherson's Ossian poems makes clear.
Cromek, on the other hand, was willing to accept Cunningham's submissions for *Remains of Nithsdale and Galloway Song*—
either in ignorance, or because he believed the authenticity of
the 'traditional' songs was unlikely to be questioned.

    On the other side of this rough divide is the composer: the
poet, the balladeer, the song-writer or the tale-teller (Allan
Ramsay, Robert Burns and James Hogg, for example, as well
as countless lost 'traditional' voices). Of course, this simple
binary barely begins to tell the story. Percy and Ritson,
though both collectors, had very different ideas about the level
of critical intervention appropriate for an editor. Ramsay,
Burns and Hogg were poets, but they were also collectors, and
editors, and bowdlerisers. As practitioners and participants in
an oral culture, as well as collectors, they did not share the
reverential attitude towards their material of someone like
Ritson, and all three cut, re-cast and made additions to their
ballads and tales as they saw fit. A different example of the
writer/collector dynamic can be seen in Walter Scott. Scott
was an antiquarian, but he was also steeped in the lore which
he gathered and published—as his stories, novels and poems

make clear (not least in their elaborate framing narratives, prefaces and footnotes). Indeed, Scott was one of the last figures to act out successfully the role of both collector and perpetuator of oral traditions.

Cunningham's own attitude to these concerns about authenticity and authorship is not straightforward. His role in the *Remains* controversy places him in the role of a composer, rather than collector, and his use of the Ossianic 'Hidallan' pseudonym in his early poems also seems to align him with Burns and other writers who felt comfortable recasting folk material in their own style. On the other hand, a comment made by De Quincey suggests that Cunningham's sense of these issues was more complicated: '[Cunningham] avowed an unqualified scorn of Ossian; such a scorn as every man that ever looked at Nature with his own eyes, and not through books, must secretly entertain.'[16]

Cunningham had praised the 'mercy-pouring song sublime' of Ossian in one of his early poems for *Literary Recreations*, but he seems to have outgrown the affection by the 1820s.[17] As he developed as a poet, Cunningham perhaps came to feel that Macpherson's error lay not so much in the morality of palming-off supposedly 'traditional' poetry on his readers, but in his failure to do so convincingly. He saw the Ossian poems as fakes which originated from outside the tradition, produced by an antiquarian for the purpose of deceiving other scholars. In contrast, Cunningham positioned himself as a writer immersed in a folk culture, and as such his works were framed as complementary additions to a popular form, rather than fraudulently imposed counterfeits. There is a sense that oral songs and tales belong to him, and he to them, and that the two are impossible to separate. There is a fair amount of arrogance in this position, but Cunningham was bullish about his own ability to navigate the tricky waters of tradition. He boasted in a letter to his brother, 'I could cheat a whole General Assembly of Antiquarians with my original manner of writing and forging ballads'.[18]

With *Traditional Tales*, Cunningham thus made his entry into an area of the publishing industry in which space could be found for both scholar and artist. At the same time, the opportunities available to authors and collectors of tales and songs were expanding. The launch of *Blackwood's Edinburgh Magazine* in 1817 was the beginning of a boom-time for the

periodical press: not only were subsequent new magazines
launched on a regular basis, but the success of *Blackwood's'*
policy of carrying numerous tales encouraged its rivals to
include more and more short fiction. The concept of the
'magazine', established during the eighteenth century, lent
itself to a certain amount of miscellaneous content, and
enabled periodicals to act as repositories for oddities and curiosities not publishable elsewhere. By the 1820s, magazines
had evolved into sophisticated vehicles, which allowed mul-
tiple voices and tones to compete within their pages and
encouraged the sort of authorial game-playing that writers
such as Cunningham relished.

Like *Blackwood's*, the *London Magazine* gave a great deal of
space to traditional literature. In the first number after its
1820 re-launch, the magazine declared 'we have a great
passion for our early poets, lyric, epic, and dramatic; and we
entreat our readers not to be offended, if we should occasionally intersperse our pages with observations, selections, or
criticisms, arising from a prevailing attachment.'[19] Over the
years, the *London* justified its claim to be a champion of early
literature by publishing antiquarian essays and notes, as well
as dozens of stories and ballads. As such, it proved the perfect
site for Cunningham. Writing for the *London* brought him
respectability, a ready-made audience and, through its continued support, a long-term residence which gave his series
stability and legitimacy.

Traditional Tales: Literature and Orality

Like many Romantic authors who worked with popular,
orally-derived material (James Hogg being a notable example), Cunningham operated in a borderland between literary invention and deference to the traditional material on
which he drew. For twentieth-century critics, this ambiguous
position can appear to lack respect for the distinctiveness of
the oral tradition. Commenting on *Traditional Tales*, Richard
Dorson is scathing about Cunningham's status as an
antiquarian:

> These verbose narrations do exhibit a sea witch who
> curses ships, the ghost of a shipwrecked lady murdered
> for her gold by a fisherman, a cupbearer to the fairies,

spectral troops that presage death. But traditional tales they are not, and they might more accurately have been titled 'Literary Tales Faintly Suggested by Oral Traditions of the Scottish Peasantry.' In 1822 the distinction between invention and tradition was not very meaningful to Cunningham, nor to most of his contemporaries.[20]

Other folklorists have been kinder. K. M. Briggs gives the work the distinction of being the first British collection of folktales, arguing that among those works 'which were the fruit of first-hand research [...] the earliest in the field was Allan Cunningham in 1822, for Scotland.'[21] As usual, the truth lies somewhere in between. Cunningham was by no means the first collector of Scottish tales, and followed writers such as Scott and Hogg in publishing volumes of more-or-less traditional material. Moreover, many of the pieces in *Traditional Tales* are not folktales by any definition of the term. Stories such as 'Elphin Irving, the Fairies' Cupbearer' have a folkloric stamp, but many others—'Placing a Scottish Minister', for instance—have no fairy or folk elements at all.

Whatever the merits or demerits of *Traditional Tales* as a folkloric collection, the fact remains that Cunningham did not regard himself as an antiquarian scholar, nor did he have any qualms about blurring 'the distinction between invention and tradition'. In the Preface to *Traditional Tales*, he positions himself as 'the collector and embellisher' of the tales, and not only recognises, but takes a deal of pride in the duality of this role and the imaginative skill it demands.[22] Despite this bold disavowal of scholarly obligations, however, there is also a discernable element of guilt. As a country-bred Scotsman who had made the journey to London, Cunningham perhaps felt that he had ended up hawking his birthright for the fleeting amusement of jaded Londoners.

The songs and legends of the Scottish Borders were a fascinating and eminently saleable commodity, but they could potentially end up as disposable curiosities for the magazine age. In 'The Ghost with the Golden Casket', the narrator, an Englishman (though with Scottish ancestry) finds it difficult to extract a legend from a local farmer:

'I am just thinking,' said he [the farmer] 'that as ye are an Englishman I should nae acquaint ye with such a story. Ye'll make it, I'm doubting, a matter of reproach

and vaunt when ye gae hame, how Willie Borlan o' Caerlaverock told ye a tale of Scottish iniquity, that cowed
all the stories in Southron book or history.' (249)

On other occasions in Cunningham's stories, tale-tellers hesi-
tate to communicate their stories and legends—perhaps
mirroring the author's fear that the audience may mock or
misappropriate the material.

This fear is connected to anxieties about the status of the
oral tradition. During the Romantic period, the transmission
of ballads and legends by word of mouth was a practice felt to
be increasingly under threat. As Penny Fielding states, 'by
the mid-nineteenth century the oral was joining the pastoral
in a sentimentalised past where it could more safely be contained'.[23] Cunningham frequently bemoaned the gradual dis-
placement of an oral with a printed tradition, and fondly
recalls the ballad-singers and raconteurs who travelled door-
to-door and effectively sang for their supper. In one of his
letters, he records a conversation with Walter Scott in which
Cunningham recalls a man ('the last of a race of district tale-
tellers') who made his living by telling stories and singing
ballads. Cunningham remembers him as having 'a devout tale
for the old, and a merry tale for the young' and describes
him as 'a sort of beggar'. To which Scott responds: 'Out upon
thee, Allan. Dost thou call that begging? Why, man, we make
our bread by story-telling, and honest bread it is.'[24]

In these stories, Cunningham vacillates between pride in
earning such 'honest bread' by extending the life of these disap-
pearing narratives, and anxiety about being 'a sort of
beggar', pawning scraps to the London Magazine. He never
managed to achieve the balance of the educated, enlightened
scholar that came so easily to Scott, and his magazine stories
often get bogged down in elaborate justifications and efforts to
describe precisely a particular circumstance or setting. His
tales make continual reference to borders: the Scottish Lowlands are described as 'the debateable land of song as well as
of the sword' (56) and their populace as 'the mixed brood of
Cumberland and Caledonia' (205), or as 'the men of the
debateable land. Men neither of predatory Scotland nor
haughty England, but begotten in the haste of a mutual
inroad—and the herald's office cannot divine by whom' (40).
Within these dubious, liminal spaces, Cunningham positions

himself as a guide: interpreting and translating the unreliable quicksand of folklore. The stories themselves are full of confusions, misapprehensions and varying accounts: all of which Cunningham tries to fix for his audience, both within the individual tales, and also through the overarching editorial structure which he builds up.

Throughout *Traditional Tales*, Cunningham expends a great deal of effort theorising the constitution of traditional literature and defending the ability of popular tales and songs to retain their power. These arguments are built up through the various framing devices and narratorial asides contained within the stories. In the Preface, he describes a triumvirate of forces—Truth, Imagination and Tradition—which unite to shed light on the nature of existence in a way that rationalism and cynicism has chased out of modern literature.

Truth is the elusive grail for Cunningham's narrators, and the term conveys not only the verifiable facts of the tales but also the drive to produce a harmonious and satisfying narrative meaning. This pleasing rightness is achieved by a combination of the other two forces: Imagination (the genius of a Romanticised poet-figure) and Tradition (the archetypal or universal qualities of each tale) must coalesce to shed light on the true nature of existence. The narrators of the stories are adamant that traditions still have much to teach us, but it is unclear just how seriously we are supposed to take these claims.

Cunningham's 'traditions' appeared first in a major periodical and were then published by a leading London bookseller. As such, they are incorporated into a fundamentally literate and educated framework, and must therefore engage with at least some degree of empirical enquiry into their origins and significance. In practice, this means that the narrator must present his tales as historical artefacts, suggesting to his readers that the primary interest of the collection lies in the ability of his stories to give an insight into a vanishing culture and philosophy. However, the rationalist restraints imposed by the narrator often begin to creak and crack under the pressure of the supernatural content. Truth, Imagination and Tradition are not always in harmony. All too often, Tradition opposes, rather than supports, the desired clarity. In many stories, Tradition emerges as an unruly force—one which threatens to undermine any sublimation and explicitly challenges the authority of rational scholarship.

In 'Ezra Peden', the first story of the collection (and perhaps significantly the last to be written), Cunningham explores both his hopes and his fears for traditions. The narrator proclaims early on in the tale that 'it is seldom that tradition requires any illustration; its voice is clear and its language simple' (5). However, as the tale progresses, the cherished notion of a tangible truth is exposed as more and more of an illusion. Peden, a late-seventeenth-century Presbyterian preacher, is to some degree the enemy of orality. He not only commits himself to ridding his parish of the pernicious influence of the fairies and their dark allies, but also to stamping out all non-authorised forms of expression:

> Wherever he sojourned, dance and song fled:—the former he accounted a devoting of limbs which God made to the worship of Satan; the latter he believed to be a sinful meting out of wanton words to a heathen measure. Satan, he said, leaped and danced, and warbled and sung, when he came to woo to perdition the giddy sons and daughters of men. (6)

Ballads and dances are aligned with witchcraft in Peden's creed, all being equally detrimental to the spiritual health of his flock. After Peden arrives too late to solicit repentance at the deathbed of a grievous sinner, the dead man's ghost returns to trigger a sequence during which the preacher apparently converses with spirits and ends up delirious in a nearby dell through unexplained circumstances.

As the events of the tale progress, their nature and cause become more cloudy. Exactly what happens to Ezra Peden is never made clear. Despite the testimony of eyewitnesses, the question of whether the entire tale 'was a fiction of the auld enemy' (28) is mooted. At the outset of the story, the narrator claims: 'I am but as an humble priest responding from the traditionary oracles, and the words of other years pass without change from between my lips' (6). The meanings of oracles, however, can prove difficult to interpret, and as the hoped-for clarity of Truth fails to emerge the narrator is forced to question his twin tools of Imagination and Tradition:

> such is the picture which tradition ever and invariably
> draws, while imagination endeavours to take up the
> tender thread of the story, and imagination must have
> this license still. Truth contents herself with the summary
> of a few and unsatisfactory particulars: the dawn of
> morning came, says Truth, and Ezra had not returned to
> his manse. Something evil hath happened, said Imagin-
> ation, scattering as she spoke a thousand tales of a thou-
> sand hues. (26–27)

Imagination proves not to be the unifying authorial force
that the narrator had hoped for, channelling and clarifying
Tradition's meaning; instead, both forces open up a host of
disparate possibilities, none of which can be satisfactorily
resolved.

These problematic negotiations between tradition and
modernity are re-enacted in many of the other tales. For
Cunningham's 'collector and embellisher', then, the initial
authorial position is straightforward. The educated, modern
writer must bring not only his poetic and imaginative skills,
but also his rational knowledge of history and philosophy to
bear upon traditional material. Such material retains the
'imagery fresh and green' (3) of early cultures, and therefore merits careful translation into a modern text, rendering
it suitable for consumption by polite society. The antiquarian
principle is a rational, modern drive, but these oral narratives
continually resist easy transformation into the ideological
safety of print culture. Quite what these stories mean to a
modern, print-based society becomes increasingly hazy,
despite their incorporation into the strictures of a printed text,
and the clearness of mind and purpose that the narrator of
the Preface expresses begins to dissolve.

The collected edition of *Traditional Tales of the English and
Scottish Peasantry* functions as an attempt to impose retrospective order and meaning on a series of magazine stories which
never fully manage to reconcile the scholarly imperatives of
the fledgling study of folklore, and a raconteur's desire to tell
the most memorable tale. Cunningham continually hesitates
between sincerity and irony, earnestness and deprecation, as
he attempts to negotiate the chasm between the fluidity of the
oral tradition with the more lucrative but less forgiving 'fixed
splendours' (307) of the printed word. As a consequence he

never managed to dismiss fully those demons which occasionally prompted him to treat his stories and ballads as curiosities
or oral relics which were patently unfit for sophisticated
literary consumption.

Tim Killick
2011

NOTE ON THE TEXT

The present volume is based on the first collected edition of *Traditional Tales of the English and Scottish Peasantry*, published in London by Taylor and Hessey in July 1822. This copy-text has been collated against the versions of the tales published in the *London Magazine* between January 1821 and June 1822, and any significant deviations are given in the notes. Several catalogues and bibliographies make reference to a second edition, produced by Taylor and Hessey in 1828, but the only listed copies are in libraries in the United States, and I have not been able to examine them. Two further editions were issued in the nineteenth century. The first by F.&W. Kerslake in 1874, and the second, with an introduction by Henry Morley, by Routledge in 1887. Neither of the Victorian editions make significant textual changes, though both regularise Cunningham's spelling and grammar to match the publishers' house style.

My intention in editing Cunningham's stories has been to retain the quality and feel of the first edition as far as possible. As with many works from the early nineteenth century, the spelling and use of grammar is not entirely consistent. Alternative spellings, such as grey/gray; rosy/rosie and ankle/ancle are often used interchangeably. Similarly, words such as kirk-yard and fireside, and geographical names such as Annan-water, are sometimes given as one word, sometimes with a hyphen, and sometimes as two separate words. These variations are in part a result of the text's origins as a collection of separately-published magazine stories, and in part reflect a generally fluid attitude towards spelling and punctuation amongst Romantic-era authors and publishers.

In the majority of instances, I have left unchanged any small variations or inconsistencies in spelling and hyphenation, as part of the text's history and publishing circumstances. I have also retained the distinctive grammatical structure of Cunningham's text, with its extensive use of dashes and slightly idiosyncratic capitalisation. Some editorial interventions have been made, however, and these are given in the Emendation List (341). The changes relate predominantly to grammatical errors and inconsistent use of speech marks, but I have also regularised proper nouns, when variations occur within a single tale, and regularised spelling and grammar within individual songs and ballads.

TRADITIONAL TALES OF THE ENGLISH AND SCOTTISH PEASANTRY

Volume I

Preface

It may be expected that something should be said concerning a series of stories for which the title-page appears to claim an oral origin. Traditional tales, interspersed with oral poetry, have long been popular among our northern peasantry. When our early written literature was filled with the thoughts, and the imagery, and the gods of the heathen, our oral or fire-side verse and prose was purely original and native, abounding with vivid presentments of action and character, an imagery fresh and green, and frequent glimpses of a sweet and a gentle fancy.

In former times, and within my own remembrance, old men wandered from house to house, chanting ballads, reciting portions of the old romances, and curious stories of real or fictitious adventure. I have listened to these oral novelists at our farmers' hearths, when they pleased many an audience, and, like the minstrel of old, 'won their food and their raiment, of which they were worthy.'[1] The stories were varied, according to the taste or talent of the reciter: every year brought a change in the plot or the succession of incidents; matters of local interest or recent occurrence found their way into the venerable narratives, and new songs displaced the original rhymes or shared with them the applause which accompanied such recitals. Sometimes it happened that the narrative remained the same, but the scene was shifted, and the little episodical embellishments were wholly altered, while the ballads which commonly pertained to the story, had their heroines removed, and some present or popular beauty was placed for the time in their stead. Such has been the change to which many of our northern lyrics have been doubtless subjected.

'We still meet with Highlanders,' says Colonel David Stewart,[2] in his interesting work, 'who can give a connected and minutely accurate detail of the history, genealogy, feuds, and battles of all the tribes and families in every district or glen for many miles round, and for a period of several hundred years; illustrating their details by reference to every remarkable stone, cairn, tree, or stream within the district;

3

connecting with each some kindred story of a fairy or a ghost, or the death of some person who perished in the snow, by any sudden disaster, or accidental encounter. In the graphic delineations of the Celtic narrator, the representation of adventures, whether romantic or domestic, was enlivened by dramatic sketches, which introduced him as speaking or conversing in an appropriate and characteristic manner.'

The attachment of our peasantry to the recital or chant of chivalrous ballads or superstitious legends, has abated by the diffusion of printed knowledge. The oral wisdom, the unwritten sallies of wit and humour, the lyric compositions and legendary histories, have begun to vanish like all unrecorded things. Information and pleasure can now be purchased and enjoyed in silence at our own fire-side.

To these humble and wandering novelists I owe the origin of many of the stories which are inserted in this collection. I am more the collector and embellisher, than the creator of these tales; and such as are not immediately copied from recitation are founded upon traditions or stories prevalent in the north. The old narrative fire-side mode of story-telling, liable as it was to interruptions and corrections from the audience, has not been departed from; and the stamp and hue which the various minds of men communicated to their various stories have been retained.

These tales and legends, rude and imperfect as they are, have sweetened for me many an hour of remission from daily labour, and, by the light of my evening fire, have given me a pleasure which the kindness or the severity of criticism can scarcely enlarge or lessen. Forbearance and gentleness need hardly be solicited for the narratives which gladdened or moved our forefathers. There is an air of reality about truth with which fiction can never invest herself, and an enjoyment in her company which passes not away. What belief the higher classes of the community may attach to these legends, I cannot pretend to foresee; but nothing is related but what is supported by popular evidence, and many stories might be collected involving more remarkable superstitions, and abounding with the chivalrous, the wild, and the supernatural.

It may be proper to add, that all these stories, with the exception of the first, appeared in different periods in the LONDON MAGAZINE.

EZRA PEDEN

I sat and watch'd while all men slept, and lo![3]
Between the green earth and the deep green sea
I saw bright spirits pass, pure as the touch
Of May's first finger on the eastern hill.
Behind them follow'd fast a little cloud;
And from the cloud an evil spirit came—
A damned shape—one who in the dark pit
Held sovereign sway; and power to him was given
To chase the blessed spirits from the earth,
And rule it for a season.   Soon he shed
His hellish slough, and many a subtle wile
Was his to seem a heavenly spirit to man.
First he a hermit, sore subdued in flesh,
O'er a cold cruse of water and a crust,
Pour'd out meek prayers abundant. Then he changed
Into a maid when she first dreams of man,
And from beneath two silken eyelids sent
The sidelong light of two such wondrous eyes,
That all the saints grew sinners. He subdued
Those wanton smiles, and grew a reverend dame,
With wintry ringlets, and grave lips, which dropt
Proverbial honey in her grandson's ear.
Then a professor of God's word he seem'd,
And o'er a multitude of upturn'd eyes
Shower'd blessed dews, and made the pitchy path,
Down which howl damned spirits, seem the bright
Thrice hallow'd way to heaven. Yet grimly through
The glorious veil of those seducing shapes
Frown'd out the fearful Spirit.

The religious legend which supplies my story with the motto,
affords me no farther assistance in arranging and interpreting
the varying traditional remembrances of the colloquies between one of the chiefs of the ancient Presbyterian kirk and
one of the inferior spirits of darkness. It is seldom that tradition requires any illustration; its voice is clear, and its lan-

guage simple—it seeks to conceal nothing—what it can explain it explains, and scorns, in the homely accuracy of its protracted details, all mystery and reservation. But in the present story there is much which the popular spirit of research would dread to have revealed; a something too mystical and hallowed to be sought into by a devout people. Often as I have listened to it, I never heard it repeated without mutual awe in the teller and the auditor. The most intrepid peasant becomes graver and graver as he proceeds, stops before the natural termination of the story, and hesitates to pry into the supernatural darkness of the tradition. It would be unwise therefore to seek to expound or embellish the legend—it shall be told as it was told to me: I am but as an humble priest responding from the traditionary oracles, and the words of other years pass without change from between my lips.

Ezra Peden was one of the shepherds of the early Presbyterian flock, and distinguished himself as an austere and enthusiastic pastor; fearless in his ministration, delighting in wholesome discipline, and guiding in the way of grace the peer as well as the peasant. He grappled boldly with the infirmities and sins of the times; he spared not the rod in the way of his ministry; and if in the time of peril he laid his hand on the sword, in the time of peace his delight was to place it on the horns of the altar. He spared no vice, he compounded with no sin, and he discussed men's claims to immortal happiness with a freedom which made them tremble. Amid the fervour of his eloquence, he aspired, like some of his fellow-professors of that period, to the prophetic mantle. Plain and simple in his own apparel, he counted the mitred glory and exterior magnificence of the hierarchy a sin and an abomination, and preferred preaching on a wild hill or in a lonesome glen to the most splendid edifice.

Wherever he sojourned, dance and song fled:—the former he accounted a devoting of limbs which God made to the worship of Satan; the latter he believed to be a sinful meting out of wanton words to a heathen measure. Satan, he said, leaped and danced, and warbled and sung, when he came to woo to perdition the giddy sons and daughters of men. He dictated the colour and the cut of men's clothes—it was seemly for those who sought salvation to seek it in a sober suit—and the ladies of his parish were obliged to humble their finery, and sober down their pride, before his sarcastic sermons on female paintings, and plumings, and perfumings, and the unloveliness of love-locks. He sought to make a modest and sedate grace abound among women; courtship was schooled and sermoned into church controversy, and love into mystical professions; the common civilities between the sexes were doled out with a suspicious hand and a jealous charity, and the primrose path through the groves of dalliance to the sober vale of marriage was planted with thorns and sown with briars.

He had other endowments not uncommon among the primitive teachers of the word. In his day, the empire of the prince of darkness was more manifest among men than now, and his ministry was distinguished, like the reign of king Saul,[4] by the persecution of witches, and elves, and evil spirits. He made himself the terror of all those who dealt in divinations, or consulted the stars, or sought to avert witchcraft by sinful spell and charm, instead of overcoming it by sorrowings and spiritual watchings. The midnight times of planetary power he held as the prime moments of Satan's glory on earth, and he punished Hallowmass revellers as chief priests in the infernal rites. He consigned to church censure and the chastening of rods a wrinkled dame who sold a full sea and a fair wind to mariners, and who insulted the apostles, and made a mystical appeal to the twelve signs of heaven in setting a brood goose with a dozen eggs. His wrath too was observed to burn against all those who compounded with witches, and people who carried evil influence in their eyes—this was giving tribute to the fiend, and bribing the bottomless pit.

He rebuked a venerable dame, during three successive Sundays, for placing a cream bowl and new-baked cake in the paths of the nocturnal elves who, she imagined, had plotted to steal her grandson from the mother's bosom. He turned loose many scripture threatenings against those diminutive and capricious beings, the fairies, and sought to preach them from the land. He prayed on every green hill, and held communings in every green valley. He wandered forth at night, as a spiritual champion, to give battle to the enemies of the light. The fairies resigned the contest with a foe equipped from such an armoury, and came no more among the sons and daughters of men. The sound of their minstrelsy ceased on the hill; their equestrian processions were seen no more sweeping past at midnight beneath the beam of the half-veiled moon; and

only a solitary and sullen elf or two remained to lament the
loss of their immemorial haunts. With the spirits of evil men
and the lesser angels of darkness he waged a fierce and a
dubious war; he evoked an ancient ghost from a ruined tower,
which it had shared for generations with the owl; and he laid
or tranquillized a fierce and troubled spirit which haunted
the abode of a miser in a neighbouring churchyard, and
seemed to gibber and mumble over his bones. All these places
were purified by prayer, and hallowed by the blessing of the
gifted pastor, Ezra Peden.

The place of his ministry seemed fitted by nature, and
largely endowed by history, for the reception and entertainment of all singular and personified beliefs. Part was maritime
and part mountainous, uniting the aerial creeds of the shepherds with the stern and more imposing beliefs of the husbandman, and the wild and characteristic superstitions of the
sailors. It often happened, when he had marched against and
vanquished a sin or a superstition of native growth, he was
summoned to wage war with a new foe; to contend with a
legion of errors, and a strange race of spirits from the haunted
coasts of Norway or Sweden. All around him on every side
were records of the mouldering influence of the enemies of
faith and charity. On the hill where the heathen Odin had
appeared to his worshippers in the circle of granite, the pillars
of his Runic temple promised to be immortal—but the god
was gone, and his worship was extinct. The sword, the spear,
and the banner, had found sanctuary from fields of blood on
several lofty promontories; but shattered towers and dismantled castles told that for a time hatred, oppression, and
revenge had ceased to triumph over religion. Persecution now
passed and gone, a demon exorcised by the sword, had hallowed three wild hills and sanctified two little green valleys
with the blood of martyrs. Their gravestones, bedded among
heather or long grass, cried up to Heaven against their oppres-
sors in verses which could not surely fail to elude the punishment awarded by the kirk against poesy. Storms, and
quicksands, and unskilful mariners, or, as common belief said,
the evil spirits of the deep, had given to the dangerous coast
the wrecks of three stately vessels; and there they made their
mansions, and raised whirlwinds, and spread quicksands, and
made sandbanks, with a wicked diligence which neither
prayer nor preaching could abate. The forms under which

these restless spirits performed their pranks have unfortunately been left undefined by a curious and a poetical peasantry.

It happened one winter, during the fifteenth year of the ministry of Ezra Peden, and in the year of grace 1705, that he sat by his fire pondering deep among the treasures of the ancient Presbyterian worthies, and listening occasionally to the chafing of the coming tide against cliff and bank, and the fitful sweep of heavy gusts of wind over the roof of his manse. During the day he had seemed more thoughtful than usual; he had consulted scripture with an anxious care, and fortified his own interpretation of the sacred text by the wisdom of some of the chiefs and masters of the calling. A Bible too, bound in black oak, and clasped with silver, from the page of which sin had received many a rebuke, and the abominations of witchcraft and sorcery had been cleansed from the land, was brought from its velvet sanctuary, and placed beside him. Thus armed and prepared, he sat like a watcher of old on the towers of Judah;[5] like one who girds up his loins and makes bare his right arm for some fierce and dubious contest.

All this stir and preparation passed not unnoticed of an old man—his predecessor's coeval, and prime minister of the household; a person thin, religious, and faithful, whose gifts in prayer were reckoned by some old people nearly equal to those of the anointed pastor. To such a distinction Josiah never thought of aspiring; he contented himself with swelling the psalm into something like melody on Sunday, visiting the sick as a forerunner of his master's approach, and pouring forth prayers and graces at burials and banquetings, as long and dreary as a hill sermon. He looked on the minister as something superior to man; a being possessed by a divine spirit, and he shook his head with all its silver hairs, and uttered a gentle groan or two, during some of the more rapt and glowing passages of Ezra's sermons.

This faithful personage stood at the door of his master's chamber, unwilling to go in, and yet loth to depart. 'Josiah, thou art called, Josiah,' said Ezra in a grave tone, 'so come hither; the soul of an evil man, a worker of iniquity, is about to depart; one who drank the blood of saints, and made himself fat with the inheritance of the righteous. It hath been revealed to me that his body is sorely troubled; but I say unto you he will not go from the body without the strong compulsion of prayer, and therefore am I summoned to war with the enemy; so I shall arm me to the task.'

Josiah was tardy in speech, and before he could reply, the clatter of a horse's hoofs was heard at the gate: the rider leaped down, and, splashed with mire and sprinkled with sleet, he stood in an instant before the minister. 'Ah! sir,' said the unceremonious messenger, 'haste—snatch up the looms of redemption, and bide not the muttering of prayer, else auld Mahoun[6] will haurl his friend Bonshaw to his cauldrons, body and saul, if he has nae him half-way hame already. God-sake, sir, start and fly, for he cannot shoot owre another hour!—he talks of perdition, and speaks about a broad road[7] and a great fire, and friends who have travelled the way before him. He's no his lane, however, that's one comfort; for I left him conversing with an old cronie, whom no one saw but himself—ane whose bones are ripe and rotten—and mickle they talked of a place called Tophet,[8] a hot enough region, if one can credit them: but I aye doubt the accounts of such travellers,—they are like the spies of the land of promise—'

'Silence thy unreverent tongue, and think of thy latter end with fear and trembling,' said Ezra, in a stern voice. 'Mount thy horse, and follow me to the evil man, thy master; brief's the time, and black's the account, and stern and inexorable will the summoning angel be.' And leaping on their horses, they passed from the manse, and sought out the bank of a little busy stream which, augmented by a fall of sleet, lifted up a voice amid its rocky and desolate glen equal to the clamour of a mightier brook. The glen or dell was rough with sharp and projecting crags, which, hanging forward at times from opposite sides, seemed to shut out all farther way; while from between their dark grey masses the rivulet leaped out in many divided streams. The brook again gathered together its waters, and subsided into several clear deep pools, on which the moon, escaping for a moment from the edge of a cloud of snow, threw a cold and wavering gleam. Along the sweeps of the stream a rough way, shaped more by nature than by the hands of man, winded among the rocks, and along this path proceeded Ezra, pondering on the vicissitudes of human life.

At length he came where the glen expanded, and the sides became steep and woody; amid a grove of decaying trees, the mansion of Bonshaw rose, square and grey. Its walls of rough granite were high and massive; the roof ascending steep and sharp carried a covering of red sand-stone flags; around the whole the rivulet poured its scanty waters in a deep moat, while a low-browed door, guarded by loopholes, gave it the character of a place of refuge and defence. Though decayed and war-worn now, it had, in former times, been a fair and a courtly spot. A sylvan nook or arbour, scooped out of the everlasting rock, was wreathed about with honeysuckles; a little pool, with a margin studded with the earliest primroses, lay at its entrance; and a garden, redeemed by the labour of man from the sterile upland, had its summer roses and its beds of lilies, all bearing token of some gentle and departed inhabitant.

As he approached the house, a candle glimmered in a small square window, and threw a line or two of straggling light along the path. At the foot of the decayed porch he observed the figure of a man kneeling, and presently he heard a voice chanting what sounded like a psalm or a lyke-wake hymn. Ezra alighted, and approached—the form seemed insensible of his presence, but stretched his hands towards the tower; and while the feathery snow descended on his grey hair, he poured his song forth, in a slow and melancholy manner. 'I protest,' said the messenger, 'here kneels old William Cameron, the Covenanter;[9] hearken, he pours out some odd old-world malison against Bonshaw. I have heard that the laird hunted him long and sore in his youth, slew his sons, burned his house, threw his two bonnie daughters desolate—that was nae gentle deed, however—and brake the old mother's heart with downright sorrow. Sae I canna much blame the dour old carle for remembering it even now, though the candles of Bonshaw are burning in the socket, and his light will be extinguished for ever. Let us hearken his psalm or his song; it is no every winter night we have minstrelsy at Bonshaw gate, I can tell ye that.' The following are the verses, which have been preserved under the title of 'Ane godly exultation of William Cameron, a chosen vessel, over Bonshaw, the persecutor.' I have adopted a plainer, but a less descriptive, title.

THE DOWNFAL OF DALZELL[10]

1.

The wind is cold, the snow falls fast,
    The night is dark and late,
As I lift aloud my voice and cry
    By the oppressor's gate.
There is a voice in every hill,
    A tongue in every stone;
The greenwood sings a song of joy,
    Since thou art dead and gone;
A poet's voice is in each mouth,
    And songs of triumph swell,
Glad songs, that tell the gladsome earth
    The downfal of Dalzell.

2.

As I raised up my voice to sing
    I heard the green earth say,
Sweet am I now to beast and bird,
    Since thou art past away:
I hear no more the battle shout,
    The martyrs' dying moans;
My cottages and cities sing
    From their foundation-stones;
The carbine and the culverin's mute—
    The deathshot and the yell
Are turn'd into a hymn of joy,
    For thy downfal, Dalzell.

3.

I've trod thy banner in the dust,
    And caused the raven call
From thy bride-chamber, to the owl
    Hatch'd on thy castle wall;
I've made thy minstrels' music dumb,
    And silent now to fame
Art thou, save when the orphan casts
    His curses on thy name.
Now thou may'st say to good men's prayers
    A long and last farewell:
There's hope for every sin save thine—
    Adieu, adieu, Dalzell!

4.

The grim pit opes for thee her gates,
     Where punish'd spirits wail,
And ghastly death throws wide her door,
     And hails thee with a Hail.
Deep from the grave there comes a voice,
     A voice with hollow tones,
Such as a spirit's tongue would have
     That spoke through hollow bones:—
'Arise, ye martyr'd men, and shout
     From earth to howling hell;
He comes, the persecutor comes!
     All hail to thee, Dalzell!'

5.

O'er an old battle-field there rush'd
     A wind, and with a moan
The sever'd limbs all rustling rose,
     Even fellow bone to bone.
'Lo! there he goes,' I heard them cry,
     'Like babe in swathing band,
Who shook the temples of the Lord,
     And pass'd them 'neath his brand.
Curs'd be the spot where he was born,
     There let the adders dwell,
And from his father's hearthstone hiss:
     All hail to thee, Dalzell!'

6.

I saw thee growing like a tree—
     Thy green head touch'd the sky—
But birds far from thy branches built,
     The wild deer pass'd thee by;
No golden dew dropt on thy bough,
     Glad summer scorned to grace
Thee with her flowers, nor shepherds wooed
     Beside thy dwelling place:
The axe has come and hewn thee down,
     Nor left one shoot to tell
Where all thy stately glory grew:
     Adieu, adieu, Dalzell!

7.

An ancient man stands by thy gate,
    His head like thine is grey;
Grey with the woes of many years,
    Years four-score and a day.
Five brave and stately sons were his;
    Two daughters, sweet and rare;
An old dame, dearer than them all,
    And lands both broad and fair:—
Two broke their hearts when two were slain,
    And three in battle fell—
An old man's curse shall cling to thee:
    Adieu, adieu, Dalzell!

8.

And yet I sigh to think of thee,
    A warrior tried and true
As ever spurr'd a steed, when thick
    The splintering lances flew.
I saw thee in thy stirrups stand,
    And hew thy foes down fast,
When Grierson fled, and Maxwell fail'd,
    And Gordon stood aghast,
And Graeme, saved by thy sword, raged fierce[11]
    As one redeem'd from hell.
I came to curse thee—and I weep:
    So go in peace, Dalzell.

When this wild and unusual rhyme concluded, the Cameronian arose and departed, and Ezra and his conductor entered the chamber of the dying man.

He found him stretched on a couch of state, more like a warrior cut in marble than a breathing being. He had still a stern and a martial look, and his tall and stalwart frame retained something of that ancient exterior beauty for which his youth was renowned. His helmet, spoiled by time of its plumage, was placed on his head; a rusty corslet was on his bosom; in his arms, like a bride, lay his broad and famous sword; and as he looked at it, the battles of his youth passed in array before him. Armour and arms hung grouped along the walls, and banners, covered with many a quaint and devotional device, waved in their places as the domestic closed the door on Ezra and the dying warrior in the chamber of presence.

The devout man stood and regarded his ancient parishioner with a meek and sorrowful look; but nothing visible or present employed Bonshaw's reflections or moved his spirit—his thoughts had wandered back to earlier years, and to scenes of peril and blood. He imagined himself at the head of his horsemen in the hottest period of the persecution, chasing the people from rock to rock, and from glen to cavern. His imagination had presented to his eye the destruction of the children of William Cameron:—he addressed their mother in a tone of ironical supplication. 'Woman, where is thy devout husband, and thy five holy sons? Are they busied in interminable prayers or everlasting sermons? Whisper it in mine ear, woman—thou hast made that reservation doubtless in thy promise of concealment. Come, else I will wrench the truth out of thee with these gentle catechists, the thumbscrew and the bootikin. Serving the Lord, sayest thou, woman? Why, that is rebelling against the king. Come, come, a better answer, else I'll make thee a bride for a saint on a bloody bed of heather.' Here he paused and waved his hand like a warrior at the head of armed men, and thus he continued: 'Come, uncock thy carbine, and harm not the woman till she hear the good tidings. Sister, saint, how many bairns have ye? I bless God, saith she, five—Reuben, Simon, Levi, Praisegod, and Patrick. A bonny generation, woman. Here, soldier, remove the bandages from the faces of those two young men before ye shoot them. There stands Patrick, and that other is Simon:—dost thou see the youngest of thy affections? The other three are in Sarah's bosom—thyself shall go to Abraham's.[12] The woman looks as if she doubted me:—here, toss to her those three heads—often have they lain in her lap, and mickle have they prayed in their time. Out, thou simpleton! canst thou not endure the sight of the heads of thine own fair-haired sons, the smell of powder, and the flash of a couple of carbines?'

The reacting of that ancient tragedy seemed to exhaust for a little while the old persecutor—he next imagined himself receiving the secret instructions of the Council. 'What, what, my lord, must all this pleasant work fall to me? A reeking house and a crowing cock shall be scarce things in Nithsdale. Weepings and wailings shall be rife—the grief of mothers, and the moaning of fatherless babes. There shall be smoking ruins

and roofless kirks, and prayers uttered in secret, and sermons
preached at a venture and a hazard on the high and solitary
places. Where is General Turner?[13]—gone where the wine is
good? And where is Grierson? has he begun to talk of repentance?—Gordon thinks of the unquenchable fire which the
martyred Cameronian raved about; and gentle Graeme vows
he will cut no more throats unless they wear laced cravats.
Awell, my lords; I am the king's servant and not Christ's, and
shall boune me to the task.'

His fancy flew over a large extent of time, and what he
uttered now may be supposed to be addressed to some invisible monitor; he seemed not aware of the presence of the
minister. 'Auld, say you, and grey headed, and the one foot in
the grave; it is time to repent, and spice and perfume over
my rottenness, and prepare for heaven? I'll tell ye, but ye
must not speak on't—I tried to pray late yestreen—I knelt
down and I held up my hands to heaven—and what think ye
I beheld? a widow woman and her five fair sons standing
between me and the Most High, and calling out "Woe, woe
on Bonshaw." I threw myself with my face to the earth, and
what got I between my hands? A gravestone which covered
five martyrs, and cried out against me for blood which I had
wantonly shed. I heard voices from the dust whispering
around me—and the angel which watched of old over the
glory of my house hid his face with his hands, and I beheld
the evil spirits arise with power to punish me for a season. I'll
tell ye what I will do—among the children of those I have
slain shall my inheritance be divided—so sit down, holy sir,
and sit down, most learned man, and hearken to my bequest.
To the children of three men slain on Iron-grey moor—to
the children of two slain on Closeburn-hill—to—no, no, all
that crowd, that multitude, cannot be the descendants of those
whom I doomed to perish by the rope, and the pistol, and
the sword. Away, I say, ye congregation of zealots and psalm-
singers!—disperse, I say, else I shall trample ye down beneath
my horse's hoofs! Peace, thou white-headed stirrer of sedition,
else I shall cleave thee to the collar!—wilt thou preach still?'

Here the departing persecutor uttered a wild imprecation,
clenched his teeth, leaped to his feet, waved his sword, and
stood for several moments, his eyes flashing from them a fierce
light, and his whole strength gathered into a blow which he
aimed at his imaginary adversary. But he stiffened as he

stood—a brief shudder passed over his frame, and he was dead before he fell on the floor, and made the hall re-echo. The minister raised him in his arms—a smile of military joy still dilated his stern face—and his hand grasped the sword hilt so firmly, that it required some strength to wrench it from his hold. Sore, sore the good pastor lamented that he had no death-bed communings with the departing chief, and he expressed this so frequently, that the peasantry said, on the day of his burial, that it would bring back his spirit to earth and vex mankind, and that Ezra would find him particularly untractable and bold. Of these whisperings he took little heed, but he became somewhat more grave and austere than usual.

It happened on an evening about the close of the following spring, when the oat beard was flourishing, and the barley shot its sharp green spikes above the clod, carrying the dew on the third morning, that Ezra Peden was returning from a wedding at Buckletiller. When he left the bridal chamber it was about ten o'clock. His presence had suppressed for a time the natural ardour for dancing and mirth which characterises the Scotch; but no sooner was he mounted, and the dilatory and departing clatter of his horse's hoofs heard, than musicians and musical instruments appeared from their hiding-places. The floor was disencumbered of the bridal dinner tables, the maids bound up their long hair, and the hinds threw aside their mantles, and, taking their places and their partners, the restrained mirth broke out like a whirlwind. Old men looked on with a sigh, and uttered a feeble and faint remonstrance, which they were not unwilling should be drowned in the abounding and augmenting merriment.

The pastor had reached the entrance of a little wild and seldom frequented glen, along which a grassy and scarce visible road winded to an ancient burial-ground. Here the graceless and ungodly merriment first reached his ears, and made the woody hollow ring and resound. Horse and rider seemed possessed of the same spirit—the former made a full halt when he heard the fiddle note, while the latter, uttering a very audible groan, and laying his bridle on his horse's neck, pondered on the wisest and most effectual way of repressing this unseemly merriment—of cleansing the parish of this ancient abomination. It was a beautiful night—the unrisen moon had yet a full hour of travel before she could reach the tops of the eastern hills—the wind was mute, and no sound was abroad save the chafing of a small runnel—and the bridal mirth.

While Ezra sat casting in his own mind a long and a dubious contest with this growing and unseemly sin, something like the shadowy outline of a horse and rider appeared in the path. The night was neither light nor dark, and the way, grassy and soft, lay broad and uninterrupted between two hazel and holly groves. As the pastor lifted up his eyes, he beheld a dark rider reining up a dark horse side by side with his own, nor did he seem to want any accoutrement necessary for ruling a fine and intractable steed. As he gazed, the figure became more distinct—it seemed a tall martial form, with a slouched hat and feather, and a dark and ample mantle, which was muffled up to his eyes. From the waist downward all was indistinct, and horse and rider seemed to melt into one dark mass visible in the outline alone. Ezra was too troubled in spirit to court the intrusion of a stranger upon his meditations; he bent on him a look particularly forbidding and stern, and having made up his mind to permit the demon of mirth and minstrelsy to triumph for the present, rode slowly down the glen.

But side by side with Ezra, and step by step, even as shadow follows substance, moved the mute and intrusive stranger —the minister looked at his companion, and stirred his steed onward—with corresponding speed moved the other, till they came where the road branched off to a ruined castle. Up this way, with the wish to avoid his new friend, Ezra turned his horse; the other did the same: the former seemed suddenly to change his mind, and returned to the path that led to the old burial-ground; the latter was instantly at his side, his face still hidden in the folds of his mantle.

Now Ezra was stern and unaccommodating in kirk controversy, and the meek and gentle spirit of religion, and a sense of spiritual interest, had enough to do to appease and sober down a temper naturally bold and even warlike. Exasperated at this intruding stranger, his natural triumphed over his acquired spirit, and lifting his riding-stick, and starting up in his stirrups, he aimed a blow equal to the unhorsing of any ordinary mortal. But the weapon met with no obstruction—it seemed to descend through air alone. The minister gazed with dread on this invulnerable being—the stranger gazed on him—and both made a halt like men preparing for

a mortal fray. Ezra, who felt his horse shuddering beneath
him, began to suspect that his companion pertained to a more
dubious state of existence than his own, and his grim look
and sable exterior induced him to rank him at once among
those infamous and evil spirits which are sometimes permitted
to trouble the earth, and to be a torment to the worthy and
the devout.

He muttered a brief and pithy prayer, and then said, 'Evil
shape, who art thou, and wherefore comest thou unto me? If
thou comest for good, speak—if for my confusion and my
harm, even do thine errand; I shall not fly from thee.' 'I come
more for mine own good than for thy harm,' responded the
figure. 'Far have I ridden, and much have I endured, that I
might visit thee and this land again.' 'Do you suffer in the
flesh, or are you tortured in the spirit?' said the pastor, desirous to know something certain of his unwelcome companion. 'In both,' replied the form: 'I have dwelt in the vale
of fire, in the den of punishment, hollow, and vast, and dread-
ful—I have ridden through the region of snow and the land
of hail—I have swam through the liquid wilderness of burning
lava—passed an illimitable sea, and all for the love of one
hour on this fair green earth, with its fresh airs and its new
sprung corn.'

Ezra looked on the figure with a steady and a penetrating
eye—the stranger endured the scrutiny. 'I must know of a
truth to whom and what I speak—I must see you face to
face—thou mayest be the grand artificer of deceit come to
practise upon my immortal soul. Unmantle thee, I pray, that
I may behold if thou art a poor and an afflicted spirit punished for a time, or that fierce and restless fiend who bears the
visible stamp of eternal reprobation.' 'I may not withstand
thy wish,' uttered the form in a tone of melancholy, and dropping his mantle, and turning round on the pastor, said, 'Hast
thou forgotten me?' 'How can I forget thee?' said Ezra, receding as he spoke; 'the stern and the haughty look of
Bonshaw has been humbled indeed. Unhappy one, thou art
sorely changed since I beheld thee on earth with the helmet
plume fanning thy hot and bloody brow as thy right hand
smote down the blessed ones of the earth. The Almighty
doom—the evil and the tormenting place—the vile companions—have each in their turn done the work of retribution
upon thee—thou art indeed more stern and more terrible,

but thou art not changed beyond the knowledge of one whom thou hast hunted and hounded, and sought to slay utterly.'

The shape or spirit of Bonshaw dilated with anger, and in a quicker and a fiercer tone said, 'Be charitable; flesh and blood, be charitable—doom not to hell-fire and grim companions one whose sins thou canst not weigh but in the balance of thine own prejudices. I tell thee, man of God, the uncharitableness of the sect to which thou pertainest has thronged the land of punishment as much as those who headed, and hanged, and stabbed, and shot, and tortured. I may be punished for a time, and not wholly reprobate.' 'Punished in part, or doomed in whole, thou needs must be,' answered the pastor, who seemed now as much at his ease as if this singular colloquy had happened with a neighbouring divine. 'A holy and a blessed spirit would have appeared in a brighter shape. I like not thy dubious words, thou half punished and half pardoned spirit. Away, vanish! shall I speak the sacred words which make the fiends howl, or wilt thou depart in peace?' 'In peace I come to thee,' said the spirit, 'and in peace let me be gone: hadst thou come sooner when I summoned thee, and not loitered away the precious death-bed moments, hearkening the wild and fanciful song of one whom I have deeply wronged, this journey might have been spared —a journey of pain to me, and peril to thyself.' 'Peril to me!' said the pastor: 'be it even as thou sayest. Shall I fly for one cast down, over whose prostrate form the purging fire has passed? Wicked was thy course on earth—many and full of evil were thy days—and now thou art loose again, thou fierce and persecuting spirit—a woe, and a woe to poor Scotland.' 'They are loose who were never bound,' answered the spirit of Bonshaw, darkening in anger, and expanding in form, 'and that I could soon show thee. But, behold, I am not permitted—there is a watcher—a holy one come nigh prepared to resist and to smite—I shall do thee no harm, holy man—I vow by the pains of punishment and the conscience-pang— now the watcher has departed.'

'Of whom speakest thou?' inquired Ezra: 'have we ministering spirits who guard the good from the plots of the wicked ones?—have we evil spirits who tempt and torment men, and teach the maidens ensnaring songs, and lighten their feet and their heads for the wanton dance?' 'Stay, I pray thee,' said the spirit; 'there are spirits of evil men and of good men made perfect who are permitted to visit the earth, and power is given them for a time to work their will with men. I behold one of the latter even now, a bold one and a noble; but he sees I mean not to harm thee, so we shall not war together.'

At this assurance of protection, the pastor inclined his shuddering steed closer to his companion, and thus he proceeded: 'You have said that my sect—my meek and lowly, and broken, and long persecuted remnant—have helped to people the profound hell—am I to credit thy words?' 'Credit them or no as thou wilt,' said the spirit: 'whoso spilleth blood by the sword, by the word, and by the pen, is there—the false witness—the misinterpreter of the gospel—the profane poet—the profane and presumptuous preacher—the slayer and the slain—the persecutor and the persecuted—he who died at the stake, and he who piled the faggot—all are there, enduring hard weird and penal fire for a time reckoned and days numbered. They are there whom thou wottest not of,' said the confiding spirit, drawing near as he spoke, and whispering the names of some of the worthies of the kirk, and the noble, and the far-descended.

'I well believe thee,' said the pastor, 'but I beseech thee to be more particular in thy information; give me the names which some of the chief ministers of woe in the nether world were known by in this—I shall hear of those who built cathedrals and strong holds, and filled thrones spiritual and temporal.' 'Ay, that thou wilt,' said the spirit, 'and the names of some of the mantled professors of God's humble Presbyterian kirk also; those who preached a burning fire and a devouring hell to their dissenting brethren, and who called out, with a loud voice, perdition to the sons and daughters of men; "draw the sword; slay and smite utterly." ' 'Thou art a false spirit assuredly,' said the pastor; 'yet tell me one thing. Thy steed and thou seem to be as one, to move as one, and I observed thee even now conversing with thy brute part; dost thou ride on a punished spirit, and is there injustice in hell as well as on earth?' The spirit laughed. 'Knowest thou not this patient and obedient spirit on whom I ride—what wouldest thou say if I named a name renowned at the holy altar?—the name of one who loosed the sword on the bodies of men, because they believed in an humble Saviour, and he believed in a lofty. I have bestrode that mitred personage before now—he is the hack to all the Presbyterians in the pit, but he cannot be

spared on a journey so distant as this.' 'So thou wilt not tell
me the name of thy steed?' said Ezra; 'well, even as thou wilt.'
'Nay,' said the spirit, 'I shall not deny so good a man so small
a matter. Knowest thou not George Johnstone, the captain
of my troop, as bold a hand as ever bore a sword and used it
among fanatics?—we lived together in life, and in death we
are not divided.' 'In persecution and in punishment, thou
mightest have said, thou scoffing spirit,' said the pastor; 'but
tell me, do men lord it in perdition as they did on earth; is
there no retributive justice among the condemned spirits?' 'I
have condescended on that already,' said the spirit, 'and I will
tell thee further: there is thy old acquaintance and mine,
George Gordon, punished and condemned though he be, he is
the scourge, and the whip, and the rod of fire to all those
brave and valiant men who served those equitable and charitable princes, Charles Stuart, and James his brother.' 'I suspect why those honourable cavaliers are tasting the cup of
punishment,' said the pastor; 'but what crime has sedate and
holy George done, that his lot is cast with the wicked?' 'Canst
thou not guess it, holy Ezra?' said the spirit; 'his crime was
so contemptible and mean that I scorn to name it: hast thou
any further questions?'

'You spoke of Charles Stuart, and James, his brother,' said
the pastor: 'when sawest thou the princes for whom thou
delugedst thy country with blood, and periledst thine own
soul?'—'Ah! thou cunning querist,' said the spirit with a
laugh, 'canst thou not ask a plain question? thou askest questions plain and pointed enough of the back-sliding damsels of
thy congregation—why shouldst thou put thy sanctified tricks
on me, a plain and a straight-forward spirit, as ever uttered
response to the godly? Nevertheless, I will tell thee, I saw
them not an hour ago—Charles saddled me my steed; wot ye
who held my stirrup?—even James his brother. I asked them
if they had any message to the devout people of their ancient
kingdom of Scotland. The former laughed, and bade me bring
him the kirk repentance-stool[14] for a throne. The latter looked
grave, and muttered over his fingers like a priest counting his
beads; and hell echoed far and wide with laughter at the two
princes.'—'Ay, ay!' said the pastor, 'so I find you have mirth
among you: have you dance and song also?'—'Ay, truly,'
answered the spirit, 'we have hymns and hallelujahs from the
lips of that holy and patriotic band who banished their native

princes, and sold their country to an alien;[15] and the alien
himself rules and reigns among them; and when they are
weary with the work of praise, certain inferior and officious
spirits moisten their lips with cupfuls of a curious and a cool-
ing liquid, and then hymn and thanksgiving recommence
again.'—'Ah, thou dissembler,' said the pastor; 'and yet I see
little cause why they should be redeemed, when so many lofty
minds must wallow with the sinful for a season. But, tell me,
it is long since I heard of Claud Hamilton; have you seen him
among you? he was the friend and follower of the alien—a
mocker of the mighty minds of his native land—a scoffer of
that gifted and immortal spirit which pours the glory of Scotland to the uttermost ends of the earth—tell me of him, I
pray.' Loud laughed the spirit, and replied in scorn, 'We take
no note of things so mean and unworthy as he; he may be in
some hole in perdition, for aught I know or care: but, stay, I
will answer thee truly; he has not passed to our kingdom yet;
he is condemned to the punishment of a long and useless life
on earth; and even now you will find him gnawing his flesh in
agony to hear the name he has sought to cast down renowned
over all the earth!'

The spirit now seemed impatient to be gone: they had
emerged from the glen; and vale, and lea, brightened by the
moon, and sown thick with evening dew, sparkled far and
wide. 'If thou wouldest question me farther,' said the frank
and communicative spirit of Bonshaw, 'and learn more of the
dead, meet me in the old burial-ground an hour before
moon-rise on Sunday night: tarry at home if thou wilt; but, I
have more to tell thee than thou knowest to ask about; and
hair of thy head shall not be harmed.' Even as he spoke, the
shape of horse and rider underwent a sudden transformation—the spirit sank into the shape of a steed, the steed rose
into the form of the rider, and wrapping his visionary mantle
about him, and speaking to his unearthly horse, away he
started, casting as he flew a sudden and fiery glance on the
astonished pastor, who muttered as he concluded a brief
prayer,—'there goes Captain George Johnstone, riding on his
fierce old master.'

The old burial-ground, the spirit's trysting place, was a fair,
but a lonely spot. All around lay scenes renowned in tradition
for blood, and broil, and secret violence. The parish was formerly a land of warriors' towers, and of houses for penance,

and vigil, and mortification. But the reformation came, and
sacked and crushed down the houses of devotion; while the
peace between the two kingdoms curbed the courage, and
extinguished for ever the military and predatory glory of those
old Galwegian chieftains. It was in a burial-ground pertaining
to one of those ancient churches, and where the peasants still
loved to have their dust laid, that Ezra trusted to meet
again the shadowy representative of the fierce old laird of
Bonshaw.

The moon, he computed, had a full hour to travel before
her beams would be shed on the place of conference, and to
that eerie and deserted spot Ezra was observed to walk like
one consecrating an evening hour to solitary musing on the
rivulet side. No house stood within half a mile; and when he
reached the little knoll on which the chapel formerly stood, he
sat down on the summit to ponder over the way to manage
this singular conference. A firm spirit, and a pure heart, he
hoped, would confound and keep at bay the enemy of man's
salvation; and he summed up, in a short historical way, the
names of those who had met and triumphed over the machin-
ations of fiends. Thus strengthened and reassured, he rose,
and looked around, but he saw no approaching shape. The
road along which he expected the steed and rider to come was
empty, and he walked towards the broken gate, to cast himself
in the way, and show with what confidence he abode his
coming.

Over the wall of the church-yard, repaired with broken
and carved stones from the tombs and altar of the chapel, he
now looked, and it was with surprise that he saw a new-made
widow, kneeling over her husband's grave, and about to pour
out her spirit in lamentation and sorrow. He knew her form
and face, and the deepest sorrow came upon him. She was the
daughter of an old and a faithful elder: she had married a seafaring youth, and borne him one fair child. Her husband was
returning from a distant voyage—had entered the sea of
Solway—his native hills—his own home, rose to his view, and
he saw the light streaming from the little chamber window,
where his wife and his sweet child sat awaiting his return. But
it was not written that they were to meet again in life. She
heard the sweep of a whirlwind, and she heard a shriek, and
going to her chamber door, she saw the ship sinking, and her
husband struggling in the agitated water. It is needless to

lengthen a sorrowful story: she now threw herself weeping over his grave, and poured out the following wail:

'He was the fairest among men, yet the sea swept him away: he was the kindest hearted, yet he was not to remain. What were all other men, compared to him—his long curling hair, and his sweet hazel eyes, and his kind and gladsome tongue? He loved me long; and he won me from many rivals; for who could see his face and not love him?—who could listen to his speech, and refuse him aught? When he danced, maids stood round, and thought his feet made richer music than the instruments. When he sang, the maids and matrons blest him; and high-born dames loved the song of my frank and gentle sailor. But there is no mercy in the ocean for the sons of men; and there is nought but sorrow for their daughters. Men go grey-headed to the grave, who, had they trusted the unstable deeps, would have perished in their prime, and left fatherless babes, and sorrowing widows. Alas, alas! in lonely night on this eerie spot, on thy low and early grave, I pour forth my heart! Who now shall speak peace to my mind, and open the latch of my little lonely home with thy kind and anxious hand? Who now shall dandle my sweet babe on his knee, or love to go with me to kirk and to preaching—to talk over our old tales of love and courtship—of the secret tryst and the bridal joy?' And, concluding her melancholy chant, she looked sorrowfully and steadfastly at the grave, and recommenced anew her wailing and her tears.

The widow's grief endured so long that the moon began to make her approach manifest by shooting up a long and a broad stream of thin, lucid, and trembling light over the eastern ridge of the Cumberland hills. She rose from her knees, shed back her moist and disordered locks, showing a face pale but lovely, while the watery light of two large dark eyes of liquid and roving blue, was cast mournfully on the way homewards, down which she now turned her steps to be gone. Of what passed in the pastor's mind at this moment, tradition, which sometimes mocks and at other times deifies the feelings of men, gives a very unsatisfactory account. He saw the hour of appointment with his shadowy messenger from the other world arrive and pass without his appearance; and he was perhaps persuaded, that the pure, and pious, and overflowing grief of the fair young widow had prevented the intrusion of a form so ungracious and unholy. As

she advanced from the burial-ground, the pastor of her parish
stood mute and sorrowful before her. She passed him as one
not wishing to be noticed, and glided along the path with a
slow step and a downcast eye.

She had reached the side of a little lonely stream, which
glided half seen, half hid, underneath its banks of broom and
honeysuckle, sprinkled at that hour with wild daisies, and
spotted with primroses—when the voice of Ezra reached her
ears. She made a full stop, like one who hears something
astounding, and turned round on the servant of the altar a
face radiant with tears, to which her tale of woe, and the wild
and lonely place, added an interest and a beauty: 'Young
woman,' he began, 'it is unseemly in thee to bewail thy loss at
this lonely hour, and in this dreary spot: the youth was given
to thee, and ye became vain. I remarked the pride of thy
looks, and the gaudiness of thine apparel, even in the house of
holiness: he is taken from thee, perhaps, to punish thy pride.
There is less meekness in thy sorrow than there was reason in
thy joy; but be ye not discomforted.' Here the weeping lady
turned the sidelong glance of her swimming eyes on Ezra, shed
back the locks which usurped a white brow and snowy
temples, and folding her hands over a bosom, the throbbings
of which made the cambric that concealed it undulate like
water, stood still, and drank in his words of comfort and
condolence.

Tradition always conducts Ezra and the mariner's widow
to this seldom frequented place: a hundred and a hundred
times have I mused over the scene in sunlight and moonlight;
a hundred and a hundred times have I hearkened to the wild
and variable accounts of the peasantry, and sought to make
bank, and bush, and stream, and tree, assist in unravelling the
mystery which must still hang over the singular and tragic
catastrophe. Standing in this romantic place, a pious man, not
overstricken in years, conversing with a rosy young widow, a
vain and a fair creature, a bank of blossomed flowers beside
them, and the new risen moon scattering her slant and ineffectual beams on the thick budded branches above them—such
is the picture which tradition ever and invariably draws, while
imagination endeavours to take up the tender thread of the
story, and imagination must have this licence still. Truth contents herself with the summary of a few and unsatisfactory
particulars: the dawn of morning came, says Truth, and Ezra

had not returned to his manse. Something evil hath happened, said Imagination, scattering as she spoke a thousand tales of a thousand hues, many of which still find credence among the pious people of Galloway.

Josiah, the old and faithful servant of Ezra, arrived in search of his master at the lonely burial-ground about the dawn of the morning. He had become alarmed at his long absence, and his alarm was not abated by the unholy voices which at midnight sailed round the manse and kirk, singing, as he imagined, a wild and infernal hymn of joy and thanks-giving. He traced his steps down the footpath by the rivulet side till he came to the little primrose bank, and found it trodden upon and pressed as if two persons had been seated among the flowers. Here all further traces ceased, and Josiah stood pondering on the power of evil spirits, and the danger of holding tryst with Beelzebub or any of the lesser spirits of darkness.

He was soon joined by an old shepherd, who told a tale which pious men refuse to believe, though they always listen to it. The bright moonlight had made him imagine it was morning, and he arose and walked forth to look at his lambs on the distant hill—the moon had been up for nearly an hour. His way lay near the little lonely primrose bank, and as he walked along he heard the whispering of tongues: he deemed it some idle piece of love-making, and he approached to see who they might be. He saw what ought not to be seen, even the reverend Ezra seated on the bank and conversing with a buxom young dame and a strange one. They were talking wondrous kindly. He observed them for a little space; the young dame was in widow's weeds; the mariner's widow wore the only weeds, praise be blest, in the parish, but she was a raven to a swan compared to the quean who conversed with the minister. She was indeed passing fair, and the longer he looked on her she became the lovelier, owre lovely for mere flesh and blood. His dog shrunk back and whimpered, and an owl that chased a bird in the grove, uttered a scream of terror as it beheld her, and forsook its prey. At length she turned the light of her eyes on himself; Will wi' the Wisp was but a proverb to them: they had a glance he should never get the better of, and he hardly thought his legs carried him home, he flew with such supernatural speed.

'But, indeed,' added the cautious peasant, 'I have some

doubts that the whole was a fiction of the auld enemy, to
make me think ill of the douce man and the godly; and if he
be spared to come home, so shall I tell him. But if Ezra, pious
man, is heard of nae mair, I shall be free to believe that what
I heard I heard, and what I saw I saw. And Josiah, man, I
may as weel give ye the benefit of my own opinion. I'll amaist
aver on my Bible, that the minister, a daring man and a
courageous—owre courageous, I doubt—has been dared out
to the lonely place by some he, or, may be, she-fiend—the
latter maist likely; and there he has been overcome by might
or temptation, and now Satan may come atween the stilts of
the gospel plough, for the right hand of Ezra will hold it no
longer; or I should nae wonder,' said the peasant, 'but that
the old dour persecutor Bonshaw has carried him away on his
fiend steed Geordie Johnstone—conscience, nought more
likely—and I'll warrant even now they are ducking him in the
dub of perdition, or picking his banes ahint the hallan o'
hell.'

The whole of this rustic prediction was not fulfilled. In a
little deep wild dell, at the distance of a gun shot, they found
Ezra Peden lying on the ground, uttering words which will
be pardoned, since they were the words of a delirious tongue.
He was carried home amid the sympathy and sorrow of his
parishioners: he answered no question nor seemed to observe a
single face, though the face of many a friend stood round
him. He only raved out words of tenderness and affection,
addressed to some imaginary person at his side; and concluded
by starting up, and raising such an outcry of horror and
amazement, as if the object of his regard had become a
demon: seven strong men could hardly hold him. He died on
the third day, after making a brief disclosure, which may be
readily divined from this hasty and imperfect narrative.

THE SELBYS OF CUMBERLAND.
PART FIRST

Thus would she sit a summer eve, and shed[16]
The wither'd tresses from her faded brow;
Stretch forth her long and feeble arm, which nursed
Three generations—moving thus her knee,
And smiling as a mother smiles who dandles
Her first-born darling mid the sunny air.
And then she chanted an old chivalrous ballad,
And mutter'd snatches of our old sad stories—
Such tales as stay the peasant at his plow—
The shepherd's sharp shears, as they reap the fleece—
The household damsel while she twines the thread—
And make the maid, even as the ewe-milk reeks
Between her whiter fingers, pause and sigh
To think of old how gentle love was crost
In green and gladsome Cumberland.

Among the pastoral mountains of Cumberland dwells an
unmingled and patriarchal race of people, who live in a primitive manner, and retain many peculiar usages different from
their neighbours of the valley and the town. They are
imagined by antiquarians to be descended from a colony of
Saxon herdsmen and warriors, who, establishing themselves
among the mountainous wastes, quitted conquest and spoliation for the peaceful vocation of tending their flocks, and
managing the barter of their rustic wealth for the luxuries
fabricated by their more ingenious neighbours. In the cultivation of corn they are unskilful or uninstructed; but in all
that regards sheep and cattle, they display a knowledge and a
tact which is the envy of all who live by the fleece and shears.
Their patriarchal wealth enables them to be hospitable, and
dispense an unstinted boon among all such people as chance,
curiosity, or barter, scatter over their inheritance.

It happened on a fine summer afternoon, that I found
myself engaged in the pursuit of an old fox, which annually
preyed on our lambs, and eluded the vigilance of the most

skilful huntsmen. Leaving Keswick far behind, I pursued my cunning adversary from glen to cavern, till, at last, he fairly struck across an extensive tract of upland, and sought refuge from the hotness of pursuit in one of the distant mountains. I had not proceeded far on this wide and desolate tract, ere I became fatigued and thirsty, and—what true sportsmen reckon a much more serious misfortune—found myself left alone and far behind—while the shout and the cheer of my late companions began to grow faint and fainter, and I at last heard only the bleat of the flocks or the calling of the curlew. The upland on which I had entered appeared boundless on all sides, while amid the brown wilderness arose innumerable green grassy knolls, with herds of small black cattle and sheep grazing or reposing on their sides and summits. They seemed so many green islands floating amid the ocean of brown blossom, with which the heath was covered.

I stood on one of the knolls, and, looking around, observed a considerable stream gushing from a small copse of hazel and lady-fern, which, seeking its way into a green and narrow glen, pursued its course with a thousand freakish windings and turnings. While following with my eye the course of the pure stream out of which I had slaked my thirst, I thought I heard something like the sound of a human voice coming up the glen; and, with the hope of finding some of my baffled companions of the chase, I proceeded along the margin of the brook. At first, a solitary and stunted alder, or hazel bush, or mountain ash, in which the hooded crow had sought shelter for her young, was all the protection the stream obtained from the rigour of the mid-day sun. The glen became broader and the stream deeper,—gliding over a bed of pebbles, shining, large, and round,—half-seen, half-hid, beneath the projection of the grassy sward it had undermined; and raising all the while that soft and simmering din, which contributes so much music to pastoral verse. A narrow footpath, seldom frequented, winded with the loops and turns of the brook. I had wandered along the margin nearly a quarter of a mile, when I approached a large and doddered tree of green holly, on the top of which sat a raven, grey-backed and bald-headed from extreme age, looking down intently on something which it thought worthy of watching beneath.

I reached the tree unheard or unheeded,—for the soft soil returned no sound to my foot; and on the sunward side I found a woman seated on the grass. She seemed bordering on seventy years of age—with an unbent and unbroken frame—a look of lady-like stateliness—and an eye of that sweet and shining hazel colour, of which neither age nor sorrow had been able to dim the glance. Her mantle,—once green, and garnished with flowers of gold thread at the extremities, lay folded at her feet, together with a broad flat straw hat—an article of dress common seventy or eighty years ago, and a long staff worn smooth as horn by daily employment. Her hair, nut-brown and remarkably long in her youth, was now become as white as December's snow, and its profusion had also yielded like its colour to time,—for it hung, or rather flowed, over her shoulders in solitary ringlets, and scarcely afforded a minute's employment to her fingers—which seemed to have been once well acquainted with arranging in all its beauty one of nature's finest ornaments. As she disposed of each tress, she accompanied the motion of her hands with the verse of a legendary ballad, which she chanted, unconscious of my presence, and which probably related to an adventure of her ancestors.

LADY SELBY[17]

1.

On the holly tree sat a raven black,
    And at its foot a lady fair
Sat singing of sorrow, and shedding down
    The tresses of her nut-brown hair:
And aye as that fair dame's voice awoke,
The raven broke in with a chorusing croak.

2.

'The steeds they are saddled on Derwent-banks;
    The banners are streaming so broad and free;
The sharp sword sits at each Selby's side,
    And all to be dyed for the love of me:
And I maun give this lily-white hand
To him who wields the wightest brand.

3.

'She coost her mantle of satin so fine,
    She kilted her gown of the deep-sea green,
She wound her locks round her brow, and flew
    Where the swords were glimmering sharp and sheen:
As she flew, the trumpet awoke with a clang,
And the sharp blades smote, and the bow-strings sang.

4.

'The streamlet that ran down the lonely vale,
    Aneath its banks, half seen, half hid,
Seem'd melted silver—at once it came down,
    From the shocking of horsemen—reeking and red;
And that lady flew—and she utter'd a cry,
As the riderless steeds came rushing by.

5.

'And many have fallen—and more have fled:—
    All in a nook of bloody ground
That lady sat by a bleeding knight,
    And strove with her fingers to stanch the wound:
Her locks, like sun-beams when summer's in pride,
She pluck'd and plac'd on his wounded side.

6.

'And aye the sorer that lady sigh'd,
    The more her golden locks she drew—
The more she pray'd—the ruddy life's-blood
    The faster and faster came trickling through:—
On a sadder sight ne'er looked the moon
That o'er the green mountain came gleaming down.

7.

'He lay with his sword in the pale moonlight;
    All mute and pale she lay at his side—
He, sheath'd in mail from brow to heel—
    She, in her maiden bloom and pride:
And their beds were made, and the lovers were laid,
All under the gentle holly's shade.

8.

'May that Selby's right hand wither and rot,
    That fails with flowers their bed to strew!
May a foreign grave be his who doth rend
    Away the shade of the holly bough!—
But let them sleep by the gentle river,
And waken in love that shall last for ever.'

As the old dame ceased her song, she opened her lap, from
which she showered a profusion of flowers—such as are gathered rather in the wood or the wild than the garden,—on two
green ridges which lay side by side beneath the shade of the
green holly. At each handful she strewed she muttered, in an
under-tone, what sounded like the remains of an ancient form
of prayer; when turning toward the path, she observed me,
and said,—'Youth, comest thou here to smile at beholding a
frail woman strew the dust of the beautiful and the brave with
mountain-thyme, wild mint, and scented hawthorn?' I soothed
her by a tone of submission and reverence. 'Eleanor Selby,
may the curse of the ballad, which thou sangest even now, be
mine, if I come to scorn those who honour the fair and the
brave. Had I known that the ancient lovers, about whom we
so often sing, slept by this lonely stream, I would have sought
Cumberland for the fairest and rarest flowers to shower on
their grassy beds.' 'I well believe thee, youth,' said the old
dame, mollified at once by my respect for the surname of
Selby,—'how could I forget the altar of Lanercost and thee?
There are few at thy wilful and froward time of life, who
would not mock the poor wandering woman, and turn her
wayward affections into ridicule; but I see thy respect for her
sitting shining in those sweet and moist eyes of hazel.'
    While she indulged in this language, she replaced her long
white locks under her bonnet, resumed her mantle and her
staff, and, having adjusted all to her liking, and taken a look
at the two graves, and at the raven, who still maintained his
seat on the summit of the bush, she addressed me again. 'But,
come, youth, come—the sun is fast walking down the side of
the western mountains: Fremmet-ha is a good mile distant;
and we shall be wise to seek the friendship of its porch, with
an unset sun above our heads.' She took my hand, and exert-
ing an energy I little expected, we descended the glen
together, keeping company with the brook, which received

and acknowledged, by an augmented murmur, the accession
of several lesser streams. At length we came where the glen,
suddenly expanding into a beautiful vale, and the brook into
a small, deep and clear lake, disclosed to my sight the whole
domestic establishment of one of the patriarchal portioners of
the mountainous regions of Cumberland.

On the northern side of the valley, and fronting the mid-
day sun, stood a large old-fashioned house, constructed of
rough and undressed stones, such as are found in abundance
on the northern uplands, and roofed with a heavy coating of
heath, near an ell in thickness,—the whole secured with bands
of wood and ropes of flax, in a manner that resembled the
checks of a highland plaid. Something which imitated a shepherd's crook and a sheathed sword was carved on a piece of
hewn stone in the front, and underneath was cut in rude
square raised letters 'RANDAL RODE, 1545'. The remains of
old defences were still visible to a person of an antiquarian
turn; but sheep-folds, cattle-folds, and swine-pens usurped the
trench and the rampart, and filled the whole southern side of
the valley. In the middle of the lake shattered walls of squared
stone were visible, and deep in the clear water a broken and
narrow causeway might be traced, which once secured to the
proprietor of the mansion a safe retreat against any hasty
incursion from the restless borderers, who, in former times,
were alternately the plunderers or defenders of their country.
The descendants of Randal Rode seemed to be sensible that
their lot was cast in securer times, and instead of practising
with the bow, or that still more fatal weapon the gun,[18] or
with the sword, or with the spear, they were collected on a
small green plat of ground on the margin of the lake, to the
number of twelve or fourteen, indulging in the rustic exercises
of wrestling, leaping, throwing the bar,[19] and casting the
stone. Several old white-headed men were seated at a small
distance on the ground, maidens continually passed backwards and forwards, with pails of milk, or with new-moulded
cheese, casting a casual glance at the pastime of the young
men—the valley all the while re-murmuring with the din of
the various contests.

As we approached, a young man who had thrown the
stone—a pebble massy and round—beyond all the marks of
his companions, perceived us coming, and came running to
welcome the old woman with all the unrestrained joyousness

of eighteen. 'Welcome, Dame Eleanor Selby, welcome to
Fremmet-ha! For thy repose I have ordered a soft warm
couch, and from no fairer hands than those of my own sister
Maude Rode—and for thy gratification, as well as mine own,
have I sought far and wide for a famous ballad of the Selbys;
but we are fallen on evil days—the memory of our oldest
men only yielded me fragments: these I have pieced together,
and shall gladly sing it with all the grace I may.'—'Fair fall
thee, youth,' said the old woman, pleased at the revival of a
traditional rhyme recording the fame of her house; 'thy companions are all clods of the valley, no better than the stones
they cast, the bars they heave, and the dull earth they leap
upon, compared to thee.—But the Selbys' blood within thee
overcomes that of the Rodes.'—The young man came close to
her ear, and in an interceding whisper said: 'It is true, Dame
Eleanor Selby, that my father is but a tender of flocks, and
nowise comparable to the renowned house of Selby, with
whom he had the fortune to intermarry—but, by the height of
Skiddaw, and the depth of Solway, he is as proud of his churl's
blood as the loftiest of the land; and the welcome of that person would be cold, and his repulse certain, who should tell
him the unwelcome tale that he wedded above his degree.'
'Youth, youth,' said the old woman, with hasty and marked
impatience, 'I shall for thy sake refrain from comparing the
churlish name of Rode with the gentle name of Selby;—but I
would rather sit a winter night on Skiddaw, than have the
best who bear the name of Rode to imagine that the hem of a
Selby's robe had not more of gentleness than seven acres of
Rodes's. But thou hast promised me a song: even let me hearken to it now in the free open air—sitting by an ancient summer seat of the Selbys—it will put me in a mood to enter thy
mother's abode.' She seated herself on the margin of the lake,
while the young man, surrounded by his companions, sung
in a rough free voice the legendary ballad of which I had the
good fortune to obtain a copy.

SIR ROLAND GRAEME[20]

1.

The trumpet has rung on Helvellyn side,
    The bugle in Derwent vale;
And an hundred steeds came hurrying fleet,
    With an hundred men in mail:
And the gathering cry, and the warning word
Was, 'Fill the quiver and sharpen the sword.'

2.

And away they bound—the mountain deer
    Starts at their helmets' flash:—
And away they go—the brooks call out
    With a hoarse and a murmuring dash;
The foam flung from their steeds as they go
Strews all their track like the drifting snow.

3.

What foe do they chase, for I see no foe;
    And yet, all spurr'd and gored:
Their good steeds fly—say, seek they work
    For the fleet hound or the sword?
I see no foe—yet a foe they pursue,
With bow and brand, and horn and halloo.

4.

Sir Richard spurs on his bonnie brown steed,
    Sir Walter on his black;
There are an hundred steeds, and each
    Has a Selby on its back:
And the meanest man there draws a brand
Has silver spurs and a Baron's land.

5.

The Eden is deep in flood—lo! look
    How it dashes from bank to bank!
To them it seems but the bonnie green lea,
    Or the vale with brackens rank.
They brave the water, and breast the banks,
And shake the flood and foam from their flanks.

6.

The winding and haunted Eske is nigh,
    With its woodlands wild and green;
'Our steeds are white with foam; shall we wash
    Their flanks in the river sheen?'
But their steeds may be doom'd to a sterner task,
Before they pass the woodland Eske.

7.

All at once they stoop on their horses' necks,
    And utter a long shrill shout;
And bury their spurs in their coursers' flanks,
    And pluck their bright blades out:
The spurn'd-up turf is scatter'd behind,
For they go as the hawk when he sails with the wind.

8.

Before them not far on the lilied lea
    There is a fair youth flying;
And at his side rides a lovely maid
    Oft looking back and sighing:—
On his basnet dances the heron's plume,
And fans the maid's cheek all of ripe rose bloom.

9.

'Now do thy best, my bonnie grey steed,
    And carry my true love over,
And thy corn shall be served in a silver dish,
    And heap'd and running over—
O bear her safe through dark Eske's fords,
And leave me to cope with her kinsmen's swords!'

10.

Proud look'd the steed, and had braved the flood,
    Had it foam'd a full mile wider;
Turn'd his head in joy, and his eye seem'd to say,
    I'm proud of my lovely rider:
And though Selbys stood thick as the leaves on the tree,
All scaithless I'd bear thee o'er mountain and lea.

11.

A rushing was heard on the river banks,
    Wide rung wood, rock, and linn—
And that instant an hundred horsemen at speed
    Came foaming and fearless in.
'Turn back, turn back, thou Scottish loon—
Let us measure our swords 'neath the light of the moon!'

12.

An hundred horsemen leap'd lightly down,
    With their silver spurs all ringing;
And drew back, as Sir Richard his good blade bared,
    While the signal trump kept singing:
Sir Roland Graeme down his mantle threw
With a martial smile, and his bright sword drew.

13.

With a measuring eye and a measured pace
    Nigher they came and nigher;
Then made a bound and made a blow,
    And the smote helms yielded fire:
December's hail, or the thunder blast,
Ne'er flash'd so bright, or fell so fast.

14.

'Now yield thee, Graeme, and give me back
    Lord Selby's beauteous daughter;
Else I shall sever thy head and heave't
    To thy light love o'er the water.'—
'My sword is steel, Sir Richard, like thine,
And thy head's as loose on thy neck as mine.'

15.

And again their dark eyes flash'd, and again
    They closed—on sweet Eske side,
The ring-doves sprung from their roosts, for the blows
    Were echoing far and wide:
Sir Richard was stark, and Sir Roland was strong;
And the combat was fierce, but it lasted not long.

16.

There's blood upon young Roland's blade,
    There's blood on Sir Richard's brand;
There's blood shower'd o'er their weeds of steel,
    And rain'd on the grassy land;
But blood to a warrior's like dew to the flow'r;
The combat but wax'd still more deadly and dour.

17.

A dash was heard in the moonlit Eske,
    And up its banks of green;
Fair Edith Selby came with a shriek,
    And knelt the knights between:
'Oh spare him, Sir Richard!' she held her white hands,
All spotted with blood 'neath the merciless brands.

18.

Young Roland look'd down on his true love and smiled,
    Sir Richard look'd also, and said—
'Curse on them that true love would sunder!' he sheath'd
    With his broad palm his berry-brown blade;
And long may the Selbys abroad and at hame,
Find a friend and a foe like the good gallant Graeme!

While the ballad proceeded, the old representative of the
house of Selby sat with a look of demure dignity and importance, and regarded this minstrel remembrance of the forcible
engrafting of the predatory name of Graeme on the stately
tree of the Selbys with a look of the darkest displeasure. When
the youth finished, she arose hastily, and, elevating herself to
her utmost stature, said, 'May that ignorant minstrel be mute
for ever—or confine his strains to the beasts of the field, and
the churls who tend them—who has presumed to fashion the
ballad of Roland Graeme's wooing of Edith Howard of
Naworth into a rhyme, reproaching with this ungentle marriage the spotless house of Selby! A gentle Selby wed a border
Graeme! may the heavens forfend! Who will lay a dog in a
deer's den?' 'No,' said she, muttering in continuance, as she
walked into the house of her ancestors, 'we have had sad
mishaps among us—but nothing like that. One branch of the
stately Selby-tree carried the kite's nest of a Forster, another
the rook's nest of a Rode—but neither scion nor bough have

sheltered the hooded-crow brood of the men of the debateable land. Men neither of predatory Scotland nor haughty England, but begotten in the haste of a mutual inroad—and the herald's office cannot divine by whom.' The mutterings of the wayward woman fell unregarded in the ear of fair Maude Rode, one of the sweetest maidens that ever pressed curd or milked ewes among the pastoral mountains of Cumberland. She welcomed old Eleanor with one of those silent glances which says so much, and spread her a seat, and ministered to her with the demeanour of the humblest handmaid of the house of Selby, when its splendour was fullest. This modest kindness soon had its effect on the mutable descendant of this ancient house; she regained her serenity; and her wild legends, and traditional tales were related to no ungrateful ears.

THE SELBYS OF CUMBERLAND.
PART SECOND

And when she came to yon kirk-yard,[21]
    Where graves are green and low,
She saw full thirty coal-black steeds
    All standing in a row.

And out she stretch'd her trembling hand,
    Their mighty sides to stroke;
And aye she reach'd, and aye she stretch'd—
    'Twas nothing all but smoke.

They were but mere delusive forms
    Of films, and sulph'ry wind;
And every wave she gave her hand
    A gap was left behind.

James Hogg

'A bright fire, a clean floor, and a pleasant company,' is one of the proverbial wishes of domestic comfort among the wilds of Cumberland. The moorland residence of Randal Rode exhibited the first and second portions of the primitive wish, and it required no very deep discernment to see that around the ample hearth we had materials for completing the proverb. In each face was reflected that singular mixture of gravity and humour, peculiar, I apprehend, to the people of the north. Before a large fire, which it is reckoned ominous ever to extinguish, lay half a dozen sheep-dogs, spreading out their white bosoms to the heat, and each placed opposite to the seat of its owner. The lord or rather portioner of Fremmet-ha himself lay apart on a large couch of oak antiquely carved, and ornamented like some of the massive furniture of the days of the olden church, with beads, and crosses, and pastoral crooks. This settee was bedded deep with sheepskins, each retaining a fleece of long white wool. At each end lay a shepherd's dog, past its prime, like its master, and, like him, enjoying a kind of half-ruminating and drowsy leisure peculiar to old age. Three or four busy wheels, guided by as many maidens, manufactured wool into yarn for rugs, and mauds, and mantles. Three other maidens, with bared arms, prepared curds for cheese, and their hands rivalled in whiteness the curdled milk itself. Under the light of a large candlestick several youths pursued the amusement of the popular game of draughts. This piece of rude furniture ought not to escape particular description. It resembled an Etruscan candelabra, and was composed of a shaft, capable of being depressed or elevated by means of a notched groove, and sunk secure in a block of wood at the floor, terminated above in a shallow cruse or plate, like a three-cocked hat, in each corner of which stood a large candle, rendering the spacious hall where we sat as light as day. On this scene of patriarchal happiness looked my old companion Eleanor Selby, contrasting, as she glanced her eye in succession over the tokens of shepherds' wealth in which the house abounded, the present day with the past; the times of the fleece, the shears, and the distaff, with those of broils and blood, and mutual inroad and invasion, when the name of Selby stood high in the chivalry of the north. One might observe in her changing looks the themes of rustic degradation and chivalrous glory on which she brooded; and the present peaceful time suffered by the comparison, as the present always does in the contemplation of old age. The constant attention of young Maude Rode, who ministered to the comfort of her ancient and wayward relative, seemed gradually to soothe and charm down the demon of proud ancestry, who maintained rule in her breast; and after inter-changing softer and softer looks of acknowledgment and kind-ness with her fair young kinswoman, she thus proceeded to relate some of the adventures she had witnessed in the time of her youth. These she poured out in a very singular manner, unconscious, apparently, at times, of the presence of others, and often addressing herself to the individuals whom her nar-rative recalled to life, as if they stood life-like and breathing before her.

'When I was young, like thee, Maude Rode, a marvel hap-pened, which amazed many:—it is, and will be, a lasting tale, and a wonder; for it came even as a vision, and I beheld it with these eyes. In those days, the crown of this land, which now stands so sure and so shining on the brows of him who rules us, was held as one of ambition's baubles, that might be transferred by the sword to some adventurous head; and men of birth and descent were ready with trumpet and with brand, to do battle for the exiled branch of the house of Stuart.[22] Rumours of rebellions and invasions were as frequent as the winds on our heaths; and each day brought a darker and more varied tale of risings in the east, and risings in the west; for the king abroad, and for the king at home; and each relater gave a colour and a substance to his tidings, even as his wishes were. The shepherd went armed to the pasturage of his flocks—the lover went armed to the meeting with his mistress—those who loved silver and gold, sought the solitary and silent place, and buried their treasure; the father and mother gazed at their sons and their daughters, and thought on the wrongs of war; and the children, armed with hazel rods for spears and swords of lath, carried on a mimic and venturous war with one another, under the hostile banners of the lion and the bonnie white rose.[23] Those who still loved the ancient church were dreaded by those who loved the new; and the sectarians[24] hated both, and hoped for the day when the jewelled mitre would be plucked off the prelate's head; and when austerity, that denies itself, yet giveth not to others, and zeal, which openeth the gates of mercy but for a tithe of mankind—should hold rule and dominion in the land. Those who had broad lands and rich heritages, wished for peace; those who had little to lose, hoped acquisitions by a convulsion; and there were many of the fiery and intractable spirits of the land who wished for strife and commotion, for the sake of variety of pursuit, and because they wished to see coronets and crowns staked on the issue of a battle. Thus, hot discussion and sore dispute divided the people of this land.

'It happened on a fine summer evening, that I stopped at the dwelling of David Forester, of Wilton-hall, along with young Walter Selby of Glamora, to refresh myself after the chase on the banks of Derwent-water. The mountain air was mild and balmy, and the lofty and rugged outline of Soutrafell appeared on a canopied background of sky so pure, so blue, and so still, that the earth and heaven seemed blended together. Eagles were visible, perched among the star-light, on the peaks of the rocks; ravens roosted at a vast distance below; and where the greensward joined the acclivity of rock and stone, the flocks lay in undisturbed repose, with their fleeces shining in dew, and reflected in a broad deep lake at the

bottom, so pure and so motionless, that it seemed a sea of
glass. The living, or rather human portion of the picture, partook of the same silent and austere character, for inanimate
nature often lends a softness or a sternness to man; the medi-
tative melancholy of the mountain, and the companionable
garrulity of the vale, have not escaped proverbial observation.
I had alighted from my horse, and, seated on a little green
hillock before the house, which the imagination of our mountaineers had not failed to people at times with fairies and
elves—tasted some of the shepherds' curds and cream, the
readiest and the sweetest beverage which rustic hospitality
supplies. Walter Selby had seated himself at my feet, and
behind me stood the proprietor of Wilton-hall and his wife,
awaiting my wishes with that ready and respectful frankness,
which those of birth and ancestry always obtain among our
mountain peasantry. A number of domestics, shepherds and
maidens, stood at a distance, as much for the purpose of listening to our conversation, as from the desire to encumber us
with their assistance in recommencing our journey.

 ' "Young lady," said David Forester, "have you heard
tidings of note from the north or from the south? The Selbys
are an ancient and renowned race, and in days of old held
rule from sunny Carlisle to the vale of Keswick—a day's flight
for a hawk. They are now lordless and landless; but the day
may soon come, when to thee I shall go hat in hand to beg a
boon, and find thee lady of thy lands again, and the noble
house of Lanercost risen anew from its briars and desolation."
I understood better than I wished to appear, this mysterious
address of my entertainer, and was saved from the confusion
of a reply, either direct or oblique, by the forward tongue of
his wife. "Marry, and God forbid," said she, "that ever old
lady Popery should hold rule in men's homes again! not that I
wholly hate the old dame either; she has really some good
points in her character; and if she would put fat flesh in her
pot o' Fridays, and no demand o' one a frank confession of
failings and frailties, she might hold rule i' the land again for
aught I care; though I cannot say I think well of the doctrine
that denies nourishment to the body, in the belief of bettering
the soul. That's a sad mistake in the nature of us moorland
people; if a shepherd lacks a meal a minute beyond the sounding of the horn, all the house hears on't: it's a religion, my
lady, that will never take root again in this wild place, where

men scorn the wheat and haver food, and make, for lack o'
kitchen—the fat mutton eat the lean."

'The good woman of the house was interrupted in her
curious speech by the arrival of one of those personages, who,
with a horse and pack, distribute the luxuries and the comforts of the city over the mountainous regions of the provinces.
His horse, loaded with heavy panniers, came foremost, anxious
for a resting-place; and behind came the owner, a middle-
aged man, tall and robust, with hair as black as the raven,
curled close beneath a very broad bonnet, and in his hand one
of those measuring rods of root grown oak, piked with iron
at the under end, and mounted with brass at the upper, which
seemed alike adapted for defending or measuring his property.
He advanced to the spot where we were seated, like an old
acquaintance, asked for, and obtained lodgings for the evening, and having disposed of his horse, he took out a small box,
resembling a casket, which he placed on the grass, and seating
himself beside it, assumed one of those looks of mingled
gravity and good humour, prepared alike for seriousness or
mirth.

'He was not permitted to remain long in silence. "Ye come
from the north, Simon Packpin," said one of the menials; "one
can know that by yere tongue—and as ye are a cannie lad at
a hard bargain, ye can tell us, in yere own sly and cannie
way, if it be true, that the Highland gentlemen are coming to
try if they can set with targe and claymore the crown of both
lands on the brow it was made for." I looked at the person
of the querist, a young man of the middle size, with a firm
limb, and a frank martial mien, and something in his bearing
which bespoke a higher ambition than that of tending flocks;
his face too I thought I had seen before, and under very different circumstances. "Good sooth, Wattie Graeme," said
another of the menials, "ye might as well try to get back
butter out o' the black dog's throat, as extract a plain answer
from Sleekie Simon; I asked him no further than a month
ago, if he thought we would have a change in the land
soon,—'The moon,' quoth he, 'will change in its season, and
so maun all things human.' 'But, do you think,' said I, 'that
the people will continue to prefer the cold blood of the man
who keeps the chair, to the warm kindly English blood o' him
that's far away?'—'Ay, ay,' quoth he, 'nae doubt, nae doubt,
when we wou'd drink ditch-water rather than red wine.'—

'But,' said I, 'would it not be better for the land that we had
the throne made steadfast under our own native king than
have it shaken by every blast that blows, as I hear it will soon
be?'—'Say ye sae?' said he, 'say ye sae? better have a finger
off, than aye wagging:'—and so he continued for an hour to
reply to every plain question with such dubious responses of
northern proverb, that I left him as wise as I found him."

'This historical sketch of the pedlar obtained the notice of
the farmer's wife, who, with the natural impatience of
womankind, thus abruptly questioned him: "We honest moorland people hate all mystery: if you are a man loyal in your
heart, and upright in your dealings, you may remain and
share our supper; but, if ye be a spy from these northern
marauders, who are coming with houghs as bare as their
swords to make a raid and a foray upon us—arise, I say, and
depart! But stay, tell us truly, when this hawk of the old
uncannie nest of the Stuarts will come to wreck and herrie
us?" To all this Simon the pedlar opposed a look of the most
impenetrable serenity, and turning over his little oaken box,
undid a broad strap and buckle, applied a key to the lock,
took out combs, and knives, and spectacles, and some of his
cheap ornaments for the bosom and the hair, and all the while
he continued chanting over the following curious song,
addressed obliquely to the good dame's queries, and perfectly
intelligible to all who knew the poetic language, and allegori-
cal meaning, which the adherents of the house of Stuart
employed to convey tidings of importance to each other.

THE CUCKOO IS A GENTLE BIRD[25]

I.

The Cuckoo is a gentle bird,
    And gentle is his note,
And April it is pleasant,
    While the sun is waxing hot;
For amid the green woods growing,
    And the fresh flowers' blooming throng,
Forth comes the gentle Cuckoo
    With his meek and modest song.

2.

The eagle slays the little lambs
    On Skiddaw high and hoar;
The hawk he covets carnage, and
    The grey glede griens for gore:
The raven croaks aloud for blood,
    Through spring and summer long;
While the bonnie Cuckoo gladdens us
    With many a merry song.

3.

The woodcock comes, and with the swan
    Brings winter on his wing;
The groves cast off their garments green,
    The small birds cease to sing:
The wild birds cease their singing, till
    The lilies scent the earth;
But the Cuckoo scatters roses round
    Whenever he goes forth.

4.

The Cuckoo is a princely bird,
    And we will wait awhile,
And welcome him with shout and song,
    In the morn of green April;
We'll lay our thighs o'er our good steeds,
    And gird our claymores on,
And chase away the hooded crows
    That croak around the throne.

'I could not help glancing my eye on this curious and demure traveller; but the perfect simplicity of his looks baffled all the scrutiny which the mysterious import of his song induced me to make. Walter Graeme, one of the shepherds, sat down at his side, desirous of purchasing some of his commodities, but the frank mountaineer was repulsed in an attempt to dip his hands among the motley contents of the pack—and had it come to the arbitration of personal strength, there could be little doubt of the issue—for the merchant had a willing hand and a frame of iron.

'Silence ensued for a little while—the pedlar, who for some time had stolen a look at me, seemed all at once to come to

some conclusion how to proceed, and fastening up his little
box, approached me with a look of submission and awe. "Fair
lady, the pedlar is but a poor man, who earns an honest
penny among the peasantry—but he has a reverence and a
love for the noble names which grace our verse and our
chivalry—and who has an English heart that knows not and
beats not high at the sound of Selby's name—and who bears a
Scottish heart that sorrows not for the wreck and the desolation of our most ancient and most noble foe. I tell thee, lady,
that I honour thee more—lady, as thou seemest to be, but of
a kirtle and a steed,—than if thou satest with a footstool of
gold—and hadst nobles' daughters bearing up thy train. This
cross and rosary,"—and he held in his hand these devotional
symbols, carved of dark wood, and slightly ornamented with
gold,—"are of no common wood—a princess has sat under
the shadow of its bough, and seen her kingdom won and
lost—and may the fair one who will now wear it, warm it in
her bosom, till she sees a kingdom long lost—won as boldly,
and as bravely, as ever the swords of the Selbys won their
land!" And throwing the rosary around my neck as he concluded—away he went—opened his pack anew, resuming
again his demure look and the arrangement of his trinkets.

'Walter Selby, who all this while—though then a hot and
forward youth—had remained mute, addressed me in a
whisper. "Fair Eleanor—mine own giddy cousin—this pedlar—
this dispenser of rosaries, made of Queen Mary's yew tree—
he, whom the churls call Simon Packpin, is no seeker of profit
from vulgar merchandise—I'll wager a kiss of thine own
ruddy lips against one of mine, that he carries swords made of
good Ripon steel, and pistols of good Swedish iron, in yon
horse-pack of his—wilt thou pledge a kiss on this wager, my
gentle cousin? And instead of a brain stored with plans for
passing an English yard for a Scottish ell, and making pieces
of homespun plaiding seem costly works from the looms of
Arras or even of Leeds, it is furnished with more perilous stuff,
pretty Eleanor—and no man can tell us better how many of
the Scottish cavaliers have their feet ready for the stirrup, and
on what day they will call on the Selbys to mount and strike
for their ancient lord and their lost inheritance." Something
of this matter had been passing in my own mind, but the
temper of the Selbys ever required more to be repressed
than encouraged—and so I endeavoured to manage thee,

poor Walter Selby!' She sighed while she named the name of
him who had guided and gladdened her youth, and in a tone
low and almost inaudible, she addressed herself to the image
which her affections had thus charmed into life,—'I saw thee,
thou last and thou bravest of all the Selbys, with thy banner
spread, thy sword bright, and thy long golden locks waving
on thy shoulders, when the barriers of Preston were lost and
won, and the gallant laird of Ashiesteel fought like a brother
by thy side—O, that this last bright picture were all I remembered of thee! But can the heart of woman, though her head
be gray, forget that she saw those long locks which made the
dames sigh, waving, soiled and bloody, on the gates of
Carlisle. There is much done in this world must be answered
for in the next, and this cruel and remorseless deed is one.'
She looked while she spoke as if her wild and agitated fancy
had given motion to the picture which she drew of her lover—
her face changed, and her eyes, from beneath their moist and
depressed lids, became fixed and frozen, like stars in a winter
night. This passed away with a smothered groan and a
moving of her hand over her bosom: she again resumed her
narrative. ' "Truly," said I, "my froward cousin, thou art the
best soldier our poor prince could peril his cause with—thou
canst make a pedlar churl into a deep plodding politician,
capable of overturning a throne; and his pack, filled with
shreds of lace and remnants of ribbon, into a magazine of
weapons fit for furnishing an army. What will thy most wise
head make of these dubious sibyl verses, which this mysterious
politician of thine has been doling out for thy especial instruction?" "By the rood, my witty Eleanor," said Walter Selby,
"I shall win a battle, and wed thee in revenge for this. But
thinkest thou not that the box which has endowed that round
white neck of thine with a cross and rosary of gold and wood
still more precious, may not contain things equally curious
and strange? Some golden information this pedlar—since pedlar thou wilt have him—carries in his looks—I wish I could
find the way to extract it." The stranger, as if guessing by our
looks and our whispers what was passing between us, proceeded to instruct us in his own singular way—he described
the excellent temper of his Sheffield whittles—praised the curious qualities of his spectacles, which might enable the wearer
to see distant events—and after soothing over some lines of a
psalm or hymn, common to the presbyterians, he proceeded

to chant the following ballad, of which I regret the loss of several verses.

THE PEDLAR'S BALLAD[26]

I.

It is pleasant to sit on green Saddleback top,
    And hearken the eagle's cry;
It is pleasant to roam in the bonnie green wood,
    When the stags go bounding by.
And it's merry to sit when the red wine goes round,
'Mid the poet's sweet song and the minstrel's sweet sound.

2.

It is merry in moonshine to lead down the dance,
    To go starting away when the string
Shakes out its deep sound, and the fair maidens fly
    Like the sunlight—or birds on the wing.
And it's merry at gloaming aneath the bows green,
To woo a young maiden and roam all unseen.

3.

But it's blither by far when the pennon is spread,
    And the lordly loud trumpet is pealing,
When the bright swords are out, and the war-courser neighs,
    As high as the top of Helvellyn.
And away spurs the warrior, and makes the rocks ring,
With the blows that he strikes for his country and king.

4.

Our gallants have sprung to their saddles, and bright
    Are the swords in a thousand hands;
I came through Carlisle, and I heard their steeds neigh
    O'er gentle Eden's sands.
And seats shall he emptied, and brands shall be wet,
Ere all these gay gallants in London are met.

5.

Lord Maxwell is mounted by winding Nith,
    Lord Kenmore by silver Dee;
The blithe lads spur on from the links of the Orr,

And Durisdeer's greenwood tree;
And the banners which waved when Judea was won,
Are all given again to the glance of the sun.

6.

The Johnstone is stirring in old Annandale,
    The Jardine—the Halliday's coming
From merry Milkwater, and haunted Dryfe bank,
    And Eske that shall list at the gloaming,
The war shout—the yell, and of squadrons the dash,
And gleam to the claymore, and carabine's flash.

7.

Then come with the war-horse, the basnet, and sword,
    And bid the big trumpet awaken;
The bright locks that stoop'd at a fair lady's feet
    'Mid the tempest of war must be shaken.
It is pleasant to spur to the battle the steed,
And cleave the proud helmet that holds a foe's head.

8.

Thy sword's rusty, Howard—hot Dacre, art thou
    So cool when the war-horse is bounding?
Come Percy, come thou, like a Percy of yore,
    When the trumpet of England is sounding:
And come, gallant Selby—thy name is a name,
While a soldier has soul, and a minstrel has flame.

9.

And come, too, ye names that are nameless—come mount,
    And win ye a name in proud story:
A thousand long years at the sock and the share
    Are not worth one moment of glory.
Come arm ye, and mount ye, and make the helms ring
Of the Whigs, as ye strike for your country and king!

'The whole household of Wilton-hall, including Walter Selby and myself, had gradually gathered around this merchant-minstrel, whose voice, from an ordinary chant, had arisen, as we became interested, into a tone of deep and martial melody. Nor was it the voice alone of the stranger that became changed—his face, which at the commencement of the ballad had a grave and a dubious expression, brightened up with enthusiasm—his frame grew erect, and his eyes gleamed with that fierce light, which has been observed in the eyes of the English soldiers on the eve of battle. "What thinkest thou, pretty Eleanor, of our merchant now?" said Walter Selby:—"I should like to have such a form on my right hand when I try to empty the saddles of the southern horse of some of the boldest Whigs."—"And I'll pledge thee, young gentleman,' said the pedlar,—raising his voice at once from the provincial drawl and obscurity of lowland Scotch into the purest English,—"any vow thou askest of me, to ride on which hand thou wilt—and be to thee as a friend and a brother, when the battle is at the hottest—and so I give thee my hand on't."—"I touch no hand," said Walter Selby, "and I vow no vow either in truce or battle, till I know thy name, if thou art of the lineage of the gentle or the churl—I am a Selby, and the Selbys—"—"The Selbys," said the stranger, in a tone, slow and deliberate, "are an ancient and a noble race—but this is no time, young gentleman, to scruple precedence of blood. In the fields where I have ridden, noble deeds have been achieved by common hands—while the gentle and the far descended have sat apart nor soiled their swords.—I neither say I am of a race churlish nor noble—but my sword is as sharp as other men's, and might do thee a friendly deed were it nigh thee in danger."—"Now God help us," said the dame of Wilton-hall, "what will old England become!—here's young Wat Selby debating lineage and blood with a packman churl:—in good truth, if I had but one drop of gentle blood in my veins, I would wrap him up in his own plaid, and beat him to death with his ell wand—which I'll warrant is a full thumb-breadth short of measure." I stood looking on Walter Selby and on the stranger—the former standing aloof with a look of haughty determination—and the latter, with an aspect of calm and intrepid resolution, enduring the scoff of the hotheaded youth, and the scorn of the vulgar matron.

'It might be now about nine o'clock—the air was balmy and mute, the sky blue and unclouded, and the moon, yet unrisen, had sent as much of her light before her as served, with the innumerable stars, to lighten the earth from the summit of the mountains to the deepest vales. I never looked upon a more lovely night, and gladly turned my face from the idle disputants to the green mountain-side, upon which that forerunner gleam which precedes the moon had begun to scatter its light. While I continued gazing, there appeared a sight on Soutra-fell side—strange, ominous, and obscure to many, at that time, but which was soon after explained in desolation and in blood. I saw all at once a body of horsemen coming swiftly down the steep and impassable side of the mountain—where no earthly horse ever rode. They amounted to many hundreds, and trooped onwards in succession—their helmets gleaming, and their drawn swords shining amid the starlight. On beholding this vision, I uttered a faint scream, and Walter Selby, who was always less or more than other men, shouted till the mountain echoed. "Saw ever man so gallant a sight? A thousand steeds and riders on the perpendicular side of old Soutra—see where they gallop along a linn, where I could hardly fly a hawk! O for a horse with so sure and so swift a foot as these, that I might match me with this elfin chivalry! My wanton brown, which can bound across the Derwent like a bird with me on its back, is but a pack-horse to one of these." Alarm was visible in every face around—for we all knew what the apparition foreboded—a lost battle, and a ruined cause. I heard my father say that the like sight appeared on Helvellyn side, before the battle of Marston-moor—with this remarkable difference—the leader wore on his head the semblance of a royal crown, whereas the leaders of the troop whom I beheld wore only earls' coronets.

' "Now his right hand protect us!" said the dame of Wilton-hall. "What are we doomed to endure?—what will follow this?"—"Misery to many," answered the pedlar, "and sudden and early death to some who are present." "Cease thy croak, thou northern raven!" said Walter Selby—"if they are phantoms, let them pass—what care we for men of mist?—and if they are flesh and bone, as I guess by their bearing they must surely be—they are good gallant soldiers of our good king, and thus do I bid them welcome with my bugle." He winded his horn till the mountain echoed far and wide—the spectre horsemen, distant nearly a quarter of a mile, seemed to halt—and the youth had his horn again at his lips to renew the note, when he was interrupted by the pedlar, who, laying his hand on the instrument, said, "Young gentleman, be wise, and be ruled—yon vision is sent for man's instruction—not for his scoff and his scorn."—The shadowy troop now advanced, and passed toward the south at the distance of an

hundred yards. I looked on them as they went, and I imagined I knew the forms of many living men—doomed speedily
to perish in the battle-field, or on the scaffold. I saw the flower
of the Jacobite chivalry—the Maxwells, the Gordons, the
Boyds, the Drummonds, the Ogilvys, the Camerons, the
Scotts, the Foresters, and the Selbys. The havoc which happened among these noble names it is needless to relate—it is
written in tale—related in ballad—sung in song—and deeper
still it is written in family feeling and national sympathy. A
supernatural light accompanied this pageant, and rendered
perfectly visible horse and man:—in the rear I saw a form that
made me shudder—a form still present to my eye, and
impressed upon my heart—old and sorrow-worn as it is—as
vividly as in early youth. I saw the shape of Walter Selby—his
short cloak, his scarlet dress—his hat and feather—his sword
by his side—and that smiling glance in his deep dark eye
which was never there but for me, and which I could know
among the looks of a thousand thousand. As he came, he laid
his bridle on his horse's neck, and leaned aside, and took at
me a long, long look. The youth himself, full of life and gladness beside me, seemed to discover the resemblance between
the spectre rider and himself, and it was only by throwing
myself in his bosom, that I hindered him from addressing the
apparition. How long I remained insensible in his arms I
know not, but when I recovered, I found myself pressed to the
youth's bosom—and a gentleman with several armed attendants standing beside me—all showing by their looks the deep
interest they took in my fate.'[27]

THE SELBYS OF CUMBERLAND.
PART THIRD.
DEATH OF WALTER SELBY

I rede ye, my lady—I rede ye, my lord,[28]
To put not your trust in trumpet and sword:
Else the proud name of Selby, which gladden'd us long,
Shall pass from the land like the sough of a song.
            Old Ballad

Before Dame Eleanor Selby had concluded her account of
the Spectre Horsemen of Soutra-fell, the sun had set—and the
twilight, warm, silent, and dewy, had succeeded—that pleasant time between light and dark, in which domestic labour
finds a brief remission. The shepherd, returned from hill or
moor, spread out his hose—moistened in morass or rivulet—
before the hearth fire, which glimmered far and wide, and
taking his accustomed seat, sat mute and motionless as a
figure of stone. The cows came lowing homewards from the
pasture-hills; others feeding out of cribs filled with rich moist
clover, yielded their milk into a score of pails; while the ewes,
folded on the sheltered side of the remote glen, submitted their
udders, not without the frequent butt and bleat, to the pressure of maidens' hands. Pastoral verse has not many finer
pictures than what it borrows from the shepherd returning
from the hill, and the shepherdess from the fold—the former
with his pipe and dogs, and the latter with her pail of reeking
milk, each singing with a hearty country freedom of voice,
and in their own peculiar way, the loves and the joys of a
pastoral life. The home of Randal Rode presented a scene of
rough plenty, and abounded in pastoral wealth; the head of
the house associated with his domestics, and maintained that
authority over their words and conduct which belonged to
simpler times; and something of the rustic dignity of the
master was observable in his men. His daughter Maude busied
herself among the maidens with a meekness and a diligence
which had more of the matron than is commonly found in so

young a dame. All this escaped not the notice of her old and
capricious kinswoman Eleanor Selby; but scenes of homely
and domestic joy seemed alien to her heart. The intrusion too
of the churlish name of Rode among the martial Selbys, never
failed to darken the picture which she would have enjoyed
had this rustic alloy mixed with the precious metal of any
other house. It was her chief delight, since all the males of her
name had perished, to chant ballads in their praise, and relate
their deeds from the time of the Norman invasion down to
their ruin in the last rebellion. Many snatches of these chivalrous ballads are still current on the Border—the debateable
land of song as well as of the sword—where minstrels sought
their themes, and entered, harp in hand, into rivalry—a kind
of contest which the sword, the critic's weapon of those days,
was often drawn to decide. Much of this stirring and heroic
border-life mingles with the traditionary tales of Eleanor
Selby. Her narratives contain, occasionally, a vivid present-
ment of character and action. I shall endeavour to preserve
something of this, and retain, at the same time, their dramatic
cast, while I prune and condense the whole, to render them
more acceptable to the impatience of modern readers. She
thus pursued her story.

'I am now to tell a tale I have related a thousand times to
the noble and the low—it is presented to me in my dreams,
for the memory of spilt blood clings to a young mind—and
the life's-blood of Walter Selby was no common blood to me.
The vision of the spectre horsemen, in which human fate was
darkly shadowed forth, passed away—and departed too, I
am afraid, from the thoughts of those to whom it came as a
signal and a warning—as a cloud passes from the face of the
summer-moon. Seated on horseback, with Walter Selby at my
bridle-rein, and before and behind me upwards of a score of
armed cavaliers, I had proceeded along the mountain side
about a mile, when a horn was winded at a small distance in
our front. We quickened our pace; but the way was rough
and difficult; and we were obliged to go a sinuous course, like
the meanderings of a brook, round rock and cairn and heathy
hill, while the horn, continuing to sound, still seemed as far
ahead as when we first heard it. It was about twelve o'clock;
and the moon, large and bright and round, gleamed down
from the summit of a green pasture mountain, and lightened
us on our way through a narrow wooded valley, where a small

stream glimmered and sparkled in the light, and ran so crooked a course, as compelled us to cross it every hundred yards. Walter Selby now addressed me in his own singular way: "Fair Eleanor, mine own grave and staid cousin, knowest thou whither thou goest? Comest thou to counsel how fifty men may do the deeds of thousands, and how the crown of this land may be shifted like a prentice's cap?" "Truly," said I, "most sage and considerate cousin, I go with thee like an afflicted damsel of yore, in the belief that thy wisdom and valour may reinstate me in my ancient domains—or else win for me some new and princely inheritance." "Thou speakest," said the youth, "like one humble in hope, and puttest thy trust in one who would willingly work miracles to oblige thee. But ponder, fair damsel—my sword, though the best blade in Cumberland, cannot cut up into relics five or six regiments of dragoons—nor is this body, though devoted to thee, made of that knight-errant stuff that can resist sword and bullet. So I counsel thee, most discreet coz, to content thyself with hearing the sound of battle afar off—for we go on a journey of no small peril." To these sensible and considerate words I answered nothing, but rode on, looking, all the while, Walter Selby in the face, and endeavouring to say something witty or wise. He resumed his converse: "Nay, nay, mine own sweet and gentle cousin—my sweet Eleanor—I am too proud of that troubled glance of thine to say one word more about separation,"—and our horses' heads and our cheeks came closer as he spoke. "That ballad of the pedlar, for pedlar shall the knight be still to oblige thee, his ballad told more truth than I reckoned a minstrel might infuse into verse. All the border cavaliers of England and Scotland are near us or with us,—and now for the game of coronets and crowns—a coffin, coz, or an earl's bauble—for we march upon Preston."

'Prepared as I was for these tidings, I could not hear them without emotion, and I looked on Walter Selby with an eye that was not calculated to inspire acts of heroism. I could not help connecting our present march on Preston with the shadowy procession I had so recently witnessed; and the resemblance which one of the phantoms bore to the youth beside me, pressed on my heart. "Now do not be afraid of our success, my fair coz," said he, "when to all the proud names of the border—names thou hast long since learned by heart, and rendered musical by repeating them—we add the names of two most wise and prudent persons, who shall hereafter be called the setters-up and pluckers-down of kings—even thy cool and chivalrous cousin, and a certain staid and sedate errant damosel." This conversation obtained for us the attention of several stranger cavaliers who happened to join us, as, emerging from the woody glen, we entered upon a green and wide moor or common. One of them, with a short cloak and slouched hat and heron's feather, rode up to my right hand, and glancing his eye on our faces, thus addressed himself to me in a kind-hearted old Scottish style:—"Fair lady, there be sights less to a warrior's liking than so sweet a face beside a wild mountain, about the full of the moon. The cause that soils one of these bright tresses in dew, must be a cause dear to man's heart—and, fair one, if thou wilt permit me to ride by thy bridle-rein, my presence may restrain sundry flouts and jests which young cavaliers, somewhat scant of grace and courtesy—and there be such in our company—may use, on seeing a lady so fair and so young, bowne on such a dangerous and unwonted journey." I thanked this northern cavalier for his charitable civility, and observed, with a smile, "I had the protection of a young person who would feel pleased in sharing the responsibility of such a task." "And, fair lady," continued he, "since Walter Selby is thy protector, my labour will be the less." My cousin, who during this conversation had ridden silent at my side, seemed to awaken from a reverie, and glancing his eye on the cavalier, and extending his hand, said, "Sir, in a strange dress, uttering strange words, and busied in a pursuit sordid and vulgar, I knew you not, and repelled your frank courtesy with rude words. I hear you now in no disguised voice, and see you with the sword of honour at your side, instead of the pedlar's staff: accept, therefore, my hand, and be assured that a Selby—as hot and as proud as the lordliest of his ancestors—feels honoured in thus touching in friendship the hand of a gallant gentleman."

'I felt much pleased with this adventure, and looked on the person of the stalwart borderer, as he received and returned the friendly grasp of Walter Selby: he had a brow serene and high, an eye of sedate resolution, and something of an ironic wit lurking amid the wrinkles which age and thought had engraven on his face. I never saw so complete a transformation; and could hardly credit, that the bold, martial-looking, and courteous cavalier at my side had but an hour or two before sung rustic songs, and chaffered with the peasants of Cumberland, about the price of ends of ribbon and two-penny toys and trinkets. He seemed to understand my thoughts, and thus resolved the riddle in a whisper:— "Fair lady, these are not days when a knight of loyal mind may ride with sound of horn, and banner displayed, summoning soldiers to fight for the good cause; of a surety, his journey would be brief. In the disguise of a calling, low, it is true, but honourable in its kind, I have obtained more useful intelligence, and enlisted more good soldiers, than some who ride aneath an earl's pennon."

'Our party, during this nocturnal march, had been insensibly augmented; and when the grey day came, I could count about three hundred horsemen—young, well-mounted, and well-armed—some giving vent to their spirit or their feelings in martial songs; others examining and proving the merits of their swords and pistols, and many marching on in grave silence, forecasting the hazards of war and the glory of success. Leaving the brown pastures of the moorlands, we descended into an open and cultivated country, and soon found ourselves upon the great military road which connects all the north country with the capital. It was still the cold and misty twilight of the morning, when I happened to observe an old man close beside me, mounted on a horse seemingly coeval with himself,—wrapped, or rather shrouded, in a grey mantle, or plaid, and all the while looking steadfastly at me from under the remains of a broad slouched hat. I had something like a dreamer's recollection of his looks; but he soon added his voice, to assist my recollection,—and I shall never forget the verses the old man chanted with a broken and melancholy, and, I think I may add, prophetic, voice:

OH! PRESTON, PROUD PRESTON[29]

I.

Oh! Preston, proud Preston, come hearken the cry
Of spilt blood against thee, it sounds to the sky;
Thy richness, a prey to the spoiler is doom'd,
Thy homes to the flame, to be smote and consumed:
Thy sage with grey locks, and thy dame with the brown
Descending long tresses, and grass-sweeping gown,

Shall shriek, when there's none for to help them: the hour
Of thy fall is not nigh, but it's certain and sure.
Proud Preston, come humble thy haughtiness—weep—
Cry aloud—for the sword it shall come in thy sleep.

2.

What deed have I done—that thou lift'st thus thy cry,
Thou bard of ill omen, and doom'st me to die?
What deed have I done, thus to forfeit the trust
In high heaven, and go to destruction and dust?
My matrons are chaste, and my daughters are fair;
Where the battle is hottest, my sword's shining there;
And my sons bow their heads, and are on their knees
    kneeling,
When the pray'r is pour'd forth and the organ is pealing:
What harm have I wrought, and to whom offer'd wrong,
That thou comest against me with shout and with song?

3.

What harm hast thou wrought! list and hearken—the hour
Of revenge may be late—but it's certain and sure:
As the flower to the field, and the leaf to the tree,
So sure is the time of destruction to thee.
What harm hast thou wrought!—haughty Preston, now
    hear—
Thou hast whetted against us the brand and the spear;
And thy steeds through our ranks rush, all foaming and hot,
And I hear thy horns sound, and the knell of thy shot:
The seal of stern judgment is fix'd on thy fate,
When the life-blood of Selby is spilt at thy gate.

4.

Oh! Selby, brave Selby, no more thy sword's braving
The foes of thy prince, when thy pennon is waving;
The Gordon shall guide and shall rule in the land;
The Boyd yet shall battle with buckler and brand;
The Maxwells shall live, though diminish'd their shine,
And the Scotts in bard's song shall be all but divine;
Even Forster of Derwent shall breathe for a time,
Ere his name it has sunk to a sound and a rhyme;
But the horn of the Selbys has blown its last blast,
And the star of their name's from the firmament cast.

'I dropt the bridle from my hand, and all the green expanse of dale and hill grew dim before me. The voice of the old man had for some time ceased before I had courage to look about; and I immediately recognized in the person of the minstrel an old and faithful soldier of my father's, whose gift at song, rude and untutored as it was, had obtained him some estimation on the border—where the strong, lively imagery, and familiar diction, of the old ballads still maintain their ground against the classic elegance and melody of modern verse. I drew back a little; and shaking the old man by the hand, said, "Many years have passed, Harpur Harberson, since I listened to thy minstrel skill at Lanercost; and I thought thou hadst gone, and I should never see thee again. Thy song has lost some of its ancient grace and military glee since thou leftest my father's hall." " 'Deed, my bonnie lady," said the borderer, with a voice suppressed and melancholy, while something of his ancient smile brightened his face for a moment, "sangs of sorrow and dule have been rifer with me than ballads of merriment and mirth. It's long now since I rode and fought by my gallant master's side, when the battle waxed fierce and desperate; and my foot is not so firm in the stirrup now, nor my hand sae steeve at the steel, as it was in those blessed and heroic days. It's altered days with Harpur Harberson, since he harped afore the nobles of the north, in the home of the gallant Selbys, and won the cup of gold. I heard that my bonnie lady and her gallant cousin were on horseback; so I e'en put my old frail body on a frail horse, to follow where I cannot lead. It's pleasant to mount at the sound of the trumpet again; and it's better for an auld man to fall with a sound of battle in his ear, and be buried in the trench with the brave, and the young, and the noble,—than beg his bread from door to door, enduring the scoff and scorn of the vulgar and sordid, and be found, some winter morning, streeked stiff and dead, on a hassock of straw in some churl's barn. So I shall e'en ride on, and see the last of a noble and a hopeless cause." He drew his hat over his brow; while I endeavoured to cheer him by describing the numbers, resources, and strength, of the party. And I expressed rather my hope, than firm belief, when I assured him "there was little doubt that the house of Selby would lift its head again and flourish, and that the grey hairs of its ancient and faithful minstrel would go down in gladness and glory to the grave." He shook his head, yet seemed almost willing to believe for a moment, against his own presentiment, in the picture of future glory I had drawn—it was but for a moment. " 'Deed no—'deed no, my bonnie, bonnie lady, it canna—canna be. Glad would I be could I credit the tale, that our house would hold up its head again, high and lordly. But I have too strong faith in minstrel prediction, and in the dreams and visions of the night, to give credence to such a pleasant thought. It was not for nought that horsemen rode in ranks on Soutra side last night, where living horseman could never urge a steed, and that the forms and semblances of living men were visible to me in this fearful procession. Nor was it for nought that my grandfather, old minstrel Harberson, caused himself to be carried in his last hour to the summit of Lanercost-hill, that he might die looking on the broad domains of his master. His harp—for his harp and he were never parted—his harp yielded involuntary sounds, and his tongue uttered unwilling words—words of sad import, the fulfilment of which is at hand. I shall repeat you the words: they are known but to few, and have been scorned too much by the noble race of Selby.

I rede ye, my lady—I rede ye, my lord,[30]
To put not your trust in the trumpet and sword;
To follow no banner that comes from the flood,
To march no more southward to battle and blood.
League not with Dalzell—no, nor seek to be fording
The clear stream of Derwent with Maxwell and Gordon,—
To a Forester's word draw nor bridle nor glaive,—
Shun the gates of proud Preston, like death and the grave—
And the Selbys shall flourish in life and in story,
While eagles love Skiddaw, and soldiers love glory.

' "These are the words of my ancestor—what must be must—I shall meet thee again at the gates of Preston." As he uttered these words he mingled with the ranks of horsemen under the banner of a border knight, and I rode up to the side of my cousin and his companion.

'It is not my wish to relate all I heard, and describe all I saw on our way southward; but our array was a sight worth seeing, and a sight we shall never see again—for war is now become a trade, and men are trained to battle like hounds to the hunting. In those days the noble and the gentle, each with his own banner,—with kinsmen and retainers, came forth to battle; and war seemed more a chivalrous effort than it seems now—when the land commits its fame and its existence to men hired by sound of trumpet and by beat of drum. It was soon broad daylight; all the adherents of the house of Stuart had moved towards Lancashire, from the south of Scotland and the north of England; and forming a junction where the Westmoreland mountains slope down to the vales, now covered the road as far as my eye could reach—not in regular companies, but in clusters and crowds, with colours displayed.— There might be, in all, one thousand horsemen and fifteen hundred foot, the former armed with sword and pistol, and carabine—the latter with musket and spear. It was a fair sight to see so many gentlemen dressed in the cavalier garb of other days, some with head and bosom pieces of burnished mail, others with slouched hats and feathers, and scarlet vests, and all with short cloaks or mantles, of velvet or woollen, clasped at the bosom with gold, and embroidered each according to their own or their mistress's fancy. A body of three hundred chosen horsemen, pertaining to my Lord Kenmore, marched in front, singing, according to the fashion of the Scotch, rude and homely ballads in honour of their leader.

1.

Kenmore's on and awa, Willie,[31]
    Kenmore's on and awa;
And Kenmore's lord is the gallantest lord
    That ever Galloway saw.

2.

Success to Kenmore's band, Willie,
    Success to Kenmore's band;
There was never a heart that fear'd a Whig,
    E'er rode by Kenmore's hand.

3.

There's a rose in Kenmore's cap, Willie,
    There's a rose in Kenmore's cap,—
He'll steep it red in ruddie life's blood,
    Afore the battle drap.

'Such were some of the verses by which the rustic minstrels
of those days sought to stimulate the valour of their country-
men. One hundred horse, conducted by Lord Nithsdale,
succeeded; those of Lord Derwentwater followed; a band,
numerous, but divided in opinion; unsteady in resolution, and
timid in the time of need and peril, like their unfortunate lord.
The foot followed: a band of warriors, strange, and even
savage in their appearance; brave and skilful, and unblench-
ing in battle, with plaid and bonnet and broadsword, bare
kneed, and marching to a kind of wild music, which, by re-
calling the airs of their ancestors, and the battles in which
they fought and bled, kindles a military fury and resolution
which destroys all against which it is directed. These were
men from the mountains of Scotland, and they were led by
chieftain Mackintosh, who was to them as a divinity; compared to whom the prince, in whose cause they fought, was a
common being, a mere mortal. I admired the rude, natural
courtesy of these people, and lamented the coward counsels
which delivered them up to the axe and the cord, without
striking a single blow. The rear, accounted, in this march,
with an enemy behind as well as before, a post of some peril,
was brought up by about two hundred border cavaliers and
their adherents; and with them rode Walter Selby and his
new companion. The command seemed divided among many;
and without obeying any one chief in particular, all seemed
zealous in the cause, and marched on with a rapidity regu-
lated by the motions of the foot.

'No serious attempt was made to impede us: some random
shots were fired from the hedge-rows and groves; till at length,
after a fatiguing journey, we came within sight of Preston;
and there the enemy made his appearance in large masses of
cavalry and foot, occupying the distant rising grounds, leaving
our entry into the town free and uninterrupted. Something
in my face showed the alarm I felt on seeing the numbers and
array of our enemies: this passed not unobserved of the cavalier at my side, who said with a smile, "Fair lady, you are
looking on the mercenary bands which sordid wealth has
marched against us; these are men bought and sold, and who
hire their best blood for a scarlet garb and a groat. I wish I
had wealth enough to tempt the avarice of men who measure
all that is good on earth by the money it brings. And yet, fair
one, I must needs own that our own little band of warriors is

brought strangely together, and bound by ties of a singular kind. It would make a curious little book, were I to write down all the motives and feelings which have put our feet in the stirrup. There's my Lord Kenmore; a hot, a brave, and a self-willed, and the Scotch maidens say a bonnie Gordon; his sword had stuck half-drawn from the scabbard, but for the white hand of his wife: but he that lives under the influence of bright eyes, Lady Eleanor, lives under a spell as powerful as loyalty. And what would the little book say of my Lord Nithsdale, with whom ride so many of the noble name of Maxwell? Can scorn for the continual cant and sordid hearts of some acres of psalm-singing covenanters, who haunt the hill-tops of Terreagles and Dalswinton, cause the good lord to put the fairest domains on the border in jeopardy? or does he hope to regain all the sway held by his ancestors of yore over the beautiful vale of Nith; humbling into dust, as he arises, the gifted weaver who preaches, the inspired cordwainer who expounds, and the upstart grocer who holds rule—the two former over men's minds, and the latter over men's bodies? There's my Lord Carnwath—."

'At this moment I heard the sounding of trumpets, and the rushing of horses behind us; and ere I could turn round, my cavalier said, in the same equal and pleasant tone in which he was making his curious communication of human character,—"Fair lady, here be strange auditors, some of my friend General Willis's troopers come to try the edges of their new swords. Halbert, lead this fair lady to a place where she may see what passes: and now for the onset, Walter Selby." The latter, exchanging a glance with me, turned his horse's head; swords were bared in a moment; and I heard the dash of their horses, as they spurred them to the contest, while a Scottish soldier hurried me towards the town. I had not the courage to look back; the clashing of swords, the knelling of carabines, the groans of the wounded, and the battle-shout of the living, came all blended in one terrible sound—my heart died within me.

'I soon came up to the Scottish mountaineers, who, with their swords drawn, and their targets shouldered, stood looking back on the contest, uttering shouts of gladness, or shrieks of sorrow, as their friends fell or prevailed. I looked about, and saw the skirmish, which at first had only extended to a few blows and shots, becoming bloody and dubious; for the

enemy, reinforced with fresh men, now fairly charged down
the open road, and the place where they contended was soon
covered with dead and dying. I shrieked aloud at this fearful
sight; and quitting my horse's bridle, held up my hands, and
cried out to the mountaineers, "O haste and rescue, else
they'll slay him! they'll slay him!" An old highlander, at
almost the same instant, exclaimed, in very corrupt English.
"God! she'll no stand and see the border lads a' cut to pieces!"
and, uttering a kind of military yell, flew off with about two
hundred men to the assistance of his friends.

'I was not allowed to remain and witness the charge of
these northern warriors, but was led into Preston, and carried
into a house half dead, where several of the ladies, who followed the fortune of their lords in this unhappy expedition,
endeavoured to soothe and comfort me. But I soon was the
gayest of them all; for in came Walter Selby, and his companion, soiled with blood and dust, from helmet to spur. I
leaped into my cousin's bosom, and sobbed with joy: he kissed
my forehead, and said, "Thank him, my Eleanor—the gallant
knight, Sir Thomas Scott; but for him, I should have been
where many brave fellows are." I recovered presence of mind
in a moment, and turning to him, said, "Accept, sir, a poor
maiden's thanks for the safety of her kinsman, and allow her
to kiss the right hand that wrought this deliverance." "Bless
thee, fair lady," said the knight, "I would fight a dozen such
fields for the honour thou profferest; but my hand is not in
trim for such lady courtesy; so let me kiss thine as a warrior
ought." I held out my hand, which he pressed to his lips; and
washing the blood from his hands, removing the soils of battle
from his dress, and resuming his mantle, he became the gayest
and most cheerful of the company.

'It was evident, from the frequent and earnest consultations
of the leaders of this rash enterprise, that information had
reached them of no pleasing kind. Couriers continually came
and went, and some of the chiefs began to resume their
weapons. As the danger pressed, advice and contradiction,
which at first were given and urged with courtesy and respect,
now became warm and loud; and the Earl of Derwentwater,
a virtuous and amiable man, but neither warrior nor leader,
instead of overawing and ruling the tumultuary elements of
his army, strode to and fro, a perfect picture of indecision and
dismay, and uttered not a word.

'All this while, Sir Thomas Scott sat beside Walter Selby and me, calm and unconcerned; conversing about our ancient house; relating anecdotes of the lords of Selby in the court and in the camp; quoting, and, in his own impressive way of reciting verse, lending all the melody of music to the old minstrel ballads which recorded our name and deeds. In a moment of less alarm I could have worshipped him for this; and my poor Walter seemed the child of his companion's will, and forgot all but me in the admiration with which he contemplated him.

'The conference of the chiefs had waxed warm and tumultuous; when Lord Nithsdale, a little, high-spirited and intrepid man, shook Sir Thomas by the shoulder, and said, "This is no time, Sir Knight, for minstrel lore, and lady's love; betake thee to thy weapon, and bring all thy wisdom with thee, for truly we are about to need both." Sir Thomas rose, and having consulted a moment with Lord Kenmore, returned to us, and said, "Come, my young friend, we have played the warrior, now let us play the scout, and go forth and examine the numbers and array of our enemies; such a list of their generals and major-generals has been laid before our leaders, as turns them pale; a mere muster-roll of a regiment would make some of them lay down their arms, and stretch out their necks to the axe. Lord Kenmore, fair Eleanor, who takes a lady's counsel now and then, will have the honour of sitting by your side till our return." So saying, Walter Selby and Sir Thomas left us, and I listened to every step in the porch, till their return, which happened within an hour.

'They came splashed with soil, their dress rent with hedge and brake; and they seemed to have owed their safety to their swords, which were hacked and dyed to the hilts. The leaders questioned them, "Have you marked the enemy's array and learned aught of their numbers?" "We have done more," said Sir Thomas; "we have learned from the tongues of two dying men, that Willis, with nine regiments of horse, and Colonel Preston, with a battalion of foot, will scarcely await for dawn to attack you." This announcement seemed to strike a damp to the hearts of several of the chiefs; and, instead of giving that consistency to their councils which mutual fear often inspires, it only served to bewilder and perplex them. "I would counsel you," said Sir Thomas, "to make an instant attack upon their position before their cannon arrive; I will lead the way; we

are inferior in number, but superior in courage; let some of
our border troopers dismount, and with the clansmen open a
passage through Colonel Preston's troops which line the hedge
rows and enclosures; the horse will follow, and there can be
no doubt of a complete victory." Some opposed this advice,
others applauded it; and the precious hours of night were consumed in unavailing debate, and passionate contradiction.

'This was only interrupted by the sound of the trumpet,
and the rushing of horse; for Willis, forcing the barriers at two
places, at once made good his entry into the principal street
of Preston. I had the courage to go into the street; and had
not proceeded far till I saw the enemy's dragoons charging at
the gallop; but their saddles were emptied fast, with shot,
and with sword; for the clansmen, bearing their bucklers over
their heads, made great havoc among the horsemen with their
claymores, and at length succeeded in repulsing them to the
fields. As soon as the enemy's trumpets sounded a retreat, our
leaders again assembled; assembled not to conquer or fall like
cavaliers, with their swords in their hands, but to yield themselves up, to beg the grace of a few days, till they prepared
their necks for the rope and the axe. The highland soldiers
wept with anger and shame, and offered to cut their way, or
perish; but the leaders of the army, unfit to follow or fight,
resolved on nothing but submission, and sent Colonel Oxburgh
with a message to General Willis to propose a capitulation.

'Sir Thomas Scott came to Walter Selby and me, and said,
with a smile of bitter scorn, "Let these valiant persons deliver
themselves up to strain the cord and prove the axe; we will
seek, Lady Eleanor, a gentler dispensation; retreat now is not
without peril; yet let us try what the good green wood will
do for poor outlaws; I have seen ladies and men too escape
from greater peril than this."

'We were in the saddle in a moment; and, accompanied
by about twenty of the border cavaliers, made our way
through several orchard enclosures, and finally entered upon
an extensive common or chase, abounding in clumps of dwarf
holly and birch, and presenting green and winding avenues,
into one of which we gladly entered, leaving Preston half a
mile behind. That pale and trembling light which precedes
day began to glimmer; it felt intensely cold; for the air was
filled with dew, and the boughs and bushes sprinkled us with
moisture. We hastened on at a sharp trot; and the soft sward

returning no sound, allowed us to hear the trumpet summons, and military din, which extended far and wide around Preston.

'As we rode along, I observed Sir Thomas motion with his hand to his companions, feel his sword and his pistols, glance to the girths of his horse, and, finally, drop his mantle from his right arm, apparently baring it for a contest. In all these preparations, he was followed by his friends, who, at the same time, closed their ranks, and proceeded with caution and silence. We had reached a kind of road, half the work of nature, and half of man's hand, which divided the chase or waste in two; it was bordered by a natural hedge of holly and thorn. All at once, from a thicket of bushes, a captain, with about thirty of Colonel Preston's dragoons, made a rush upon us, calling out, "Yield! down with the traitors!" Swords were bare in a moment, pistols and carabines were flashing, and both parties spurred, alike eager for blood.

'Of this unexpected and fatal contest I have but an indistinct remembrance; the glittering of the helmets, the shining of drawn swords, the flashing of pistols and carabines, the knell of shot, the rushing of horses, and the outcry of wounded men, come all in confusion before me; but I cannot give a regular account of such a scene of terror and blood. It was of brief duration. I laid my bridle on my horse's neck, and wrung my hands, and followed with my looks every motion of Walter Selby. He was in the pride of strength and youth, and spurred against the boldest; and putting soul and might into every blow, made several saddles empty; I held up my hands, and prayed audibly for success. A dragoon, who had that moment killed a cavalier, rode to my side, and exclaimed, "Down with thy hands, thou cursed nun, down with thy hands; woot pray yet, woot thou; curse tha then;" and he made a stroke at me with his sword. The eyes of Walter Selby seemed to lighten as a cloud does on a day of thunder, and at one blow he severed the dragoon's head, bone and helmet, down to his steel collar. As the trooper fell, a pistol and carabine flashed together, and Walter Selby reeled in the saddle, dropt his head, and his sword, and saying, faintly, "Oh, Eleanor!" fell to the ground, stretching both hands towards me. I sprang to the ground, clasped him to my bosom, which he covered with his blood, and entreated Heaven to save him; and oh, I doubt I upbraided the Eternal with his death! but Heaven will pity the ravings of despair.

He pressed my hand faintly, and lay looking on my face alone, though swords were clashing, and pistols were discharged over us.

'Ere the contest had ceased, Sir Thomas sprang from his horse, took Walter Selby in his arms, and tears sparkled in his eyes, as he saw the blood flowing from his bosom. "Alas! alas!" said he, "that such a spirit, so lofty and heroic, should be quenched so soon, and in a skirmish such as this! Haste, Frank, Elliot, haste, and frame us a litter of green boughs; cover it thick with our mantles; place this noble youth upon it, and we will bear him northward on our horses' necks. Ere I leave his body here, I will leave mine own aside it; and you, minstrel Harberson, bring some water from the brook for this fair and fainting lady."

'All these orders, so promptly given, were as quickly executed; and we recommenced our journey to the north, with sorrowful hearts, and diminished numbers. I rode by the side of the litter, which, alas! became a bier, ere we reached the green hills of Cumberland. We halted in a lonely glen; a grave was prepared; and there, without priest, prayer, or requiem, was all that I loved of man consigned to a sylvan grave. "The dust of our young hero," said Sir Thomas, "must lie here till the sun shines again on our cause, and it shall be placed in consecrated earth." The minstrel of the ancient name of Selby stood gazing on the grave, and burst out into the following wail or burial song, which is still to be heard from the lips of the maids and matrons of Cumberland:

LAMENT FOR WALTER SELBY[32]

I.

Mourn, all ye noble warriors—
    Lo! here is lying low
As brave a youth as ever
    Spurr'd a courser on the foe:
Hope is a sweet thing to the heart,
    And light unto the ee,
But no sweeter and no dearer
    Than my warrior was to me:
He rode a good steed gallantly,
    And on his foes came down

With a war-cry like the eagle's,
    From Helvellyn's haughty crown:
His hand was wight, and his dark eye
    Seem'd born for wide command;
Young Selby has nae left his like
    In all the northern land.

2.

Weep for him, all ye maidens—
    And weep for him, all ye dames;
He was the sweetest gentleman
    From silver Tweed to Thames.
Wail all for Walter Selby,
    Let your tears come dropping down;
Wail all for my young warrior,
    In cottage, tower, and town.
Curs'd be the hand that fired the shot;
    And may it never know
What beauty it has blighted,
    And what glory it laid low!
Shall some rude peasant sit and sing,
    How his rude hand could tame
Thy pride, my Walter Selby,
    And the last of all thy name?

3.

And mourn too, all ye minstrels good,
    And make your harp-strings wail,
And pour his worth through every song,
    His deeds through every tale.
His life was brief, but wond'rous bright:
    Awake your minstrel story!
Lo! there the noble warrior lies,
    So give him all his glory.
When Skiddaw lays its head as low,
    As now 'tis green and high—
And the Solway sea grows to a brook,
    Now sweeping proudly by—
When the soldier scorns the trumpet sound,
    Nor loves the temper'd brand—
Then thy name, my Walter Selby,
    Shall be mute in Cumberland.'

'But, alas! the form of the lovely and the brave was not permitted to sink silently into dust—it was plucked out of its lonely and obscure grave—displayed on a gibbet, and the head, separated from the body, was placed on the gate of Carlisle. All day I sat looking, in sadness and tears, on this sorrowful sight, and all night I wandered wild and distracted about, conjuring all men who passed by to win me but one tress of the long bright hair of Walter Selby. Even the rude sentinels were moved by my grief, but no one dared to do a deed so daring and so perilous.

'I remember it well—it was on a wild and stormy night— the rain fell fast—the thunder rocked the walls, and the lightnings flashing far and wide showed the castle's shattered towers, and the river Eden rolling deep in flood. I wrapped my robe about me, and approached the gate. The sentinels, obeying the storm, had sought shelter in the turrets, and no living soul seemed abroad but my own unhappy self. I gazed up to the gate where, alas! I had often gazed, and I thought I beheld a human form—a flash of lightning passed, and I saw it was a living being—it descended and approached me, motioning me back with its hand. I retired in awe, and still the figure followed. I turned suddenly round and said, "Whether thou comest for evil or for good, farther shall I not go till I know thy errand."

' "Fair and unhappy lady," said a voice which I had often heard before, "I have come, not without peril, from a distant place; for I heard the story of your daily and nightly sorrowings, and I vowed I would not leave a relique of the noble and the brave to gladden the eyes of vulgar men, and feast the fowls of heaven. Here, take this tress of thy lover's hair, and mourn over it as thou wilt—men shall look on the morrow for the golden locks of Walter Selby waving on Carlisle gate, and when they see nothing there they shall know that the faithful and the valiant are never without friends. His body has been won, and his head removed, and his dust shall mingle with the knightly and the far descended, even as I vowed when we laid him in his early grave." With these words Sir Thomas Scott departed, and I placed the ringlet in my bosom, from which it shall never be separated.'

Such was the story of Eleanor Selby. In a later day some unknown Scottish minstrel heard the uncertain and varying tradition, and, with a minstrel's licence, wove it into verse,

suppressing the name of Selby and giving the whole a colour
and character most vehemently Scottish. A northern lady is
made to sing the following rude and simple lament:

CARLISLE YETTS[33]

1.

White was the rose in my love's hat,
 While he rowed me in his lowland plaidy,
His heart was true as death in love,
 His hand was aye in battle ready;
His lang lang hair in yellow hanks
 Waved o'er his cheeks sae sweet and ruddy,
But now it waves o'er Carlisle yetts,
 In dripping ringlets soiled and bloody.

2.

When I came first through fair Carlisle
 Ne'er was a town sae gladsome seeming,
The white rose flaunted o'er the wall,
 The thistled pennons far were streaming.
When I came next through fair Carlisle
 O! sad, sad seemed the town and eerie;
The old men sobbed, and grey dames wept,
 O! lady, come ye to seek your dearie?

3.

I tarried on a heathery hill,
 My tresses to my cheeks were frozen,
And far adown the midnight wind
 I heard the din of battle closing.
The grey day dawned, where 'mang the snow
 Lay many a young and gallant fellow,
But the sun came visiting in vain
 Two lovely een tween locks of yellow.

4.

There's a tress of soiled and yellow hair
 Close in my bosom I am keeping,
Oh! I have done with delight and love,
 So welcome want, and woe, and weeping.

Woe, woe upon that cruel heart,
    Woe, woe, upon that hand so bloody,
That lordless leaves my true love's hall,
    And makes me wail a virgin widow.

PLACING A SCOTTISH MINISTER

Lang patronage, wi' rod of airn,[34]
    Has shored the kirk's undoin,
As lately Fenwick, sair forfairn,
    Has proven to its ruin;
Our patron, honest man! Glencairn,
    He saw mischief was brewin;
And, like a godly elect bairn,
    He's waled us out a true ane,
        And sound this day.

Burns

'The pleasantest hour, perhaps, of human life, is when a man, becoming master of his own actions, and with his first earned money in his hand, gazes along the opening vista of existence, and sees, in silent speculation, the objects of his ambition appearing before him in their shadowy succession of peace, and enjoyment, and glory. Out of a few hard-won shillings, the peasant frames visions of rustic wealth, whitens the mountains with his flocks, and covers the plain with clover and corn. The seaman casts his future anchor on a coast of silver, and gold, and precious stones; and sees his going and returning sails wafting luxury and riches. The poet, in his first verse, feels a thrill of unbounded joy he is never to experience again; he hears Fame sounding her trumpet at his approach, and imagines his songs descending through the most delightful of all modes of publication—the sweet lips of millions of fair maidens, now and for evermore. It was with feelings of this kind that I arranged the purchases my first wealth made, in a handsome pack secured with bolt and lock; and proceeded to follow the gainful and healthful calling of a packman among the dales of Dumfrieshire and the green hills of Galloway. On the first morning of my trade, I halted in every green lane, spread out the motley contents of my box in orderly array before me, surveyed them with silent and growing joy, then placed them again in the box, and recommenced my march, amid busy calculation of the probable proceeds of my industry.

'A little before noon, on a sweet morning of summer, I had seated myself on the summit of a little green fairy hill which overlooks the ancient abbey of Bleeding-Heart; and, spreading out all the articles I had to offer for sale before me, I indulged, unconsciously, in the following audible speculation:—"A pleasant story and a merry look will do much among the young; and a sedate face and a grave tale will win me a lodging from the staid and devout. For the bonnie lass and the merry lad, have I not the choicest ballads and songs? For the wise and the grave, do I lack works of solemn import, from the Prophecies of Peden,[35] and the Crumb of Comfort, up to Salvation's Vantage-Ground, or a Louping-on-Stone for Heavy Believers? Then for those who are neither lax on the one hand, nor devout on the other, but stand as a stone in the wall, neither in the kirk nor out of it, have I not books of as motley a nature as they? And look at these golden laces, these silken snoods, and these ivory bosom-busks,—though I will not deny that a well-faured lass has a chance to wheedle me out of a lace, or a ribbon, with no other money than a current kiss, and reduce my profit,—yet I must even lay it the heavier on new-married wives, rosy young widows, and lasses with fee and bounty in their laps. It would be a sad thing if love for a sonsie lass should make me a loser."

'An old dame in a grey linsey-woolsey gown, a black silk riding hood pinned beneath her chin, with a large calf-skin-covered Bible under her arm, had approached me unseen. She fell upon me like a whirlwind:—"O! thou beardless trickster, thou seventeen year old scant-o'-grace, wilt thou sit planning among God's daylight how to overreach thy neighbour? My sooth lad, but thou art a gleg one. I question if William Mackfen himself, who has cheated my good man and me these twenty-seven summers, is half such a wily loon as thyself. A night's lodging ye need never ask at Airnaumrie. And yet it would be a sore matter to my conscience to turn out a face so young, and so well faured, to the bensel of the midnight blast." And away the old lady walked, and left me to arrange the treasures of my pack at my leisure.

'Her words were still ringing in my ears, when an old man, dressed in the antique Scottish fashion—a grey plaid wound about his bosom, a broad westland bonnet on his head, which shaded, but did not conceal, a few shining white hairs, and with a long white staff in his hand, came up, and addressed me:—"Gather up thy books and thy baubles, young man; this is not the time to spread out these worldly toys to the eyes of human infirmity. Gather them together, and cast them into that brook, and follow me. Alas!" said he, touching my treasures with the end of his staff, "here are gauds for our young and our rosie madams,—bosom-busks, brow-snoods, and shining brooches for ensnaring the eyes of youth. I tell thee, young man, woman will fall soon enough from her bright station by her own infirmities, without thy helping hand to pluck her down. Much do I fear thou hast been disposing of sundry of thy snares to the vain old dame of Airnaumrie. She is half saint and half sinner; and the thoughts of her giddy youth are still too strong for her grey hairs: seest thou not that she carries the book of redemption in her hand, when she should bear it in her head? But she gleaned her scanty knowledge on an Erastian field among the Egyptian stubble.[36] Ah! had she been tightly targed by a sound professor on the Proof Catechism, she had not needed that printed auxiliary under her arm. But I waste precious time on an unprofiting youth. I hasten whither I am called,—for patronage, with its armed hand, will give the kirk of Galloway a sad stroke to-day, if there be no blessed interposition." And my male followed my female monitor, leaving me to wonder what all this religious bustle and preparation might mean.

'I was about to follow, when loud talk, and louder laughter, came towards me through the green avenue of a neighbouring wood. A bevy of lads and lasses in holiday clothes, with books of devotion in their hands, soon appeared; and they were not slack in indulging themselves in week-day merriment. "A pretty whig, indeed!" said a handsome girl with brown locks, and coats kilted half-way up a pair of very white legs; "a pretty whig, indeed!—I'll tell thee, lad, thou'lt never be the shining star in the firmament thy aunt speaks of when she prays. I have seen a lad with as much grace in his eye as thyself, endure a sore sermon by himself when the kirk should have scaled." "And I have seen," retorted the swain, "as great a marvel as a pair of white legs, rosie lips, and mischievous eyes, making as wise a man as myself pay dear for an hour's daffin." "Daffin," said the maiden, laughing till the woods rung again; "daffin will be scant when a lass seeks for't

with such a world's wonder as thee. It sets thy mother's oldest
son well to speak of daffin." "I have climbed a higher tree,
and harried a richer nest," murmured the plowman: "but
what, in the name of patronage, have we here? Here's an
abstract personification, as somebody called John Goudie the
Cameronian, of old Willie Mackfen the pedlar—in the days of
his youth." So saying, a crowd of lads and lasses surrounded
my pack and me, and proceeded to examine and comment on
my commodities, with an absence of ceremony which would
have vexed even a veteran traveller.

' "As I shall answer for it," said one youth, "here's the very
snood Jenny Birkwhistle lost amang Andrew Lorrance's
broom." "And I protest," retorted the maiden, justly offended
at this allusion to the emblem of maidenhood, "I protest,
here's the wisest of all printed things—even A Groat's Worth
of Wit for a Penny, which thy mother longed to read ere she
was lightened of thee. Thy father has much to answer for." A
loud laugh told that truth was mingled with the wit of the
maiden. Utter ruin seemed to wait on my affairs, when a
woman, with a sour sharp visage, and a tongue that rang like
a steel hammer on a smith's anvil, came up, and interposed.
"Ye utterly castaway and graceless creatures, are ye making
godless mirth on a green hill side?" said she, stretching forth
her hands, garnished with long finger-nails, over the crowd—
like a hawk over a brood of chickens, "is not this the day
when patronage seeks to be mighty, and will prevail? Put
yourselves, therefore, in array. The preaching man of Belial,
with his red dragons,[37] even now approaches the afflicted kirk
of Bleeding-Heart. Have ye not heard how they threaten to
cast the cope-stone of the kirk into the deep sink, where our
forefathers of yore threw the lady of Babylon,[38] and her
painted and mitred minions? But it is ever this way. Ye would
barter the soul's welfare for the body's folly. Ah!" said she to
a young peasant, "what would Hezekiah Graneaway, thy
devout grandfather, say, were he to see his descendant, on a
day of trial like this, standing making mouths at a poor
packman-lad, with a bevy of petticoated temptresses around
him? Get along, I say, lest I tear those curled love-locks from
thy temples. And as for thee, thou young money-changer,—
thou dealer in maiden trickery and idle gauds, knowest thou
not that this is ORDINATION DAY—so buckle up thy merchandise, and follow. Verily, none can tell from whose hand the

blow shall come this day, that will save us from the sinful compliance with that offspring of old Mahoun,[39] even patronage." I was glad of any pretext for withdrawing my goods from the hands of my unwelcome visitors; so I huddled them together, secured them with the lock, and followed the zealous dame, who, with a proud look, walked down the hill, to unite herself to a multitude of all ranks and sexes, which the placing of the parish minister had collected together.

'The place where this multitude of motley beliefs and feelings had assembled, was one of singular beauty. At the bottom of a woody glen, the margin of a beautiful lake, and the foot of a high green mountain, with the sea of Solway seen rolling and sparkling in the distance, stood a populous and straggling village, through which a clear stream, and a paved road, winded side by side. Each house had its garden behind, and a bare-headed progeny running wild about the banks of the rivulet; beside which, many old men and matrons, seated according to their convenience, enjoyed the light of the sun, and the sweetness of the summer air. At the eastern extremity of the village, a noble religious ruin, in the purest style of the Saxons, raised its shattered towers and minarets far above all other buildings; while the wall-flowers, shooting forth in the spring at every joint and crevice, perfumed the air for several roods around. The buttresses, and exterior auxiliary walls, were covered with a thick tapestry of ivy; which, with its close-clinging and smooth shining leaf, resembled a covering of velvet. One bell, which tradition declares to be of pure silver, remained on the top of one of the highest turrets, beyond the reach of man. It is never rung, save by a violent storm; and its ringing is reckoned ominous—deaths at land, and drownings at sea, follow the sound of the silver bell of Bleeding-Heart Abbey. Innumerable swarms of pigeons and daws shared the upper region of the ruin among them, and built and brought forth their young in the deserted niches of saints, and the holes from which corbals of carved wood had supported the painted ceiling. At the very foot of this majestic edifice stood the parish kirk, built in utter contempt of the beautiful proportions of its ancient neighbour; and for the purpose, perhaps, of proving in how mean a sanctuary the pure and stern devotion of the Presbyterians could humble itself. Men thrash their grain, stall their horses, feed their cattle, and even lodge themselves, in houses dry and comfortable—but, for religion, they erect edifices which resemble the grave: the moist clay of the floor, the dampness, and frequent droppings of water from the walls, are prime matters of satisfaction to the parish grave-digger, and preserve his spade from rust.

'Into this ancient abbey, and the beautiful region around it, the whole population of the parish appeared to have poured itself, for the purpose of witnessing, and perhaps resisting, the ordination of a new and obnoxious pastor, whom patronage had provided for their instruction. Youths, more eager for a pleasant sight than religious controversy, had ascended into the abbey towers;—the thick-piled grave-stones of the kirk-yard—each ruined buttress—the broken altar stone, and the tops of the trees, were filled with aged or with youthful spectators. Presbyterians of the established kirk, Burghers, Antiburghers, Cameronians, and seceders of all denominations,[40] paraded the long crooked street of the village, and whiled away the heavy time, and amused their fancy, and soothed their conscience, by splitting anew the straws scattered about by the idle wind of controversy. Something like an attempt to obstruct the entrance to the kirk appeared to have been made. The spirit of opposition had hewn down some stately trees which shaded the kirk-yard, and these, with broken ploughs and carts, were cast into the road—the kirk door itself had been nailed up, and the bell silenced by the removal of the rope. The silver bell on the abbey alone, swept by a sudden wind, gave one gentle toll; and, at that moment, a loud outcry, from end to end of the village, announced the approach of the future pastor. The peasants thickened round on all sides; and some proceeded to wall up the door of the kirk with a rampart of loose stones. "Let Dagon defend Dagon,"[41] said one rustic, misapplying the Scripture he quoted, while he threw the remains of the abbey altar-stone into the path. "And here is the through-stone of the last abbot, Willie Bell. It makes a capital cope-stone to the defences—I kenn'd it by the drinking cup aside the death's head—he liked to do penance with a stoup of wine at his elbow," said another boor, adding the broken stone to the other incumbrances. "A drinking cup! ye coof," said an old man, pressing through the crowd, "it is a sand-glass—and cut too on the head-stone of thy own grandfather—black will be thy end for this." The boor turned away with a shudder; while the dame of Airnaumrie, with the black hood, and large

Bible, exclaimed, "Take away that foul memorial of old Gomorrha Gunson. The cause can never prosper that borrows defence from that never-do-good's grave. Remove the stone, I say, else I shall brain thee with this precious book." And she shook the religious missile at the descendant of old Gomorrha, who carried off the stone; and no farther attempt was made, after this ominous circumstance, to augment the rampart.

'Amid all this stir and preparation, I had obtained but an indistinct knowledge of the cause which called into action all the grave, impatient, and turbulent spirits of the district. This was partly divulged in a conversation between two persons, to which there were many auditors. One was the male broad bonneted disciplinarian, who rebuked me for displaying the contents of my pack; and the other was the sour-visaged, shrilled-tongued dame, who rescued my pack from the peril of pillage on the road, and with the true antique spirit of the reformed church, lent her voice to swell the clamour of controversy. Their faces were inflamed, and their voices exalted, by the rancour of mutual contradiction: and it was thus I heard the male stickler for the kirk's freedom of election, express himself: "I tell thee once, woman, and I tell thee again, that the kirk of Bleeding-Heart there, where it stands so proud and so bonnie, by the side of that auld carcase of the woman of Rome,—I tell thee it shall stand empty and deserted, shall send forth on Sunday a dumb silence, and the harmony of her voice be heard no more in the land,— rather than she shall take, like a bridegroom to her bosom, that sapless slip of the soul-misleading and Latin-quoting University. Instead of drinking from the pure and fresh well-head, we shall have to drink from the muddy ditch which men have dug for themselves with the spades and shovels of learning. Instead of the down-pouring of the frank and heaven-communicated spirit, we shall have the earthly spirit—the gross invention and fancy of man—a long, dull, down-come of a read sermon, which falls as seed on the ocean, and chaff on the furrowed land. Besides all this, is not this youth—this Joel Kirkpatrick, a slip or scion from the poison-ous tree of patronage, that last legacy from the scarlet lady of Rome?" "I say no to that—the back of my hand to that," interrupted the woman, in red and visible wrath; "I have heard him preach, and I have profited by his prayers; he is a precious youth, and has a happy gift at unravelling the

puzzled skein of controversy. He will be a fixed and a splendid
star, and that ye will soon see. And here he comes, blessings
upon his head; ye shall hear a sermon soon, such as has not
been heard in the land since that chosen youth, John Ruther-
ford, preached on the text, 'I shall kiss thee with kisses of my
mouth.' "[42] "Woman, woman," said her antagonist, "thou
art the slipperiest of thy kind; and opposition and controversy
turn thee round, even as the bush bends to the blast. To-day
hast thou stood for the kirk in its ancient purity; and lo! now
thou wilt take her defiled by patronage, because of that
goodly youth Joel Kirkpatrick." "Silence, ye fule-fowk," said
a young plowman at their side; "ye'll no let me hear the
sound of the soldiers' bugle; they are coming to plant the
gospel with spear and with sword. I have seen many a priest
placed, some with pith of the tongue, and some with the pith
of malt: Black Ned of the parish of Slokendrouth, was placed
in his pulpit by the aid of the brown spirit of malt; and there
the same spirit supports him still. But, on my conscience, I
never saw a parson guarded to the pulpit with cold steel
before. It's a sight worth seeing."

'A stir and a movement was now observed at the extremity
of the village; and presently the helmets, and plumes, and
drawn swords, of two hundred horsemen, appeared, shining
and waving above the crowd. This unusual accompaniment of
the ministerial functions was greeted with hissings and hootings: and the scorn and anger of the multitude burst at once
into one loud yell. The women and the children, gathering
the summer dust in their hands, showered it as thick and as
blinding as winter-drift, on the persons of the troopers. The
anger of people did not rest here; pebbles were thrown, and
symptoms of fiercer hostility began to manifest themselves; for
many of the peasants were armed, and seemed to threaten to
dispute the entrance to the kirk. In the midst of all this
tumult, mounted on a little white horse, and dressed in black,
rode a young man, around whom the dust ascended and
descended as if agitated by a whirlwind. This was the minister. He passed on, nor looked to the right or left, but with
singular meekness, and a look of sorrow and resignation,
endured the tumultuous scorn of the crowd. Long before he
reached the limit of the village, he seemed more a pillar of
dust than a human being. "Is the kirk a dog, that thou comest
against her with staves?" said one: "Or is she a besieged city,

that thou bringest against her thy horsemen and thy cha-
riots?" cried a second: "Or comest thou to slay, whom thou
canst not convince?" shouted a third: "Or dost thou come to
wash thy garments in the blood of saints?" bawled a fourth:
"Or to teach thy flock the exercise of the sword rather than
the exercise of devotion?" yelled a fifth: "Or come ye," exclaimed a sixth, at the very limit of the human voice, "to mix
the voice of the psalm with that of the trumpet, and to hear
how divinity and slaughter will sound together?" Others
expressed their anger in hissings and hootings; while an old
mendicant ballad-singer paraded, step by step with the minister, through the crowd, and sung to a licentious tune the
following rustic lampoon:—

PLACING THE PARSON[43]

1.

Come hasten, and see, for the kirk, like a bride,
Is array'd for her spouse in sedateness and pride.
Comes he in meek mood, with his hands clasp'd and sighing
For the godless and doom'd, with his hopes set on Zion?
Comes he with the grave, the austere, and the sage,—
A warfare with those who scoff Scripture to wage?
He comes—hark! the reins of his war-steeds are ringing;
His trumpet—but 'tis not God's trumpet, is singing.

2.

Clap your hands, all ye graceless; sing loud, and rejoice,
Ye young men of Rimmon;[44] and lift up your voice
All ye who love wantonness, wassail, and sinning
With the dame deck'd in scarlet and fine-twined linen.
Scoff louder, thou scoffer; scorn on, thou proud scorner;
Satan comes to build kirks, and has laid the first corner.
The Babylon dame, from perdition's deep pool,
Sings and cradles her babes in the kirk's cuttie stool.[45]

3.

He comes! of all parsons the swatch and the pattern,
Shaped out to save souls by the shears of his patron.
He comes steep'd in learning's dark puddle, and chatters
Greek words, and tears all Calvin's creed into tatters,

And vows the hot pit shall shut up its grim portals,
Nor devour to a tithe the sum-total of mortals;
Talks of works, and morality's Will-o'-wisp glimmer,
And showers reason's frost on our spiritual simmer.

4.

He comes! lo! behind on their war-horses ranking,
Ride his bands of the faithful, their steel weapons clanking;
Proud hour for religion, when God's chosen word
Is proclaim'd by the trump, and confirm'd by the sword.
Proud hour, when with bayonet, and banner, and brand,
The kirk spreads her sway o'er old Galloway's land,
Where of yore, Sandie Peden look'd down on the vales,
Crying—Clap me hell's flame to their heathenish tails.

'Over this minstrel discordance a far louder din now prevailed; though the mendicant raised his voice to its loftiest
pitch, and all those who purchased his ballad swelled the noise
with their utmost strength. A grove of elm and oak, old and
stately, whose broad green branches had shaded the splendid
processions of the hierarchy of the church of Rome, when in
the height of its glory, presented a short avenue from the end
of the village to the door of the parish kirk. Here the peasantry posted themselves in great numbers; and here the horsemen halted to form for the charge, which they expected to
make before they could obtain access to the church. Nor did
this promise to be an easy task. Many of the peasants were
well armed; and boat-poles, pitchforks, fish-spears, and
hedging-bills—all excellent weapons for resistance and annoyance,—began to thicken near the bosoms of the horses; while
behind, fowling-pieces, and pistols, and swords, appeared prepared in hands that knew well how to use them. In a remoter
line still, the women, their aprons charged with pebbles and
staves, stood ready to succour, with hand and with voice, the
maintainers of kirk purity.

'The casting of dust—the showering of gravel and stones,
and the loud outcry of the multitude, every moment augmented. John Cargill, a gifted Cameronian weaver, from one
of the wildest Galloway mountains, brandished an oaken
treddle, with which he had armed himself, like a quarter-staff,
and cried, "Down with the men of Moab."[46] Tom Gunson,
a smuggler, shouted till he was heard a mile distant, "Down

with them, my handy chaps, and we'll drink the auld kirk's
health out of the troopers' helmets;" and, to crown their audacity, Ill Will Tennan, the poacher, halloed, "Ise shoot the whole
troop at a grey groat the pair, and give ye the raven priest to
the mends." Open hostility seemed almost unavoidable, when
an old farmer, throwing his hat aside, advanced suddenly from
the crowd to the side of the minister, and said, "Did I ever think
I should behold the son of my soothfast friend, Hebron Kirkpatrick, going to glorify God's name at the head of a band of
daily brawlers and paid stabbers?—his horse's feet shall pass
over this frail body first;" and he bent himself down at the feet of
the minister's horse, with his grey locks nearly touching the dust.

'At this unexpected address, and remarkable action, Joel
Kirkpatrick wakened as from a reverie of despondency, and
lighting from his horse, took the old man in his arms with
looks of concern and affection. The multitude was hushed
while the minister said, "May my head be borne by the scoffer
to the grave, and my name serve for a proverb of shame and
reproach, if I step another step this day other than thou
willest. Thou hast long been an exemplar and a guide to me,
John Halberson; and, though God's appointed preacher, and
called to the tending of his flock, be assured I will have thy
sanction, else my ministry may be barren of fruit." The venerable old man gazed on the young preacher with the light of
gladness in his eyes, and taking his hand, said, "Joel Kirkpatrick, heed my words; I question not the authority of the
voice permitted by Him whom we serve to call thee to his
ministry. The word of the multitude is not always with the
wisest, nor the cry of the people with the sound divine and the
gifted preacher. I push thee not forward, neither do I pluck
thee back; but surely, surely, young man of God, he never
ordained the glory of his blessed kirk to be sustained by the
sword, and that he whom he called should come blowing the
trumpet against it. Much do I fear for the honour of that
ministry which is entered upon with banner and brand." As
John Halberson spoke, a sudden light seemed to break upon
the preacher—he motioned the soldiers back; and, taking off
his hat, advanced firmly and meekly down the avenue towards
the kirk-door, one time busied in silent prayer, another time
endeavouring to address the multitude.

' "Hear him not," said one matron; "for he comes schooled
from the university of guile and deceit; and his words, sweet

as honey in the mouth, may prove bitter in the belly, even as
wormwood." "I say hear him, hear him," said another
matron, shaking her Bible at her neighbour's head, to enforce
submission—"ye think him bitterer than the gourd, but he
will be sweeter than the honey-comb." "Absolve thee," said
one old man, the garrulity of age making a speech out of what
he meant for an exclamation, "Absolve thee of the foul guilt,
the burning sin, and the black shame of that bane and wormwood of God's kirk, even patronage; and come unto us—not
with the array of horsemen and the affeir of war; but come
with the humility of tears, and the contrition of sighs, and we
will put thee in the pulpit; for we know thou art a gifted
youth." Another old man, with a bonnet and plaid, and bearing a staff to reinforce his lack of argument, answered the
enemy of patronage, "Who wishes for the choice of the foolish
many, in preference to the election of the one-wise? The
choice of our pastor will be as foolishness for our hearts and a
stumbling-block to our feet. When did ignorance lift up its
voice as a judge, and the sick heart become its own physician?
We are as men who know nothing—each expounding scripture as seemeth wise in vain eyes; and yet shall we go to say
this man, and no other, hath the wisdom to teach and instruct
us?" "Well spoken and wisely, laird of Birkenloan," shouted
a plowman from the summit of the old abbey; "more by
token, our nearest neighbours, in their love for the lad who
could preach a sappy spiritual sermon, elected to the ministry
a sworn and ordained bender of the bicker,[47] whose pulpit,
instead of the odour of sanctity, sends forth the odour of
smuggled gin."—A loud burst of laughter from the multitude
acknowledged the truth of the plowman's sarcasm; while Jock
Gillock, one of the most noted smugglers of the coast of Solway, shook his hand in defiance at the rustic advocate of
patronage, and said, "If I don't make ye the best thrashed
Robson ever stept in black leather shoon, may I be foundered
in half a fathom of fresh water." "And if ye fail to know and
fear the smell of a plowman's hand from this day forthwith,
compared to that of all meaner men's," cried the undaunted
agriculturist, "I will give ye leave to chop me into ballast for
your smuggling cutter:" and he descended to the ground with
the agility of a cat, while the mariner hastened to encounter
him; and all the impetuous and intractable spirits on both
sides followed to witness the battle.

' "So now," said an old peasant, "doth not the wicked slacken their array? Doth not the demon of secession, who hath so long laid waste our kirk, draw off his forces of his own free will? Let us fight the fight of righteousness, while the workers of wickedness fight their own battles. Let us open the kirk portals, blocked up and barricaded by the Shimeis of the land."[48] Several times the young preacher attempted to address the crowd, who had conceived a sudden affection for him since the salutary dismissal of the dragoons—but his flock were far too clamorous, impatient, and elated, to heed what he had to say. They were unaccustomed to be addressed, save from the pulpit; and the wisest speech from a minister without the imposing accompaniments of pulpits and pews, and ranks of douce unbonneted listeners, is sure to fail in making a forcible impression. It was wise, perhaps, in the minister to follow the counsel of grave John Halberson, and let the multitude work their own way. They lifted him from the ground; and, borne along by a crowd of old and young, he approached the kirk—the obstacles which impeded the way vanished before the activity of a thousand willing hands. The kirk-door, fastened with iron spikes by a band of smugglers on the preceding evening, was next assailed, and burst against the wall with a clang that made the old ruin ring again, and in rushed a multitude of heads, filling every seat, as water fills a vessel, from one end of the building to the other. The preacher was borne aloft by this living tide to the door of the pulpit; while the divine, to whom was deputed the honour of ordaining and placing him in his ministry, was welcomed by a free passage, though he had to listen to many admonitions as he passed. "O admonish him to preach in the ancient spirit of the reformed kirk—in a spirit that was wonderful to hear and awful to understand!" said one old man, shaking a head of grey hair as he spoke. "And O," said another peasant, as the divine turned his head, unwilling thus to be schooled in his calling—"targe him tightly anent chambering and wantonness, the glory of youth and the pride of life; for the follies of the land multiply exceedingly." From him the divine turned away in displeasure; but received in the other ear the cross-fire of an old woman, whose nose and chin could have held a hazel-nut, and almost cracked it between their extremities; and whose upper lip was garnished with a beard matching in length and strength the whiskers of a cat. "And O, sir, he's in a state of

single-innocence and sore temptation even now—warn him,
I beseech thee; warn him of the pit into which that singular
and pious man fell in the hour of evil—even him whom the
scoffers call sleepy Samuel.[49] Bid him beware of painted flesh
and languishing eyes—of which there be enough in this
wicked parish. Tell him to beware of one whose love-locks
and whose lures will soon pluck him down from his high calling, even the fair daughter of the old dour trunk of the tree
of papistry, bonnie Bess Glendinning." Here her words were
drowned in the more audible counsel of another of the burning and shining lights of the parish, from whose lips escaped,
in a tone resembling a voice from a cavern, the alarming
words, "Socinians, Arminians, Dioclesians, Erastians, Arians,
and Episcopalians."—"Episcopalians!" ejaculated an old
woman in dismay and astonishment, who mistook, perhaps,
this curtailed catalogue of schismatics for some tremendous
anathema or exorcism—"Episcopalians! God protect me,
what's that?"

'I have no wish to attempt to describe the effects which a
very happy, pithy, and fervent inauguration sermon had on
the multitude. The topics of election, redemption, predestination, and the duties which he called his brother to perform,
with a judicious mind, a christian feeling, and an ardent but
temperate spirit, were handled, perilous as the topics were,
with singular tact, and discrimination, and delicacy. The
happy mixture of active morality and spiritual belief, of work-
day-world practice, and elegant theory, which this address
contained, deserves a lasting remembrance.

'The summary of the preacher's duties, and the description
of the impetuous and mistempered spirits of the parish, and
the contradictory creeds which he had to soothe and to solder,
form still a traditionary treasure to the parish. To minds
young and giddy as mine, these healthy and solacing things
were not so attractive as the follies and outrages of a disap-
pointed crowd; and let not an old man, without reflecting
that he too was once eighteen, condemn me for forsaking the
presence and precepts of the preacher, for the less spiritual
and less moral, but no less instructive drama which was acting
in the open air.

'The dragoons were still in their saddles, but had retired
to the extremity of the village, where they emptied bottles of
ale, and sung English ballads, with a gaiety and a life which

obtained the notice of sundry of the young maidens; who are
observed to feel a regard for scarlet and lace, which I leave to
those who love not their pleasant company to explain. As they
began to gather round, not unobserved by the sons of Mars,
some of the village matrons proceeded to remonstrate.
"Wherefore gaze ye on the men with whiskers, pruned and
laundered, and with coats of scarlet, and with lace laid on the
skirts thereof?" said one old woman, pulling at the same time
her reluctant niece by the hand, while her eyes, notwithstand-
ing her retrograde motion, were fixed on a brawny trooper.
"And Deborah," said a mother to her daughter, whose white
hand and whiter neck, shaded with tresses of glossy auburn,
the hands of another trooper had invaded, "what wouldst
thou do with him who wears the helmet of brass upon his
head?—He is an able-bodied man, but a great covenant-
breaker, and he putteth trust in the spear and in the sword."
The maiden struggled with that earnestness with which a
virgin of eighteen strives to escape from the kindness of a
handsome man; and kiss succeeding kiss told what penalty she
incurred in delaying to follow her mother.

'Of the dissenting portion of the multitude, some disposed
of themselves in the readiest ale-houses; where the themes of
patronage, free-will, and predestination, emptied many
barrels; and the clouds of mystery and doubt darkened down
with the progress of the tankard. Others, of a more flexible
system of morality, went to arrange, far from the tumult of
tongues and opinions in which the district gauger figured, a
midnight importation of choice Geneva,[50] the rapid consumption of which was hastened by the burning spark of controversy, which raged unquenchably in their throats. Many
retired sullenly homeward, lamenting that a concourse of men
of hostile opinions could collect, controvert, and quarrel, and
then coolly separate without blows and bloodshed, cursing the
monotony of human existence now, compared with the stirring times of border forays and covenant-raids. A moiety
nearly of the seceding crowd remained in clumps on the village green. They were men chiefly of that glowing zeal, to
whom mere charity, and the silent operations of religious feeling, seem cold and unfruitful; those pure and fortunate beings,
who find nothing praise-worthy, or meriting the hope of salvation, in the actions of mere men; who discover new interpreta-
tions of scripture, and rend anew the party-coloured and

patched garments of sect and schism every time they meet, when the liquor is abundant. Their hope of the complete reform in the discipline of the parish kirk, or the creation of a new meeting-house to enjoy the eloquence of a preacher, the choice of their own wisdom, seemed now nearly blasted; and they uttered their discontent at the result, while they praised the dexterity or cunning with which they opposed the ordination of that protégé of patronage, Joel Kirkpatrick. "The kirk session may buy a new bell-rope," said a Cameronian weaver, "for I cut away the tow from their tinkling brass yestreen; more by token, it now tethers my hummel cow on the unmowed side of John Allan's park—he had no business to set himself up against the will of the parish, and the word of God." Gilbert Glass, the village glazier, found a topic of worldly consolation amid the spiritual misfortunes of the day: "The kirk windows will cost them a fine penny to repair! some one, whom I'll not name, left not a single pane whole; and each pane will cost the heritors a silver sixpence; that's work my way. It is an evil wind, Saunders Bazely, that blows nobody good; a profitable proverb to you."—"All that I know of the proverb," replied Saunders the slater, "is, that it will be the sweet licking of a creamy finger to thee; but alake! what shall I get out of the pain of riding stride-legs over the clouted roof of the old kirk, patching a few broken slates? I have heard of many a wind blowing for one's good, but I never heard of a wind that uncovered a kirk yet." To all this answered Micah Meen, a sectarian[51] mason, "Plague on't! I wish there were not a slate on its roof, or one stone of its wall above another. This old kirk, built out of the spare stones of the old abbey, is but a bastard-bairn of the old lady of Rome, and deserves no good to come on't. Look ye to the upshot of my words. Seventeen year have I been kirk-mason, and am still as poor as one of its mice. But bide ye, let us lay our heads together, and build a brent new meeting-house. I will build the walls, and no be too hard about the siller, if I have the letting of the seats. And we will have a preacher to our own liking, one who shall not preach a word save sound doctrine, else let me never bed a stone in mortar more."—"Eh, man, but ye speak soundly," said Charlie Goudge, the village carpenter, "in all, save the article of kirk-seats, which, being of timber, pertain more to my calling. Howsomever, I would put a roof of red Norway fir over your heads, and erect ye such seats as no man sits in who lends his ears to a read sermon."—"And as for us two," said the slater and the glazier, clubbing their callings together, for the sake of making a more serious impression, "we would counsel ye to cover your kirk with blue Lancashire slate, instead of that spongy stone from Locherbrighill, which besides, coming from a hill of witch and devil-trysting, is fit for nought, save laying above a dead man's dwelling, who never complains of a bad roof; and farther, put none of your dull green glass in the windows, but clear pure glass, through which a half-blind body might see to expound the word."—"And I would counsel ye to begin a subscription incontinent," said the keeper of a neighbouring ale-house; "and if ye will come into my home, we can commence the business with moistened throats; and," continued mine host in an under-tone, "I can kittle up your spirits with some rare Geneva from the bosom of my sloop the Bonnie Nelly Lawson there, where she lies cosy among Cairnhowrie birks, and the gauger never the wiser."

'A flood of sectarians inundated the parlour of the Thistle and Hand-Hammer, and a noise, rivalling the descent of a Galloway stream down one of its wildest glens, issued ringing far and wide from the change-house. "Subscribe!" said Gilpin Johnstone, a farmer of Annandale descent, "I would not give seven placks, and these are but small coins, for the fairest kirk that ever bore a roof above the walls. There's the goodman of Hoshenfoot, a full farmer, who hopes to be saved in his own way, he may subscribe. No but that I am willing to come and listen if the pew-rates be moderate."—"Me subscribe!" said he of the Hoshenfoot, buttoning his pockets as he spoke, to fortify his resolution, "where in the wide world, think ye, have I got gold to build into kirk-walls. Besides, I have been a follower of that ancient poetical mode of worship, preaching on the mountain side; and if ye will give me a day or two's reaping in the throng of harvest, I will lend ye the green hill of Knockhoolie to preach an hour's sound doctrine on any time; save, I should have said, when the peas are in the pod; and then deil have me if I would trust a hungry congregation near them." Similar evasions came from the lips of several more of the wealthy seceders; and, one by one, they dissented and dispersed: not without a severe contest with the landlord, whether they were responsible for all the liquor they had consumed, seeing it was for the spiritual welfare of the parish.

'If the entry of the minister into his ministry was stormy and troubled, ample reparation was made by the mass of the parishioners, who, after the ordination, escorted him home to the Manse, giving frequent testimony of that sedate joy and tranquil satisfaction, which the people of Scotland are remarkable for expressing. "Reverend sir, you have had but a cold and a wintry welcome to your ministry," said an old and substantial dame, "and if ye will oblige me by accepting of such a hansel, I will send ye what will make a gallant house-heating."—"And ye mauna have all the joy of giving gifts to yourself, goodwife," said an old man with a broad bonnet, and stooping over a staff, "for I shall send our ain Joel Kirkpatrick such a present as no minister o' Bleeding-Heart ever received since Mirk-Monday,[52] and all too little to atone for the din that my old and graceless tongue raised against God's gifted servant this blessed morning."—"And talking of atonements," interrupted an old woman, whose hands were yet unwashen from the dust which she had lately thrown on the minister, "I have an atoning offering to make for having wickedly testified against a minister of God's kirk this morning. I shall send him a stone weight of ewe-milk cheese tomorrow." But no one of the multitude seemed more delighted, or stood higher in general favour, than John Halberson, the wise and venerable man who had given the first check to the fiery spirit that blazed so fiercely in the morning. He walked by the minister's side, his head uncovered, and his remaining white hairs glittering in the descending sun. His words were not many; but they were laid up in the heart, and practised in the future life of the excellent person to whom they were addressed. "Young man and reverend, thy lot is cast in a stormy season, and in a stony land. There be days for sowing, and days for reaping, and days for gathering into the garner. Thou hast a mind gifted with natural wisdom, and stored with written knowledge; a tongue fluent and sweet in utterance, and thou hast drunk of the word at the well-head. But trust not thy gifts alone for working deliverance among the people. Thou must know each man and woman by face and by name: pass into their abodes, acquaint thyself with their feelings and their failings, and move them, and win them, to the paths of holiness, as a young man woos his bride. Thou must dandle their young ones on thy knees, for thy MASTER loved little children, and it is a seemly thing to be beloved of babes.

Should youth go astray, in the way in which youth is prone, take it gently and tenderly to task; severity maketh the kirk rancorous enemies, and persecution turneth love into deadly hate; humanity and kindness are the leading strings of the human heart. One counsel more, and I have done: take unto thee a wife. Ministers are not too good for such a sweet company as woman's, neither are they too steadfast not to fear a fall. Wed, saith the Scripture, and replenish the earth; and I wish not the good, the brave, and ancient name of Kirkpatrick to pass from among us. Peace be with thee, and many days." By following the wise counsel of his venerable parishioner, Joel Kirkpatrick became one of the most popular pastors of the Presbytery, and one of the chief luminaries of the ancient province of Galloway. His eloquence, his kindliness of heart, and the active charity of his nature, will be proverbial in parish tradition, while eloquence, and kindness, and charity, are reverenced on earth.'

THE KING OF THE PEAK.
A DERBYSHIRE TALE

What time the bird wakes in its bower,[53]
He stood, and look'd on Haddon tower;
High rose it o'er the woodland height,
With portals strong, and turrets bright,
And gardens green, with swirl and sweep,
Round rush'd the Wye, both broad and deep.
Leaping and looking for the sun,
He saw the red-deer and the dun;
The warders with their weapons sheen,
The watchers with their mantles green;
The deer-hounds at their feet were flung,
The red blood at their dew-laps hung.
Adown he leap'd, and awhile he stood,
With a downcast look, and pondering mood,
Then made a step, and his bright sword drew,
And cleft a stone at a stroke in two—
So shall the heads of my foemen be,
Who seek to sunder my love from me.

Derbyshire Rhyme of Dora Vernon

Remains of the ancient frank and open-hearted hospitality of old England linger yet among her vales and mountains; and travellers are not unfrequently greeted with a patriarchal welcome, and a well-spread table, without the chilling formality of a fair-penned and prudently-worded introduction. The open bounty of hill, and wood, and vale, and sea, is poured in wholesale profusion on many of the fortunate dwellers in the country; while, on those who forsake the wonders of God for the works of man—the green land, and the glorious air, for the confusion of the city—nature sprinkles her favours with a sparing and a niggard hand. The city strives in vain to emulate the frank kindness of the country, and opens her doors, but opens them with a sad civility, and a constrained and suspicious courtesy. In the country, the door stands open, the table is spread, and the bidden guest is the way-wearied man, or the fugitive and the wanderer. He enters, he refreshes himself, he reposes, and on the morrow he renews his journey.

It happened once in a northern county, that I found myself at a farmer's fire-side, and in company which the four winds of heaven seemed to have blown together. The farmer was a joyous old man; and the evening, a wintry one, and wild with wind and snow, flew away with jest, and mirth, and tale, and song. Our entertainer had no wish that our joy should subside: for he heaped the fire till the house shone to its remotest rafter; loaded his table with rustic delicacies, and once, when a pause ensued after the chanting of one of Robin Hood's ballads, he called out, 'Why stays the story, and what stops the rhyme? Have I heated my hearth, have I spread my tables, and poured forth my strong drink for the poor in fancy, and the lame in speech? Up, up; and give me a grave tale or a gay, to gladden or sadden the present moment, and lend wings to the leaden feet of evening time. Rise, I say; else may the fire that flames so high—the table which groans with food, for which water, and air, and earth, have been sought; and the board that perfumes you with the odour of ale and mead—may the first cease to warm, and the rest to nourish ye.'

'Master,' said a hail and joyous personage, whose shining and gladsome looks showed sympathy and alliance with the good cheer and fervent blood of merry old England; 'since thy table smokes, and thy brown ale flows more frankly for the telling of a true old tale, then a true old tale thou shalt have— shame fall me if I balk thee, as the pleasant folk say in the dales of bonny Derby.[54]

'Those who have never seen Haddon Hall, the ancient residence of the Vernons of Derbyshire, can have but an imperfect notion of the golden days of old England. Though now deserted and dilapidated—its halls silent—the sacred bell of its chapel mute—though its tables no longer send up the cheering smell of roasted boars, and spitted oxen—though the music and the voice of the minstrel are silenced, and the light foot of the dancer no longer sounds on the floor—though no gentle knights and gentler dames go trooping hand in hand, and whispering among the twilight groves—and the portal no longer sends out its shining helms, and its barbed steeds;— where is the place that can recall the stately hospitality and glory of former times, like the Hall of OLD HADDON?

'It happened on a summer evening, when I was a boy, that
several curious old people had seated themselves on a little
round knoll near the gate of Haddon Hall; and their talk was
of the Vernons, the Cavendishes, the Manners, and many
old names once renowned in Derbyshire. I had fastened myself
to the apron-string of a venerable dame, at whose girdle hung
a mighty iron key, which commanded the entrance of the hall;
her name was Dolly Foljambe; and she boasted her descent
from an ancient red cross knight of that name, whose alabaster figure, in mail, may be found in Bakewell church. This
high origin, which, on consulting family history, I find had
not the concurrence of clergy, seemed not an idle vanity of the
humble   portress;   she   had   the   straight   frame,   and   rigid,
demure, and even warlike cast of face, which alabaster still
retains of her ancestor; and had she laid herself by his side, she
might have passed muster, with an ordinary antiquarian, for
a coeval figure. At our feet the river Wye ran winding and
deep; at our side rose the hall, huge and grey; and the rough
heathy hills, renowned in Druidic, and Roman, and Saxon,
and Norman story, bounded our wish for distant prospects,
and gave us the mansion of the Vernons for our contemplation, clear of all meaner encumbrances of landscape.

' "Ah! dame Foljambe," said an old husbandman, whose
hair was whitened by acquaintance with seventy winters; "it's
a sore and a sad sight to look at that fair tower, and see no
smoke ascending. I remember it in a brighter day, when many
a fair face gazed out at the windows, and many a gallant form
appeared at the gate. Then were the days when the husbandman could live—could whistle as he sowed; dance and sing
as he reaped; and could pay his rent in fatted oxen to my lord,
and in fatted fowls to my lady. Ah! dame Foljambe, we
remember when men could cast their lines in the Wye; could
feast on the red deer and the fallow deer, on the plover and
the ptarmigan; had right of the common for their flocks, of
the flood for their nets, and of the air for their harquebuss.
Ah! dame, old England is no more the old England it was,
than that hall, dark, and silent, and desolate, is the proud hall
that held Sir George Vernon, the King of the Peak, and his
two lovely daughters, Margaret and Dora. Those were days,
dame; those were days!" And as he ceased, he looked up to
the tower, with an eye of sorrow, and shook and smoothed
down his white hairs.

' "I tell thee," replied the ancient portress, sorely moved in mind, between present duty and service to the noble owner of Haddon, and her lingering affection for the good old times of which memory shapes so many paradises, "I tell thee the tower looks as high and as lordly as ever; and there is something about its silent porch, and its crumbling turrets, which gives it a deeper hold of our affections, than if an hundred knights even now came prancing forth at its porch, with trumpets blowing, and banners displayed."

' "Ah! dame Foljambe," said the husbandman; "yon deer now bounding so blithely down the old chase, with his horny head held high, and an eye that seems to make nought of mountain and vale; it is a fair creature. Look at him! see how he cools his feet in the Wye, surveys his shadow in the stream, and now he contemplates his native hills again. So! away he goes, and we gaze after him, and admire his speed and his beauty. But were the hounds at his flanks, and the bullets in his side, and the swords of the hunters bared for the brittling; Ah! dame, we should change our cheer; we should think that such shapely limbs, and such stately antlers, might have reigned in wood and on hill for many summers. Even so we think of that stately old hall, and lament its destruction."

' "Dame Foljambe thinks not so deeply on the matter," said a rustic; "she thinks, the less the hall fire, the less is the chance of the hall being consumed; the less the company, the longer will the old hall floor last, which she sweeps so clean, telling so many stories of the tree that made it;—that the seven Virtues in tapestry would do well in avoiding wild company; and that the lass with the long shanks, Diana, and her nymphs, will hunt more to her fancy on her dusty acre of old arras, than in the dubious society of the lords and the heroes of the court gazette. Moreover, the key at her girdle is the commission by which she is keeper of this cast-off and moth-eaten garment of the noble name of Manners; and think ye that she holds that power lightly, which makes her governess of ten thousand bats and owls, and gives her the awful responsibility of an armoury, containing almost an entire harquebuss, the remains of a pair of boots, and the relique of a buff jerkin?"

'What answer to this unceremonious attack on ancient things committed to her keeping the portress might have made, I had not an opportunity to learn; her darkening brow indicated little meekness of reply; a voice, however, much sweeter than the dame's, intruded on the debate. In the vicinity of the hall, at the foot of a limestone rock, the summer visitors of Haddon may and do refresh themselves at a small fount of pure water, which love of the clear element induced one of the old ladies to confine within the limits of a large stone basin. Virtues were imputed to the spring, and the superstition of another proprietor erected beside it a cross of stone, lately mutilated, and now removed, but once covered with sculptures and rude emblems, which conveyed religious instruction to an ignorant people. Towards this fountain, a maiden from a neighbouring cottage was observed to proceed, warbling, as she went, a fragment of one of those legendary ballads which the old minstrels, illiterate or learned, scattered so abundantly over the country.

DORA VERNON[55]

I.

It happen'd between March and May-day,
    When wood-buds wake which slumber'd late,
When hill and valley grow green and gaily,
    And every wight longs for a mate;
When lovers sleep with an open eye-lid,
    Like nightingales on the orchard tree,
And sorely wish they had wings for flying,
    So they might with their true love be.

2.

A knight all worthy, in this sweet season
    Went out to Carcliff with bow and gun,
Not to chase the roebuck, nor shoot the pheasant,
    But hunt the fierce fox so wild and dun.
And, by his side, was a young maid riding,
    With laughing blue eyes, and sunny hair;
And who was it but young Dora Vernon,
    Young Rutland's true love, and Haddon's heir.

3.

Her gentle hand was a good bow bearing,—
    The deer at speed, or the fowl on wing,
Stay'd in their flight, when the bearded arrow

Her white hand loosed from the sounding string.
Old men made bare their locks, and blest her
    As blithe she rode down the Durwood side,
Her steed rejoiced in his lovely rider,
    Arch'd his neck proudly, and pranced in pride.

'This unexpected minstrelsy was soon interrupted by dame
Foljambe, whose total devotion to the family of Rutland rendered her averse to hear the story of Dora Vernon's elopement, profaned in the familiar ballad strain of a forgotten
minstrel. "I wonder at the presumption of that rude minion,"
said the offended portress, "in chanting such ungentle strains
in my ear. Home to thy milk-pails, idle hussy—home to thy
distaff, foolish maiden; or if thou wilt sing, come over to my
lodge when the sun is down, and I will teach thee a strain of a
higher sort, made by a great court lord, on the marriage of
her late Grace. It is none of your rustic chants, but full of fine
words, both long and lordly; it begins,

Come, burn your incense, ye god-like graces,[56]
    Come, Cupid, dip your darts in light;
Unloose her starry zone, chaste Venus,
    And trim the bride for the bridal night.

' "None of your vulgar chants, minion, I tell thee; but stuffed
with spiced words, and shining with gods, and garters, and stars,
and precious stones, and odours thickly dropping; a noble strain
indeed." The maiden smiled, nodded acquiescence, and trip-
ping homewards, renewed her homely and interrupted song,
till the river bank and the ancient towers acknowledged, with
their sweetest echoes, the native charms of her voice.
    ' "I marvel much," said the hoary portress, "at the idle
love for strange and incredible stories which possesses as with
a demon the peasants of this district. Not only have they given
a saint, with a shirt of hair cloth and a scourge, to every
cavern, and a druid with his golden sickle and his mistletoe to
every circle of shapeless stones; but they have made the
Vernons, the Cavendishes, the Cockaynes, and the Foljambes,
erect on every wild place crosses or altars of atonement for
crimes which they never committed; unless fighting ankle-
deep in heathen blood, for the recovery of Jerusalem and the
holy sepulchre, required such outlandish penance. They cast

too a supernatural light round the commonest story; if you
credit them, the ancient chapel bell of Haddon, safely lodged
on the floor for a century, is carried to the top of the turret,
and, touched by some invisible hand, is made to toll forth
midnight notes of dolour and woe, when any misfortune is
about to befall the noble family of Rutland. They tell you too
that wailings of no earthly voice are heard around the
decayed towers, and along the garden terraces, on the festival
night of the saint who presided of old over the fortunes of the
name of Vernon. And no longer agone than yesterday, old
Edgar Ferrars assured me that he had nearly as good as seen
the apparition of the King of the Peak himself, mounted on
his visionary steed, and, with imaginary horn, and hound,
and halloo, pursuing a spectre stag over the wild chase of
Haddon. Nay, so far has vulgar credulity and assurance gone,
that the great garden entrance, called the Knight's Porch,
through which Dora Vernon descended step by step among
her twenty attendant maidens, all rustling in embroidered
silks, and shining and sparkling like a winter sky, in diamonds,
and such like costly stones—to welcome her noble bridegroom, Lord John Manners, who came cap in hand with his
company of gallant gentlemen—"

' "Nay, now, dame Foljambe," interrupted the husbandman, "all this is fine enough, and lordly too, I'll warrant; but
thou must not apparel a plain old tale in the embroidered
raiment of thy own brain, nor adorn it in the precious stones
of thy own fancy. Dora Vernon was a lovely lass, and as
proud as she was lovely; she bore her head high, dame; and
well she might, for she was a gallant Knight's daughter; and
lords and dukes, and what not, have descended from her. But,
for all that, I cannot forget that she ran away in the middle
of a moonlight night, with young Lord John Manners, and no
other attendant than her own sweet self. Ay, dame, and for
the diamonds, and what not, which thy story showers on her
locks and her garments, she tied up her berry brown locks in a
menial's cap, and ran away in a mantle of Bakewell brown,
three yards for a groat. Ay, dame, and instead of going out
regularly by the door, she leapt out of a window; more by
token she left one of her silver heeled slippers fastened in the
grating, and the place has ever since been called the Lady's
Leap."

'Dame Foljambe, like an inexperienced rider, whose steed

refuses obedience to voice and hand, resigned the contest in despair, and allowed her rustic companion to enter full career into the debatable land, where she had so often fought and vanquished in defence of the decorum of the mode of alliance between the houses of Haddon and Rutland.

' "And now, dame," said the husbandman, "I will tell thee the story in my own and my father's way. The last of the name of Vernon was renowned far and wide for the hospitality and magnificence of his house, for the splendour of his retinue, and more for the beauty of his daughters, Margaret and Dorothy. This is speaking in thy own manner, dame Foljambe; but truth's truth. He was much given to hunting and hawking, and jousting, with lances either blunt or sharp; and though a harquebuss generally was found in the hand of the gallant hunters of that time, the year of grace 1560, Sir George Vernon despised that foreign weapon; and well he might, for he bent the strongest bow, and shot the surest shaft, of any man in England. His chase-dogs too were all of the most expert and famous kinds—his falcons had the fairest and most certain flight; and though he had seen foreign lands, he chiefly prided himself in maintaining unimpaired the old baronial grandeur of his house. I have heard my grandsire say, how his great grandsire told him, that the like of the knight of Haddon, for a stately form, and a noble, free, and natural grace of manner, was not to be seen in court or camp. He was hailed, in common tale, and in minstrel song, by the name of the KING OF THE PEAK; and it is said, his handsome person and witchery of tongue chiefly prevented his mistress, good Queen Bess, from abridging his provincial designation with the headsman's axe.

' "It happened in the fifth year of the reign of his young and sovereign mistress, that a great hunting festival was held at Haddon, where all the beauty and high blood of Derbyshire assembled. Lords of distant counties came; for to bend a bow, or brittle the deer, under the eye of Sir George Vernon, was an honour sought for by many. Over the chase of Haddon, over the hill of Stanton, over Bakewell-edge, over Chatsworth hill and Hardwicke plain, and beneath the ancient castle of Bolsover, as far as the edge of the forest of old Sherwood, were the sounds of harquebuss and bowstring heard, and the cry of dogs and the cheering of men. The brown-mouthed and white-footed dogs of Derbyshire were there among the foremost; the snow-white hound and the coal-black, from the Scottish border and bonny Westmoreland, preserved or augmented their ancient fame; nor were the dappled hounds of old Godfrey Foljambe, of Bakewell bank, far from the throat of the red deer when they turned at bay, and gored horses and riders. The great hall floor of Haddon was soon covered with the produce of wood and wild.

' "Nor were the preparations for feasting this noble hunting party unworthy of the reputation for solid hospitality which characterised the ancient King of the Peak. Minstrels had come from distant parts, as far even as the Scottish border; bold, free-spoken, rude, rough witted men; 'for the selvage of the web,' says the northern proverb, 'is aye the coarsest cloth.'[57] But in the larder the skill of man was chiefly employed, and a thousand rarities were prepared for pleasing the eye and appeasing the appetite. In the kitchen, with its huge chimneys and prodigious spits, the menial maidens were flooded nigh ankle deep in the richness of roasted oxen and deer; and along the passage, communicating with the hall of state, men might have slided along, because of the fat droppings of that prodigious feast, like a slider on the frozen Wye. The kitchen tables, of solid plank, groaned and yielded beneath the roasted beeves and the spitted deer; while a stream of rich smoke, massy, and slow, and savoury, sallied out at the grated windows, and sailed round the mansion, like a mist exhaled by the influence of the moon. I tell thee, dame Foljambe, I call those the golden days of old England.

' "But I wish you had seen the hall prepared for this princely feast. The floor, of hard and solid stone, was strewn deep with rushes and fern; and there lay the dogs of the chase in couples, their mouths still red with the blood of stags, and panting yet from the fervour and length of their pursuit. At the lower end of the hall, where the floor subsided a step, was spread a table for the stewards and other chiefs over the menials. There sat the keeper of the bows, the warder of the chase, and the head falconer, together with many others of lower degree, but mighty men among the retainers of the noble name of Vernon. Over their heads were hung the horns of stags, the jaws of boars, the skulls of the enormous bisons, and the foreheads of foxes. Nor were there wanting trophies, where the contest had been more bloody and obstinate—

banners, and shields, and helmets, won in the Civil, and Scottish, and Crusading wars, together with many strange weapons of annoyance or defence, borne in the Norwegian and Saxon broils. Beside them were hung rude paintings of the most renowned of these rustic heroes, all in the picturesque habiliments of the times. Horns, and harquebusses, and swords, and bows, and buff coats, and caps, were thrown in negligent groups all about the floor; while their owners sat in expectation of an immediate and ample feast, which they hoped to wash down with floods of that salutary beverage, the brown blood of barley.

‘ "At the upper end of the hall, where the floor was elevated exactly as much in respect, as it was lowered in submission at the other, there the table for feasting the nobles stood; and well was it worthy of its station. It was one solid plank of white sycamore, shaped from the entire shaft of an enormous tree, and supported on squat columns of oak, ornamented with the arms of the Vernons, and grooved into the stone floor, beyond all chance of being upset by human powers. Benches of wood, curiously carved, and covered, in times of more than ordinary ceremony, with cushions of embroidered velvet, surrounded this ample table;—while in the recess behind appeared a curious work in arras, consisting of festivals and processions, and bridals, executed from the ancient poets; and for the more staid and grave, a more devout hand had wrought some scenes from the controversial fathers and the monkish legends of the ancient church. The former employed the white hands of Dora Vernon herself; while the latter were the labours of her sister Margaret, who was of a serious turn, and never happened to be so far in love as to leap from a window.'

‘ "And now," said dame Foljambe, "I will describe the Knight of Haddon, with his fair daughters and principal guests, myself." "A task that will last thee to doomsday, dame," muttered the husbandman. The portress heeded not this ejaculation, but with a particular stateliness of delivery proceeded. "The silver dinner bell rang on the summit of Haddon Hall, the warder thrice wound his horn, and straightway the sound of silver spurs was heard in the passage, the folding door opened, and in marched my own ancestor, Ferrars Foljambe by name. I have heard his dress too often described not to remember it. A buff jerkin, with slashed and

ornamented sleeves, a mantle of fine Lincoln green, fastened
round his neck with wolf-claws of pure gold, a pair of gilt
spurs on the heels of his brown hunting-boots, garnished above
with taslets of silver, and at the square and turned-up toes,
with links of the same metal connected with the taslets. On his
head was a boar-skin cap, on which the white teeth of the
boar were set tipt with gold. At his side, was a hunting horn,
called the white hunting horn of Tutbury, banded with silver
in the middle, belted with black silk at the ends, set with
buckles of silver, and bearing the arms of Edmund, the warlike brother of Edward Longshanks. This fair horn descended
by marriage to Stanhope, of Elvaston, who sold it to Foxlowe,
of Staveley. The gift of a king and the property of heroes
was sold for some paltry pieces of gold."

' "Dame Foljambe," said the old man, "the march of thy
tale is like the course of the Wye, seventeen miles of links and
windings down a fair valley five miles long. A man might
carve thy ancestor's figure in alabaster in the time thou
describest him. I must resume my story, dame; so let thy
description of old Ferrars Foljambe stand; and suppose the
table filled about with the gallants of the chase and many fair
ladies, while at the head sat the King of the Peak himself, his
beard descending to his broad girdle, his own natural hair of
dark brown—blessings on the head that keeps God's own
covering on it, and scorns the curled inventions of man—
falling in thick masses on his broad, manly shoulders. Nor silver, nor gold, wore he; the natural nobleness of his looks
maintained his rank and pre-eminence among men; the step
of Sir George Vernon was one that many imitated, but few
could attain—at once manly and graceful. I have heard it
said, that he carried privately in his bosom a small rosary of
precious metal, in which his favourite daughter Dora had
entwined one of her mother's tresses. The ewer-bearers
entered with silver basins full of water; the element came pure
and returned red; for the hands of the guests were stained with
the blood of the chase. The attendant minstrels vowed, that
no hands so shapely, nor fingers so taper, and long, and white,
and round, as those of the Knight of Haddon, were that day
dipped in water.

' "There is wondrous little pleasure in describing a feast of
which we have not partaken; so pass we on to the time when
the fair dames retired, and the red wine in cups of gold, and

the ale in silver flagons, shone and sparkled as they passed
from hand to lip beneath the blaze of seven massy lamps. The
knights toasted their mistresses, the retainers told their
exploits, and the minstrels with harp and tongue made music
and song abound. The gentles struck their drinking vessels on
the table till they rang again; the menials stamped with the
heels of their ponderous boots on the solid floor; while the
hounds, imagining they heard the call to the chase, leaped up,
and bayed in hoarse but appropriate chorus.

' "The ladies now re-appeared, in the side galleries, and
overlooked the scene of festivity below. The loveliest of many
counties were there; but the fairest was a young maid of
middle size, in a dress disencumbered of ornament, and possessed of one of those free and graceful forms which may be
met with in other counties, but for which our own Derbyshire
alone is famous. Those who admired the grace of her person
were no less charmed with her simplicity and natural meekness of deportment. Nature did much for her, and art strove
in vain to rival her with others; while health, that handmaid
of beauty, supplied her eye and her cheek with the purest light
and the freshest roses. Her short and rosy upper-lip was
slightly curled, with as much of maiden sanctity, perhaps, as
pride; her white high forehead was shaded with locks of sunny
brown, while her large and dark hazel eyes beamed with free
and unaffected modesty. Those who observed her closely
might see her eyes, as she glanced about, sparkling for a
moment with other lights, but scarce less holy, than those of
devotion and awe. Of all the knights present, it was impossible
to say, who inspired her with those love-fits of flushing joy
and delicious agitation; each hoped himself the happy person,
for none could look on Dora Vernon without awe and love.
She leaned her white bosom, shining through the veil which
shaded it, near one of the minstrels' harps; and looking round
on the presence, her eyes grew brighter as she looked; at least,
so vowed the knights, and so sang the minstrels.

' "All the knights arose when Dora Vernon appeared. 'Fill
all your wine-cups, knights,' said Sir Lucas Peverel. 'Fill them
to the brim,' said Sir Henry Avenel. 'And drain them out,
were they deeper than the Wye,' said Sir Godfrey Gernon.
'To the health of the Princess of the Peak,' said Sir Ralph
Cavendish. 'To the health of Dora Vernon,' said Sir Hugh de
Wodensley; 'beauty is above titles, she is the loveliest maiden

a knight ever looked on, with the sweetest name too.' 'And yet, Sir Knight,' said Peverel, filling his cup, 'I know one who thinks so humbly of the fair name of Vernon, as to wish it charmed into that of De Wodensley.' 'He is not master of a spell so profound,' said Avenel. 'And yet he is master of his sword,' answered De Wodensley, with a darkening brow. 'I counsel him to keep it in its sheath,' said Cavendish, 'lest it prove a wayward servant.' 'I will prove its service on thy bosom where and when thou wilt, Lord of Chatsworth,' said De Wodensley. 'Lord of Darley,' answered Cavendish, 'it is a tempting moonlight, but there is a charm over Haddon to-night it would be unseemly to dispel. To-morrow, I meet Lord John Manners to try whose hawk has the fairer flight, and whose love the whiter hand. That can be soon seen; for who has so fair a hand as the love of young Rutland? I shall be found by Durwood-Tor when the sun is three hours up, with my sword drawn—there's my hand on't, De Wodensley;' and he wrung the knight's hand till the blood seemed starting from beneath his finger nails.

' " 'By the saints, Sir Knights,' said Sir Godfrey Gernon, 'you may as well beard one another about the love of "some bright particular star and think to wed it,"[58] as the wild wizard of Warwick says, as quarrel about this unattainable love. Hearken, minstrels: while we drain our cups to this beauteous lass, sing some of you a kindly love strain, wondrously mirthful and melancholy. Here's a cup of Rhenish, and a good gold Harry[59] in the bottom on't, for the minstrel who pleases me.' The minstrels laid their hands on the strings, and a sound was heard like the swarming of bees before summer thunder. 'Sir Knight,' said one, 'I will sing ye, Cannie Johnnie Armstrong with all the seventeen variations.' 'He was hanged for cattle stealing,' answered the knight: 'I'll have none of him.' 'What say you to Dick of the Cow, or the Harper of Lochmaben?' said another, with something of a tone of diffidence: 'What! you northern knaves, can you sing of nothing but thievery and jail-breaking?' 'Perhaps, your knightship,' humbly suggested a third, 'may have a turn for the supernatural, and I'm thinking the Fairy Legend of young Tamlane is just the thing that suits your fancy.' 'I like the naïveté of the young lady very much,' answered the knight; 'but the fair dames of Derbyshire prize the charms of lovers with flesh and blood, before the gayest Elfin-knight that ever

ran a course from Carlisle to Caerlaverock.'—'What would
your worship say to William of Cloudesley?' said a Cumberland minstrel. 'Or to the Friar of Orders Grey?' said a harper
from the halls of the Percys.

' " 'Minstrels,' said Sir Ralph Cavendish, 'the invention of
sweet and gentle poesy is dead among you. Every churl in the
Peak can chant us these beautiful but common ditties. Have
you nothing new for the honour of the sacred calling of verse,
and the beauty of Dora Vernon? Fellow—harper,—what's
your name? you with the long hair and the green mantle,' said
the knight, beckoning to a young minstrel who sat with his
harp held before him, and his face half buried in his mantle's
fold: 'come, touch your strings and sing; I'll wager my gold-
hilted sword against that pheasant feather in thy cap, that
thou hast a new and a gallant strain; for I have seen thee
measure more than once the form of fair Dora Vernon with a
ballad-maker's eye.—Sing, man, sing.'

' "The young minstrel, as he bowed his head to this singular mode of request, blushed from brow to bosom; nor were
the face and neck of Dora Vernon without an acknowledgment of how deeply she sympathised in his embarrassment. A
finer instrument, a truer hand, or a more sweet and manly
voice, hardly ever united to lend grace to rhyme.

THE MINSTREL'S SONG[60]

1.

Last night a proud page came to me;
Sir Knight, he said, I greet you free;
The moon is up at midnight hour,
All mute and lonely is the bower:
To rouse the deer my lord is gone,
And his fair daughter's all alone,
As lily fair, and as sweet to see,—
Arise, Sir Knight, and follow me.

2.

The stars stream'd out, the new-woke moon
O'er Chatsworth hill gleam'd brightly down,
And my love's cheeks, half-seen, half-hid,
With love and joy blush'd deeply red:

Short was our time, and chaste our bliss,
A whisper'd vow and a gentle kiss;
And one of those long looks, which earth
With all its glory is not worth.

3.

The stars beam'd lovelier from the sky,
The smiling brook flow'd gentlier by;
Life, fly thou on; I'll mind that hour
Of sacred love in greenwood bower;
Let seas between us swell and sound,
Still at her name my heart shall bound;
Her name—which like a spell I'll keep,
To soothe me and to charm my sleep.

' " 'Fellow,' said Sir Ralph Cavendish, 'thou hast not
shamed my belief of thy skill; keep that piece of gold, and
drink thy cup of wine in quiet, to the health of the lass who
inspired thy strain, be she lordly, or be she low.' The minstrel
seated himself, and the interrupted mirth recommenced,
which was not long to continue. When the minstrel began to
sing, the King of the Peak fixed his large and searching eyes
on his person with a scrutiny from which nothing could
escape, and which called a flush of apprehension to the face of
his daughter Dora. Something like a cloud came upon his
brow at the first verse, which, darkening down through the
second, became as dark as a December night at the close of
the third, when rising, and motioning Sir Ralph Cavendish to
follow, he retired into the recess of the southern window.
' " 'Sir Knight,' said the lord of Haddon, 'thou art the
sworn friend of John Manners, and well thou knowest what
his presumption dares at, and what are the letts between him
and me. *Cavendo tutus!*[61] ponder on thy own motto well.—"Let
seas between us swell and sound:"[62]—let his song be prophetic, for Derbyshire—for England has no river deep enough
and broad enough to preserve him from a father's sword,
whose peace he seeks to wound.' 'Knight of Haddon,' said Sir
Ralph, 'John Manners is indeed my friend; and the friend of
a Cavendish can be no mean person; a braver and a better
spirit never aspired after beauty.' 'Sir Knight,' said the King
of the Peak, 'I court no man's counsel; hearken to my words.
Look at the moon's shadow on Haddon-dial; there it is beside

the casement; the shadow falls short of twelve. If it darkens the midnight hour, and John Manners be found here, he shall be cast, fettered, neck and heel, into the deepest dungeon of Haddon.'

' "All this passed not unobserved of Dora Vernon, whose fears and affections divined immediate mischief from the calm speech and darkened brow of her father. Her heart sank within her when he beckoned her to withdraw; she followed him into the great tapestried room. 'My daughter,—my love Dora,' said the not idle fears of a father, 'wine has done more than its usual good office with the wits of our guests to-night; they look on thee with bolder eyes, and speak of thee with a bolder tongue, than a father can wish. Retire, therefore, to thy chamber. One of thy wisest attendants shall be thy companion.—Adieu, my love, till sun-rise!' He kissed her white temples and white brow; and Dora clung to his neck, and sobbed in his bosom;—while the secret of her heart rose near her lips. He returned to his guests, and mirth and music, and the march of the wine-cup, recommenced with a vigour which promised reparation for the late intermission.

' "The chamber, or rather temporary prison, of Dora Vernon, was nigh the cross-bow room, and had a window which looked out on the terraced garden, and the extensive chase towards the hill of Haddon. All that side of the hall lay in deep shadow, and the moon, sunk to the very summit of the western heath, threw a level and a farewell beam over river and tower. The young lady of Haddon seated herself in the recessed window, and lent her ear to every sound, and her eye to every shadow that flitted over the garden and chase. Her attendant maiden—shrewd, demure, and suspicious,—of the ripe age of thirty—yet of a merry pleasant look, which had its admirers—sat watching every motion with the eye of an owl.

' "It was past midnight, when a foot came gliding along the passage, and a finger gave three slight scratches on the door of the chamber. The maid went out, and after a brief conference suddenly returned, red with blushes from ear to ear. 'Oh, my lady!' said the trusty maiden,—'oh, my sweet young lady,—here's that poor young lad—ye know his name—who gave me three yards of crimson ribbon to trim my peach-bloom mantle, last Bakewell fair.—An honester or a kinder heart never kept a promise; and yet I may not give him the meeting. Oh, my young lady, my sweet young lady, my beautiful young lady, could you not stay here for half an hour by yourself?' Ere her young mistress could answer, the notice of the lover's presence was renewed.—The maiden again went—whispers were heard—and the audible salutation of lips; she returned again more resolute than ever to oblige her lover.—'Oh, my lady—my young lady; if ye ever hope to prosper in true love yourself—spare me but one half hour with this harmless kind lad.—He has come seven long miles to see my fair face, he says;—and, oh, my lady, he has a handsome face of his own.—Oh, never let it be said that Dora Vernon sundered true lovers!—but I see consent written in your own lovely face—so I will run—and, oh, my lady, take care of your own sweet handsome self, when your faithful Nan's away.' And the maiden retired with her lover.

' "It was half an hour after midnight, when one of the keepers of the chase, as he lay beneath a holly bush listening, with a prolonged groan, to the audible voice of revelry in the hall, from which his duty had lately excluded him, happened to observe two forms approaching: one of low stature, a light step, and muffled in a common mantle;—the other with the air, and in the dress, of a forester—a sword at his side, and pistols in his belt. The ale and the wine had invaded the keeper's brain, and impaired his sight; yet he roused himself up with a hiccup and a 'hilloah,' and 'where go ye, my masters?'—The lesser form whispered to the other—who immediately said, 'Jasper Jugg, is this you? Heaven be praised I have found you so soon;—here's that north country pedlar, with his beads and blue ribbon—he has come and whistled out pretty Nan Malkin, the lady's favourite, and the lord's trusty maid.—I left them under the terrace, and came to tell you.'

' "The enraged keeper scarce heard this account of the faithlessness of his love to an end,—he started off with the swiftness of one of the deer which he watched, making the boughs crash, as he forced his way through bush and glade direct for the hall, vowing desertion to the girl, and destruction to the pedlar. 'Let us hasten our steps, my love,' said the lesser figure, in a sweet voice; and, unmantling as she spoke, turned back to the towers of Haddon the fairest face that ever left them—the face of Dora Vernon herself. 'My men and my horses are nigh, my love,' said the taller figure; and taking a silver call from his pocket, he imitated the sharp shrill cry of the plover; then turning round, he stood and gazed towards Haddon, scarcely darkened by the setting of the moon, for the festal lights flashed from turret and casement, and the sound of mirth and revelry rang with augmenting din. 'Ah, fair and stately Haddon,' said Lord John Manners, 'little dost thou know thou hast lost thy jewel from thy brow—else thy lights would be dimmed, thy mirth would turn to wailing, and swords would be flashing from thy portals in all the haste of hot pursuit. Farewell, for a while, fair tower, farewell for a while.—I shall return, and bless the time I harped among thy menials and sang of my love—and charmed her out of thy little chamber window.' Several armed men now came suddenly down from the hill of Haddon, horses richly caparisoned were brought from among the trees of the chase, and the ancestors of the present family of Rutland sought shelter, for a time, in a distant land, from the wrath of the King of the Peak." '

THE MOTHER'S DREAM

She slept—and there was vision'd to her eye[63]
A stately mountain, green it seem'd, and high;
She sought to climb it—lo! a river dark
Roll'd at its foot; there came a gallant bark,
And in the bark were forms the eldest fiend
Had shaped to mock God's image; fierce they lean'd
O'er the ship's side, and, seizing her, rush'd through
The river wave, which kindled as they flew.
Then to the bank came one and laugh'd aloud;
Bright robes he wore, stern was his look and proud,
He stretch'd his arm, and hail'd her for his bride;
The shuddering waters wash'd his robe aside,
And show'd a shape the fiend's tormenting flame
Had sorely vex'd; she shriek'd, and faintness came.
Then shouts she heard, and sound of gladsome song,
And saw a stream of torches flash along.
The feast was spread, the bridal couch prepared,
Dread forms stood round, with naked swords to guard;
Nor look'd she long; one whisper'd in her ear,
Come, climb thy bed; for lo! the bridegroom's near.
She cried to heaven—at once the wedding joy
Was changed to war shout and to funeral cry;
Swords in the air, as sunshine, flash'd and fell,
Then rose all crimson'd; loud came groan and yell,
And from the middle tumult started out
A form that seiz'd her—blow, and shriek, and shout
Came thick behind: down to the Solway flood
Fast was she borne, it seem'd a sea of blood;
She felt it touch her knees, and with a scream
She started back, and waken'd from her dream.

Legend of Lady Beatrice

Were the Mother's Dream a traditionary fiction, and its predictions unfulfilled, gladness would be diffused around many
hearths, and the tears wiped away from many matrons'
cheeks. It was related to me by a Dumfriesshire lady: her
voice was slow and gentle, and possessed that devotional

Scottish melody of expression which gives so much antique richness and grace to speech. Under the shade of a long veil she sought to conceal a face, where early grief had bleached the roses, and impressed a sedate and settled sorrow on a brow particularly white and high. But her eye still retained something of the light of early life, which darkened or brightened as the joys, the sufferings, or the sorrows of wedded and maternal love gave a deeper interest or passion to her story.

'When woman is young,' said she, with a sigh, but not of regret, 'she loves to walk in the crowded streets, and near the dwellings of men; when she becomes wiser, has seen the vanities, and drunk of the miseries and woes of life, she chooses her walks in more lonely places, and, seeking converse with her spirit, shuns the joy and the mirth of the world. When sorrow, which misses few, had found me out, and made me a mateless bird, I once walked out to the margin of that beautiful sheet of water, the Ladye's Lowe. It was the heart of summer; the hills in which the lake lay embosomed were bright and green; sheep were scattered upon their sides; shepherds sat on their summits; while the grassy sward, descending to the quiet pure water, gave it so much of its own vernal hue, that the eye could not always distinguish where the land and lake met. Its long green water flags, and broad lilies, which lay so flat and so light along the surface, were unmoved, save by the course of a pair of wild swans, which for many years had grazed on the grassy margin, or found food in the bottom of the lake.

'This pastoral quietness pertained more to modern than to ancient times. When the summer heat was high, and the waters of the lake low, the remains of a broken but narrow causeway, composed of square stones, indented in a framework of massy oak, might still be traced, starting from a little bay on the northern side, and diving directly towards the centre of the lake. Tradition, in pursuing the history of this causeway, supplied the lake with an island, the island with a tower, and the tower with narratives of perils, and bloodshed, and chivalry, and love. These fire-side traditions, varying according to the fancy of the peasantry, all concluded in a story too wild for ordinary belief. A battle is invariably described by some grey-headed narrator, fought on the southern side of the lake, and sufficiently perilous and bloody. A lady's voice is heard, and a lady's form is seen, among the armed men, in the middle of the fight. She is described as borne off towards the causeway by the lord of the tower, while the margin of the water is strewed with dead or dying men. She sees her father, her brother, fall in her defence; her lover, to whom she had been betrothed, and from whom she had been torn, die by her side; and the deep and lasting curse which she denounced against her ravisher, and the tower, and the lake which gave him shelter, is not forgotten, but it is too awful to mingle with the stories of a grave and a devout people. That night, it is said, a voice was heard as of a spirit running round and round the lake, and pronouncing a curse against it; the waters became agitated, and a shriek was heard at midnight. In the morning, the castle of the Ladye's Lowe was sunk, and the waters of the lake slept seven fathoms deep over the cope-stone.

'They who attach credence to this wild legend are willing to support it by much curious testimony. They tell that, when the waters are pure in summer time, or when the winter's ice lies clear beneath the foot of the curler, the walls of the tower are distinctly seen without a stone displaced; while those who connect tales of wonder with every remarkable place, say, that once a year the castle arises at midnight from the bosom of the lake, with lights, not like the lights of this world, streaming from loophole and turret, while on the summit, like a banner spread, stands a lady clad in white, holding her hands to heaven, and shrieking. This vision is said to precede, by a night or two, the annual destruction of some person by the waters of the lake. The influence of this superstition has made the Ladye's Lowe a solitary and a desolate place, has preserved its fish, which are both delicious and numerous, from the fisher's net and hook, and its wild swans from the gun of the fowler. The peasantry seldom seek the solitude of its beautiful banks, and avoid bathing in its waters; and when the winter gives its bosom to the curler or the skater, old men look grave and say, "The Ladye's Lowe will have its yearly victim;" and its yearly victim, tradition tells us, it has ever had since the sinking of the tower.

'I had reached the margin of the lake, and sat looking on its wide pure expanse of water. Here and there the remains of an old tree, or a stunted hawthorn, broke and beautified the winding line of its border; while cattle, coming to drink and gaze at their shadows, took away from the solitude of the

place. As my eye pursued the sinuous line of the lake, it was
arrested by the appearance of a form, which seemed that of a
human being, stretched motionless on the margin. I rose,
and on going nearer, I saw it was a man; the face cast upon
the earth, and the hands spread. I thought death had been
there; and while I was waving my hand for a shepherd, who
sat on the hill-side, to approach and assist me, I heard a
groan, and a low and melancholy cry; and presently he
started up, and, seating himself on an old tree-root, rested a
cheek on the palm of either hand, and gazed intently on the
lake. He was a young man; the remains of health and beauty
were still about him; but his locks, once curling and long,
which maidens loved to look at, were now matted, and wild,
and withered; his cheeks were hollow and pale, and his eyes,
once the merriest and brightest in the district, shone now with
a grey, wild, and unearthly light. As I looked upon this
melancholy wreck of youth and strength, the unhappy being
put both hands in the lake, and lifting up water in his palms,
scattered it in the air; then dipping both hands again,
showered the water about his locks like rain. He continued,
during this singular employment, to chant some strange and
broken words with a wild tone and a faltering tongue.

SONG OF BENJIE SPEDLANDS[64]

1.

Cursed be thou, O water, for my sake;
    Misery to them who dip their hands in thee!
May the wild fowl forsake thy margin,
    The fish leap no more in thy waves;
May the whirlwind scatter thee utterly,
    And the lightning scorch thee up;
May the lily bloom no more on thy bosom,
    And the white swan fly from thy floods!

2.

Cursed be thou, O water, for my sake;
    The babe unborn shall never bless thee;
May the flocks that taste of thee perish;
    May the man who bathes in thy flood
Be cross'd and cursed with unrequited love,

And go childless down to the grave,
As I curse thee with my delirious tongue.
    I will mar thee with my unhappy hands!

3.

As this water, cast on the passing wind,
    Shall return to thy bosom no more,
So shall the light of morning forsake thee,
    And night-darkness devour thee up.
As that pebble descends into thy deeps,
    And that feather floats on thy waves,
So shall the good and the holy curse thee,
    And the madman mar thee with dust.

4.

Cursed may'st thou continue, for my sake,
    For the sake of those thou hast slain;
For the father who mourn'd for his son,
    For the mother who wail'd for her child.
I heard the voice of sorrow on thy banks,
    And a mother mourning by thy waters;
I saw her stretch her white hands over thee,
    And weep for her fair-hair'd son!

'The sound of the song rolled low and melancholy over the surface of the lake. I never heard a sound so dismal. During the third verse, the singer took up water in the hollow of his hand, and threw it on the wind. Then he threw a pebble and a feather into the lake; and, gathering up the dust among the margin stones, strewed it over the surface of the water. When he concluded his wild verses, he uttered a loud cry, and throwing himself suddenly on his face, spread out his hands, and lay, and quivered, and moaned like one in mortal agony.

'A young woman, in widow's weeds, and with a face still deeper in woe than her mourning dress, now came towards me, along the border of the lake. She had the face and the form of one whom I knew in my youth, the companion of my teens, and the life and love of all who had hearts worth a woman's wish. She was the grace of the preaching, the joy of the dance, through her native valley, and had the kindest and the gayest heart in the wide holms of Annandale. I rode at her wedding, and a gay woman was I; I danced at her wedding as if sorrow was never to come; and when I went to the kirking, and saw her so fair, and her husband so handsome, I said, in the simplicity of my heart, they will live long and happy on the earth. When I saw him again, he was stretched in his shroud, and she was weeping with an infant son on her knee, beside the coffin of her husband. Such remembrances can never pass away from the heart, and they came thick upon me as the companion of my early years approached. We had been long separated. I had resided in a distant part, till the loss of all I loved brought me back to seek for happiness in my native place, in the dwellings of departed friends, and the haunts of early joys.

'Something of a smile passed over her face when she saw me, but it darkened suddenly down; we said little for awhile; the histories of our own sorrows were written on our faces; there was no need for speech. "Alas! alas!" said she, "a kind husband, and three sweet bairns, all gone to the green churchyard! but ye were blest in the departure of your children compared to me. A mother's eye wept over them, a mother's knees nursed them, and a mother's hand did all that a mother's hand could do, till the breath went to heaven from between their sweet lips: O, woman, woman, ye were blest compared with me!" And she sobbed aloud, and looked upon the lake, which lay clear and unruffled before us. At the sound of her voice the young man raised himself from the ground, gave one wild look at my companion, and uttering a cry, and covering his face with his hands, dropt flat on the earth, and lay mute and without motion.

' "See him, see him," said she to me; "his name is Benjie Spedlands, he was once the sweetest youth in the parish, but now the hand of Heaven is heavy upon him and sore; he is enduring punishment for a season and a time; and heavy as was his trespass, so heavy has been his chastening." I entreated her to tell me how he had offended, and also how it happened that her appearance gave him such pain, and made him cry and cover his face. "It is a strange and a mournful story," she answered, "but it eases my spirit to relate it. O woman, I was once a merry and a happy creature, with a face as gladsome as the light of day; but for these eight long years I have had nought but cheerless days and joyless nights; sad thoughts and terrible dreams. Sorrow came in a dream to me, but it will not pass from me till I go to the grave.

' "It happened during the summer time, after I had lost
my husband, that I was very down-spirited and lonesome,
and my chief and only consolation was to watch over my
fatherless son. He was a sweet child; and on the day he was
two years old, when I ought to have been glad, and praised
HIM who had protected the widow and the orphan, I became
more than usually melancholy, for evil forebodings kept down
my spirits sorely, and caused me to wet the cheeks of my child
with tears. You have been a mother, and may have known
the tenderness and love which an infant will show her when
she is distressed. He hung his little arms round my neck, hid
his head in my bosom, and raised up such a murmur and a
song of sorrow and sympathy, that I blessed him and smiled,
and the bairn smiled, and so we fell asleep. It was about midnight that I dreamed a dream.

' "I dreamed myself seated at my own threshold, dandling
my boy in the sun: sleep gives us many joys which are taken
from us when we wake, and shadows out to us many woes
which are interrupted by sorrow. I thought my husband was
beside me; but, though he smiled, his look was more grave
than in life, and there seemed a light about him, a purer light
than that of day. I thought I saw the sun setting on the green
hills before me. I heard the song of the maidens as they
returned from the folds; saw the rooks flying in a long black
and wavering train towards their customary pines; and beheld
first one large star, and then another, arising in the firmament. And I looked again, and saw a little black cloud hanging between heaven and earth; it became larger and darker
till it filled all the air, from the sky down to the bosom of the
Ladye's Lowe. I wondered what this might mean, when presently the cloud began to move and roll along the earth, coming nearer and nearer, and it covered all the green fields,
and shut out the light of heaven. And as it came closer, I
thought I beheld shapes of men, and heard voices more shrill
than human tongue. And the cloud stood still at the distance
of a stone-cast. I grew sore afraid, and clasped my child to my
bosom, and sought to fly, but I could not move; the form of
my husband had fled, and there was no one to comfort me.
And I looked again, and, lo! the cloud seemed cleft asunder,
and I saw a black chariot, drawn by six black steeds, issue
from the cloud. And I saw a shadow seated for a driver, and
heard a voice say, 'I am the bearer of woes to the sons and

daughters of men; carry these SORROWS abroad, they are in number eight.' And all the steeds started forward; and when the chariot came to my threshold, the phantom tarried and said, 'A woe and a woe for the son of the widow Rachel.' And I arose and beheld in a chariot the coffins of seven children; and their names, and their years, were written thereon. And there lay another coffin; and, as I bent over it, I read the name of my son, and his years were numbered six; a tear fell from my cheek, and the letters vanished. And I heard the shadow say, 'Woman, what hast thou done? Can thy tears contend with me?' and I saw a hand pass, as a hand when it writes, over the coffin again. And I looked, and I saw the name of my son, and his years were numbered nine. And a faintness came into my heart, and a dimness into mine eye, and I sought to wash the words out with my tears, when the shadow said, 'Woman, woman, take forth thy woe and go thy ways, I have houses seven to visit, and may not tarry for thy tears; three years have I given for thy weeping, and I may give no more.'

' "I have often wondered at my own strength, though it was all in a dream; 'Vision,' I said, 'if thy commission is from the evil one, lash thy fiend-steeds and begone.' The shadow darkened as I spoke: 'Vision,' I said, 'if thy mission is from Him who sits on the holy hill,—"the Lord giveth and taketh away, blessed be his name;" do thy message and depart.' And suddenly the coffin was laid at my door, the steeds and chariot fled, the thick clouds followed, and I beheld him no more. I gazed upon the name, and the years nine; and as I looked it vanished from my sight; and I awoke weeping, and found my locks drenched in sweat, and the band of my bosom burst asunder with the leaping of my heart.

' "And I told my dream, and all the people of the parish wondered; and those who had children waxed sorrowful, and were dismayed. And a woman who dwells by the Rowantree-burn came unto me, and said, 'I hear that you have dreamed an evil dream; know ye how ye may eschew it?' And I answered, 'I have dreamed an evil dream, and I know not how I may eschew it, save by prayers and humiliation.' And the woman said to me, 'Marvel not at what I may say: I am old, and the wisdom of ancient times is with me; such wisdom as foolish men formerly accounted evil—listen to my words. Take the under garment of thy child, and dip it at midnight in that water called the Ladye's Lowe, and hang it forth to dry in the new moon-beam. Take thy Bible on thy knees, and keep watch beside it; mickle is the courage of a woman when the child that milked her bosom is in danger. And a form, like unto the form of a lady, will arise from the lake, and will seek to turn the garment of thy son; see that ye quail not, but arise and say, "Spirit, by all the salvation contained between the boards of this book, I order thee to depart and touch not the garment." '

' "And while this woman spake, there came another woman, the wife of one who had sailed to a distant land, and had left her with two sweet children, and the name of the one was Samuel, and the name of the other John. Now John was a fair and comely child, the image of her husband, but he was not his mother's joy, for she loved Samuel, who bore the image of one she had loved in her youth; and this made her husband sorrowful, and caused him to sail to a far country. And when she came in, she said: 'So ye have dreamed a bad dream, and ye have sought this ill woman of the Rowantree-burn to give the interpretation thereof; if evil is threatened, evil is the way you seek to avert it. Now listen unto me; "the wind bloweth as it listeth;"[65] the ways of God will not be changed by the wisdom of man; providence may seek thy child for a saint; see that ye cast him not to the fiends by dealing with unholy charms and spells, and with graceless hags. I have two fair children; one of them is his father's love, the other is mine; say, saw ye not the name of John written on one of those visionary coffins? for I hope my Samuel will long be the grace of the green earth before he goes to the dowie mools.' And the eyes of the woman of the Rowantree-burn flashed with anger, and she said, 'Hearken to the words of this shameless woman; she seeks the destruction of the child of wedlock, and wishes life to the child of wantonness and sin. Lo! I say, hearken unto her. But the evil of her ways shall be to her as sadness, and what has given her joy shall be to the world a hissing and a scorn; to her a scourge, and a curse. She will lose the sweet youth John, even as she wishes, but long and full of evil shall be the life of the child she loves.' And upon this, these two foolish women reproached each other with works of sin and with deeds of darkness; and waxing wroth with their words, they tore each other's raiment and hair, and smote and bruised one another, and the clamour of their tongues increased exceedingly.

' "Now, in the midst of all this folly, there came to my fire-
side a man cunning in the culture of corn, and versed in the
cure of those evils which afflict dumb creatures. And when he
saw the strife between the woman of the Rowantree-burn
and the mariner's wife, he laughed aloud in the fulness of his
joy. 'Strong may the strife be, and long may it continue,' said
he, 'for pleasant is the feud between the raven and the
hooded-crow, and the small birds sing when the hawks of
heaven fight. That woman has destroyed the firstlings of the
flock, has dried up the udders to the sucking lambs, and
lessened the riches of men who live by sweet cheese and
fattened herds. She hath also cast her spells over the deep
waters of Annan and Ae; the fish have fled, and the nets of the
fishermen are dipped in vain. The fowls of heaven too have
felt the cunning of her hand; the wild swans have left the
Ladye's Lowe, the wild geese have fled from the royal lakes of
Lochmaben; and the black-cock and the ptarmigan come no
more to the snare of the fowler. Let her therefore scream and
weep under the strong hand and sharp nails of her bitter
enemy. And for the other woman, even she whose husband
lives on the deep waters, and to whom she bears children in
the image of other men, let her, I say, suffer from the fingers
of witchcraft: pleasant is the strife between workers of wickedness; and woe to the wit, and sorrow to the hand, that seeks
to sunder them. Now, touching this singular dream of thine, I
have a word to say, and it is this: believe it not, it is the work
of the grand architect of human misery, who seeks to draw
people to sin in the dreams and shadows of the night. To men
whose hearts are warm, and whose blood is young, he descends in soft and voluptuous visions. I have myself beheld a
maiden with a languishing look and an eye blue and ensnaring, standing at my bed-side, clothed out in a midnight dream
with the shadowy beauty of a sleeping imagination; and this
appeared too on that very night when my inward gifts and
graces had raised me from a humble sower of seed-corn to
become an elder of our godly kirk; praise be blest, and may
the deed be lauded of men. But it is not alone to the staid and
the devout that the enemy appears in dreams; he presents
the soldier with imaginary fields of peril and blood, and
blesses his ear with the yell and the outcry of battle, and the
trumpet sound. To the maiden he comes in gallant shapes and
costly raiment, with becks and bows, and feet which pace

gracefully over the floor to the sound of the flute and dulcimer, and all manner of music. To the sleeping eye of a
mother he digs a deep pit for the babe of her bosom, and lays
the child that sucks her breast by the side of a fathomless
stream. He shows her shrouds, and empty coffins; figures
stretched in white linen, and kirk-yard processions, and raises
in her ear the wail of the matrons and the lyke-wake song.
Heed not dreams therefore; they are the delusions of him who
seeks to sink our souls. But bless thy God, and cherish thy
child; keep his feet from the evil path, and his hand from the
evil thing, and his tongue from uttering foolishness; and the
boy shalt become a stripling, and the stripling a man, wise in
all his ways, and renowned in his generation, and thou shalt
rejoice with abundance of joy.'

' "While this devout person cheered my heart with his
counsel, he was not unheard of those two foolish women; they
liked not the wisdom of his words, nor his sayings concerning
themselves, and they began with a fierce and sudden outcry.
'A pretty elder indeed,' said the woman of the Rowantree-
burn, 'to come here in the shades and darkness of night to
expound dreams to a rosie young widow. I'll warrant he
would not care if the man-child were at the bottom of the
Ladye's Lowe, so long as a full farm, a well plenished house,
and a loving dame in lily-white linen were to the fore. I wish
I were a real witch for his sake, he should dree a kittle cast.'
The words of the mariner's wife chimed in with those of her
antagonist. 'A pretty elder, truly,' said she, smiting her hands
together close to his nose, 'he'll come here to talk of sinful
dreams, and flutes and dulcimers, and shaking of wanton legs,
and the smiling of ensnaring eyes. And yet should the bairn
of a poor body have a fairer look than ane's ain husband, he
will threaten us with kirk censure and session rebuke, though
it's weel kenned that mothers cannot command the com-
plexion of their babes, nor controul the time when it pleases
Providence to send them weeping into the world. There was
my ain son Samuel; his father had sailed but ten months and
a day when the sweet wean came; where was the marvel of
that? If there was not an indulgence, and acts of wondrous
bounty and kindness, and blessings in the shape of babes
showered upon mariners, sorrowful would their lives be,
dwelling so far from their wives in the deep wide waters.'

' " 'Woman, woman,' said the elder, 'I came not hither to

hearken to thy confession; go home and repent, and leave me
to admonish the owner of this house, touching the dream with
which her spirit is sorely troubled.' 'Admonish!' said the
mariner's spouse, 'I dare ye, sir, to use that word of scorn and
kirk scandal to the widow of as douce a man as ever stepped
in a black-leather shoe—admonish, indeed! If ye are so full of
the gracious spirit of counsel and admonition, wherefore have
ye not come to cheer me in my lonesome home, where all I
have is two bairns to keep sadness from my fireside? My husband is sailing on the great deep, and has not blest my sight
these three long years; mickle need have I of some one to
soothe my widow-like lot; I could find ye something like scripture warrant for such kindness which ye wot not of.' And the
woman went her ways; the man tarried but a little while; and
the woman of the Rowantree-burn departed also, admonishing me to remember her words, and do as she had desired.

' "It was on the third evening after I dreamed my dream,
that I thought on the woman's words; and I debated with
myself, if such seekings after future events by means of charms
and spells were wise, and according to the word. But old
beliefs, and legendary stories, and the assurances of many wise
and venerable people, have ever proved too hard for the cunning of wisdom and the pure light of the gospel; and I thought
on my grandmother, to whom the person of my grandfather,
then in a remote land, was shown in a vision one hallowmass-
eve, and so I went my ways. It was near midnight when I
reached the Ladye's Lowe, and, seating myself on the place
where I now sit, I looked sadly to the heaven, and sorrowfully
to the waters. The moon had arisen with her horns half filled;
the stars had gathered around her; the sheep lay white and
clustering on the hill sides; the wild swans sailed in pairs along
the quiet bosom of the lake; and the only sound I heard was
that of the mother-duck, as she led her swarm of yellow young
ones to graze on the tender herbage on the margin of the lake.
I had wetted, as the woman bade me, the under garment of
my child, and hung it forth to dry on a little bush of broom,
and there I sat watching it and ruminating on my lot, on the
sorrows and joys of a mother. Midnight came; the lake lay still
and beautiful; the wind was heard by fits among the bushes,
and gushed gently over the bosom of the water with a sweet
and a lulling sound. I looked and thought, and I thought and
looked, till mine eyes waxed weary with watching, and I

closed them for a time against the dazzling undulation of the
water, which swelled and subsided beneath the clear moonlight. As I sat, something came before me as a vision in a
dream, and I know not yet whether I slumbered or waked.
Summer I thought was changed into winter, the reeds were
frozen by the brook, snow lay white and dazzling on the
ground, and a sheet of thick and transparent ice was spread
over the bosom of the Ladye's Lowe. And, as I looked, the
lake became crowded with men; I beheld the faces of many
whom I knew, and heard the curling-stones rattle and ring, as
they glided along the ice or smote upon one another; and the
din and clamour of men flew far and wide. And my son
appeared unto me, a child no more, but a stripling tall and
fair and graceful, his fair hair curling on his shoulders—my
heart leapt with joy. And seven young men were with him; I
knew them all, his school companions; and their seven
mothers came, I thought, and stood by my side, and as we
looked we talked of our children. As they glided along the ice,
they held by each other's hands and sang a song; above them
all, I heard the voice of my son, and my heart rejoiced. As
the song concluded, I heard a shriek as of many drowning,
but I saw nothing, for the ice was fled from the bosom of the
lake, and all that was visible was the wild swans with the
lesser water fowl. But all at once, I saw my son come from the
bottom of the lake; his locks were disordered and drenched;
and deadly paleness was in his looks. One bore him out of the
water in his arms, and laid him at my feet on the bank. I
swooned away; and when I came to myself, I found the morning light approaching, the lake fowl sheltering themselves
among the reeds; and, stiff with cold, and with a heavy heart,
I returned home.

' "Years passed on, my son grew fair and comely, out-rivalled
his comrades at school, and became the joy of the young,
and the delight of the old. I often thought of my dream as I
gazed on the child; and I said, in the fulness of a mother's
pride, surely it was a vain and an idle vision, coloured into
sadness by my fears; for a creature so full of life, and strength,
and spirit, cannot pass away from the earth before his prime.
Still at other times the vision pressed on my heart, and I had
sore combats with a misgiving mind; but I confided in Him
above, and cheered my spirit as well as I might. I went with
my son to the kirk, I accompanied him to the market, I walked

with him on the green hills, and on the banks of the deep
rivers; I was with him in the dance, and my heart rejoiced to
see him surpass the children of others: wherever he went, a
mother's fears, and a mother's feet, followed him. Some
derided my imaginings, and called me the dreaming widow;
while others spoke with joy of his beauty and attainments,
and said he was a happy son who had so tender and so
prudent a mother.

' "It happened in the seventh year from my dream, that a
great curling bonspiel was to be played between the youths
and the wedded men of the parish; and a controversy arose
concerning the lake on which the game should be decided. It
was the middle of December; the winter had been open and
green; till suddenly the storm set in, and the lakes were frozen
equal to bear the weight of a heavy man in the first night's
frost. Several sheets of frozen water were mentioned: ancient
tale, and ancient belief, had given a charm to the Ladye's
Lowe which few people were willing to break; and the older
and graver portion of the peasantry looked on it as a place of
evil omen, where many might meet, but few would part. All
this was withstood by a vain and froward youth, who despised
ancient beliefs as idle superstitions—traditionary legends as
the labour of credulous men; and who, in the pride and vanity
of human knowledge, made it his boast that he believed nothing. He proposed to play the bonspiel on the Ladye's
Lowe—the foolish young men his companions supported his
wish; and not a few among the sedater sort consented to dismiss proverbial fears, and to play their game on these ominous
waters. I thought it was a sad sight to see so many grey heads
pass my threshold, and so many young heads following, to
sport on so perilous a place; but curiosity could not be
restrained—young and old, the dame and the damsel,
crowded the banks of the lake to behold the contest; and I
heard the mirth of their tongues and the sound of their
curling-stones, as I sat at my hearth fire. One of the foremost was Benjie Spedlands.'

'The unhappy mother had proceeded thus far, when the
demented youth, who till now had lain silent and motionless
by the side of the lake, uttered a groan, and starting suddenly
to his feet, came and stood beside us. He shed back his long
and moistened locks from a burning and bewildered brow,
and looking stedfastly in her face, for a moment, said, "Rachel,

dost thou know me?" She answered only with a flood of tears, and a wave of her hand to be gone. "Know me! ay, how can ye but know me—since for me that deadly water opened its lips, and swallowed thy darling up. If ye have a tongue to curse, and a heart to scorn me—scorn me then, and curse me; and let me be seen no more on this blessed earth. For the light of day is misery to me, and the cloud of night is full of sorrow and trouble. My reason departs, and I go and sojourn with the beasts of the field—it returns, and I fly from the face of man; but wherever I go, I hear the death-shriek of eight sweet youths in my ear, and the curses of mothers' lips on my name." "Young man," she said, "I shall not curse thee, though thy folly has made me childless; nor shall I scorn thee, for I may not scorn the image of Him above; but go from my presence, and herd with the brutes that perish, or stay among men, and seek to soothe thy smitten conscience by holy converse, and by sincere repentance." "Repentance!" he said, with a wildness of eye that made me start—"of what have I to repent? Did I make that deep lake, and cast thy son, and the sons of seven others, bound into its bosom. Repentance belongs to him who does a deed of evil—sorrow is his who witlessly brings misfortunes on others; and such mishap was mine. Hearken, and ye shall judge."

'And he sat down by the side of the lake; and taking up eight smooth stones in his hand, dropped them one by one into the water; then turning round to us, he said: "Even as the waters have closed over those eight pebbles, so did I see them close over eight sweet children. The ice crashed, and the children yelled; and as they sunk, one of them, even thy son, put forth his hand, and seizing me by the foot, said: 'Oh! Benjie, save me—save me;' but the love of life was too strong in me, for I saw the deep, the fathomless water; and, far below, I beheld the walls of the old tower, and I thought on those doomed yearly to perish in this haunted lake, and I sought to free my foot from the hand of the innocent youth. But he held me fast, and looking in my face, said, 'Oh! Benjie, save me, save me!' And I thought how I had wiled him away from his mother's threshold, and carried him and his seven companions to the middle of the lake, with the promise of showing him the haunted towers and courts of the drowned castle; but the fears for my own life were too strong; so putting down my hand, I freed my foot, and, escaping over the ice, left him

to sink with his seven companions. Brief, brief was his
struggle—a crash of the faithless ice—a plunge in the fathomless water, and a sharp shrill shriek of youthful agony, and
all was over for him—but for me—broken slumbers, and a
burning brain, and a vision that will not pass from me, of
eight fair creatures drowning."

'Ere he had concluded, the unhappy mother had leaped to
her feet, and stretched forth her hands over him, and, with
every feature dilated with agony, gathered up her strength to
curse and to confound him. "Oh! wretched and contemptible
creature," she said, "were I a man as I am but a feeble
woman, I would tread thee as dust aneath my feet, for thou
art unworthy to live. God gave thee his own form, and gave
thee hands to save, not to destroy his fairest handy works; but
what heart, save thine, could have resisted a cry for mercy
from one so fair and so innocent? Depart from my presence—
crawl—for thou art unworthy to walk like man—crawl as
the reptiles do, and let the hills cover thee, or the deeps
devour thee; for who can wish thy base existence prolonged?
The mother is unblest that bare thee, and hapless is he who
owns thy name. Hereafter shall men scorn to count kindred
with thee. Thou hast no brother to feel for a brother's shame,
no sister to feel for thee a sister's sorrow—no kinsman to
mourn for the reproach of kindred blood. Cursed be she who
would bear for thee the sacred name of wife. Seven sons would
I behold—and I saw one,—wae's me!—dragged from the
bottom of that fatal lake; see them borne over my threshold
with their long hanks of fair hair wetting the pavement, as the
lovely locks of my sweet boy did; and stretch their lily limbs
in linen which my own hands had spun for their bridal
sheets, even as I stretched my own blessed child,—rather
than be the mother of such a wretch as thou!" From this fearful malediction, the delirious youth sought not to escape; he
threw himself with his face to the earth, spread out his hands
on the turf, and renewed his sobbings and his moans, while
the sorrowful mother returned to a cheerless home and an
empty fireside.

'Such was her fearful dream; and such was its slow, but sure
and unhappy fulfilment. She did not long survive the desolation of her house. Her footsteps were too frequent by the lake,
and by the grave of her husband and child, for the peace of
her spirit; she faded, and sank away; and now the churchyard

grass grows green and long above her. Old people stop by
her grave, and relate with a low voice, and many a sigh, her
sad and remarkable story. But grass will never grow over the
body of Benjie Spedlands. He was shunned by the old, and
loathed by the young; and the selfish cruelty of his nature met
with the singular punishment of a mental alienation, dead to
all other feeling save that of agony for the death of the eight
children. He wandered into all lonesome places, and sought to
escape from the company of all living things. His favourite
seat was on a little hill top, which overlooks the head of the
Ladye's Lowe. There he sat watching the water, with an
intensity of gaze which nothing could interrupt. Sometimes he
was observed to descend with the swiftness of a bird in its
flight, and dash into the lake, and snatch and struggle in the
water like one saving a creature from drowning. One winter
evening, a twelvemonth from the day of the fatal catastrophe
on the lake, he was seen to run round its bank like one in
agony, stretching out his hands, and shouting to something he
imagined he saw in the water. The night grew dark and
stormy—the sleet fell, and thick hail came, and the winds augmented. Still his voice was heard at times far shriller than
the tempest—old men shuddered at the sound—about midnight it ceased, and was never heard more. His hat was found
floating by the side of the water, but he was never more seen
nor heard of—his death-lights,[66] glimmering for a season on
the lake, told to many that he had found, perhaps sought, a
grave in the deepest part of the Ladye's Lowe.'

ALLAN-A-MAUT

1.

Good Allan-a-Maut lay on the rigg,[67]
One call'd him bear, one call'd him bigg;
An old dame slipp'd on her glasses: 'Aha!
He'll waken,' quoth she, 'with joy to us a'.'
The sun shone out, down dropp'd the rain,
He laugh'd as he came to life again;
And carles and carlins sung who saw't,
Good luck to your rising Allan-a-Maut.

2.

Good Allan-a-Maut grew green and rank,
With a golden beard and a shapely shank,
And rose sae steeve, and wax'd sae stark.
He whomelt the maid, and coupit the clark;
The sick and lame leap'd hale and weel,
The faint of heart grew firm as steel,
The douce nae mair call'd mirth a faut,
Such charms are mine, quoth Allan-a-Maut.

The person who chanted this famous border bousing-rhyme was a tall young man, whose shaggy great coat, brass-headed riding whip, and long sharp spurs projecting from behind his massy and iron-heeled boots, might denote him to be a dealer in horses, accoutred for Rosley-hill or Dumfries fairs. But his inner coat, lined with silk, and studded with silver buttons, a small gold chain round his neck, from which depended a heart of rock crystal, enclosing a tress of nut-brown hair, and half concealed among ruffles of the finest cambric, edged with rich lace, might belong to an opulent and fantastic youth fond of finery, proud of a handsome person, and vain of his influence among the border maidens.

His singular song, and remarkable dress, attracted instant attention. His character was thus hit off by a demure old dame in a whisper to me, during the applause which followed his song. 'He's a frank and a concerted youth, Sir; the owner of a fair estate, and well known among the merry maids of

Cumberland and Dumfriesshire at fairs and dancings, when
his patrimony is showered down among the gay and the
cherry-lipped, in the shape of snoods, and ribbons, and gloves.
Nor will ye hinder him to reign the chief of chaps in the
change-house, when the tale and the strong drink circulate
together: who like Lacie Dacre, I should be glad to know, for
chanting bousing-ballads, and telling merry adventures? He's
the wildest of all our border spirits, and his exploits with the
brandy-cup and the ale-flagon have obtained him the name of
Allan-a-Maut; a scrap of an old-world song, Sir, with which
young Spend-pelf ever commences and concludes his merriment. I have said my worst of the lad—I believe he's a kind-
hearted chield, and as true to his word as the cup is to his
lip. And now listen to his story, for I'll warrant it a queer
one.' And as she concluded, he commenced.

'That song,' said the youth, 'rude and uncouth though it
seems, pitches, as a musician would say, the natural tone or
key of the tale I have to tell; it was far from unwise in me to
sing it; and so with this explanation I will proceed. It happened some summers ago, as I was returning, during the grey
of the morning, from a love tryste in a green glen on the banks
of Annan water, I fell into a kind of reverie; and what should
the subject of it be, but the many attachments my heart had
formed among the maidens, and the very limited requital the
law allows one to make to so many sweet and gentle creatures.
My spirit was greatly perturbed, as ye may guess, with this
sorrowful subject; and a thick mist, which the coming sun
seemed unable to dispel, aided me in totally mistaking my
way; and I could not well mistake it further, for I found
myself in a region with which I had formed no previous
acquaintance: I had wandered into a brown and desolate
heath, the mist rolled away in heavy wreaths before me, and
followed close on my heels, with the diligence of an evil
spirit.

'All hill and woodland mark, our usual country guides,
were obscured, and I strayed on till I came to the banks of a
moorland brook, stained by the soil through which it passed,
till it flowed the colour of the brownest brandy. The tenants
of this desert stream partook of the congenial nature of the
region—they were not of that swift and silver-speckled sort
described by the pastoral verse-makers, but of a dull and dark
mottled kind, and so lean and haggard as to be wholly

unworthy of a fisher's bait. I caught one under the mossy bank, and returned it again to the stream as unfit for food. I saw no living thing in my course across this desert; the heron, that beautiful and solitary bird, rejected it for a haunt; and even the wild moorfowl, which in the fowler's proverb feeds on the heather top, sought neither food nor shelter amid the brown and dreary wilderness.

'I came at last to a thick and gloomy plantation of Scotch firs, which, varying the bleak desolation of the moor, gave me the assurance that some thirty years before, the hand of man had been busied in the region. A fence of loose stone, sur-mounted by a rude cope or cornice of rough sharp rock, pre-sented an effectual barrier to sheep and even deer. The latter animals will over-leap a high wall of firm masonry, but turn back from a very slender impediment which threatens insecure footing.

'The soil had in many places proved ungenial to Scotch firs, the hardiest of all forest trees; they grew in dwarfish and stunted clumps, and exceeded not the altitude of ordinary shrubs. In passing along the side of the fence, I came to a hollow, where the masses of high green bracken betokened a richer soil. Here the trees, striking deep into the mossy loam, towered up into a beautiful and extensive grove, relieved in their gloomy appearance by the wild cherry and mountain ash, at that time covered with bloom. Behind me, the moor spread out high and uneven, full of quagmires and pits, out of which the peasants of Annan-vale cut peats for fuel.

'I observed, winding through the field of bracken, a kind of trodden way, resembling a hare-road, which, passing over the fence, by the removal of the cope-stone, dived directly into the bosom of the wood. The path too seemed marked with men's feet; and with the hope of its leading me to some human abode I entered the plantation. The wood, fair and open at first, became thick and difficult; the road too grew sinuous and perplexing; and I was compelled to pull aside the thick masses of boughs, and, gliding gently into the aperture, make the best of my way by sleight and stratagem.

'I had proceeded in this way nearly half a mile, when I came to the foot of one of those vast rocks which tower up so abrupt and unexpectedly on many of the Scottish heaths. It seemed a pile of prodigious stones huddled rudely together in the careless haste of creation, rather than a regular rock. Deep chasms, and openings resembling caves, were visible in many places, shagged round the entrance with heath-berry; and where the plant that bears this delicious fruit failed to grow, the hardier ivy took root, and with little nourishment shot up into small round masses, called fairy-seats by the peasantry. At the foot of the precipice, some hundreds of high and shivered stones stood on end, like a Druidic grove, but in seven-fold confusion, and here and there a fir inserted in the cliffs of the rock struggled for life; while the ivy, shooting its stems to the summit of the crag, shook down a profusion of green tendrils, and crawled along the ground again, till the mossy soil, which bubbled up water at every step, arrested the march of the beautiful evergreen. Around the crag, a circle of spruce firs was planted; while high over the whole the rock rose savage and grey, and gave the eagles, which not infrequently visited its summit, a view over some of the fairest pasture lands in Annandale.

'The desolation of the place was heightened by the absence of living water—the voice of the brook, which lends the tongue of life to many a dreary place. A little puddle of brown moorish water supplied the place of a fountain; around its margin the bones of hares and fowls were strewn; while in a recess in the rock the fox had sought a lair, and heaped it high with wool and feathers. But the proverbial lord of craft and cunning had for some time forsaken this once favourite abode; the presence of man had intruded on his wild domain, and driven him to the neighbouring mountains.

'I climbed to the summit of the rock, and gazed down the vale of Annan as far as the sea of Solway, and westward as far as the green hills of Nithsdale. To enable me more pleasantly to enjoy the beauty of a scene which Turner, or Callcott, or Dewint,[68] would love to consecrate, I proceeded to discuss the merits of some ewe-milk cheese, made for me by the lily-white hand of Jessie Johnstone, of Snipeflosh; and the gift of the maiden began to vanish before the sharp-set perseverance of youth. The sun too, dispelling the fog, gleamed over the green heads of the groves in all his summer glory, and I proceeded to examine how I might find out the way to Ae water, to the dwelling of bonnie Bess Dinwoodie.

'While I sat gazing about me, I observed a thin and curling line of smoke ascending from the base of the crag; it rose up thicker and blacker, and, wafted by the wind, gushed against my face; I never felt a vapour so strange and offensive. As I proceeded to consider the various kinds of exhalations which arise from forest or fen, I saw a large and hungry dog come out of the wood. It uttered a cry of discovery, half howl and half bark, and coming near, seemed willing to leap at my throat. I threw it a piece of cheese; it caught and devoured it, and renewed its clamour. It was soon joined, to my utter dismay, by a human being. I never beheld a man with a look so startled and threatening. He was tall and strong-built, with hair long and matted, the colour of ashes, while his eyes, large, and staring, and raw, looked, as Lancie Lauborde the tailor said, "like scored collops bordered with red plush."

'He addressed me in a tone that in nowise redeemed his savage appearance. "Weel met, quoth the wolf to the fox; weel met, my crafty lad; so ye have found out the bonnie bee-byke at last, as the boy said when he thrust his hand into the adder's den. I maun ken more about ye, my lad; so tell me thy tale cleverly; else, I swear by the metal worm through which my precious drink dribbles,[69] I will feast the fox and her five cubs on thy spool-bane. On my conscience, lad, as ye brew, so shall ye drink; and that's o'er fair a law for a gauger." What this depraved being meant by his mysterious language, and what calling he followed, were alike matters of conjecture; his manner was certainly hostile and threatening. I told him I was passing towards the vale of Ae, and had lost my way in the mist. "Lost your way in the mist, and found the way ye were seeking for, my wylie lad, I'll warrant; but I shall come at the bare truth presently." So saying, he laid the flap of his shaggy coat aside, and, showing me a brace of pistols, and the hilt of a dirk stuck in a belt of rough leather, motioned me to follow him.

'Resistance was hopeless; we descended from the rock by a winding and secret way, concealed among the ivy, and the branches of a spreading spruce fir. This brought us to a rude structure, resembling a shepherd's shed, half cavern and half building, and nearly hidden under the involving branches of two luxuriant firs. My guide half pushed me into this un-promising abode; a miserable hovel, loathsome and foul, and filled with a thick and noisome vapour. I was greeted on my entrance by a squat, thick-set, and squalid being, who, start-ing up from a couch of straw, exclaimed, "Wha in the fiend's name's this ye have driven into our bit den of refuge in the

desert, as ane wad drive a ratton into a trap? Deil drown me
in a strong distillation, and that's an enviable death, if this
lad's no a stripling exciseman, whelped in our unhappy land
by the evil spirits of the government. If he's a gauger, take ye
the spade and dig, and I'll take the sword and strike; for he
shall never craw day again, else my name's nae mair Jock
Mackleg." And the wretch, as he spoke, proceeded to sharpen
an old sword on the strake of a scythe.

    ' "Hooly, man, hooly with thy bit of rusty airn," said his
companion, "ye're no sae handy with it when its warse
needed, Jock, ye ken. I shall allow the young lad to live, be he
devil, or be he gauger, and that's meikle waur, were it only
that he might partake of that glorious spirit which I call
'stupefy,' but which wiser Jock Mackleg christened 'heart's-
blood,' and learn of what a princely beverage he would
deprive this poor taxed and bleeding land." It happened well
for me that these two wretches, though born for each other's
society, like bosom bones, and necessary to each other in their
detestable pursuits as the bark is to the bush, chose to be of
different opinions respecting the mode of managing me, and
thus John Mackleg expressed his dissent from his more moderate as well as powerful associate. "And so he's to live and to
taste of the 'heart's-blood!' deil turn him into our distilling-
worm first, that the liquid consolation the gauger tribe seek to
deprive us of may run reeking through him. Ah, Mungo
Macubin, ye're soft, ye're soft; ye would give the supervisor
himself our hain'd drops of distillery dew; and for fear he
should drop into a ditch, ye would carry him hame. I'll tell ye
what—were ye Mungo Macubin seven times told, I will cease
to be longer conjunct and several with you; else may I be
whipt through the lang burgh of Lochmaben, with the halter
of a gauger's horse." And still growling out anger, which
he dared not more openly express, he threw himself down
on a litter bed, while his companion, with a look of scorn,
answered.—"Thou predestined blockhead, am I a blind stab-
ber behind backs in the dark, like thyself? Am I to harm the
white skin of this young raw haspen of a lad, unless I ken why
and wherefore? Spill his sweet life indeed! Faith, if this lad
threatened ye with six inches of cauld steel in his hand, though
water five fathoms deep and seven mile wide divided ye, ye
would be less free of your threats. So lie still there, and put
thy bonnet on thy bald scalp, from which whisky has scalded

the hair: Ay, that will do. Now sit down, my wandering man of the mist, let me have a look at thee; but first hold this cup of 'stupefy' to thy head. Faith, my birkie, if I thought ye kenn'd the might of whisky by mathematical measuring, or any other dangerous government mode of ascertaining spirituous strength, I'd make ye swallow yere gauging sticks. So sit down; else, by the spirit of malt and the heart of corn, I will make thee obedient."

'I sat down on an empty cask, and holding in my hand a cup full of the hot and untaken-down liquor, which my entertainers were busied in preparing, I could not but give a few hurried glances round this wretched lodge in the wilderness. The cabin itself seemed more the creation of distempered or intoxicated intellects, than the work of consideration and sobriety. At the entrance of a kind of cavern in the rock, a rude enclosure of stone was raised, the whole covered over with boughs and turf, with an opening in the side capable of admitting one person at a time. The floor was bedded with rushes and bracken, but trodden into mire, and moistened with a liquor of a flavour so detestable that I felt half suffocated; while the steam of a boiling caldron, mingling with the bitter smoke of green fir-wood, eddied round and round, and then gushed out into the morning air through the aperture by which I entered. In the cavern itself, I observed a fire glimmering, and something of the shape of a human being stretched motionless before it. This personage was clad in a garb of rough sheep-skin, the wool shorn, or rather singed close, and an old fur-cap slouched over his ears, while his feet, wholly bare, and nearly soot-black, were heated among the warm ashes which he raked from the caldron fire. He lay on his belly, supporting his head with his hands; and about all his person nothing was white but the white of his eye. Beside him stood what seemed an old tobacco-box; he dipped it frequently into a pail of liquor, and each time he carried it to his head, a strong smell of whisky was diffused over the place.

'On the right hand of this menial drudge, lay the person of John Mackleg: an old Sanquhar rug[70] interposed between him and the foul litter below; a small cask, the spigot of which was worn by frequent use, stood within reach; while a new-drained cup lay at his head, with a crust of bread beside it. On the other side sat Mungo Macubin, on a seat covered with a sheep-skin; and compared to his debased and brutish

companions he seemed a spirit of light. In spite of his disordered locks, and the habitual intoxication in which his eyes
swam, his look was inviting, and even commanding. Something of better days and brighter hopes appeared about him.
But in his eye frequently glimmered that transient and equivo-
cal light, suspicious and fierce, which, influenced by drink,
and inflamed by contradiction, rendered him an insecure
companion. A sword lay on a shelf beside him, with several
tattered books, a fish-spear, a fishing-rod, and a fowling-piece;
and a fiddle, tuned perhaps during the delirium of drink, hung
there with its disordered strings. I observed too the machinery
of a wooden clock, the labour, I afterwards learned, of his
knife; together with several spoons, and cups of sycamore,
which he wanted the patience rather than the skill to finish.
The notice which I took of this part of the establishment
seemed far from displeasing to the proprietor.

'Around the shealing stood kegs and vessels for containing
liquor, all of portable dimensions, such as a man might readily
carry; and I wanted not this to convince me that a whisky-still
of considerable magnitude was busy in the bosom of this
wilderness. In the middle of the floor stood a rude table, the
top of which had belonged to some neighbouring orchard,
and still threatened in large letters the penalties of traps and
guns to nightly depredators. It was swimming with liquor,
and strewn with broken cups; and in the midst of the whole
lay several of those popular publications which preach up the
equality of human intellect and estate, and recommend, along
with a general division of worldly goods, a more tolerant
system of intercourse between the sexes. No doubt the excellent authors of those works would regard this appearance of
their labours amid the Caledonian desert as a certain proof
of fame; they would seek more than ever to attract men's
affections to a more flexible system of morality; to awaken a
kind of devotion which affords more scope to the natural
passions of the multitude, and to wean human regard from
that austere doctrine which inculcates self-denial, and sundry
other such unreasonable matters. On a paper which contained
a printed list of rewards given by government, to men who
had laboured for the good of their country, I observed a calculation of the proceeds of illicit distillations; while on the
floor lay the skin of a fat wether recently killed, which still
bore the mark of a neighbouring farmer, whose consent to this

appropriation my companions, in the full relish of liberty, had not thought it necessary to obtain.

'During this examination, the eye of John Mackleg dwelt upon all my motions with increasing jealousy and distrust. At length, when my glance settled on the sheep-skin, he exclaimed, in a tone reproving and harsh, "Deil be in ye, Mungo Macubin; will ye let that fiend's baited hook of a gauger sit quietly there, and take an inventory of the only world's goods the oppression of man has left us? Take tent, lad, take tent; ye think him a bird that means nae mischief in his sang; bide ye a bit, ye may find him worse than a water-adder, and as cunning as lang Sandie Frizel the sautman, who praised the tone of your fiddle, and your skill in cup-making, and having proven the excellence of our distillation, sent auld Wylie Metestick, the gauger, to look at our cavern of curiosities!" "I'll tell ye what, John," said his companion; "guide your tongue in a less graceless manner, else it may bring your foreteeth and my right-hand knuckles acquainted. Gauger! what puts it into thy gowk's head that the lad's a gauger? Thinkest thou that a single exciseman, and ane both soft and slim, would have dropped down into the adder's den? But where's the profit of carousing with such a clod of the valley as thee?" Here the chief manager of this illicit establishment rose, and looked out into the wood; returned to his seat; and thus he resumed his conversation.

' "But where's the profit of putting trust in such a capon as thee? When the day comes that we have long looked for, you will put your hand to the full tankard rather than to the sharpened steel. And such a desirable day is not far distant, else let man believe no longer in white paper and black print. What says Ringan Alarum, of the Cowgate, in his strong paper called Liberty's Lighted Match, which auld Davie Dustyhause, the west-country skin-man, gave us when we sold him our cannily-come-by skins of three mug ewes. Does he not say as much as that the sceptre will soon be more harmless than a shepherd's staff; the mitre as little reverenced as grey hairs, or a scone-bonnet; a coronet as empty as a drunkard's drained cup; and that Sunday shall be as Saturday, and Saturday as Sunday; that a silken gown, flounced and fur-belowed, will rustle as common in a peasant's sheal as the plaiden kirtle of maid Margery; and that Meg Milligan, in her linsey-woolsey, will be as good and as lordly as our

madames with their perfumes and pearlins? Now John, my
man, should all these pleasant things come to pass, I will build
a whisky-still as big as Wamphray-kirk, with a distillation-
pipe large enough to pour a flood of pure spirit over the land,
in which we might float a revenue cutter."

'Flooded as the brain of John Mackleg seemed to be with
the spirit which his own industry had produced, he had intellect enough remaining to appear visibly delighted with this
promised picture of enjoyment. But his natural want of courage withheld him from indulging in his comrade's strain of
unguarded rapture. "O Lord, send it soon and sudden,
Mungo! O man, soon and sudden! But I conjure ye, by the
pith and power of malt, to speak lowne; O, man, speak
lowne." "Then," said his comrade, "await the coming of the
blessed time in silence. When it comes we shall have whisky-
stills in every kirk, and he that drinks longest shall rule and
reign among us. I will choose myself out a warm home in a
fertile land. The justice of the peace shall be dumb, and the
gauger silent, and his measuring rods regarded no more. Our
young men shall drink, and our young maidens dance; the
minister of the parish shall fill our cups, and the pulpit and
repentance-stool shall hold flagons and mutchkin stoups. I will
go to bed with six pint stoups placed at my feet and six at
my head; and when I grow doited and dizzy, the sweetest lass
in the country-side shall sit and hold my head." "And I," said
John Mackleg, in a low and cautious tone, "shall be the first
laird of my whole kin; whisky-brose shall be my breakfast,
and my supper shall be the untaken-down spirit, with strength
enough to float a pistol-bullet. I shall be the first of the name
of Mackleg who owned more land than they measured in the
dowie kirk-yard."

'His companion eyed him with a look particularly merry
and ironical; "Oh thou ambitious knave," said Mungo
Macubin, "dost thou long to be lord of all the land which
thou hast measured with thy drunken carcass? Why, man,
thou hast meted out with that genealogical ell-wand half the
land 'tween the sea-sand of Caerlaverock and the brown
heathy hills of Durisdeer. And so thou thinkest a drunkard's
fall on the earth has given thee possession of it? Plague take
me, if I give my consent to such a dangerous monopoly." The
perverse being to whom this speech was addressed made light
of its irony, and seizing a large two-eared quaigh, stooped his

face into it till nothing remained above the brim save a fleece of sooty uncombed locks, and drained out the liquor at a breath. He hurled the empty cup to the figure before the fire, and, though opposed by violent hiccupings, exclaimed, "More! bring me more! that was delicious. Jock, Jenny Mason's Jock, fill that cog, my man, and hear ye me; come hither and haud it to my head, for I am no sae sicker as I should be; and that whin-stone rock seems as if it would whomble aboon me. And d'ye hear me, Jock Laggengird, let me have none of the dyke-water additions which Mungo Macubin makes to the prime spirit which he drinks. Taxes and stents have made Scotland's crowdie thin, and turned her warm brose into cauld steerie. If ye covet the present length of your lugs, let me have none of your penitential potations."

'While Jenny Mason's descendant crawled to a cask, and turned a pin from which a pure liquid dribbled drop by drop into the cup, Mungo Macubin took down his fiddle, arranged the disordered strings, played a pleasant air, and accompanied it by singing the following rustic verses, which I have since learned were of his own composition.

MUNGO MACUBIN'S SONG[71]

1.

Come toom the stoup! let the merry sun shine
On sculptured cups and the merry man's wine;
Come toom the stoup! from the bearded bear,
And the heart of corn, comes this life-drink dear.
The reap-hook, the sheaf, and the flail for me;
Away with the drink of the slave's vine tree.
The spirit of malt sae free and sae frank,
Is my minted money and bonds in the Bank.

2.

Come toom up the stoup; what must be must,
I'm cauld and canker'd, and dry as dust;
A simmering stoup of this glorious weet
Gives soaring plumes to Time's leaden feet.
Let yon stately madam, so mim and so shy,
Arch her white neck proud, and sail prouder by;
The spirit of maut, so frank and so free,
Is daintier than midnight madam to me.

3.

Drink fills us with joy and gladness, and soon
Hangs canker'd care on the horns of the moon;
Is bed and bedding; and love and mirth
Dip their wings in drink ere they mount from the earth.
Come toom the stoup—it's delightful to see
The world run round, fit to whomel on me;
And yon bonnie bright star, by my sooth it's a shiner,
Ilka drop that I drink it seems glowing diviner.

4.

Away with your lordships of mosses and mools,
With your women, the plague and the plaything of fools;
Away with your crowns, and your sceptres, and mitres;
Lay the parson's back bare to the rod of the smiters;
For wisdom wastes time, and reflection is folly,
Let learning descend to the score and the tally.
Lo! the floor's running round, the roof's swimming in glory,
And I have but breath for to finish my story.

'The arch, and something of a drunken gravity, with which this rhyme was chanted, with the accompanying "thrum, thrum," on the fiddle, rendered it far from unpleasant. John Mackleg, whether desirous of emulating his companion, or smitten, perhaps, with a wayward desire of song, raised himself up from his lair, and improved the melody of a wild and indecorous rhyme, by the hollow sound extracted by means of his drinking quaigh from the head of an empty barrel. I can trust myself with repeating four of the verses only; the others, when the drink is at home and the understanding gone out, may be endured at midnight by the lee-side of a howl of punch;—but I see by the gathering storm in the brow of that sedate dame, that I have said enough about the graceless song,—yet she will endure a specimen, I have some suspicion.

JOHN MACKLEG'S SONG[72]

1.

Good evening to thee, madam moon,
    Sing brown barley bree,
Good evening to thee, madam moon,
    Sing bree;
So gladsomely ye're glowering down,
Fu' loth am I to part so soon,
But all the world is running roun'
    With me.

2.

A fair good morrow to thee, sun,
    Sing brown barley bree;
A fair good morrow to thee, sun,
    Sing bree;
Ye laugh and glory in the fun,—
But look, my stoup is nearly run,
And, 'las! my cash is mair than done,
    With me.

3.

Good morrow to thee, lovesome lass,
    Sing brown barley bree,
Good morrow to thee, lovesome lass,
    Sing bree;
Who wooes thee on the gowany grass,
Ere he has cool'd him with the tass,
Should through a three-fold penance pass,
    For me.

4.

O fair's the falcon in his flight,
    Sing brown barley bree;
And sweet's a maiden at midnight,
    Sing bree;
And welcome is the sweet sun-light,—
But here's a sweeter, blither sight,
The blood of barley pouring bright,
    For me.

'Such was a part of the song, and the better part of it. As
soon as he had ended his unmelodious chant, he silently raised
the quaigh of liquor to his lips, and laying his head back, the
liquid descended into the crevice, as water drops into the
chink of a rock. In a moment he started up, with curses mur-
muring on his lips, and hurling the quaigh, half full of liquor,
at the head of the son of Janet Mason, exclaimed,—"Sinner
that thou art, thou hast filled my cup out of the barrel of
reduced spirit prepared for Andrew Erngrey, the Cameronian.
It is as cauld and fizzenless as snow-water, though good
enough to cheer the saints at a mountain preaching. I tell ye,
my man, if you indulge yourself in such unsonsie pranks, I
shall bait Mungo Macubin's fox-trap with your left lug."
'The drunkard's missile was hurled by a hand which it
had helped to render unsteady; it flew over the prostrate descendant of Janet Mason, and striking against the furnace,
poured its contents into the fire. Such was the strength of the
liquid, that, subdued as it was for a devout person's use, the
moment it touched the fire a sudden and bright flame gushed
up to the roof of the shealing, and, kindling the dried grassy
turf, flashed along it like gunpowder. I started up, and seizing
the raw sheep-skin, fairly smothered and struck out the flame,
which would soon have consumed the whole illicit establishment. As I resumed my seat, Mungo Macubin seized my
hand, and nearly wringing it from my wrist, in joy exclaimed,
"By my faith, lad, ye are a rid-handed one, and well do ye
deserve a share in the profits of our distillation. Who would
have thought that a stolen sheep skin, or rather the skin of a
stolen sheep, could have quenched such a furious flame? And
now, let me tell you, John Mackleg, if you touch whisky or let
whisky touch you, for these four-and-twenty hours, I will
surely measure out your inheritance with that scoundrel
carcass of yours." And with a stamp of his foot, and a lour of
his brow, he awed his companion into fear and submission.
'I could see that the chief conductor of this wild establishment no longer regarded me with distrust or suspicion. He
seated himself between his fiercer comrade and me, as if he
dreaded outrage; and pulling a soiled book from his bosom,
appeared to examine it with some attention. It was one of
those political labours of the London press, where the author,
addressing himself to the multitude, had called in the powerful
aid of engraving to render the obscurity of language intelli-

gible. Our southern peasantry, with that love of the simplicity
of ancient days which regards instruction as a trick of state,
and wishes to reduce the tyranny of learning to the primitive
score and tally, have maintained their natural condition in
such entire purity, that literature in addressing them is fain to
make use of sensible signs and tokens. Of these this book was
full; but its owner turned over the leaves with a dissatisfied
and disdainful eye, and at last threw it in contempt into the
caldron fire. He took up his fiddle again, and after playing
snatches of several serious airs, sang some verses with a tone of
bitter sorrow which showed little sympathy with the poetry.
I remember several stanzas.

MY MIND TO ME A KINGDOM IS[73]

1.

Full thirty winter snows, last yule,
Have fallen on me mid pine and dool,
My clothing scant, my living spare,
I've reckon'd kin with woe and care;
I count my days and mete my grave;
While Fortune to some brainless knave
Holds up her strumpet cheek to kiss:
My mind to me my kingdom is.

2.

For faded friendship need I sigh,
Or love's warm raptures long flown by,
When fancy sits and fondly frames
Her angels out of soulless dames?
Sick of ripe lips and sagemen's rules,
The faith of knaves and fash of fools;
And scorning that, and loathing this,
My mind to me my kingdom is.

3.

The Muse with laurel'd brow in vain
Sweeps by me with her vision'd train;
I've bow'd my head and ruled my hand
Too long beneath her magic wand.
Shall I go shrouded to my hearse,

Full of the folly of vain verse?
I'll court some soberer, surer bliss;
My mind to me my kingdom is.

'Something in the song of Mungo Macubin had awakened
a train of thought of a nature too soft for his present hazardous calling; his looks darkened down in a kind of moody sorrow, and I could imagine that retrospection was busy with
him. He observed the interest which my looks testified I took
in his fate, took me by the hand with much kindness, and said
in a mingled tone of bitterness and sorrow, "I have often
thought that we have less control over our fate than we ought,
and that an evil destiny dogs us through life, and pursues us
to perdition. Take counsel, I beseech ye, from my words, and
warning from my conduct; this shealing contains a being
whose fate may be a text for you to preach from till these
black locks grow grey.—Listen, and then say with the Word,
'surely one vessel is made for honour, and another for dishonour.'[74] All I have cherished, or loved, or looked with kindness upon, have passed away, departed, and sunk to death or
dishonour; and all I have saved from the stream of destiny is
the wretched wreck on which you look. I beheld men of dull
and untutorable intellects blessed and doubly blessed. I saw
the portion of folly growing as lordly as the inheritance of
wisdom, and I in the vanity of my heart, shall I not also be
beloved and happy? But man's success is not of his own
shaping:—my cattle died, my crops failed, my means perished,
and one I loved dearly forgot me; I could have forgiven
that—she forgot herself. I have nothing now to solace or cheer
me—I look forward without hope, and the present moment
is so miserable that I seek to forget myself in the company of
two wretches who are not disturbed with those forebodings
which are as a demon to me. This stringed instrument, the
carving of these cups, and the making of that wooden time-
piece, with that caldron brimful to me of the liquor of ob-
livion, form the sum of all existing enjoyment. But from them,
from this sodded sheal, from this barren spot, and this lonesome desert, I shall soon be dragged or driven; for, sorrowful
and miserable as I am, my lot is far too happy to last."
'Never were words more ominously true than the last words
of poor Mungo Macubin; even as he spoke a human shadow
darkened the door, another succeeded, and a third, and a fourth,

followed close behind; he saw all this with a composure of face and an alacrity of resource truly surprising. He drew his pistol, he bared his sword, and, at the motion of his hand, the silent and prostrate being at the caldron snatched a piece of blazing fir from the fire, and sought counsel from the conduct or motions of his leader. I heard a sort of suppressed parley at the door, and presently several armed men made a dash through the aperture, exchanging blow and shot with Macubin, who, overthrowing one of the boldest of the officers, forced his way unhurt through all opposition, and disappeared in the thick wood. Meanwhile his companion applying the fir-torch to the roof, the shealing was filled with smoke, and flame, and human outcry. The fire seized the combustible wood, touched the inflammable spirit, and, wrapping all in a flame, ascended in a high and bright column above the green forest. I escaped into the wood, and never saw that wild spot, nor one of those men, more.'

END OF VOLUME I

TRADITIONAL TALES OF THE
ENGLISH AND SCOTTISH PEASANTRY

Volume II

MILES COLVINE,
THE CUMBERLAND MARINER

'William Glen was our captain's name;[75]
He was a bold and a tall young man,
As brave a sailor as e'er sailed the sea,
And he was bound for New Barbarie.

'The first of April we spread our sail,
To a low, a sweet, and a pleasant gale;
With a welcome wind on a sunny sea,
Away we sailed for New Barbarie.

'We had not sailed more days than two,
Till the sky waxed dark and the tempest blew;
The lightning flashed, and loud roared the sea,
As we were bound for New Barbarie.'
                              Old Ballad

On the Cumberland side of the firth of Solway lies a long line
of flat and unelevated coast, where the sea-fowl find refuge
from the gun of the fowler, and which, save the barren land
and the deep sea, presents but one object to our notice,—the
ruins of a rude cottage, once the residence of MILES COLVINE,
the Mariner. The person who built this little house of
refuge,—a seaman, a soldier, a scholar, and a gentleman,—
suffered shipwreck on the coast; and it was not known for a
time that any one else had escaped from the fatal storm. His
vessel was from a foreign land—had no merchandise aboard,
nor seemed constructed for traffic; and when the tempest
drove her along the Allanbay shore, three persons only were
visible on deck. Something mysterious hung over the fate of
the vessel and crew. The conduct of Miles Colvine was less
likely to remove than confirm suspicion; he was a silent and
melancholy man; and when the peasantry who saved him
from the storm inquired concerning the history of his ship and
seamen, he heard them, but answered them not, and seemed
anxious to elude all conversation on the subject. As they stood

on the beach, looking at the bursting of the billows, and listening to the howling of the storm, the remains of the ship were
shivered to pieces, and a large portion of the deck floated
ashore at their feet. The planks seemed stained with blood
and with wine; and as the peasants hauled it out to the dry
land, one of them asked him if it was wet with the blood of
beasts or men. 'With the blood of both,' was the answer. They
left the shore, and sought no further intercourse with him.

Where the vessel was wrecked, there he seemed determined
to remain;—he built a little hut, fenced it round with a wall
of loose stone, and lived in it without molestation from any
one. He shunned the fishermen of Allanbay and the seamen of
Skinverness; nor seemed pleased when the children of the
peasantry carried him little presents of food;—he sought and
found his subsistence in the water. It was the common remark
of the fishermen, that no man dipped a hook, or wetted a
net, between Skinverness and Saint Bees, with greater skill
and success. In this solitude, exposed to every storm that
swept the beach from sea or land, amid much seeming
wretchedness and privation, he resided during a summer and
autumn: winter, a season of great severity on an unsheltered
coast, was expected either to destroy or drive him from his
dwelling; but he braved every storm, and resisted all offers of
food or raiment.

The first winter of his abode was one of prodigious storm
and infinite hardship. The snow lay long and deep on the
ground, the ice was thick on lake and pool, and the Solway
presented one continual scene of commotion and distress. The
shore was covered with the wrecks of ships, the eddies choked
with drowned men, and the sea itself so rough and boisterous,
that the fishermen suspended their customary labours, and
sat with their families at the hearth-fire, listening to the
sounding of the surge, and relating tales of maritime disaster
and shipwreck. But on Miles Colvine the severe and continued
storm seemed to have no influence. He ranged the shore, collecting for his fire the wrecks of ships; he committed his nets
and hooks to the sea with his usual skill; and having found a
drifted boat, which belonged to some unfortunate vessel, he
obtained command over the element most congenial to his
heart, and wandered about on the bosom of the waters noon
and night, more like a troubled spirit than a human being.
When the severity of winter had passed away, and sea-birds

laid their eggs in the sand, the Mariner remitted his excursions at sea, and commenced a labour which surprised many. The sea shore, or that portion of the coast which lies between the margin of the sea and the cultivated land,—a region of shells, drift sand, and pebbles,—has ever been regarded as a kind of common; and the right of suspending nets, hauling boats aground, and constructing huts for the summer residence of the fishermen, has never been disputed by the owners of those thriftless domains. It was on this debateable ground, between the barren sea and the cultivated field, that the Mariner fixed his abode; but it soon appeared that he wished to extend his possessions, and augment his household accommodation. He constructed a larger and more substantial house, with equal attention to durability and neatness; he fenced off the sea by a barrier of large stones, and scattered around his dwelling a few of the common flowers which love to blossom near the sea breeze. The smoke of his chimney, and the unremitting clank of his hammer finishing the interior accommodations, were seen and heard from afar. When all this was concluded, he launched his boat and took to the sea again, and became known from the Mull of Galloway to the foot of Annan-water.

I remember, the first time that ever I saw him was in the market-place of Dumfries: his beard seemed of more than a year's growth,—his clothes, once rich and fine, were darned and patched,—and over the whole he wore a kind of boat-cloak, which, fastened round his neck, descended nigh the ground; but all this penury could not conceal the step and air of other and better days. He seldom looked in the face of any one; man he seemed to regard with an eye of scorn, and even deadly hatred; but on women he looked with softness and regard: and when he happened to meet a mother and child, he gazed on them with an eye of settled sorrow and affection. He once made a full stop, and gazed on a beautiful girl of four or five years old, who was gathering primroses on the margin of the Nith; the child, alarmed at his uncouth appearance, shrieked, and fell, in its fright, into the deep stream; the Mariner made but one spring from the bank into the river, saved the child, replaced it in its mother's bosom, and resumed his journey, apparently unconscious that he had done aught remarkable. Ever after this, the children of Dumfries pursued him with the hue and cry, 'Eh!

come and see the wild bearded man, who saved Mary
Lawson.'

On another occasion, I was hunting on the Scottish mountain of Criffel, and, having reached its summit, I sat down to
look around on the fine prospect of sea and land below me,
and take some refreshment. At a little distance I saw something like the figure of a human being, bedded in the heath,
and lying looking on the Solway from a projecting rock, so
still and motionless that it seemed dead. I went near: it was
Miles Colvine. He seemed unconscious of my approach, and,
looking steadfastly on the sea, remained fixed, and muttering,
as long as I continued on the mountain. Indeed, wherever he
went, he talked more like a man holding communion with
his own mind, than one sharing his thoughts with others; and
the general purport of such imperfect sentences as could be
heard was, that he had doomed many men to perish for some
irreparable wrong they had offered to a lady. Sometimes he
spoke of the lady as his wife, or his love, and the men he had
destroyed as the lawless crew of his own vessel. At other times
he addressed his seamen as spirits, whom he had sent to be
tortured for wrongs done in the body, and his lady as an angel
that still visited his daily dreams and his nightly visions.
Through the whole of these wayward musings the cry of
revenge, and the sense of deep injury, were heard and understood by all.

When Miles Colvine had fairly finished his new residence,
and the flowers and fruits had returned to field and tree, he
was observed to launch his boat: this was a common occurrence, but a small lair of seal-skins, a jar of water, and some
dried fish, called kippered salmon by the Scotch, looked like
preparation for a long voyage. The voyage was begun, for he
was seen scudding away southward, by the light of the stars,
and no more was seen or heard of him for some time. Day
after day his door continued shut, his chimney ceased to
smoke, and his nets hung unemployed. At length the revenue
cutter from Saint Bees arrived at Allanbay, to land a cargo of
fine Holland gin, which the officers had taken from an Irish
smuggler, between Carrickfergus and the Isle of Man. They
had been terribly alarmed, they said, on their way, by the
appearance, about the third watch of the night, of a visionary
boat, navigated by a bearded fiend, which scudded with
supernatural swiftness along the surface of the water. This

tale, with all the variations which a poetical peasantry readily
supply, found its way from cottage to hamlet, and from
hamlet to hall. Old men shook their heads, and talked of the
exploits of the great fiend by sea and land, and wished that
good might happen to Old England from the visit of such a
circumnavigator. Others, who were willing to believe that the
apparition was Miles Colvine on a coasting voyage, seemed
no less ready to confound the maritime recluse with an evil
being, who had murdered a whole ship's crew, sunk their ship,
and dwelt on the coast of 'cannie Cumberland,' for the express
purpose of raising storms, shaking corn, and making
unwedded mothers of half the fair damsels between Sarkfoot
and Saint Bees. Several misfortunes of the latter kind, which
happened about this time, confirmed this suspicion, and his
departure from the coast was as welcome as rain to the farmer
after a long drought.

About a fortnight after this event, I happened to be on a
moonlight excursion by water, as far as the ruined castle of
Comlongan. I was accompanied by an idle friend or two, and,
on our return, we allowed the receding tide to carry us along
the Cumberland coast, till we came nearly opposite the cottage of Miles Colvine. As we directed our boat to the shelter
of a small bank, I observed a light glimmering in the Mariner's house; and landing and approaching closer, I saw plainly
the shadows of two persons, one tall and manly, the other slim
and sylph-like, passing and repassing on the wall. I soon
obtained a fairer view. I saw the Mariner himself; his dress,
once rude and sordid, was replaced by one of the coarsest
materials, but remarkably clean; his beard was removed, and
his hair, lately matted and wild, now hung orderly about his
neck and temples. The natural colour was black; but it had
been changed by grief to snow-white; his look was hale, but
sorrowful, and he seemed about forty years of age. The figure
of the creature that accompanied him was much too tender
and beautiful to last long in a situation so rude and un-
protected as the cottage of a fisherman. It was a female, richly
dressed, and of a beauty so exquisite, and a look so full of
sweetness and grace, that the rude scene around was not
wanted to exalt her above all other maidens I had ever seen.
She glided about the cottage, arranging the various articles of
furniture, and passing two white hands, out-rivalling the fairest creations of the sculptor, over the rude chairs and tables,

and every moment giving a glance at the Mariner, like one
who took delight in pleasing him, and seemed to work for his
sake. And he was pleased. I saw him smile, and no one had
ever seen him smile before; he passed his hand over the long
clustering tresses of the maiden; caused her to sit down beside
him, and looked on her face, which outgrowing the child,
had not yet grown into woman, with a look of affection, and
reverence, and joy.

I was pondering on what I witnessed, and imagining an
interview with the unhappy Mariner and his beautiful child,
for such his companion was, when I observed the latter take
out a small musical instrument from a chest. She touched its
well-ordered strings with a light and a ready hand, and
played several of the simple and plaintive airs so common
among the peasantry of the Scottish and English coasts. After
a pause she resumed her music, and, to an air singularly wild
and melancholy, sang the following ballad, which relates, no
doubt, to the story of her father's and mother's misfortunes;
but the minstrel has observed a mystery in his narrative which
excites suspicion rather than gratifies curiosity:—

O MARINER, O MARINER[76]

1.

O mariner, O mariner,
    When will our gallant men
Make our cliffs and woodlands ring
    With their homeward hail agen?
Full fifteen paced the stately deck,
    And fifteen stood below,
And maidens waved them from the shore,
    With hands more white than snow;
All underneath them flash'd the wave,
    The sun laugh'd out aboon,
Will they come bounding homeward
    By the waning of yon moon?

2.

O maid, the moon shines lovely down,
    The stars all brightly burn,
And they may shine till doomsday comes

Ere your true love return;
O'er his white forehead roll the waves,
    The wind sighs lowne and low,
And the cry the sea-fowl uttereth
    Is one of wail and woe;
So wail they on, I tell thee, maid,
    One of thy tresses dark
Is worth all the souls who perish'd
    In that good and gallant bark.

3.

O mariner, O mariner,
    It's whisper'd in the hall,
And sung upon the mountain side
    Among our maidens all,
That the waves which fill the measure
    Of that wide and fatal flood,
Cannot cleanse the decks of thy good ship,
    Or wash thy hands from blood;
And sailors meet, and shake their heads,
    And, ere they sunder, say,
God keep us from Miles Colvine,
    On the wide and watery way!

4.

And up then spoke he, Miles Colvine,
    His thigh thus smiting soon,
By all that's dark aneath the deep,
    By all that's bright aboon,
By all that's blessed on the earth,
    Or blessed on the flood,
And by my sharp and stalwart blade
    That revel'd in their blood—
I could not spare them; for there came
    My loved one's spirit nigh,
With a shriek of joy at every stroke
    That doom'd her foes to die.

5.

'O mariner, O mariner,
    There was a lovely dame,
Went down with thee unto the deep,

And left her fathers hame.'—
His dark eyes, like a thunder cloud,
    Did rain and lighten fast,
And, oh! his bold and martial face
    All grimly grew and ghast:
I loved her, and those evil men
    Wrong'd her as far we ranged;
But were ever woman's woes and wrongs
    More fearfully avenged?

The ballad had proceeded thus far, when a band of smugglers, from the coasts of Ireland and Scotland, uniting the
reckless desperation of the former with the craft and tact of
the latter, attracted by the secure and naked coast, and perhaps by the lonely house, which presented hope of plunder
with little appearance of resistance, landed to the number of
seven, and, leaping over the exterior wall, seized the door and
shook it violently, calling loudly for admittance. I lay down,
with my two companions, behind a small hillock covered with
furze, to see the issue of this visit; for at that time l imagined
the Mariner maintained some mysterious correspondence with
these fierce and lawless men.

'Open the door,' said one, in a strong Irish accent, 'or, by
the powers, I'll blow your cabin to peelings of potatoes about
your ears, my darlings.'

'Hout, Patrick, or what's your name,' said one of his comrades, in Lowland Scotch, 'ye mauna gang that rough way to
wark; we maun speak kindly and cannilie, man, till we get
in our hand, and then we can take it a' our ain way, like
Willie Wilson's sow, when she ran off with the knife in her
neck.'

The Mariner, on hearing this dialogue, prepared himself
for resistance, like one perfectly well acquainted with such
rencounters. With a sword in one hand, a cocked pistol in the
other, and a brace in his belt, he posted himself behind the
door, and, in a low voice, admonished his daughter to retire
to a little chamber constructed for her accommodation. With
a voice which, though quivering with emotion, lost nothing of
its native sweetness, the young maiden answered, 'Oh, let me
be near you!—let me but be near you!'

Her low and gentle voice was drowned in the wild exclamations of one of the smugglers. 'Och, my dears, let us break

the door, and clap a red turf to the roof, and all to give me
light to see to kiss this maiden with the sweet voice. By the
holy poker that stirred the turf fire beneath the first potatoe, I
have not been within seven acres broad of a woman since we
sailed with Miles Colvine's lady. And, by the bagpiper, she
was a bouncer; and a pretty din she made about it, after all,
and took it into her head to shriek till the shores rang, and
pray till the saints grew deaf; ah, my hearties, it wouldn't
do.—What the devil holds this door?—stand by till I show
you how handsomely I'll pitch it against the wall. Ah, I wish
you had seen me when I upset the house of Ranald Mullagen,
in Lurgen, and made the bonniest blaze you ever saw in the
wide world, at all, at all.'

And, setting his shoulders to the door, he thrust with all
his might; but, though seconded by his comrades, who seemed
all alike eager for violence, the door resisted his utmost
efforts.

'Stand back, my darlings,' said the miscreant, 'I'll show
you a trick worth two of this; I'll teach you how we bring out
a bonnie lass from a bolted chamber in little Ireland.'

So saying, he proceeded to prime a pistol, having previously
hammered the flint with a little steel cross, curiously chased
and ornamented, which he took from his bosom. 'Ah,' said he,
'may the devil cork me up in a stone bottle, and send me to
seek out the latitude of the lake of darkness, if I don't carve
up that old he-goat into relics!—Now, come on, my early
boys—my souls of boys; the boy that won't do as I do deserves
to be whipped through Purgatory with the tail of St. Patrick's
ass. Thack and thunder! hell's to hinder us when I snap my
pistol under the thatch.'

In a moment the door opened, Miles Colvine stood on the
threshold, a cocked pistol in his right hand, his sword gleaming in his left, his eyes shooting from them a fierce dark light,
but his manner perfectly calm and collected. Behind him came
the beautiful form of his daughter, with a pistol in her hand,
and shuddering from head to foot at the immediate peril
which seemed to beset her father. These maritime desperadoes
started back at this sudden apparition of an armed man; and
even their miscreant leader, forward as he was, recoiled a pace
or two. The Mariner eyed him for a moment, and said, 'Did
my sword then do its work slovenly, and did the deep sea not
devour thee, thou immeasurable villain? but God has given

thee back to earth, to become a warning how sure and how certain just vengeance is.' And leaping on him as he spoke, I saw the pistol flash, and the gleam of the descending sword, in almost the same instant. I instantly started up with my companions, and the smugglers, perceiving this reinforcement, carried off their companion, groaning, and cursing, and praying; and pushing their boat from the shore, vanished along the misty bosom of the summer sea.

I found Miles Colvine standing on the threshold of his house, and his daughter on her knees beside him. He knew me, for we had often passed each other on the beach and on the sea, and he was aware that I was a friend, for I had endeavoured in vain to oblige him in his forlorn state with little acts of kindness.

'Come hither, sir,' said the Mariner, 'I have to thank you for aid this night.' He paused for a moment, and then said in a lower tone, 'I know your faith is not my faith, and that your life is not embittered with what has embittered mine. But tell me, sir, tell me, do you believe that the events of our life are ordained? for what hath happened to-night seems of a wise Being's ordering.'

'Surely, sir,' I said, 'God knoweth all things, present and to come; but, whether he permits evil deeds to be wrought, or ordains good ones to be done'—

'Enough, enough,' said the Mariner. 'May Colvine, my love, trim thy father's shealing, and set the supper-table in array, for it is ordained that our deliverers shall rest with us, and break bread at our board; so come in.'

And into the Mariner's cottage we walked, not unawed by the presence of a being of whose temper and courage we had seen such a proof.

If the exterior of the cottage was rude and unskilfully built, the interior was wonderfully commodious and neat. The floor was laid of drifted ship timber, and the walls were hung with nets as with tapestry; and fish-spears, and gaff-hooks of steel, sharp and bright, were grouped like weapons for battle in a chieftain's hall of old. The fruits of the fisherman's skill were every where visible; the chimney-mantel, a beam of wood which extended from side to side of the cottage, was covered with kippered salmon, large, and red, and savoury, and various kegs were filled with salted fish of the many excellent kinds which the Solway affords. A small bed stood near the chimney, swelled with the feathers of sea-fowl, and hillocked high with quilts and mantles, from beneath which some linen looked out, only rivalled in whiteness by the snow. A very small chamber was constructed at the farther end, into which May Colvine disappeared for a moment to re-adjust her dress, and, perhaps, add some other of those artificial attractions which women always bring in to the aid of their natural charms. The Mariner seated himself, motioned me to a seat, over which a seal-skin was thrown, while a lamp, fed plentifully with oil, and suspended from the roof, diffused light over the apartment. Nor was the place devoted to brute comfort alone: several books, among which I observed *Robinson Crusoe*, and Homer's *Odyssey* in Greek, with a curious collection of Northern legendary ballads, were scattered about, and a shepherd's pipe and a fiddle were there to bring music to assist in the dissipation of melancholy thought.

May Colvine now came forth from her little chamber, with an increase of loveliness, such as a rose appears when refreshed in dew. She had laid aside the snood of silk and pearl which enclosed her hair, and the curling luxuriance of her ringlets descended over her shoulders, while her white temples, and whiter neck, were seen through the waving fleece which fell so profusely over them. Her father gazed on her like one who recalls the lovely past in the beautiful present; and his thoughts had flitted to other days and remoter climes, for after a brief reverie he said, 'Come, my love, the vessel is ready, the mariners aboard, the sails spread to the wind, and we must pass the haunted headland before the moon goes down.'

The maiden meanwhile had filled the supper-board with such coarse fare as the cabin afforded, and addressing her father, said, 'Sir, the table is prepared, your guests are waiting, and will expect you to bless the fare which is set before them.'

The Mariner laid his hat aside, and sitting in his place, after the manner of the Presbyterians, said, 'Thou who spreadest thy table on the deep waters, and rainest down abundance in the desert places, make this coarse food seem savoury and delicate unto these three men, and this tender virgin; but my hands, on which the blood of man yet reeks unatoned for, may not presume to touch blessed food.' And spreading the fold of his mantle over his face, and stooping down, he appeared to busy himself in mental devotion, while, tasting the supper set before us, and obeying the mute invitation of the maiden to a glass of water, we complied with all the forms which this extraordinary audience seemed to impose upon us.

After this was past, the young woman took up one of the instruments, and singing as she played, with inexpressible sweetness and grace, her father gradually uncovered his face,—his looks began to brighten, and uttering a deep sigh, he waved his hand, the minstrelsy ceased, and he thus addressed us:—

'I was not always an unhappy man,—I had fair domains, a stately house, a beauteous wife, and a sweet daughter; but it is not what we have, but what we enjoy, that blesseth man's heart, and makes him as one of the angels. I dwelt on a wild sea-coast, far from here, full of woods and caverns, the haunt of a banditti of smugglers, those fierce, and vulgar, and intractable spirits, who find subsistence in fraud and violence, and, from a continued perseverance in hostility to human law, become daily more hardened of heart and fierce of nature. I was young and romantic; and though I did not approve of the course of these men's lives, there appeared glimpses of generosity, and courage, and fortitude, about them, which shed a halo over a life of immorality and crime. I protected them not, neither did I associate with them; but they soon saw in the passive manner in which I regarded their nocturnal intercourse with the coast, and the ready and delighted ear which I lent to the narratives of their adventures by sea and land, that they had nothing to fear and much to hope. Their confidence increased, and their numbers augmented; and they soon found a leader capable of giving an aim to all their movements, and who brought something like regular craft and ability to their counsels.

'I was reputed rich, and was rich; my treasures were mostly of gold and silver plate, and bars of the former metal, the gain of a relative who had shared with the Buccaneers in the plunder of Panama. I had also been wedded for a number of years, my wife was young and beautiful, and our daughter, an only child, my own May Colvine, here where she sits, was in her thirteenth year, with a frame that seemed much too delicate to survive the disasters she has since been doomed to meet. We were counselled to carry her to warmer climates, and were preparing for our voyage, and my wife was ready to accompany me; when a large smuggling cutter cast anchor in a deep woody bay which belonged to my estate, and as I sat on the top of my house, looking towards the sea, a person in a naval dress came and accosted me. He was, he said, the captain of the free trader lying in the bay, with a cargo of choice wine, and his mariners, bold lads and true, had periled themselves freely by land and water, and often experienced the protection of Miles Colvine's bay, and the hospitality of his menials. They had heard of my intention to carry my wife and daughter to a more genial climate; and, if we wished to touch at Lisbon, or to go to any of the islands where Europeans seek for health, they would give us a passage, for they honoured us next to commerce without law or restraint.

'But, I must tell you, that the chief of this band, knowing my love for marvellous tales, hinted, that he had men on board, who, to the traditionary lore of their maritime ancestors, added their own adventures and deeds; and could, with the romantic ballads of Denmark and Sweden, mingle the Troubadour tales of France, the Moorish legends of Spain, and the singular narratives which survive among the peasantry on my native coast. To soothe and propitiate my wife, he had recourse to another charm; from the pocket of a long boat-cloak he produced a mantle of the most precious fabric, and spreading it out before her, with all its rich variety of colour, and Eastern profusion of ornament, offered it as a humble present from himself and his mariners. I need not prolong this part of my narrative; we embarked at twilight, and standing out of the bay, dropped anchor till morning dawn. The captain sat armed beside us; this excited no suspicion, for he went commonly armed, and related adventures of a daring and remarkable kind which had befallen him on foreign shores, with a liveliness, and a kind of maritime grace, which were perfectly captivating. All night we heard overhead the tramp and the din of sailors passing and repassing, and with the grey of the morning we plucked up our anchor, spread our sails to a shrill wind, shot away seaward, and my native land vanished from my view. All was life and gladness; we danced and we sang on deck, and drained cups of the purest wine; while the breeze favoured us, and the sky remained unclouded and serene.

'When the spice groves of one of the Portuguese islands appeared before us, the sun was setting, and it was resolved

we should remain at the entrance of a bay till day-light. We
were crowded on the deck, looking on the green and beauteous land, and a gentle seaward wind wafted the perfume of
the forest about us. My wife was in the bloom of youth and
beauty, full of health, and life, and love; and as she stood leaning on my arm, the sailors smoothed their rough looks, and
refrained from curses, so much were they touched by her
beauty; but this awe lasted but a little while. The captain was
merry far beyond his usual measure of delight, and drained
one wine cup after another to my wife's health and mine; he
vowed I was as a god among his men, and that my wife was
reverenced as a divinity. "But come," said he, "Miles Colvine,
I have a curious and a cunning thing to show you, which
you alone deserve to see; I got it among the Moors, so come,
and come alone."

'I rose, and followed him, for my curiosity was unbounded;
he conducted me below, and, opening a small wicket in the
wall of his cabin with a key, ushered me in, and closing it suddenly upon me, locked it; and then I heard him bounding up
the stair to the deck. I stood half imagining this to be a jest,
or something, at least, of a light nature; but shriek after shriek
of my wife, uttered in the piercing agony of anguish and despair, soon undeceived me. I called, I entreated, I used force,
and though I was armed by anger and despair with almost
supernatural might, the door withstood all my efforts. But
why should I dwell upon a scene of such unutterable misery?
What I endured, and what the woman I loved and adored
suffered, are fit only to be imagined, not, surely, to be spoken.
Her wrongs were remembered, and her shrieks numbered, by
a POWER far more terrible than man; and a certain doom
and deplorable death was pronounced against them, at the
moment their joy was fullest.

'The evening passed away, and morning came; and,
through a little wicket which looked upon the sea, the light
showed me that my chamber was the treasure-room of the
pirates, for such they were, as well as smugglers; at the same
moment a hole opened above, and a piece of bread and an
antique silver cup filled with wine were lowered down. Amid
the misery of my situation it seemed but a light evil that I
recognized the silver vessel to be part of the treasure I had left
at home; and in seeking for a weapon to force the wicket, I
found that my whole riches, in gold as well as silver, had been

seized and put on board. I could now measure the extent of my calamity, and prepared myself for a fate, which, among such miscreants, could not be deemed far distant. The morning was not much advanced when the sun dipped at once into a dark and tempestuous ocean of clouds, the wind began to whistle shriller and shriller among our sails, and the sea, upturned by sudden and heavy gusts of wind, showed, as far as the eye could reach, those dark and tremendous furrows so fatal to mariners. The wind was from the land, and I could both see and feel that the vessel was unable to gain the harbour, and had sought security from the approaching tempest by standing out to sea. I heard the wind wax louder, and saw the billows roll, with a joy that arises from the hope of revenge: the sky became darker, the sea flashed over the decks, and the tempest hurried the ship onward with a rapidity which alarmed the sailors, accustomed as they were to the element. The seams of the vessel began to admit the sea, and every where symptoms appeared of her immediate destruction.

'I heard a conversation overhead I shall never forget. "I tell you," said a voice in lowland Scotch, "good can never come of such evil as your captain and you have wrought; had you taken Miles Colvine's gold and silver alone, the sin had been but little, and a grey-headed repentance might have mended all. But the bonnie lady! her voice has been heard to-day, and tremble all you that touched her sweet body, for here has come an avenging tempest. The sea will soon devour us, and hot hell will hold us; and the mother who bore, and the wife who loved me, and the bonnie babes I have nursed on my knee, will behold me no more; and all for being in company with such hell-hounds as you."

'A voice replied to all this, in a tone too low and suppressed to be audible; and the Scotchman answered again:—"Lo, look, did ever eyes behold such a sight; all around us the sea is smooth as glass, and other ships pass by us under a gentle breeze, without a wetted sail; but we! the anger of Heaven has found us, for on us the thick tempest beats, and the evil one is pursuing us to destruction. O thou eternal villain—captain, shall I call thee no more—and you!—you fifteen wretches, who shared with him in his crime, make you ready, for that storm will neither leave you, nor forsake you, till you are buried in the ocean."

'At the very moment when ruin seemed inevitable, the tempest ceased, the clouds passed away, and the descending sun shone brightly down, making the shoreless waters sparkle as far as the eye could reach. No bounds were now set to the joy of the crew; they crowded the deck, made a circle round several vessels of wine and baskets of biscuit; and before the twilight had passed away, a few only were capable of guiding the vessel. The night grew very dark, and as I sat in utter despair, I heard the same friendly voice, that I had so lately heard, say, "Miles Colvine, put your trust in Him who can still the tempest; thy time is come."

'In a moment the wicket opened, and the same voice said, "Take this sword, and come with me. If you have courage to avenge the miseries and the death of your beautiful and wretched wife, come, for the hour is at hand, and as sure as I hate sin, and love immortal happiness, I shall help you."

'I took the sword, followed in silence, and, coming on deck, I beheld a scene which the hope of sure and immediate revenge rendered inexpressibly sweet. The captain and five sailors, though nearly overcome with wine, were seated on deck; the remainder of the crew had retired below; some shouted, some sang, all blasphemed, and one loud din of cursing and carousal echoed far and wide: the mingled clamour that ascended from this scene of wickedness and debauchery, partook of all the evil qualities of debased minds, and the most infamous pursuits, and cannot be described. Discord had its full share in the conference on deck between the captain and his confederates; they were debating about their shares in the plunder of my house.

' "Share! by my saul, man," said a Scottish sailor to the captain, "your share in Miles Colvine's pure gold can be but small; one hour of his sweet lady, a hundred leagues from land, was worth all the gold that ever shone."

' "I shall share all fairly," said the captain, laying his hand on the hilt of his cutlass; "and first I shall share thy scoundrel carcase among the fishes of the sea, if I hear such a word again. Did I plan the glorious plot of carrying away the fair lady and her lord's treasure, to share either with such a Scotch sawney as thee?"

'The wrath of the Scotchman burnt on his brow, far redder than the flush of the wine he had drunk. "Fiend seethe my

saul in his chief cauldron, if ye taste na' cauld iron for this!"
And out came his cutlass as he spoke.

' "That's my hearty Caledonian," said one of his comrades,
"give him a touch of the toasting iron; didn't he give a blow
on the head to my mother's own son, this blessed morning, for
only playing pluck at the lady's garment. Ah, give him the
cold piece of steel, my hearty."

'A blow from the captain's cutlass was the answer to this;
several drunkards drew their swords, and ill-directed blows,
and ineffectual stabs, were given and received in the dark.
"Now," said my sailor, laying his hand on mine, to stay me
till I received his admonition, "say not one word, for words
slay not, but glide in among them like a spirit; thrust your
blade, for anger strikes, but revenge stabs; and I will secure
the gangway, and fight along with you."

'I heard and obeyed, and gliding among them, thrust one
of them through and through; a second, and a third, dropped,
ere they saw who was among them. The captain attempted
to draw a pistol, but my sword, and my friend's, entered at
back and bosom; and though two yet remained unhurt, I
struck my sword a second time through the bosom of my
mortal enemy, as he lay beneath me; and the last expiring
glance of his eye was a look worth remembering. Ere this was
accomplished, the other two were both lying with their companions. I have frequently imagined that a firmness and
strength, more than my own, were given me during this
desperate encounter. Meanwhile the remainder of the crew
below set no bounds to their merriment and shouting, and
seemed, as my Scottish friend remarked, ordained to die by
my hand, since their clamour, by drowning the groans of their
comrades, prevented them from providing for their safety.
We fastened the cabin door, and barricaded the gangway,
keeping watch for many days with pistol and sword, with the
hope of seeing some friendly shore, or a compassionate sail;
while the vessel, urged onward by a strong wind, scudded with
supernatural swiftness through the midnight waters. We had
entered the Solway sea, when a storm came on, which, augmenting every moment, carried us rapidly along. When opposite Allanbay, a whirlwind seizing our ship by the rigging,
whirled her fairly round, and dashed her against a sand bank.
As the planks sundered, and the waters rushed in, I beheld
an armed man, one of the band of wretches from below, rise

up before me with a look of fury which a fiend might envy.
Our hatred was superior to the tempest and the scene of desolation around, and, drawing our cutlasses, we sought each
other's bosom. There is a fate in all things—the planks parted
beneath our feet, and the sea broke over us, and he escaped
me then, to perish by my hand to-night. Revenge is sweetest
when it comes unhoped for. As we sank in the waves, a
passing vessel, it seems, saved my sweet May Colvine, while
the remainder of the crew went to the bottom, without the
chance of swimming for an existence they deserved not to
prolong. Such is my story.'

Little more is known with certainty of the life of this
remarkable man. He forsook his house soon after, and went to
another—perhaps his native land. The peasantry and the
fishermen, from awe as well as respect to his fortitude and misfortunes, permitted his cottage to remain untouched; and the
seamen, as they sailed by, looked with something of a superstitious regard on the residence of Miles Colvine. Many years
afterwards—on a summer morning, a peasant went to the
sea, to examine his nets and lines. The sun had just risen, and
was slanting his first beams over the green hills behind—a
few long and narrow lines of dewy light fell across the Solway,
and the mountains on the Scottish side were brightened from
their summits midway down. He saw a man seated by the
door of the Mariner's cottage, dressed in a garb resembling
that of a pilgrim, and leaning over a staff. He went closer,
and addressed him—no answer was returned—the stranger
was cold and dead—his hands were clasped together on the
head of his staff, and his eyes were wide open, and looking
seaward. Some old men came, and said, 'A woeful man was
Miles Colvine, the Mariner,' and interred him among their
ancestors in the parish churchyard.

HONEST MAN
JOHN OCHILTREE

'A gay young lad frae Locherben[77]
Came galloping late to our gate en;
He doft his hat, and came bouncing ben,
    Saying, Maiden, I come to wooe.
His brow was brent, his glance was gleg,
A snaw-white skin an' a wanton leg;
A gallant young lad, quo' I, by my feg,
    He's welcome here to wooe.

'Aboon the fire upon the bink,
He had bread to eat an' wine to drink,
But ne'er a blithe styme wad he blink
    Till he was warm and fou;
Syne by the hand I have him ta'en,
Ye coldrife lover now get ye gane,
I'd liefer lie a year my lane
    Than lie an hour wi' you.'

Old Scottish Song

'I was not always an old man, with a lank leg and a grey head; there was a time before I began the pleasant trade of cheering the dames and maidens with my merry tales. I was then young, my leg was firm and shapely, my locks were bushy and black; and I could have pitched the bar, or played a fiddle, with the youth of seven parishes. But a sad cough, which I caught among the damp broom on Quarrelwood Hill hearkening a sectarian sermon, plucked strength and spirit down, and drove me to win the bread by my wit, which more favoured men purchase by the sweat of their brow. But the world is an altered world to me since I commenced my calling; it is a white half-crown, a week the worse for the wear; people are grown too wise to be delighted—they laugh not at my wittiest story, nor shed one tear at my saddest. I have seen when ye might have tied seven strong men with a straw, as they shouted and laughed, and lay down and laughed at my narratives; a smile is as hard to earn as a sixpence now, and tears are dried up on the earth. My saddest story would bring red wine out of a rock, or strong drink from a log of Memel fir, sooner than extract one tear from the brightest eye of the present generation.

'But I scatter none of those antique pearls—those tender and touching narratives, before the eyes of the self-sufficient husbandman and the critical mechanic. I steep not my story now in the dark and fathomless stream of superstition: I have seen the time when tales and ballads of fairies and elves, and witches and warlocks, and elve candles and water spunkies, and wraiths and ghosts, and goblins and foul fiends, horned or cloven-footed, would have been to one as food and raiment and white money. But the wisdom of man so much abounds, that he is pleased with nought; he laughs at ancient beliefs, and calls for ocular proof, and testimony on oath, and the assurance of many witnesses, for all oral or recorded things. The poetry has departed from story-telling, conjured away by the wand of that sorcerer, education. Not that I mean to aver that all else is as husks and bran, compared to the white and the purified grain. I have had curious adventures of my own, in which the most querulous matter-of-fact man could detect neither superstition nor poetry. These, falling from the lips of one blessed with a natural grace of utterance, might go far to move men to mirth; but I can hope for no such consummation.'

The old man adjusted his mantle, stood perpendicularly up, and, combing his white locks with his fingers, commenced his narrative with something of a look and tone at once grave and shrewd.

'The adventures I shall relate commenced with my seventeenth year: I had learned to sing, and also to dance; but nature, which lavishes so many notable gifts, denied me that ready and familiar grace of address which wins its way to woman's regard: I conversed with the maids, whom the music of the fiddle surrendered to my company, with such manifest confusion, and even alarm, that they soon reckoned me a creature equally uncouth and ungracious; and I was subjected to abundance of scorn, and caprice, and wit, when I endeavoured at gallantry. When I led them to the floor, they would examine me from head to foot, with an eye sparkling in malicious wit; and even their grandmothers regarded me with a glance of the most mortifying compassion. It was sometimes a matter of rivalry among the girls to obtain my hand: to dance with such a cutter of uncouth capers, such a marvellous piece of human imperfection as me, was made a matter of boast and a subject for laughter; and any expressions of respect or love which I hazarded were parodied and distorted into all that was absurd and ridiculous by these capricious spirits. They all seemed to possess, for my mortification and sorrow, a talent for humour and ridicule, which broke out on every occasion. I became the most exalted personage in the parish, if my merit might be estimated by the notice I received; and to this "bad eminence"[78] I was raised by the wit, and the fun, and folly of women.

'To one of those meetings at the conclusion of harvest, which, taking farewell of autumn, welcome the winter with drinking and dancing, and all sorts of rustic festivity, I was about this time invited. I dressed myself out for the occasion in my newest dress, and in the vanity of my heart I counted myself captivating. My aunt assisted me much in this; she possessed an antique taste, and so far back did her intelligence in apparel reach, that she sought to revive, and that on my person, the motley dress of the minstrels at the ancient border tournaments. One mistake was, that I had no turn for poetry, so I was soon doomed to endure the malice of verse without the power of inflicting it on others; and another was, that I had nothing of a romantic turn about me, so that the dress sat on me with an evil grace. To the dance, however, I went, waving my right arm gallantly as I marched along, and look-ing oftentimes back at my shadow in the moonlight; the luminary I could not help thinking neglected to do justice to my form, but that planet is certainly the most capricious of all the lesser lights. I was received with a general stare; and then with a burst of universal and spontaneous mirth. The old men surveyed me with looks in which compassion struggled with curiosity; but the maidens gathered about me, com-mended the head that imagined my dress, and the hand that fashioned it: the young men joined in this praise with a gravity which I mistook for envy, and the roof rocked and rang to another peal of laughter.

'The fiddler, wholly blind, and seated apart from this scene of merriment and mortification, seemed incensed to think that any one should be the cause of mirth but himself. He stayed his hand, laid down his instrument, and while he rosined his bow, inquired what all this laughter meant. "Thy curiosity shall be gratified," said a wicked young girl; and taking my unreluctant hand, she led me up to this producer of sounds, and guided his hand to my person. He felt my dress from head to heel, vowed by his bow he had never touched a garment of such rich device as my coat, swore by his fiddle my bonnet was worth all the money his instrument had ever earned, and hoped I would leave the land before I ruined the mystery of thairms,[79] for there was no need of instrumental mirth where I came. And dismissing me with a suppressed laugh, for open merriment might have diminished his evening's gain, he recommenced his music, and the discontinued dance began.

'My torment now commenced: the lasses danced round me in a ring. I had the misfortune to be so much in request that I was never off the floor; though I danced six and thirty reels without let or pause; and though the drops fell from my brows like rain: I saw no end to such perpetual capering. This ridiculous exertion is still remembered among the dames of Annandale; and I lately heard a girl reproach her lover with his listlessness for mirth, saying, "When will ye dance six and thirty reels like daft John Ochiltree?" I grew an inch taller with this proof of my fame. All this was to come to an end. The blind fiddler had been smit in his youth with the disease of tune-making: he had mingled the notes of half a dozen tunes together, from which he extracted a kind of musical square root, and this singular progeny he was desirous of baptizing; much it seems depends on having a fine sounding name. At present he was hesitating between "Prince Charles's Delight," or "Duke William's Welcome," when a peasant demanded the tune; "the new tune, plague on't, the tune without a name." "A tune without a name," said a girl, "cannot ye christen it, man? here, fiddler, play up Honest Man John Ochiltree." A shout of laughter succeeded: "A name, by my faith," exclaimed many voices at once; and the new name was shouted by a hundred tongues, to the infinite mortification of the fiddler and me: our vanity was wounded. The name of the tune was fixed as unalterably as the laws of the Medes,[80] and from that hour forward it haunted me through life; while the popularity of the air was increased by the noises which a rustic minstrel soon caused to jingle in rude chorus to the air. Thus I got the name of "Honest Man

John Ochiltree," and the story was a winter's laugh to the parish.

'But there is no sour without its sweet: all this had been witnessed by a farmer's daughter, whom the pursuit of many lovers had not rendered capricious, and who thought she perceived in the patience with which I endured all this musical persecution the materials for making a quiet and tractable husband. She trod on my foot returning from a hill-preaching, and apologized with so much grace, that I thought her the fairest maiden of the whole valley; and after touching on the sermon, and quoting the Song of Solomon,[81] we parted with a mutual promise of meeting in her father's barn at midnight. I was punctual to my tryste, and so accurate was the devout maiden, that the clock struck twelve as she turned the key in the granary door. She opened a little wicket, and let in the summer moonlight; and seating ourselves on two inverted bushels, we sat in collateral splendour, side by side, amid the silent light of the luminary.

'I looked at the maiden, who kept looking on the opposite wall with an aspect of demure but arch composure, and seemed to count the stones of which it was built. Had I been afflicted with the cureless evil of verse making, I had now a matchless opportunity of displaying my gift. The silence of the place,—the glow of the moon,—the beauty of the maiden, Mary Anderson by name,—her white hands clasped over a whiter bosom, her locks a glistering and a golden brown, escaping from the comb, descending in ringlets down her left cheek and shoulder, and taking a silvery or a golden hue as they moved to her breath amid the pure moonlight! This was my first attempt at courtship. I trembled much, and the words of love, too, trembled on my tongue. Let no man sit many minutes silent in the presence of his mistress: he will be forgiven for folly, for more serious offences, but never for silence. Had I made my début in darkness, I think I should have spoken, and spoken, too, with much tenderness and true love. But the fault lay with the moon, plague on the capricious planet! I never see her fickle light glimmering through the chink of a barn wall, but I think on the time when I lost my first love through her influence. We sat mute for the space of a quarter of an hour; and I had nearly vanquished my aversion to the moon's presence, when an owl rested from her flight on the roof above us for a moment, and just as the words had assembled on my lips, uttered a long and melancholy "whoop hoo." I wished not to pitch the tone of courtship by a sound so ominous, and remained mute. I mustered my resolution again, and the first word (I would give the world to remember what word it was) was actually escaping from my lips, when a sucking calf lowed, perhaps for its dam, in a stall near us, and the voices of the four and the two footed animals were blended so curiously in utterance, that a judge of natural music would have found difficulty in awarding to each their own proper notes. This was a sound much more mischievous than the voice of the owl: the maiden, devout as she was, could not suppress a smile, and rising said, "I think we know enough of one another's minds for one night," and vanished from my side; so I closed my first night's wooing. I once had the courage to propose to her the endurance of another vigil; she set her hands to her mouth, and "whooted out whoots three:" we never met again.

'But I was an inextinguishable lover. I disciplined my mind, pampered up my courage, and having, as I hoped, inured myself to the sharp encounter of female wit, boldly resolved to go in quest of an adventure. I have travelled much in the world; but all parts of the earth are surpassed by Scotland in the amorous spirit of its peasantry: there a maiden has many lovers, and a peasant many mistresses: adventures equalling those of romance are encountered; and the effusion of men's blood, as well as maiden's tears, not unfrequently follows those nocturnal excursions. I walked resolutely abroad, and hoped the achievement of some notable adventure. For some time I was without success; but at last a long stream of light from a farmer's window led me up to the casement, within which I observed his eldest daughter, a gay damsel of eighteen, couched on the watch, and waiting the approach of some happy wooer. She opened the window when I appeared, but seeing a form she had not hoped for, stood holding the sash in her hand, pondering whether she should take the earliest blessing which heaven had sent in human shape.

'At this moment her expected lover appeared, a spruce youth from the neighbouring city, pruned and landered, and scenting the way with musk and frankincense. The maiden wrung her hands with vexation: her wit could not deal with more than one at a time; and as I was never of a quarrelsome nature, and had an aversion to intrude upon true love, I turned suddenly to retreat. The young man started off too; and as my road lay the very way he ran, he imagined I pursued him with some sinister intention, so he augmented his speed; I still gained on him; a lake was in the way: I have ever had an affection for running water since it received my rival in its bosom, plump over head and ears, with a dash that startled the wild ducks for a mile round. He swam through like an evil spirit, while I returned to his mistress, and found her holding the casement open, perhaps for the successful lover; so I leaped gaily into the chamber, and, seated by the maiden's side, began to hope I was conquering my fate.

'The night, gloomy before, became tenfold darker now; the wind, accompanied by heavy gushes of rain, shook window and door, and raised in the chimney-top that long and melancholy whine which so many of the peasants reckon ominous. The night waxed wilder and wilder; and, to augment the tempest, the fires flashed and the thunder roared in such rapid succession, that the walls of the chamber appeared in continual flame, and the furniture shook and clattered. Now I have heard of lovers who considered a stormy tryste night as a kind gift of fortune, and who could enlist the tempest which "roared and rustled"[82] around them into the service of love, and compel it to make a pathetic supplication in their behalf to an unmerciful mistress. I never liked these cloudy influences, and instead of making a vassal of elemental commotion, it always made a servant of me; a high wind and a storm, accompanied by thunder and fire, made me quiver and quake. I gave ample proof on this unfortunate night of my submission to the genius of the blast: the maid laid her white arm round my neck, and when she was soothing my terrors with soft words, the door of the chamber opened, and in glided her mother, saying, "Lassie, are ye waking?" To find a lover in her daughter's chamber was, perhaps, neither uncommon nor unexpected; but to find a new face, to find me, "Honest Man John Ochiltree," whose name was doomed to descend to posterity at the top of a ridiculous reel tune, the disclosure was to be dreaded; so the subtle maiden, unloosing a comb from a thick fleece of long auburn hair, threw such a profusion of ringlets over my face, as nearly suffocated me; waving her hand at the same time for her mother to retire.

'The prudent mother, however, advanced, saying, "Bless

me, lassie, this is a fearful night to have love-trystes and
wooester-daffin in. I have trysted on mony a queer night
myself, but on none that equalled this; yet I think nae the
waur of the lad who keeps his faith on a night that makes the
wide world tremble." The daughter still waved her hand,
but the dame was not to be daunted; and thus she persisted:
"But Jenny, my bonny bairn, when will ye put an end to these
dallyings; no that I would have ye to make your election
rashly, in the calf-love, as the rude proverb says, for ye're
young and no at the end of your teens till the bud be on the
bush; but when will ye quit these dallyings, I say, and single
out a discreet husband and a devout? Ye have rich lovers,
more than one or two, yet set not thy heart on the siller, lass,
though I would hardly counsel ye to wed without it. A loving
lad in lily white linen looks weel enough in a fule sang, but
give me the lad with bills and bonds, and good set siller, who
can fill and fetch mair. Yet make not gowd a god in the choice
of thy heart; though to give ye mair for a bridal-tocher than
three hundred pounds, and put ye into a fu' farm, is what I
wadnae counsel thy father to do." The daughter still waved
her mother to be gone; but the covering of my face excited the
good dame's suspicions, and she resolved to see me face to face,
though it might diminish the amount of Jenny's admirers.

'No resolution was ever carried more quickly into execu-
tion. "But Jenny, woman, what ails the lad that he hides his
face? if he has nae a face worth looking at, he's no a lad for
thee. And I ken not a lad in the parish who might wish to hide
his head, except that daft chield, Jock Ochiltree,—Jock
Gomeral[83] would suit him better. His grand-dame was burnt
for a witch at the West-bow port of Edinburgh; and if the
grandson was burnt for a fool, there would be no waste of fuel
on the family." And removing a handful of her daughter's
hair as she spoke, she saw me, and shouted, till her voice fairly
exceeded the tempest that still raged without: "Nay, but the
Lord preserve me! his presence be near! here's that gaping
goose, Jock Gowk himself; for my lips I wadnae defile with his
name, much less my arms with his person. Oh, to think that
ever thy mother's daughter thought of lending credit to such a
race, or bearing a bonnie bairntime to a born gomeral. Out
of my house, I say, out of my house; start, else I shall write
the notes of thy ain tune on thy face, seven crotchets to the
bar."

' "O mother," said the submissive daughter, "turn not the poor lad out on such a night as this: the thunder and fire, the flash and the din, will kill him; for he shakes at every clap like the leaf o' the linn."

' "Na, worse than all," shouted the dame, in a tone where scorn was blended with anger; "na, worse than all: to be but a fool is no such a failing; there's Captain what's his name? whose whole wit lies in feeding capons, and who is hardly fit for watching the worms from the kale, yet he's made a justice o' the peace: but what can one do with a coward? I'm wasting words; I'm whistling a reel tune to a mile-stone: out of my house, I say; I will not defile both window and door with thee, so leap and vanish." And holding up the casement, I leaped gladly out, happy at escaping from the wicked wagging of her tongue into the more endurable evil of wind, and rain, and fire.

'This unlucky repulse, with many a mischievous embellishment, flew over the parish; but I was not to be daunted. On the third evening after this mixed adventure of good and evil, I made an excursion beyond the limits of my parish; and entered upon the wild moorlands, where the dwellings are few and far between. A young man finds ready access among marriageable maidens; so I soon found myself seated at a sheep farmer's fire, in company of the good man's only daughter, a maid both ripe and rosy, with her father and mother, and some fifteen sheep dogs, as auditors of our conversation. At first, our talk was of that kind which newspapers call desultory; the weather, with all its variations; the fruits in their season; and the cattle after their kind; and contracting the circle of our scrutiny as we proceeded, we at last settled upon the cares of a pasture farm. We talked of sheep after their sorts, the Cheviot breed, the auld stock of Tinwald, the lang sheep and the short mug ewes, gimmers, crocks, and dinmans; nor did we fail to discuss the diseases which preyed on this patriarchal wealth; mawks and moorill, rot and leaping-illness; and so extensive was my knowledge in all this, and also on the more mysterious mischief of evil e'en, elf-arrows, and witchcraft, that the old dame grew astonished, and whispered to her husband: "This lad's words are worth drops of gold; speak him cannilie, Sandie, speak him cannilie." Her daughter, too, had her own thoughts: she appeared to employ herself with the intricacies of a skein of thread; but contrived at every

motion of her hand, to steal a glance at me from beneath a
thick mass of natural curls which rivalled in density, and
nearly in colour, the fairest fleece of any of her father's flock.
Her hand, too, unwittingly paused in its work, and shed back
the curls from her ears that she might hear more accurately
my ideas of fire-side economy and joy. The old man alone
seemed slow in entering into the prospect of wedding his
daughter's visible wealth, to one whose chief substance was
speculative. He sat solacing his thoughts with a scheme which
had no connexion with my happiness. I saw something sinister
in his looks; I heard him utter many a dry and dubious cough
as his wife urged his admission of me as a suitor; and perceived, like the half hope of bliss held out by the Puritans, that
I might be elected, but should never be chosen.

At this moment the latch of the door was lifted, and a
human figure tottered in, leaning twofold over a staff polished
like glass with long use. It was a neighbouring moorland
farmer, and a suitor to the maiden. He was dressed, or rather
encumbered with clothes, which in the shape of two coats, a
large one and a less, showed the antique skill of cloth-cutting
at the time of the Scottish persecution.[84] Over all these a large
plaid extended, and a bonnet that nearly overshaded the
plaid, crowned the whole. He removed this last mentioned
article, and displayed a face as sharp and biting as a northern
frost, and a couple of small, keen, and inquisitive grey eyes,
which seemed only acquainted with arithmetical calculation.
He smoothed back his locks, which seemed to have long
rebelled against the comb, and casting his eyes over us, said
with a prefatory cough;

' "Hale be thy heart, goodman, and happy be thine, good-
wife, and merry may thine be, Penney, my winsome quean,
mair by token I have sold seven score of dinmans, every cloot,
and all to buy thee a bridal garment, lass, and a horse to ride
on to the kirking; the fellow of whilk ye'll no find from Annan
to Nith. But who, in the name of all that's holy, can this
strange tyke be?" said this venerable gallant, casting a look of
no great delight on me; "his dress would scare the sheep, so
he can be no shepherd; and he seems to lack wit to watch the
hooded crows from his flock, so he cannot be wealthy;" and
with this unceremonious notice of me, he drew in a chair by
the side of the maiden, and stroked down her innumerable
curls with his hand, which smelled of tar equal to the suffoca-

tion of any town damsel. She smiled, for the smell was
frankincense to her; the ancient suitor smiled also,—a smile,
rivalling that of a death's head on a grave-stone, and said,
"Well may ye laugh, lassie; that's the right hand that lays on
the tar with mair skill than the proudest man in Tiviotdale,
and has more flocks to lay tar on, lassie,—seventy score of
brood ewes; but why need I brag? A man may ride a summer-
day on my farm and no get far over the boundary."

'I sat confounded at this display of opulence, which I saw
had a strong influence on the maiden's heart; while her father,
drawing near her, whispered, "Take him, Penney, take
him—he's a rich man and well arrayed—he has two tap-coats
and a plaid on."

'The shepherd maiden looked on this antiquated suitor,
and she looked on me; but the glow which unrequited love
spread over a face of eighteen barely balanced the matter
against territorial wealth and its grey-bearded owner. I had
no resource save in youth and health; but my adversary came
armed in the charms and might of property, and my more
modern looks made but a poor battle against the appeal
which riches made to maiden vanity. "Foolish lassie," said my
rival, in a tone which sounded like the first shovel-full of
churchyard earth thrown on the lid of a coffin,—"Foolish
lassie, why makest thou thy bright een glance from side to side
on this stripling and me, as if thou wouldst weigh us in a
balance? Who is this raw youth, thinkest thou? The owner of
his own proper person, the laird of no-town-brae, as the proverb says, and lord of windy-wa's,[85] as singeth the auld sang.
He may wooe you with fine words, but will he drop a bonnet
piece of beaten gold in thy lap for every sigh he gives? he
may please thee with his face, and, bating that he looks like a
fool, his looks are well enough; but can he cast cantraips over
ye as I can do? can he scatter golden spells and paper charms
in thy lap, and make ye lady of as mickle land as a hooded
crow will fly over when he seeks to prey on the earliest lamb
of spring?"

'And as the old man spoke, he produced from the nook-
pouch of his plaid a kind of wallet of rough calf-skin, secured
with many a strap and string, which he unloosed with a kind
of prolonged delight, and then diving into the bosom of this
mouldy sanctuary of Mammon, fished up the remains of an
old stocking. "Haud thy lap, Penney, my woman," said the

owner; and he emptied with a clang into the maiden's lap
upwards of an hundred antique pieces of Scottish gold, which
avarice had arrested in their circulation before the accession
of the house of Stuart. "There's as mickle as will array thee
for the bridal, and here's documents for property which I will
give thee the moment the kirk buckles us." An old piece of
leather, which the diligence of the owner had fashioned from
a saddle-lap into a pocket-book, supplied him with sundry
papers, which he described as he submitted them to her
examination. "That's a haud-fast bond on the lands of the
laird of Sloken-drouth for seven hundred pounds Scots, a' sure
siller; that's the rights of the lands of Knockhoolie, thirty-five
pounds yearly, and ye'll be called the dame of Knockhoolie, a
bonnie title and weel sounding."

'But why should I prolong a story of which all who hearken
must know the upshot? I saw the wicked speed that Mammon
made in the maiden's affections, and sat dumbfounded and
despairing. Her look, which was one of grave consideration at
first, gradually brightened and expanded; she looked at the
riches and she looked at him, and said, "But I'm to have the
cheese-siller, and the siller for the udder-locks;[86] a riding
habit, brown or blue, or one of both; a grey horse and a side
saddle. I am to gang to the two fairs of Dumfries, the St.
James's fair of Lanark, to the Cameronian sacrament, and to
have a dance twice a year—once at Beltane, and once at
Hallowmass."[87]

' "All shall be as thou sayest, Penney, my princess," said
her lover, interrupting, probably, a long list of expected
luxuries; "so name the bridal-day."

'My vexation now exceeded all bounds of decorum, and I
spoke: "I would counsel ye to name the day soon, for the
bridegroom has not an hour to lose; the bridal cups will barely
be dry before they're lacked for his lyke wake; he has little
time to spare."

'The bride, as I may safely call her, laughed till her eyes
were wet, and said, "Well spoken, young man, that's the most
sensible thing ye have said this blessed night; and so, as there
is no time to be lost, ye say, let us be married on Saturday;
let the fault fall on the lag end of the week." For this mention
of early joy the bridegroom endeavoured to inflict the penance
of a kiss on the lips which uttered it.—"Haud off," said the
damsel, "filthy body, ye stink of tar; bide off till the blessing's

said, till the meat be consecrated; go home, and nurse your breath, for it's wondrous feeble."

'I now rose to depart; the bride conducted me to the door, and endeavoured to console me in a departing whisper: "This is Monday,—I'm to be wed on Saturday,—let me see,—my father and mother will be frae hame on Thursday, so come owre here in the braw moonlight, and let us have an hour's running round the haystacks, and daffin in the darksome nooks. Auld Worlds-worm,—Auld Simon Setsiller,—him there with the twa tap-coats and the plaid on, wha has not as much breath as would bless his breakfast, he'll ne'er be the wiser on't: what he disnae ken will give him no manner of trouble." We parted, but we met no more.

'After this unsuccessful inroad on the moorlands, I resolved to push my fortune no farther, without some more sensible assurance of success. I was, therefore, on the look out for the young and the handsome: I frequented fairs with the fidelity of a horse dealer; attended all the merry-makings round, with the punctuality of a fiddler; and went devoutly to the kirk, with the regularity of an ancient maiden whose thoughts had been weaned, by the counsel of aching bones and the elo-quence of wrinkles, from free love to religion. But I was doomed to every species of mortification and repulse, and had actually in despair procured a copy of the register of maidens' baptisms in the parish, with the serious resolution of courting them regularly forward, according to their seniority of claim, when the wheel of fortune turned up one of her brightest spokes.

'As I sat pondering on my luckless lot, a slender fair-haired girl of fourteen, the daughter of a respectable and opulent farmer, came gliding like a sylph to my side, and, with a manner conscious and sly, said, that her father and her mother were gone to a bridal, and that her elder sister, Bess, desired my company to curds and cream, and to help her to while away the fore-night. Now her sister was one of the merriest and rosiest girls in the district; had a dancing foot and a fine ankle, and a voice which lent a grace to old songs which the best of your theatrical quaverers fail to impart. I need not say that her invitation charmed me: I lavished ribands, as well as thanks, on the bearer of this pleasing news, and passed my hand over her long and curling hair, saying, "An' thou be spared, some lad will sigh at his supper for thee

yet." She set out a fair chin and a white bosom to the motion
of my hand, and seemed perfectly aware, though young now,
that she would be older in summer. She tripped to the door,
and looking back with an archness of manner, and a roguish
glance of her eye, said, "Ye might have done waur than given
me a kiss to carry to my sister, and ane to myself for carrying
it;" and uttering a loud laugh as she saw me rise to follow,
away she bounded as light and graceful as a woodland fairy.
An old beggar woman looked after her as she fled, and shook
her crutch at her: "Ah, thou young wanton, I heard thy
words: they who learn young learn fair, and it's worse to keep
the kitten frae the kirn than the auld cat; but see what it all
comes to; a lamiter's crutch and an awmous-powk: nought
will be a warning!" and the old woman groaned bitterly as
she halted along at the memory of merrier days.

'I was true to tryste, and turned my steps to the farmer's
residence a little after twilight; the windows were gleaming
with light, and the din of merriment resounded far and wide.
My fairy messenger met me at the door, and standing on
tiptoe, whispered in my ear, "Come away, ye have been lang
looked for: there's naebody here but Jock Gordon of Goose-
dub, Rab Robson of Rowantree-burn, and Davie Wilson of
Ballacraig; ye ken all the rest except the young laird of
Moorbirn and his cousin, whom men call Daunering John." I
entered, and found my knowledge was much more limited
than the girl imagined; the farmer's hall was filled with
strange faces, for three parishes round had each sent its contribution of youthful flesh and blood.

Ten came east, and ten came west,[88]
    And ten came rowing o'er the water;
Twa came down the long dike side,
    There's twa and thirty wooing at her.

'But if the heroine of Tintock-top[89] rivalled bonnie Bess in
the amount of her wooers, I question if she excelled her in the
native tact and good management with which she kept in sub-
ordination so many fiery and intractable dispositions. We
were all seated round a large table, at the head of which the
maiden herself presided, distributing her glances among her
admirers with an equal and a judicious diligence. Curds and
cream, and tea, were in succession handed round; she partook

of both, uniting in her own person the pastoral taste of the mountains with the refinement of the vales: songs were sung; she assisted in the strain, and her voice was sweet and delightful; and thus the evening hours flew by. But amid all this show of harmony and good fellowship, an experienced eye might observe, by the clouding brow and restrained joy of many, that the breeze of love which blew so soft and so balmy would soon burst out into tempest and storm. It is certainly a hazardous policy in such matters to collect a number of admirers face to face: in the silent darkness of a solitary tryste, the lover imagines himself the sole, or at least, the favoured admirer; and after breathing a brief vow, and tasting the joy of a half yielded kiss, he returns home, leaving his mistress to the nocturnal hardihood and superior address of a more artful lover. But seated with your rivals at your side, your jealousy of affection rises in arms against your peace, and you begin to sum up the hours you have been blessed in her company, and to multiply them by the number of her admirers, conceding in despair a fractional part of affection to yourself, while it is plain your rivals have revelled in round numbers. There is no temper can long endure this; and it seemed plain that my fellow suitors regarded our meeting as a general field-day,—a numbering of the people, that she might wonder over the amount of her admirers and the force of her own charms.

'Conversation began at last to flag, and silence ensued. "For my own part," said an upland shepherd, "I came here for an hour of quiet joy in a dark nook, the darker the better; but here's nought but an assembly of fools from the four winds of heaven, bending their darkening brows at one another, and a young lass sitting to count the strokes they strike, and to reckon every bruised brow a sure sign of her influence among men. Deil have me if I like it; so let short peace and long strife be among ye; and for you, my bonnie dame, the less ye make sport of honest hearts, the less sport will evil hearts make of you, and so I leave you:" and away he strode, whistling manfully the tune of the gallant Graemes, in token of defiance. "Let him go, the rough-footed moorcock, that can clap his wings, but never crow," said a ploughman from the vale of Ae; "the smell of tar and tainted mutton is diminished since his departure." This was touching on a perilous theme,—the old feud which exists between the pastoral and agricultural districts. "I would advise ye lads," said a youth of moorland

descent, "to eat well of wether mutton and moorcocks afore
ye speak lightly of aught that's bred among mosses; ye may
need all your strength to maintain unguarded words. Lord, if
my cousin of Blackhagg were here, he would make ye eat your
own words, though every one were as ill to swallow as a
pound of hiplock wool." The incensed tiller of the holms of Ae
started to his feet, his utterance nearly choked with rage:
"Rise, ye moorland coof, ye two-footed tender of four-footed
brutes, lacking as much in sense as ye lack in number of limbs;
rise this precious moment, else I'll give ye the blow where ye
sit." The man of the moors was not slow in attempting to rise;
the brawny arm of a brother shepherd, which clutched his
gorget with a grasp equal to the tethering of a bull, alone
retarded his rising. "Let him alone, I say, Sandie; just let him
alone," said the shepherd; "be civil at a douce man's hearth
before his weelfaured daughter: ye ken the auld say; Be the
saint in the hall, and the devil on the greensward; meaning,
nae doubt, that we should carry our mischief out of doors: I'll
stretch him as straight as one of his own furrows before an
hour blow by, and on the same place too, the lily lea." The
wrath of the husbandman was turned on this doughty auxiliary, and, having a divided aim, it burnt fiercely between
them, without harming either. Meantime, other tongues took
part in the commotion: parochial nick-names, and family failings, and personal defects, were bandied from side to side,
with all the keenness of rustic wit, and the malice of rivalry;
while, on the whole, the maiden sat and looked as one would
on a fire burning too fiercely to be quenched.

'It was not my wish to distinguish myself in this strife of
tongues, and therefore I sat still, maintaining an expression of
face which I hoped would carry me quietly through this
stormy tide of contention. I was only deceiving myself.

' "And ye'll sit mute and motionless there, and hear the
bonnie green hills of Annandale turned, by the malice of
man's wit, into moudie-tammocks," said a shepherd to me;
"Up and speak, for I have spoken till I'm as hoarse as a
raven; or rise and fight; if ye have not a tongue in your head,
ye may have a soul in your body."

'All turned their eyes on me at this address, and the uproar
subsided for a time to hear my answer to this singular
appeal.

' "A soul in his body," shouted a rustic, in a tone which

implied something like a suspicion of my right to the spark immortal, "Have ye not heard the scoffing sang that's ringing from side to side of the country? I wonder the subject of such verses presumed to show his face among sponsible folk."

'And to my utter shame and confusion of face, he proceeded to chant the following rude verse, looking all the while on me with an eye sparkling with scorn and derision:

O, have ye not heard of John Ochiltree?[90]
    That dainty chield John Ochiltree?
The owl has a voice, and the cat an ee,
    And so has sonsie John Ochiltree.
An ancient woman wonn'd in Colean,
She had never a tooth 'tween her lips but ane,
She mumbled her meat with a horn spoon,
Yet she fell in love with a bonnie new tune;
She bobb'd on her crutches so frank and so free,
To the dainty tune of John Ochiltree.

'As the verse ended, a laugh burst out which made the roof shake over our heads, to show how fickle men's passions are, and the mortification I was doomed to endure. To be the subject of ludicrous rhymes is to have an infection about one equal to the plague. My fellow suitors shunned me, and the capricious maiden herself assumed an air so haughty and decided that I saw my cause was cureless. All this was witnessed by one who sympathized in my sufferings, and whose ready wit suggested an instant remedy. The milkiness of my nature had already given way to the accumulating reproach; I had started to my feet, and taken one stride towards my rhyming persecutor with a clenched fist, and a face burning in anger, when the young girl who brought me the invitation to this unlucky tryste, uttered a scream, and holding up her hand, laid her ear to the floor like one listening intensely. We all stood mute and motionless: she darted to the door with the rapidity of light, returned in a moment half-breathless, and exclaimed in a voice of seeming despair, "Oh! Bess, Bess, what will become of ye? Here's Hazelbank; here's our ain father coming up the road. If he sees what I see, he'll burn Solway, be it for him or against him."

'Like a brood of chickens when the hawk descends, so started, so fluttered, and so flew in all directions this meeting

of rivals; the door seemed far too narrow for escape. Seven
bounded over the stack-yard dike, and three leaped over a
quickset hedge six feet high; two ran down the middle of a
corn-field, with half the dogs of the place pursuing them; and
two, who were strangers, in the haste of escape, fairly leaped
into a pond, or small lake, and made good their retreat by
swimming to the opposite side. In one minute the clamorous
hall of Hazelbank was as mute as a kirk at midnight. As I
hastened to retreat with the others, a white hand twitched me
cunningly by the sleeve, and pulled me aside into a little
closet, where two very warm and ripe lips whispered close in
my ear, "Let the gowks flee, they know not the goose's quack
from the eagle's cry; my father's far from home:"—and, shutting the chamber-door as she spoke, my bonnie and discreet
messenger added:—"My sister Bess is in her grand moods this
night; she carries her head o'er high, and winna speak to ye,
for the foolery of that silly sang. A pretty thing, to lose a weel-
faured lad for the sake of an idle rhyme: sae bide with me; I
am almost as tall as Bess is; and I'll be fifteen at midsummer."

'And now,' said this representative of the rustic name of
Ochiltree, 'I shall stay my narrative; feeling something of the
distress of a traveller who comes to the shedlands of sundry
roads, and knows not which one to elect; for the adventures
which befell me were manifold, and seem in my sight all alike
curious and important. But I cannot expect douce greyheaded
folk will listen to the idle tales of youthful times. I might have
made far more imposing stories of my misadventures among
the maidens; for they are not unsusceptible of poetical embellishment; but I despise fictions, and laugh at "the idly feigned
poetic pains"[91] of metre ballad makers; I abide by the old
proverb, "truth tells aye best." '

'Truth tells aye best indeed,' re-echoed an ancient dame,
as she sat by the hall fire, 'and yet, idle fictions, and the
embellishments,—I think that's the word ye used,—of a poetic
fancy, seem to flow off as glibly as the current of truth itself.
Ah! thou auld-farrand ane, dost thou think to pass off the
pleasant inventions of thy own fertile brain for the well-known
tales of thy early courtship? Ah, my lad,'—and she eyed him
with a look where humour and seriousness seemed striving for
mastery,—'ye are kenned where ye least hope it; far kenned
and noted is thy name, as the rhyme-maker said of Satan.[92]

And so ye say, you are John Ochiltree, and suffered in your youth from maiden's scorn and minstrel's sang? A bonnie tale, indeed! D'ye think I don't know the merry goodman of Dootagen, Simon Rodan by name, whom I have known since he was the height of a pint-stoup. More by token, he plundered my plum-trees when he was a boy, and climbed in at my chamber windows afore the beard was on his chin, and all to woo three of my servant maidens, and my own cousin, bonnie Jeanie Carruthers.—Scorned by the lasses, indeed! Mickle scorn have they endured for thee. Ah! thou flatterer, and bonnie tale teller. Many a good advice hast thou received from the parish minister and elders, in full session assembled. A lad the like of Simon Rodan, with all the failings he had, was not to be seen in seven hours' riding.—A straighter, or a more taper leg never set its foot in a black leather shoe; and it's not much the worse o' the wear yet.'

ELPHIN IRVING,
THE FAIRIES' CUPBEARER

'The lady kilted her kirtle green,[93]
    A little aboon her knee,
The lady snooded her yellow hair
    A little aboon her bree,
And she's gane to the good green wood
    As fast as she could hie.

'And first she let the black steed pass,
    And syne she let the brown,
And then she flew to the milk-white steed,
    And pull'd the rider down:
Syne out then sang the queen o' the fairies,
    Frae 'midst a hank of broom,
She that has won him, young Tamlane,
    Has gotten a gallant groom.'
               Old Ballad

The romantic vale of Corriewater, in Annandale, is regarded by the inhabitants, a pastoral and unmingled people, as the last border refuge of those beautiful and capricious beings, the fairies. Many old people, yet living, imagine they have had intercourse of good words and good deeds with the 'good folk;' and continue to tell that in the ancient of days the fairies danced on the hill, and revelled in the glen, and showed themselves, like the mysterious children of the deity of old, among the sons and daughters of men. Their visits to the earth were periods of joy and mirth to mankind, rather than of sorrow and apprehension. They played on musical instruments of wonderful sweetness and variety of note, spread unexpected feasts, the supernatural flavour of which overpowered on many occasions the religious scruples of the Presbyterian shepherds, performed wonderful deeds of horsemanship, and marched in midnight processions, when the sound of their elfin minstrelsy charmed youths and maidens into love for their persons and pursuits; and more than one family of Corriewater have the fame of augmenting the numbers of the elfin chivalry. Faces of friends and relatives, long since doomed to the battle-trench, or the deep sea, have been recognized by those who dared to gaze on the fairy march. The maid has seen her lost lover, and the mother her stolen child; and the courage to plan and achieve their deliverance has been possessed by, at least, one border maiden. In the legends of the people of Corrievale there is a singular mixture of elfin and human adventure, and the traditional story of the Cupbearer to the Queen of the Fairies appeals alike to our domestic feelings and imagination.

In one of the little green loops, or bends, on the banks of Corriewater, mouldered walls, and a few stunted wild plum-trees, and vagrant roses, still point out the site of a cottage and garden. A well of pure spring-water leaps out from an old tree-root before the door; and here the shepherds, shading themselves in summer from the influence of the sun, tell to their children the wild tale of Elphin Irving, and his sister Phemie; and, singular as the story seems, it has gained full credence among the people where the scene is laid.

'I ken the tale and the place weel,' interrupted an old Scottish woman, who, from the predominance of scarlet in her apparel, seemed to have been a follower of the camp,[94] 'I ken them weel, and the tale's as true as a bullet to its aim, and a spark to powder. Oh, bonnie Corriewater, a thousand times have I pulled gowans on its banks wi' ane that lies stiff and stark on a foreign shore in a bloody grave:' and sobbing audibly, she drew the remains of a military cloak over her face, and allowed the story to proceed.

When Elphin Irving and his sister Phemie were in their six-teenth year, for tradition says they were twins, their father was drowned in Corriewater, attempting to save his sheep from a sudden swell, to which all mountain streams are liable; and their mother, on the day of her husband's burial, laid down her head on the pillow, from which, on the seventh day, it was lifted to be dressed for the same grave. The inheritance left to the orphans may be briefly described: seventeen acres of plough and pasture land, seven milk cows, and seven pet sheep (many old people take delight in odd numbers;) and to this may be added, seven bonnet-pieces of Scottish gold, and a broad sword and spear, which their ancestor had wielded with such strength and courage in the battle of Dryfe-sands,

that the minstrel who sang of that deed of arms ranked him
only second to the Scotts and Johnstones.

The youth and his sister grew in stature and in beauty.
The brent bright brow, the clear blue eye, and frank and
blithe deportment of the former, gave him some influence
among the young women of the valley; while the latter was no
less the admiration of the young men, and at fair and dance,
and at bridal, happy was he who touched but her hand, or
received the benediction of her eye. Like all other Scottish
beauties, she was the theme of many a song; and while tradition is yet busy with the singular history of her brother, song
has taken all the care that rustic minstrelsy can of the gentleness of her spirit, and the charms of her person.

'Now I vow,' exclaimed a wandering piper, 'by mine own
honoured instrument, and by all other instruments, that ever
yielded music for the joy and delight of mankind, that there
are more bonnie songs made about fair Phemie Irving than
about all other dames of Annandale, and many of them are
both high and bonnie. A proud lass maun she be, if her spirit
hears; and men say, the dust lies not insensible of beautiful
verse; for her charms are breathed through a thousand sweet
lips, and no farther gone than yestermorn, I heard a lass singing on a green hill-side what I shall not readily forget. If ye
like to listen, ye shall judge; and it will not stay the story long,
nor mar it much, for it is short, and about Phemie Irving;'
and accordingly he chanted the following rude verses, not
unaccompanied by his honoured instrument, as he called his
pipe, which chimed in with great effect, and gave richness to
a voice which felt better than it could express:—

FAIR PHEMIE IRVING[95]

I.

Gay is thy glen, Corrie,
    With all thy groves flowering;
Green is thy glen, Corrie,
    When July is showering;
And sweet is yon wood where
    The small birds are bowering,
And there dwells the sweet one
    Whom I am adoring.

2.

Her round neck is whiter
        Than winter when snowing;
Her meek voice is milder
        Than Ae in its flowing;
The glad ground yields music
        Where she goes by the river;
One kind glance would charm me
        For ever and ever.

3.

The proud and the wealthy
        To Phemie are bowing;
No looks of love win they
        With sighing or suing;
Far away maun I stand
        With my rude wooing,
She's a flow'ret too lovely
        To bloom for my pu'ing.

4.

O were I yon violet,
        On which she is walking;
O were I yon small bird,
        To which she is talking;
Or yon rose in her hand,
        With its ripe ruddy blossom;
Or some pure gentle thought,
        To be blest with her bosom.

This minstrel interruption, while it established Phemie
Irving's claim to grace and to beauty, gave me additional
confidence to pursue the story—

But minstrel skill, and true love tale, seemed to want their
usual influence, when they sought to win her attention; she
was only observed to pay most respect to those youths who
were most beloved by her brother; and the same hour that
brought these twins to the world, seemed to have breathed
through them a sweetness and an affection of heart and mind,
which nothing could divide. If, like the virgin queen of the
immortal poet, she walked 'in maiden meditation fancy
free,'[96] her brother Elphin seemed alike untouched with the

charms of the fairest virgins in Corrie. He ploughed his field,
he reaped his grain, he leaped, he ran, and wrestled, and
danced, and sang, with more skill, and life, and grace, than
all other youths of the district; but he had no twilight and
stolen interviews: when all other young men had their loves
by their side, he was single, though not unsought; and his joy
seemed never perfect, save when his sister was near him. If
he loved to share his time with her, she loved to share her time
with him alone, or with the beasts of the field, or the birds of
the air. She watched her little flock late, and she tended it
early; not for the sordid love of the fleece, unless it was to
make mantles for her brother, but with the look of one who
had joy in its company. The very wild creatures, the deer and
the hares, seldom sought to shun her approach, and the bird
forsook not its nest, nor stinted its song, when she drew nigh;
such is the confidence which maiden innocence and beauty
inspire.

It happened one summer, about three years after they
became orphans, that rain had been for awhile withheld from
the earth, the hill-sides began to parch, the grass in the vales
to wither, and the stream of Corrie was diminished between
its banks to the size of an ordinary rill. The shepherds drove
their flocks to moor lands, and marsh and tarn had their reeds
invaded by the scythe, to supply the cattle with food. The
sheep of his sister were Elphin's constant care; he drove them
to the moistest pastures during the day, and he often watched
them at midnight, when flocks, tempted by the sweet dewy
grass, are known to browse eagerly, that he might guard them
from the fox, and lead them to the choicest herbage. In these
nocturnal watchings he sometimes drove his little flock over
the water of Corrie, for the fords were hardly ankle-deep; or
permitted his sheep to cool themselves in the stream, and taste
the grass which grew along the brink. All this time not a drop
of rain fell, nor did a cloud appear in the sky.

One evening, during her brother's absence with the flock,
Phemie sat at her cottage-door, listening to the bleatings of
the distant folds, and the lessened murmur of the water of
Corrie, now scarcely audible beyond its banks. Her eyes,
weary with watching along the accustomed line of road for
the return of Elphin, were turned on the pool beside her, in
which the stars were glimmering fitful and faint. As she looked
she imagined the water grew brighter and brighter; a wild

illumination presently shone upon the pool, and leaped from
bank to bank, and suddenly changing into a human form,
ascended the margin, and, passing her, glided swiftly into the
cottage. The visionary form was so like her brother in shape
and air, that starting up, she flew into the house, with the
hope of finding him in his customary seat. She found him not,
and impressed with the terror which a wraith or apparition
seldom fails to inspire, she uttered a shriek so loud and so
piercing as to be heard at Johnstone bank, on the other side of
the vale of Corrie.

An old woman now rose suddenly from her seat in the
window-sill, the living dread of shepherds, for she travelled
the country with a brilliant reputation for witchcraft, and thus
she broke in upon the narrative: 'I vow, young man, ye tell
us the truth upset and down-thrust. I heard my douce grandmother say, that on the night when Elphin Irving disappeared—disappeared I shall call it, for the bairn can but be
gone for a season, to return to us in his own appointed
time,—she was seated at the fire-side at Johnstone bank; the
laird had laid aside his bonnet to take the book, when a shriek
mair loud, believe me, than a mere woman's shriek,—and
they can shriek loud enough, else they're sair wranged,—came
over the water of Corrie, so sharp and shrilling, that the
pewter plates dinneled on the wall: such a shriek, my douce
grandmother said, as rang in her ear till the hour of her death,
and she lived till she was aughty and aught, forty full ripe
years after the event. But there is another matter, which,
doubtless, I cannot compel ye to believe; it was the common
rumour that Elphin Irving came not into the world like the
other sinful creatures of the earth, but was one of the Kane-
bairns of the fairies, whilk they had to pay to the enemy of
man's salvation, every seventh year. The poor lady-fairy,—a
mother's aye a mother, be she Elve's flesh or Eve's flesh,—hid
her Elf son beside the christened flesh in Marion Irving's
cradle, and the auld enemy lost his prey for a time. Now hasten on with your story, which is not a bodle the waur for
me. The maiden saw the shape of her brother,—fell into a
faint, or a trance, and the neighbours came flocking in:—gang
on with your tale, young man, and dinna be affronted because
an auld woman helped ye wi't.'

It is hardly known, I resumed, how long Phemie Irving
continued in a state of insensibility. The morning was far

advanced, when a neighbouring maiden found her seated in an old chair, as white as monumental marble; her hair, about which she had always been solicitous, loosened from its curls, and hanging disordered over her neck and bosom, her hands and forehead; the maiden touched the one, and kissed the other; they were as cold as snow: and her eyes, wide open, were fixed on her brother's empty chair, with the intensity of gaze of one who had witnessed the appearance of a spirit. She seemed insensible of any one's presence, and sat fixed, and still, and motionless. The maiden, alarmed at her looks, thus addressed her:—'Phemie, lass, Phemie Irving! dear me, but this be awful! I have come to tell ye that seven of your pet sheep have escaped drowning in the water; for Corrie, sae quiet and sae gentle yestreen, is rolling and dashing frae bank to bank this morning. Dear me, woman, dinna let the loss of the world's gear bereave ye of your senses. I would rather make ye a present of a dozen mug-ewes of the Tinwald brood myself; and now I think on't, if ye'll send over Elphin, I will help him hame with them in the gloaming myself. So, Phemie, woman, be comforted.'

At the mention of her brother's name she cried out, 'Where is he? Oh, where is he?'—gazed wildly round, and shuddering from head to foot, fell senseless on the floor. Other inhabitants of the valley, alarmed by the sudden swell of the river, which had augmented to a torrent, deep and impassable, now came in to inquire if any loss had been sustained, for numbers of sheep and teds of hay had been observed floating down about the dawn of the morning. They assisted in reclaiming the unhappy maiden from her swoon; but insensibility was joy, compared to the sorrow to which she awakened. 'They have ta'en him away, they have ta'en him away,' she chanted, in a tone of delirious pathos; 'him that was whiter and fairer than the lily on Lyddal-lee. They have long sought, and they have long sued, and they had the power to prevail against my prayers at last. They have ta'en him away; the flower is plucked from among the weeds, and the dove is slain amid a flock of ravens. They came with shout, and they came with song, and they spread the charm, and they placed the spell, and the baptized brow has been bowed down to the unbaptized hand. They have ta'en him away, they have ta'en him away; he was too lovely, and too good, and too noble, to bless us with his continuance on earth; for what are the sons of men compared to him?—the light of the moon-beam to the morning sun; the glow-worm to the eastern star. They have ta'en him away; the invisible dwellers of the earth. I saw them come on him with shouting and with singing, and they charmed him where he sat, and away they bore him; and the horse he rode was never shod with iron, nor owned, before, the mastery of human hand. They have ta'en him away over the water, and over the wood, and over the hill. I got but ae look of his bonnie blue ee, but ae, ae look. But as I have endured what never maiden endured, so will I undertake what never maiden undertook, I will win him from them all. I know the invisible ones of the earth; I have heard their wild and wondrous music in the wild woods, and there shall a christened maiden seek him, and achieve his deliverance.' She paused, and glancing around a circle of condoling faces, down which the tears were dropping like rain, said, in a calm and altered, but still delirious tone—'Why do you weep, Mary Halliday? and why do you weep, John Graeme? Ye think that Elphin Irving,—oh, it's a bonnie, bonnie name, and dear to many a maiden's heart as well as mine,—ye think he is drowned in Corrie, and ye will seek in the deep, deep pools for the bonnie, bonnie corse, that ye may weep over it, as it lies in its last linen, and lay it, amid weeping and wailing, in the dowie kirk-yard. Ye may seek, but ye shall never find; so leave me to trim up my hair, and prepare my dwelling, and make myself ready to watch for the hour of his return to upper earth.' And she resumed her household labours with an alacrity which lessened not the sorrow of her friends.

Meanwhile the rumour flew over the vale that Elphin Irving was drowned in Corriewater. Matron and maid, old man and young, collected suddenly along the banks of the river, which now began to subside to its natural summer limits, and commenced their search; interrupted every now and then by calling from side to side, and from pool to pool, and by exclamations of sorrow for this misfortune. The search was fruitless: five sheep, pertaining to the flock which he conducted to pasture, were found drowned in one of the deep eddies; but the river was still too brown, from the soil of its moorland sources, to enable them to see what its deep shelves, its pools, and its overhanging and hazely banks concealed. They remitted farther search till the stream should become pure; and old man taking old man aside, began to whisper about the mystery of the youth's disappearance: old women laid their lips to the ears of their coevals, and talked of Elphin Irving's fairy parentage, and his having been dropped by an unearthly hand into a Christian cradle. The young men and maids conversed on other themes; they grieved for the loss of the friend and the lover, and while the former thought that a heart so kind and true was not left in the vale, the latter thought, as maidens will, on his handsome person, gentle manners, and merry blue eye, and speculated with a sigh on the time when they might have hoped a return for their love. They were soon joined by others who had heard the wild and delirious language of his sister: the old belief was added to the new assurance, and both again commented upon by minds full of superstitious feeling, and hearts full of supernatural fears, till the youths and maidens of Corrievale held no more love trystes for seven days and nights, lest, like Elphin Irving, they should be carried away to augment the ranks of the unchristened chivalry.

It was curious to listen to the speculations of the peasantry. 'For my part,' said a youth, 'if I were sure that poor Elphin escaped from that perilous water, I would not give the fairies a pound of hiplock wool for their chance of him. There has not been a fairy seen in the land since Donald Cargil, the Cameronian, conjured them into the Solway for playing on their pipes during one of his nocturnal preachings on the hip of the Burnswark hill.'

'Preserve me, bairn,' said an old woman, justly exasperated at the incredulity of her nephew, 'if ye winna believe what I both heard and saw at the moonlight end of Craigyburnwood on a summer night, rank after rank of the fairy folk; ye'll at least believe a douce man and a ghostly professor, even the late minister of Tinwaldkirk: his only son, I mind the lad weel with his long yellow locks and his bonnie blue eyes, when I was but a gilpie of a lassie, *he* was stolen away from off the horse at his father's elbow, as they crossed that false and fearsome water, even Locherbriggflow, on the night of the Midsummer fair of Dumfries. Aye, aye, who can doubt the truth of that; have not the godly inhabitants of Almsfieldtown and Tinwaldkirk seen the sweet youth riding at midnight, in the midst of the unhallowed troop, to the sound of flute and of dulcimer; and though meikle they prayed, naebody tried to achieve his deliverance.'

'I have heard it said by douce folk and sponsible,' interrupted another, 'that every seven years the elves and fairies pay kane, or make an offering of one of their children to the grand enemy of salvation, and that they are permitted to purloin one of the children of men to present to the fiend; a more acceptable offering, I'll warrant, than one of their own infernal brood that are Satan's sib allies, and drink a drop of the deil's blood every May morning. And touching this lost lad, ye all ken his mother was a hawk of an uncannie nest, a second cousin of Kate Kimmer, of Barfloshan, as rank a witch as ever rode on ragwort. Aye, Sirs, what's bred in the bone is ill to come out of the flesh.'

On these and similar topics, which a peasantry full of ancient tradition and enthusiasm, and superstition, readily associate with the commonest occurrences of life, the people of Corrievale continued to converse till the fall of evening; when each seeking their home, renewed again the wondrous subject, and illustrated it with all that popular belief and poetic imagination could so abundantly supply.

The night which followed this melancholy day was wild with wind and rain; the river came down broader and deeper than before, and the lightning, flashing by fits over the green woods of Corrie, showed the ungovernable and perilous flood sweeping above its banks. It happened that a farmer, returning from one of the border fairs, encountered the full swing of the storm; but mounted on an excellent horse, and mantled from chin to heel in a good grey plaid, beneath which he had the farther security of a thick great-coat, he sat dry in his saddle, and proceeded in the anticipated joy of a subsided tempest and a glowing morning sun. As he entered the long grove, or rather remains of the old Galwegian forest, which lines for some space the banks of the Corriewater, the storm began to abate, the wind sighed milder and milder among the trees; and here and there a star, twinkling momentarily through the sudden rack of the clouds, showed the river raging from bank to brae. As he shook the moisture from his clothes, he was not without a wish that the day would dawn, and that he might be preserved on a road which his imagination beset with greater perils than the raging river; for his superstitious feeling let loose upon his path elf and goblin, and the current traditions of the district supplied very largely to his apprehension the ready materials of fear.

Just as he emerged from the wood, where a fine sloping bank, covered with short green sward, skirts the limit of the forest, his horse made a full pause, snorted, trembled, and started from side to side, stooped his head, erected his ears, and seemed to scrutinize every tree and bush. The rider, too, it may be imagined, gazed round and round, and peered warily into every suspicious looking place. His dread of a supernatural visitation was not much allayed, when he observed a female shape seated on the ground at the root of a huge old oak-tree, which stood in the centre of one of those patches of verdant sward, known by the name of 'fairy rings,' and avoided by all peasants who wish to prosper. A long thin gleam of eastern daylight enabled him to examine accurately the being who, in this wild place and unusual hour, gave additional terror to this haunted spot. She was dressed in white from the neck to the knees; her arms, long, and round, and white, were perfectly bare; her head, uncovered, allowed her long hair to descend in ringlet succeeding ringlet, till the half of her person was nearly concealed in the fleece. Amidst the whole, her hands were constantly busy in shedding aside the tresses which interposed between her steady and uninterrupted gaze, down a line of old road which winded among the hills to an ancient burial ground.

As the traveller continued to gaze, the figure suddenly rose, and wringing the rain from her long locks, paced round and round the tree, chanting in a wild and melancholy manner an equally wild and delirious song.

THE FAIRY OAK OF CORRIEWATER[97]

I.

The small bird's head is under its wing,
　　The deer sleeps on the grass;
The moon comes out, and the stars shine down,
　　The dew gleams like the glass:
There is no sound in the world so wide,
　　Save the sound of the smitten brass,
With the merry cittern and the pipe
　　Of the fairies as they pass.—
But oh! the fire maun burn and burn,
And the hour is gone, and will never return.

2.

The green hill cleaves, and forth, with a bound,
    Comes elf and elfin steed;
The moon dives down in a golden cloud,
    The stars grow dim with dread;
But a light is running along the earth,
    So of heaven's they have no need:
O'er moor and moss with a shout they pass,
    And the word is spur and speed—
But the fire maun burn, and I maun quake,
And the hour is gone that will never come back.

3.

And when they came to Craigyburnwood,
    The Queen of the fairies spoke;
'Come, bind your steeds to the rushes so green,
    And dance by the haunted oak:
I found the acorn on Heshbon-hill,
    In the nook of a palmer's poke,[98]
A thousand years since; here it grows!'
    And they danced till the greenwood shook—
But oh! the fire, the burning fire,
The longer it burns, it but blazes the higher.

4.

'I have won me a youth,' the Elf-queen said,
    'The fairest that earth may see;
This night I have won young Elph Irving
    My cup-bearer to be.
His service lasts but for seven sweet years,
    And his wage is a kiss of me.'
And merrily, merrily, laugh'd the wild elves
    Round Corrie's greenwood tree.—
But oh! the fire it glows in my brain,
And the hour is gone, and comes not again.

5.

The Queen she has whisper'd a secret word,
    'Come hither, my Elphin sweet,
And bring that cup of the charmed wine,
    Thy lips and mine to weet.'
But a brown elf shouted a loud loud shout,

'Come, leap on your coursers fleet,
For here comes the smell of some baptized flesh,
    And the sounding of baptized feet.'—
But oh! the fire that burns, and maun burn;
For the time that is gone will never return.

6.

On a steed as white as the new-milk'd milk,
    The Elf-queen leap'd with a bound,
And young Elphin a steed like December snow
    'Neath him at the word he found.
But a maiden came, and her christened arms
    She linked her brother around,
And called on God, and the steed with a snort
    Sank into the gaping ground.—
But the fire maun burn, and I maun quake,
And the time that is gone will no more come back.

7.

And she held her brother, and lo! he grew
    A wild bull waked in ire;
And she held her brother, and lo! he changed
    To a river roaring higher;
And she held her brother, and he became
    A flood of the raging fire;
She shrieked and sank, and the wild elves laughed
    Till the mountain rang and mire.—
But oh! the fire yet burns in my brain,
And the hour is gone, and comes not again.

8.

'O maiden, why waxed thy faith so faint,
    Thy spirit so slack and slaw?
Thy courage kept good till the flame wax'd wud,
    Then thy might began to thaw;
Had ye kissed him with thy christen'd lip,
    Ye had wan him frae 'mang us a'.
Now bless the fire, the elfin fire,
    That made thee faint and fa';
Now bless the fire, the elfin fire,
The longer it burns it blazes the higher.'

At the close of this unusual strain, the figure sat down on the grass, and proceeded to bind up her long and disordered tresses, gazing along the old and unfrequented road. 'Now God be my helper,' said the traveller, who happened to be the laird of Johnstone bank, 'can this be a trick of the fiend, or can it be bonnie Phemie Irving, who chants this dolorous sang? Something sad has befallen, that makes her seek her seat in this eerie nook amid the darkness and tempest: through might from aboon I will go on and see.' And the horse, feeling something of the owner's reviving spirit in the application of spur-steel, bore him at once to the foot of the tree. The poor delirious maiden uttered a yell of piercing joy as she beheld him, and with the swiftness of a creature winged, linked her arms round the rider's waist, and shrieked till the woods rang. 'Oh, I have ye now, Elphin, I have ye now,' and she strained him to her bosom with a convulsive grasp. 'What ails ye, my bonnie lass?' said the laird of Johnstone bank, his fears of the supernatural vanishing, when he beheld her sad and bewildered look. She raised her eyes at the sound, and seeing a strange face, her arms slipped their hold, and she dropped with a groan on the ground.

The morning had now fairly broke: the flocks shook the rain from their sides, the shepherds hastened to inspect their charges, and a thin blue smoke began to stream from the cottages of the valley into the brightening air. The laird carried Phemie Irving in his arms, till he observed two shepherds ascending from one of the loops of Corriewater, bearing the lifeless body of her brother. They had found him whirling round and round in one of the numerous eddies, and his hands, clutched and filled with wool, showed that he had lost his life in attempting to save the flock of his sister. A plaid was laid over the body, which, along with the unhappy maiden in a half lifeless state, was carried into a cottage, and laid in that apartment distinguished among the peasantry by the name of the chamber. While the peasant's wife was left to take care of Phemie,—old man and matron, and maid, had collected around the drowned youth, and each began to relate the circumstances of his death, when the door suddenly opened, and his sister, advancing to the corpse with a look of delirious serenity, broke out into a wild laugh and said: 'O, it is wonderful, it's truly wonderful! that bare and death-cold body, dragged from the darkest pool of Corrie, with its hands

filled with fine wool, wears the perfect similitude of my own
Elphin! I'll tell ye—the spiritual dwellers of the earth, the
Fairyfolk of our evening tale, have stolen the living body, and
fashioned this cold and inanimate clod to mislead your pursuit. In common eyes this seems all that Elphin Irving would
be, had he sunk in Corriewater; but so it seems not to me. Ye
have sought the living soul, and ye have found only its garment. But oh, if ye had beheld him, as I beheld him to-night,
riding among the elfin troop, the fairest of them all; had you
clasped him in your arms, and wrestled for him with spirits
and terrible shapes from the other world, till your heart
quailed and your flesh was subdued, then would ye yield no
credit to the semblance which this cold and apparent flesh
bears to my brother. But hearken,—on Hallowmass-eve, when
the spiritual people are let loose on earth for a season, I will
take my stand in the burial-ground of Corrie; and when my
Elphin and his unchristened troop come past with the sound
of all their minstrelsy, I will leap on him and win him, or
perish for ever.'

All gazed aghast on the delirious maiden, and many of her
auditors gave more credence to her distempered speech than
to the visible evidence before them. As she turned to depart,
she looked round, and suddenly sunk upon the body, with
tears streaming from her eyes, and sobbed out, 'My brother!
Oh, my brother!' She was carried out insensible, and again
recovered; but relapsed into her ordinary delirium, to which
she continued till the Hallow-eve after her brother's burial.
She was found seated in the ancient burial-ground, her back
against a broken grave-stone, her locks white with frost-rime,
watching with intensity of look the road to the kirk-yard: but
the spirit which gave life to the fairest form of all the maids
of Annandale was fled for ever.—Such is the singular story
which the peasants know by the name of Elphin Irving, the
Fairies' Cupbearer; and the title, in its fullest and most supernatural sense, still obtains credence among the industrious
and virtuous dames of the romantic vale of Corrie.

RICHARD FAULDER, MARINER

'It's sweet to go with hound and hawk,[99]
　　O'er moor and mountain roamin';
It's sweeter to walk on the Solway side,
　　With a fair maid at the gloamin';
But its sweeter to bound o'er the deep green sea,
　　When the flood is chafed and foamin';
For the seaboy has then the prayer of good men,
　　And the sighing of lovesome woman.

'The wind is up, and the sail is spread,
　　And look at the foaming furrow,
Behind the bark as she shoots away,
　　As fleet as the outlaw's arrow;
And the tears drop fast from lovely eyes,
　　And hands are wrung in sorrow;—
But when we come back, there is shout and clap,
　　And mirth both night and morrow.'
　　　　　　　Old Ballad

On a harvest afternoon, when the ripe grain, which clothed
the western slope of the Cumberland hills, had partly submitted to the sickle, a party of reapers were seated on a small
green knoll, enjoying the brief luxury of the dinner hour.
The young men lay stretched on the grass; the maidens sat
plaiting and arranging their locks into more graceful and
seducing ringlets; while three hoary old men sat abreast and
upright, looking on the Sea of Solway, which was spread out,
with all its romantic variety of headland, and rock, and bay,
below them. The mid-day sun had been unusually sultry,
accompanied with hot and suffocating rushings of wind; and
the appearance of a huge and dark cloud, which hung, like a
canopy of smoke and flame over a burning city, betokened,
to an experienced swain, an approaching storm. One of the
old reapers shook his head, and combing the remainder snow
over his forehead with his fingers, said, 'Woe's me! one token
comes, and another token arises, of tempest and wrath on that
darkening water. It comes to my memory like a dream—for

I was but a boy then groping trouts in Ellenwater—that it was on such a day, some fifty years ago, that the Bonnie Babie Allan, of Saint Bees, was wrecked on that rock, o'er the top of which the tide is whirling and boiling,—and the father and three brethren of Richard Faulder were drowned. How can I forget such a sea!—It leaped on the shore, among these shells and pebbles, as high as the mast of a brig; and threw its foam as far as the corn ricks of Walter Selby's stackyard,—and that's a good half mile.'

'Ise warrant,' interrupted a squat and demure old man, whose speech was a singular mixture of Cumbrian English and Border Scotch,—'Ise warrant, Willie, your memory will be rifer o' the loss of the lovely Lass of Annanwater, who whomel'd, keel upward, on the hip of the Mermaid rock, and spilt her wameful of rare brandy into the thankless Solway. Faith, mickle good liquor has been thrown into that punch-bowl; but fiend a drop of grog was ever made out of such a thriftless basin. It will aiblens be long afore such a gude-send comes to our coast again. There was Saunders Macmichael was drunk between yule and yule—forbye—'

'Wae's me, well may I remember that duleful day,' interrupted the third bandsman: 'it cost me a fair son—my youngest, and my best—I had seven once—alas, what have I now!—three were devoured by that false and unstable water—three perished by the sharp swords of those Highland invaders who slew so many of the gallant Dacres at Clifton and Carlisle—but the Cumberland ravens had their revenge!—I mind the head and lang yellow hair of him who slew my son, hanging over the Scottish gate of Carlisle.[100] Ay, I was avenged no doubt. But the son I have left has disgraced, for ever, our pure blood, by wedding a border Gordon, with as mickle Gypsey blood in her veins as would make plebeians of all the Howards and the Percies. I would rather have stretched him in the church-ground of Allanbay, with the mark of a Hielandman's brand on his brow, as was the lot of his brave brothers—or gathered his body from among these rocks, as I did those of my other children!—But oh, Sirs, when did man witness so fearful a coming on as yon dark sky forebodes?'

While this conversation went on, the clouds had assembled on the summits of the Scottish and Cumbrian mountains, and a thick canopy of vapour, which hung over the Isle of Man, waxed more ominous and vast. A light, as of a fierce fire burning, dropped frequent from its bosom,—throwing a sort of supernatural flame along the surface of the water,—and showing distinctly the haven, and houses, and shipping, and haunted castle, of the Isle. The old men sat silently gazing on the scene, while cloud succeeded cloud, till the whole congregating vapour, unable to sustain itself longer, stooped suddenly down from the opposing peaks of Criffel and Skiddaw, filling up the mighty space between the mountains, and approaching so close to the bosom of the ocean, as to leave room alone for the visible flight of the seamew and cormorant.

The water-fowl, starting from the sea, flew landward in a flock, fanning the waves with their wings, and uttering that wild and piercing scream, which distinguishes them from all other fowls, when their haunts are disturbed. The clouds and darkness increased, and the bird on the rock, the cattle in the fold, and the reapers in the field, all looked upward, and seaward, expecting the coming of the storm.

'Benjamin Forster,' said an old reaper to me, as I approached his side, and stood gazing on the sea—'I counsel thee, youth, to go home, and shelter these young hairs beneath thy mother's roof. The mountains have covered their heads—and hearken, too,—that hollow moan running among the cliffs!—There is a voice of mourning, my child, goes along the seacliffs of Solway before she swallows up the seafaring man. Seven times have I heard that warning voice in one season—and it cries, woe to the wives and the maids of Cumberland!'

On the summit of a knoll, which swelled gently from the margin of a small beck or rivulet, and which was about a dozen yards apart from the main body of the reapers,—sat a young Cumbrian maiden, who seemed wholly intent on the arrangement of a profusion of nut-brown locks, which descended, in clustering masses, upon her back and shoulders. This wilderness of ringlets owed, apparently, as much of its curling elegance to nature as to art, and flowed down on all sides with a profusion rivalling the luxuriant tresses of the Madonnas of the Roman painters. Half in coquetry, and half in willingness to restrain her tresses under a small fillet of green silk, her fingers, long, round, and white, continued shedding and disposing this beautiful fleece. At length the

locks were fastened under the fillet—a band denoting maidenhood—and her lily-looking hands, dropping across each other
in repose from their toil, allowed the eye to admire a smooth
and swan-white neck, which presented one of those natural
and elegant sinuous lines, that sculptors desire so much to communicate to marble. Amid all this sweetness and simplicity,
there appeared something of rustic archness and coquetry;—
but it was a kind of natural and born vanity, a little of which
gives a grace and joyousness to beauty. Those pure creations
of female simplicity, which shine in pastoral speculations, are
unknown among the ruddy and buxom damsels of Cumberland. The maritime nymphs of Allanbay are not unconscious
of their charms, or careless about their preservation; and to
this sweet maiden, nature had given so much female tact, as
enabled her to know that a beautiful face, and large dark
hazel eyes, have some influence among men.—When she had
wreathed up her tresses to her own satisfaction, she began to
cast around her such glances,—suddenly shot, and as suddenly
withdrawn—as would have been dangerous, concentrated on
one object, but which, divided with care, even to the fractional part of a glance, among several hinds, infused a sort of
limited joy, without exciting hope. Indeed, this was the work
of the maiden's eyes alone, for her heart was employed about
its own peculiar care, and its concern was fixed on a distant
and different object. She pulled from her bosom a silken case,
curiously wrought with the needle: A youth sat on the figured
prow of a bark, and beneath him a mermaid swam on the
green silken sea, waving back her long tresses with one hand,
and supplicating the young seaman with the other.—This
singular production seemed the sanctuary of her triumphs
over the hearts of men. She began to empty out its contents in
her lap; and the jealousy of many a Cumbrian maiden, from
Allanbay to Saint Bees'-head, would have been excited by
learning whose loves these emblems represented. There were
letters expressing the ardour of rustic affection—locks of hair,
both black and brown, tied up in shreds of silk,—and keepsakes, from the magnitude of a simple brass pin, watered with
gold, to a massy brooch of price and beauty. She arranged
these primitive treasures, and seemed to ponder over the
vicissitudes of her youthful affections. Her eyes, after lending a
brief scrutiny to each keepsake and symbol, finally fixed their
attention upon a brooch of pure gold: as she gazed on it, she

gave a sigh, and looked seaward, with a glance which showed that her eye was following in the train of her affections. The maiden's brow saddened at once, as she beheld the thick gathering of the clouds; and, depositing her treasure in her bosom, she continued to gaze on the darkening sea, with a look of increasing emotion.

The experienced mariners on the Scottish and Cumbrian coasts appeared busy mooring, and double mooring their vessels. Some sought a securer haven; and those who allowed their barks to remain, prepared them, with all their skill, for the encounter of a storm, which no one reckoned distant. Something now appeared in the space between the sea and the cloud, and emerging more fully, and keeping the centre of the sea, it was soon known to be a heavily laden ship, apparently making for the haven of Allanbay. When the cry of 'A ship! a ship!' arose among the reapers,—one of the old men, whose eyes were something faded, after gazing intently, said, with a tone of sympathy,—'It *is* a ship indeed,—and woe's me but the path it is in be perilous in a moment like this!'

'She'll never pass the sunken rocks of Saint Bees'-head,' said one old man: 'Nor weather the headland of Barnhourie, and the caverns of Colvend,' said another:—'And should she pass both,' said a third, 'the coming tempest, which now heaves up the sea within a cable's length of her stern, will devour her ere she finds shelter in kindly Allanbay!'

'Gude send,' said he of the mixed brood of Cumberland and Caledonia,—'since she maun be wrecked, that she spills nae her treasure on the thankless shores of Galloway! These northerns be a keen people, with a ready hand, and a clutch like steel: besides, she seems a Cumberland bark, and it's meet that we have our ain fish-guts to our ain sea-maws.'

'Oh, see, see!' said the old man, three of whose children had perished when the Bonnie Babie Allan sank,—'see how the waves are beginning to be lifted up! Hearken how deep calls to deep; and hear, and see, how the winds and the windows of heaven are loosened! Save thy servants—even those seafaring men—should there be but one righteous person on board!'—And the old reaper rose, and stretched out his hands in supplication as he spoke.

The ship came boldly down the middle of the bay, the masts bending and quivering, and the small deck crowded

with busy men, who looked wistfully to the coast of Cumberland.

'She is the Lady Johnstone of Annanwater,' said one,
'coming with wood from Norway.'

'She is the Buxom Bess of Allanbay,' said another, 'laden
with the best of West India rum.'—

'And I,' said the third old man, 'would have thought her
the Mermaid of Richard Faulder,—but,' added he, in a lower
tone, 'the Mermaid has not been heard of, nor seen, for many
months;—and the Faulders are a doomed race:—his bonny
brig and he are in the bottom of the sea; and with them sleeps
the pride of Cumberland, Frank Forster of Derwentwater.'

The subject of their conversation approached within a
couple of miles, turned her head for Allanbay, and, though
the darkness almost covered her as a shroud, there seemed
every chance that she would reach the port ere the tempest
burst. But just as she turned for the Cumbrian shore, a rush of
wind shot across the bay, furrowing the sea as hollow as the
deepest glen, and heaving it up mast-head high. The cloud,
too, dropt down upon the surface of the sea; the winds,
loosened at once, lifted the waves in multitudes against the
cliffs; and the foam fell upon the reapers, like a shower of
snow. The loud chafing of the waters on the rocks prevented
the peasants from hearing the cries of men whom they had
given up to destruction. At length the wind, which came in
whirlwind gusts, becoming silent for a little while, the voice of
a person singing was heard from the sea, far above the turbulence of the waves. Old William Dacre uttered a shout, and
said—

'That is the voice of Richard Faulder, if ever I heard it in
the body. He is a fearful man, and never sings in the hour of
gladness, but in the hour of danger—terror and death are
beside him when he lifts his voice to sing. This is the third
time I have listened to his melody,—and many mothers will
weep, and maidens too, if his song have the same ending as of
old.'

The voice waxed bolder, and approached the shore; and,
as nothing could be discerned, so thick was the darkness, the
song was impressive, and even awful.

THE SONG OF RICHARD FAULDER[101]

I.

It's merry, it's merry, among the moonlight,
    When the pipe and the cittern are sounding—
To rein, like a war-steed, my shallop, and go
    O'er the bright waters merrily bounding.
It's merry, it's merry, when fair Allanbay,
    With its bridal candles is glancing—
To spread the white sails of my vessel, and go
    Among the wild sea-waters dancing.

2.

And it's blythesomer still, when the storm is come on,
    And the Solway's wild waves are ascending
In huge and dark curls—and the shaven masts groan,
    And the canvas to ribbons is rending;—
When the dark heaven stoops down unto the dark deep,
    And the thunder speaks 'mid the commotion,
Awaken and see, ye who slumber and sleep,
    The might of the Lord on the ocean!

3.

This frail bark, so late growing green in the wood,
    Where the roebuck is joyously ranging,—
Now doomed for to roam o'er the wild fishy flood,
    When the wind to all quarters is changing—
Is as safe to thy feet as the proud palace floor,
    And as firm as green Skiddaw below thee,—
For God has come down to the ocean's dread deeps,
    His might and his mercy to show thee.

As the voice ceased, the ship appeared, through the cloud,
approaching the coast in full swing; her sails rent, and the
wave and foam flashing over her, mid-mast high. The maiden,
who has already been introduced to the affection of the
reader, gazed on the ship, and, half suppressing a shriek of
joy, flew down to the shore, where the cliffs, sloping backwards from the sea, presented a ready landing-place, when
the waves were more tranquil than now. Her fellow-reapers
came crowding to her side, and looked on the address and
hardihood of the crew,—who, with great skill and success,

navigated their little bark through and among the sand-banks, and sunken rocks, which make the Solway so perilous and fatal to seamen. At last they obtained the shelter of a huge cliff, which, stretching like a promontory into the sea, broke the impetuosity of the waves, and afforded them hopes of communicating with their friends, who, with ropes and horses, were seen hastening to the shore.

But, although Richard Faulder and his Mermaid were now little more than a cable-length distant from the land, the peril of their situation seemed little lessened. The winds had greatly abated; but the sea, with that impulse communicated by the storm, threw itself against the rocks, elevating its waters high over the summits of the highest cliffs, and leaping and foaming around the bark, with a force that made her reel and quiver, and threatened to stave her to pieces.—The old and skilful mariner himself was observed, amid the confusion and danger, as collected and self-possessed as if he had been entering the bay in the tranquillity of a summer evening, with a hundred hands waving and welcoming his return. His spirit and deliberation seemed more or less communicated to his little crew; but chiefly to Frank Forster, who, in the ardent buoyancy of youth, moved as he moved, thought as he thought, and acted from his looks alone, as if they had been both informed with one soul. In those times, the benevolence of individuals had not been turned to multiply the means of preserving seamen's lives; and the mariner, in the hour of peril, owed his life to chance—his own endeavours—or the intrepid exertions of the humane peasantry.

The extreme agitation of the sea rendered it difficult to moor or abandon the bark with safety; and several young men ventured fearlessly into the flood on horseback, but could not reach the rope which the crew threw out to form a communication with the land. Young Forster, whose eye seemed to have singled out some object of regard on shore, seized the rope; then leaping, with a plunge, into the sea, he made the waters flash! Though for a moment he seemed swallowed up, he emerged from the billows like a waterfowl, and swam shoreward with unexpected agility and strength. The old mariner gazed after him with a look of deep concern; but none seemed more alarmed than the maiden with many keepsakes. As he seized the rope, the lily suddenly chased the rose from her cheek, and uttering a loud scream, and crying out, 'Oh, help him, save him!' she flew down to the shore, and plunged into the water, holding out her arms, while the flood burst against her, breast high.

'God guide me, Maud Marchbank,' cried William Dacre, 'ye'll drown the poor lad out of pure love,—I think,' continued he, stepping back, and shaking the brine from his clothes, 'I am the mad person myself—a caress and a kiss from young Frank of Derwentwater is making her comfortable enough. Alas! but youth be easily pleased—it is as the northern song says—

'Contented wi' little and cantie wi' mair;'[102]

but old age is a delightless time!'

To moor the bark was the labour of a few moments; and fathers, and mothers, and sisters, and sweethearts, welcomed the youths they had long reckoned among the dead, with affection and tears. All had some friendly hand and eye to welcome and rejoice in them, save the brave old mariner, Richard Faulder alone. To him no one spoke, on him no eye was turned; all seemed desirous of shunning communication with a man to whom common belief attributed endowments and powers, which came not as knowledge and might come to other men; and whose wisdom was of that kind against which the most prudent divines, and the most skilful legislators, directed the rebuke of church and law. I remember hearing my father say, that when Richard Faulder, who was equally skilful in horsemanship and navigation, offered to stand on his grey horse's bare back, and gallop down the street of Allanbay, he was prevented from betting against the accomplishment of this equestrian vaunt by a wary Scotchman, who, in the brief manner of his country, said, 'Dinna wager, Thomas—God guide your wits—that man's no cannie!'—At that time, though a stripling of seventeen, and possessed strongly with the belief of the mariner's singular powers, I could not avoid sympathizing with his fortune, and the forlorn look with which he stood on the deck, while his companions were welcomed and caressed on shore. Nothing, indeed, could equal the joy which fathers and mothers manifested towards their children,—but the affection and tenderness with which they were hailed by the bright eyes of the Cumbrian maidens.

'His name be praised!' said one old man, to whose bosom a son had been unexpectedly delivered from the waves.

'And blessed be the hour ye were saved from the salt sea, and that fearful man,'—said a maiden, whose blushing cheek and brightening eye, indicated more than common sympathy.

'And oh! Stephen Porter, my son,' resumed the father, 'never set foot on shipboard with that mariner more!'

In another group stood a young seaman with his sister's arms linked round his neck; receiving the blessings and the admonitions which female lips shower so vainly upon the sterner sex:—'This is the third time, Giles, thou hast sailed with Richard Faulder: and every time my alarm and thy perils increase.—Many a fair face he has witnessed the fate of,—and many a fair ship has he survived the wreck of:—think of the sea, since think of it thou must—but never more think of it with such a companion.'

In another group, a young woman stood gazing on a sailor's face, and, in her looks, fear and love held equal mastery. 'Oh! William Rowanberry,' said she, and her hand trembled with affection in his while she spoke,—'I would have held my heart widowed for one year and a day, in memory of thee—and though there be fair lads in Ullswater, and fairer still in Allanbay,—I'll no say they would have prevailed against my regard for thee before the summer.—But I warn thee,' and she whispered, waving her hand seaward to give importance to her words,—'never be found on the great deep with that man again!'—

Meanwhile, the subject of this singular conversation kept pacing from stem to stern of the Mermaid—gazing, now and then, wistfully shoreward—though he saw not a soul with whom he might share his affections. His grey hair, and his melancholy look, won their way to my youthful regard, while his hale and stalwart frame could not fail of making an impression on one not wholly insensible to the merits of the exterior person. A powerful mind should in poetical justice have a noble place of abode. I detached myself a little from the mass of people that filled the shore, and seeming to busy myself with some drift wood, which the storm had brought to the hollow of a small rock, I had an opportunity of hearing the old mariner chant, as he paced to and fro, the fragment of an old maritime ballad, part of which is still current among

the seamen of Solway, along with many other singular rhymes
full of marine superstition and adventure.

SIR RICHARD'S VOYAGE[103]

1.

Sir Richard shot swift from the shore, and sailed
    Till he reached Barnhourie's steep,
And a voice came to him from the green land,
    And one from the barren deep.
The green sea shuddered, and he did shake,
For the words were those which no mortals make.

2.

Away he sailed—and the lightning came,
    And streamed from the top of his mast;
Away he sailed, and the thunder came,
    And spoke from the depth of the blast:—
'O God!' he said,—and his tresses so hoar
Shone bright i' the flame, as he shot from the shore.

3.

Away he sailed—and the green isles smiled,
    And the sea-birds sang around:
He sought to land—and down sank the shores,
    With a loud and a murmuring sound—
And where the green wood and the sweet sod should be,
There tumbled a wild and a shoreless sea.

4.

Away he sailed—and the moon looked out,
    With one large star by her side—
Down shot the star, and upsprang the sea-fowl
    With a shriek—and roared the tide!
The bark, with a leap, seemed the stars to sweep,
And then to dive in the hollowest deep.

5.

Criffel's green mountain towered on his right—
    Upon his left, Saint Bees—
Behind,—Caerlaverock's charmed ground—

Before,—the wild wide seas:—
And there a witch-fire, broad and bright,
Shed far a wild unworldly light!—

6.
A lady sat high on Saint Bees's-head,
    With her pale cheek on her hand;
She gazed forth on the troubled sea,
    And on the troubled land:
She lifted her hands to heaven—her eyes
Rained down bright tears—still the shallop flies.

7.
The shallop shoulders the surge and flies,—
    But at that lady's prayer,
The charmed wind fell mute, nor stirr'd
    The rings of her golden hair:—
And over the sea there pass'd a breath
From heaven—the sea lay mute as death.

8.
And the shallop sunders the gentle flood,
    No breathing wind is near:
And the shallop sunders the gentle flood,
    And the flood lies still with fear—
And the ocean, the earth, and the heaven smile sweet
As Sir Richard kneels low at that lady's feet!

While the old mariner chanted this maritime rhyme, he
looked upon me from time to time,—and, perhaps, felt
pleased in exciting the interest of a youthful mind, and
obtaining a regard which had been but sparingly bestowed
in his native land. He loosed a little skiff, and, stepping into
it, pushed through the surge to the place where I stood,
and was in a moment beside me. I could not help gazing,
with an eye reflecting wonder and respect, on a face—bold,
mournful, and martial, as his was,—which had braved so
long 'the battle and the breeze.'[104] He threw across my
shoulders a mantle of leopard skin,—and said, as he walked
towards his little cottage on the rock,—'Youth, I promised
that mantle to the first one who welcomed me from a voyage
of great peril:—take it, and be happier than the giver,—and

glad am I to be welcomed by the son of my old Captain Randal Forster.'

Such were the circumstances under which I became acquainted with Richard Faulder of Allanbay. At his lonely hearth I was afterwards a frequent and welcome guest, and an attentive and wondering auditor to his wild maritime legends, gathered on many an isle and mainland coast; but none of all his stories made a deeper impression on my memory than the Tale of the LAST LORD OF HELVELLYN.[105]

THE LAST LORD OF
HELVELLYN

'An ancient curse still clings to their name.'[106]

'It was, I think, in the year seventeen hundred and thirty-three, that, one fine summer evening, I sat on the summit of Rosefoster-cliff, gazing on the multitudes of waves which, swelled by the breeze, and whitened by the moonlight, undulated as far as the eye could reach. The many lights, gleaming from Allanbay, were extinguished one by one; the twinklings of remote Saint Bees glimmered fainter and fainter on the Solway; while the villages and mansions on the Scottish coast, from Annand to Kirkcudbright, were perfectly silent and dark, as beseemed their devout and frugal inhabitants. As I sat and thought on the perils I had encountered and braved on the great deep, I observed a low dark mist arise from the middle of the Solway; which, swelling out, suddenly came rolling huge and sable towards the Cumberland shore. Nor was fear or fancy long in supplying this exhalation with sails, and pennons, and the busy hum and murmur of mariners. As it approached the cliff on which I had seated myself, it was not without dismay that I observed it become more dark, and assume more distinctly the shape of a barge, with a shroud for a sail.[107] It left the sea, and settled on the beach within sea-mark, maintaining still its form, and still sending forth the merry din of mariners. In a moment the voices were changed from mirth to sorrow; and I heard a sound and outcry like the shriek of a ship's company whom the sea is swallowing. The cloud dissolved away, and in its place I beheld, as it were, the forms of seven men, shaped from the cloud, and stretched black on the beach; even as corses are prepared for the coffin. I was then young, and not conversant with the ways in which He above reveals and shadows out approaching sorrow to man. I went down to the beach, and though the moon, nigh the full, and in mid-heaven, threw down an unbroken light,—rendering visible mountain, and headland, and sea, so that I might count the pebbles and shells on the shore,—the seven black shadows of men had not departed, and there appeared a space in the middle, like room measured out for an eighth. A strange terror came upon me; and I began to dread that this vision was sent for my warning; for be assured, Heaven hath many and singular revelations for the welfare and instruction of man. I prayed, and, while I prayed, the seven shadows began to move—filling up the space prepared for another: then they waxed dimmer and dimmer, and then wholly vanished!

'I was much moved; and, deeming it the revelation of approaching sorrow, in which I was to be a sharer, it was past midnight before I could fall asleep. The sun had been some time risen when I was awakened by Simon Forester, who, coming to my bed-side, said, "Richard Faulder, arise, for young Lord William of Helvellyn-Hall has launched his new barge on the Solway, and seven of the best and boldest mariners of Allanbay must bear him company to bring his fair bride from Preston-Hall—even at the foot of the mountain Criffel; hasten and come, for he sails not, be sure, without Richard Faulder!"[108]

'It was a gallant sight to see a shallop, with her halsers and sails of silk, covered with streamers, and damasked with gold, pushing gaily from the bay. It was gallant, too, to behold the lordly bridegroom, as he stood on the prow, looking towards his true-love's land; not heeding the shout, and the song, and the music-swell, with which his departure was hailed. It was gallant to see the maids and the matrons of Cumberland, standing in crowds, on headland and cliff, waving their white hands seaward, as we spread our sails to the wind, and shot away into the Solway, with our streamers dancing and fluttering like the mane of a steed as he gallops against the wind. Proud of our charge, and glorying in our skill, we made the good ship go through the surge as we willed; and every turn we made, and every time we wetted her silken sails, there came shout and trumpet-sound from the shore, applauding the seven merry mariners of Allanbay.

'Helvellyn-Hall, of which there is now no stone standing, save an old sun-dial around which herdsmen gather at noon-day, to hear of old marvels of the Foresters,—was an extensive mansion, built in the times when perils from the pirate and the Scot were dreaded,—and stood on a swelling knoll, encompassed with wood, visible from afar to mariners. In the

centre was a tower, and on the summit of the tower was a
seat, and in that seat tradition will yet tell you that the good
Lord Walter Forester sat for a certain time, in every day of
the year, looking on the sea. The swallows and other birds
which made their nests and their roosts on the castle-top,
became so accustomed to his presence, that they built, and
sang, and brought forth their young beside him; and old men,
as they beheld him, shook their heads, and muttered over
the ancient prophecy, which a saint, who suffered from persecution, had uttered against the house of Helvellyn.

Let the Lord of Helvellyn look long on the sea—[109]
For a sound shall he hear, and a sight shall he see;
The sight he shall see is a bonnie ship sailing,
The sound he shall hear is of weeping and wailing;
A sight shall he see on the green Solway shore,
And no lord of Helvellyn shall ever see more.

'As we scudded swiftly through the water, I looked towards
the shore of Cumberland, stretching far and near, with all its
winding outline, interrupted with woody promontories; and
there I beheld the old Lord Walter of Helvellyn, seated on the
topmost tower of his castle, looking towards the Scottish shore.
I thought on the dying man's rhyme; and thought on the
vision of last night: and I counted the mariners, and looked
again on the castle and Lord Walter; and I saw that the ful-
filling of the prophecy and the vision was approaching.
Though deeply affected, I managed the barge with my
customary skill, and she flew across the bay, leaving a long
furrow of foam behind. Michael Halmer, an old mariner of
Allanbay, afterwards told me, he never beheld a fairer sight
than the barge that day, breasting the billows; and he stood,
warding off the sun with his hands from his fading eyes, till we
reached the middle of the bay. At that time, he said, he
beheld something like a ship formed of a black cloud, sailing
beside us, which moved as we moved, and tacked as we
tacked; had the semblance of the same number of mariners,
and, in every way appeared like the bridegroom's barge! He
trembled with dismay, for he knew the spectre shallop of
Solway, which always sails by the side of the ship which the
sea is about to swallow. It was not my fortune to behold fully
this fearful vision; but, while I gazed towards Helvellyn-Hall,

I felt a dread, and although I saw nothing on which my fears could fix, I remember that a kind of haze or exhalation, resembling the thin shooting of a distant light, floated through the air at our side, which I could not long endure to look upon. The old Lord still preserved his position on the tower, and sat gazing towards us, as still and motionless as a marble statue, and with an intensity of gaze like one who is watching the coming of destiny.

'The acclamations which greeted our departure from Cumberland, were exceeded by those which welcomed us to the Scottish shore. The romantic and mountainous coast of Colvend and Siddick was crowded with shepherd, and matron, and maid, who stood as motionless as their native rocks, and as silent too, till we approached within reach of their voices, and then such a shout arose, as startled the gulls and cormorants from rock and cavern for a full mile. The Scotch are a demure, a careful, and a singular people; and, amid much homeliness of manner, have something of a poetical way of displaying their affections, which they treasure too for great occasions, or, as they say, "daimen times". There are certain of their rustics much given to the composition of song and of ballad, in which a natural elegance occasionally glimmers among their antique and liquid dialect. I have been told the Lowland language of Scotland is more soft and persuasive than even that of England; and, assuredly there was Martin Robson, a mariner of mine, in the Mermaid, whose wily Scotch tongue made the hearts of half the damsels of Cumberland dance to their lips. But many of their ballads are of a barbarous jingle, and can only be admired because the names of those whom their authors love and hate, and the names of hill, and dale, and coast, and stream, are interwoven with a ready ease unknown among the rustic rhymes of any other people.

'Preston-Hall—the plough has long since passed over its foundation stones!—was long the residence of a branch of the powerful and ancient name of Maxwell; and such was its fame for generosity, that the beggar or pilgrim who went in at the eastern gate empty, always came out at the western gate full, and blessing the bounty of the proprietor. It stood at the bottom of a deep and beautiful bay, at the entrance of which two knolls, slow in their swell from the land, and abrupt in their rise from the sea,—seemed, almost, to shut out all

approach. In former times, they had been crowned with slight
towers of defence. It was a fairy nook for beauty; and tradition, which loves to embellish the scenes on which nature has
been lavish of her bounty, asserted that the twin hillocks of
Preston-bay were formerly one green hill, till a wizard, whose
name has not yet ceased to work marvels,[110] cleft the knoll
asunder with his wand, and poured the sea into the aperture,—
laying, at the same time, the foundation-stone of Preston-Hall,
with his own hand.* On the sides and summits of these small
hills, stood two crowds of peasants, who welcomed the coming
of Lord William with the sounding of instruments of no
remarkable harmony. As this clamorous hail ceased, the melody of maidens' tongues made ample amends for the instrumental discord. They greeted us as we passed with this
poetical welcome, after the manner of their country.

THE MAIDENS' SONG[111]

Maids of Colvend

Ye maidens of Allanbay, sore may ye mourn,
For your lover is gone—and will wedded return;
His white sail is fill'd, and the barge cannot stay,
Wide flashes the water—she shoots through the bay.
Weep, maidens of Cumberland, shower your tears salter,—
The priest is prepared, and the bride's at the altar!

---

* Scotland is rife with the labours of wizard and witch. The beautiful green
mountain of Criffel, and its lesser and immediate companions, were
created by a singular disaster which befell Dame Ailie Gunson. This noted
and malignant witch had sustained an insult from the sea of Solway, as she
crossed it in her wizard shallop, formed from a cast-off slipper; she, therefore, gathered a huge creelful of earth and rock, and, stride after stride, was
advancing to close up for ever the entrance of that beautiful bay! An old
and devout mariner who witnessed her approach, thrice blessed himself,
and at each time a small mountain fell out of the witch's creel; the last
was the largest, and formed the mountain Criffel, which certain rustic
antiquarians say is softened from 'creel fell,' for the witch dropped earth
and creel in despair.

Maids of Siddick

The bride she is gone to the altar—and far,
And in wrath, flies gay Gordon of green Lochinvar;
Young Maxwell of Munshes, thy gold spur is dyed
In thy steed, and thy heart leaps in anguish and pride—
The bold men of Annand and proud Niddisdale
Have lost her they loved, and may join in the wail.

Maids of Colvend

Lord William is come; and the bird on the pine,
The leaf on the tree, and the ship on the brine,
The blue heaven above, and below the green earth,
Seem proud of his presence, and burst into mirth.
Then come, thou proud fair one, in meek modest mood—
The bridal bed's ready—unloosen thy snood!

Maids of Siddick

The bridal bed's ready;—but hearken, high lord!
Though strong be thy right arm, and sharp be thy sword,—
Mock not Beatrice Maxwell!—else there shall be sorrow
Through Helvellyn's valleys, ere sun-rise to-morrow:
Away, haste away! can a gallant groom falter,
When the bridal wine's pour'd, and the bride's at the altar!

'During this minstrel salutation, the barge floated into the
bosom of Preston-bay; and, through all its woody links, and
greenwood nooks, the song sounded mellow and more mellow,
as it was flung from point to point over the sunny water.
The barge soon approached the green sward, which, sloping
downwards from the hall, bordering with its livelier hue the
dull deep green of the ocean, presented a ready landing place.
When we were within a lance's length of the shore, there
appeared, coming towards us from a deep grove of holly, a
female figure, attired in the manner of the farmer matrons of
Scotland,—with a small plaid, or mantle, fastened over her
grey lint-and-woollen gown, and a white cap, or mutch, sur-
mounting, rather than covering, a profusion of lyart locks
which came over her brow and neck, like remains of winter
snow. She aided her steps with a staff, and descending to the

prow of the barge, till the sea touched her feet, stretched her staff seaward, and said with a deep voice and an unembarrassed tone:—"What wouldest thou, William Forster, the doomed son of a doomed house, with Beatrice Maxwell, the blessed child of a house whose name shall live, and whose children shall breathe, while green woods grow, and clear streams run? Return as thou camest, nor touch a shore hostile to thee and thine. If thy foot displaces but one blade of grass—thy life will be as brief as the endurance of thy name, which that giddy boy is even now writing on the sand within sea-mark:— the next tide will pass over THEE—and blot IT out for ever and for ever! Thy father, even now watching thy course from his castle top, shall soon cease to be the warder of his house's destiny; and the Cumberland boor, as he gazes into the bosom of the Solway, shall sigh for the ancient and valiant name of Forster."[112]

'While this singular speech was uttering, I gazed on the person of the speaker—from whom no one, who once looked, could well withdraw his eyes. She seemed some seventy years old, but unbowed or unbroken by age,—and had that kind of commanding look which common spirits dread. Lord William listened to her words with a look of kindness and respect:— "Margery Forsythe," he said, "thou couldest have prophesied more fortunately and wisely, hadst thou wished it—but thou art a faithful friend and servant to my Beatrice—accept this broad piece of gold, and imagine a more pleasant tale, when, with the evening tide, I return with my love to Helvellyn."

'The gold fell at the old woman's feet, but it lay glittering and untouched among the grass, for her mind and eye seemed intent on matters connected with the glory of her master's house.

' "Friend am I to Beatrice Maxwell, but no servant," said Margery, in a haughty tone, "though it's sweet to serve a face so beautiful. Touch not this shore, I say again, William Forster—but it's vain to forbid—the thing that must be must—we are fore-ordained to run our course—and this is the last course of the gallant house of Forster."

'She then stepped aside, opposing Lord William no longer, who, impatient at her opposition, was preparing to leap ashore. Dipping her staff in the water as a fisher dips his rod, she held it dripping towards the Solway, to which she now addressed herself:—"False and fathomless sea—slumbering now in the sweet summer sun, like a new lulled babe, I have lived by thy side for years of sin that I shall not sum; and every year hast thou craved and yearned for thy morsel, and made the maids and matrons wail in green Galloway and Nithsdale. When wilt thou be satisfied, thou hungry sea?— even now, sunny and sweet as thou seemest, dost thou crave for the mouthful ordained to thee by ancient prophecy, and the fair and the dainty morsel is at hand."[113]

'Her eyes, dim and spiritless at first, became filled, while she uttered this apostrophe to the sea, with a wild and agitated light—her stature seemed to augment, and her face to dilate with more of grief than joy; and her locks, snowy and sapless with age, writhed on her forehead and temples, as if possessed with a distinct life of their own. Throwing her staff into the sea, she then went into the grove of holly, and disappeared.

' "May I be buried beyond the plummet sound," said Sam Dacre of Skiddawbeck,[114] "if I fail to prove if that dame's tartan kirtle will flatten swan-shot,—I never listened to such unblessed language," and he presented his carbine after her—while William Macgowan, a Galloway sailor, laid his hand on the muzzle, and said,

' "I'll tell thee what, Margery Forsythe has mair forecast in the concerns o' the great deep than a wise mariner ought to despise. Swan-shot, man!—she would shake it off her charmed calimanco kirtle as a swan shakes snow from its wings. I see ye're scantly acquaint with the uncannie pranks of our Colvend dame. But gang up to the Boran point, and down to Barnhourie bank, and if the crews of two bonnie ships, buried under fifteen fathom of quicksand and running water, winna waken and tell ye whose uncannie skill sunk them there, the simplest hind will whisper ye that Margery Forsythe kens mair about it than a God-fearing woman should. So ye see, Lord William Forster, I would even counsel ye to make yere presence scarce on this kittle coast—just wyse yersel warily owre the salt water again. And true-love's no like a new-killed kid in summer—it will keep, ye see; it will keep. This cross cummer will grow kindly, and we shall come snoring back in our barge, some bonnie moonlight summer night, and carry away my young lady with a sweeping oar and a wetted sail. For if we persist when she resists, we shall have wet sarks and droukit hair. Sae ye laugh and listen not? Aweel, aweel, them that will to Couper will to Couper![115]—a doomed man's easily drowned!—the thing that maun be maun be!—and sic things shall be if we sell ale!"

'These predestinating exclamations were abridged by a long train of bridal guests hurrying from the hall to receive the bridegroom, who, disregarding all admonition, leaped gaily ashore, and was welcomed with trumpet flourish and the continued sound of the lowland pipe. He was followed by six of his seven mariners; I alone remained, overawed by the vision I had beheld on the preceding night, by the prophetic words of the sorceress of Siddick, and by that boding forecast of disaster, which the wise would do well to regard.

'On all sides people were seated on the rising grounds: the tree tops, the immemorial resting places of ravens and rooks, were filled with young men, anxious to see the procession to the chapel of Preston, and to hearken the bridal joy; and even the rough and dizzy cliff of Barnhourie burn, which overlooks the Solway for many miles, had the possession of its summit disputed with its native cormorants and eagles, by some venturous schoolboys, who thus showed that love of adventure which belongs to the children of the sea-coast. The sun was in noon when we landed in Preston-bay, and its edge was touching the grassy tops of the western hills of Galloway, when shout above shout, from wood and eminence, the waving of white hands from field and knoll, and the sudden awakening of all manner of clamorous and mirthful melody, announced the coming of the bridal crowd. The gates of Preston-Hall burst suddenly open; out upon the level lawn gushed an inundation of youths and maidens clad in their richest dresses, and the living stream flowed down to the Solway side. As they approached, a shallop, covered from the mast-head to the water with streamers, and pennons, and garlands, came suddenly from a small anchorage scooped out of the bosom of the garden, making the coming tide gleam to a distance, with the gold and silver lavished in its decoration. But my admiration of this beautiful shallop was soon interrupted by the appearance of a lady, who, standing on the ground by the prow of the bride's barge, looked earnestly seaward, and trembled so much that the white satin dress which covered her from bosom to heel, studded, and sown, and flowered with the most costly stones and metals, shook as if touched by an ungentle wind. Her long tresses, of raven black hair, and

which, in the boast of maidenhood of my early days, descended till she could sit upon them, partook of her agitation.
Her eyes alone, large and bright, and fringed with long lashes
of a black still deeper than that of her hair, were calm and
contemplative, and seemed with her mind meditating on some
perilous thing. While she stood thus, a maiden came to her
side, and casting a long white veil, a present from the bridegroom, over her head, shrouded her to the feet; but the
elegance of her form, and the deep dark glance of her expressive eyes, triumphed over the costly gift;—though the fringe
was of diamonds, and the disastrous tale of the youth who
perished swimming over the Solway to his love, was wrought,
or rather damasked, in the middle. I could have gazed from
that hour till this on this beautiful vision; but, while I looked,
there came slowly from the wood a figure of a woman, bent
with age or distress to the ground, and entirely covered in a
black mantle: she approached the bride unperceived, and lay
down at her feet—as a footstool on which she must tread
before she could enter the shallop. This was unheeded of
many, or of all; for the blessings showered by all ranks on the
departing pair,—the bustle of the mariners preparing to sail
with the tide, which now filled Preston-bay, the sounding of
bugle and pipe, and the unremitting rivalry in song and
ballad, between the mariners in the barges of the bridegroom
and bride, successively filled every mind, save mine, over-
clouded then, and as it has ever since been, before some
coming calamity. Ballad and song passed over my memory
without leaving a verse behind; one song alone, sung by a
mariner of Allanbay, and which has long been popular on the
coast, interested me much,—more, I confess from the dark
and mysterious manner in which it figured or shadowed forth
our catastrophe, than from its poetical merit, the last verse
alone approaching to the true tone of the lyric.

MICHAEL HALMER'S SONG[116]

1.

Upon the bonnie mountain side,
    Upon the leafy trees,
Upon the rich and golden fields,
    Upon the deep green seas,
The wind comes breathing freshly forth—
    Ho! pluck up from the sand
Our anchor, and go shooting as
    A wing'd shaft from the land!
The sheep love Skiddaw's lonesome top—
    The shepherd loves his hill—
The throstle loves the budding bush—
    Sweet woman loves her will—
The lark loves heaven for visiting,
    But green earth for her home;
And I love the good ship, singing
    Through the billows in their foam.

2.

My son, a grey-hair'd peasant said,
    Leap on the grassy land,
And deeper than five fathom sink
    Thine anchor in the sand;
And meek and humble make thy heart;
    For ere yon bright'ning moon
Lifts her wond'rous lamp above the wave
    Amid night's lonely noon,
There shall be shriekings heard at sea—
    Lamentings heard ashore—
My son, go pluck thy main-sail down,
    And tempt the heav'n no more.
Come forth and weep, come forth and pray,
    Grey dame and hoary swain—
All ye who have got sons to-night
    Upon the faithless main.

3.

And wherefore, old man, should I turn?
    Dost hear the merry pipe,
The harvest bugle winding

Among Scotland's corn fields ripe?
And see her dark-eyed maidens dance,
 Whose willing arms alway
Are open for the merry lads
 Of bonnie Allanbay?
Full sore the old man sigh'd—and said,
 Go bid the mountain wind
Breathe softer, and the deep waves hear
 The prayers of frail mankind,
And mar the whirlwind in his might;—
 His hoary head he shook,
Gazed on the youth, and on the sea,
 And sadder wax'd his look.

4.

Lo! look! here comes our lovely bride—
 Breathes there a wind so rude
As chafe the billows when she goes
 In beauty o'er the flood?
The raven fleece that dances
 On her round and swan-white neck;
The white foot that wakes music
 On the smooth and shaven deck;
The white hand that goes waving thus,
 As if it told the brine—
Be gentle in your ministry,
 O'er you I rule and reign;
The eye that looks so lovely,
 Yet so lofty in its sway—
Old man, the sea adores them—
 So adieu, sweet Allanbay!

'During the continuance of this song, an old gentleman of the house of Maxwell, advancing through the press to the barges, said aloud—"A challenge, ye gallants, a challenge!— let the bridegroom take his merry mariners of England—let the bride take her mariners of old Galloway—push the barges from Preston-bay, as the signal-pipe sounds; and a pipe of blood-red wine to a cupful of cold water, that *we* reach Allanbay first." As the old man finished his challenge, hundreds of hats, and bonnets too, were thrown into the air, and the bridegroom, with a smile, took his offered hand and said,—

"What! Sir Marmaduke Maxwell,[117] wilt thou brave us
too?—A pipe of the richest wine to a drink of the saltest brine
in the centre of Solway, that the merry lads of Allanbay
exceed thee at least by ten strokes of the oar." The English
mariners replied, as is their wont, with a shout, threw aside
their jackets and caps, and prepared gladly for the coming
contest: nor were the mariners of Siddick and Colvend slow in
preparing; they made themselves ready with that silent and
sedate alacrity peculiar to that singular people. "May I never
see Skiddaw again," said William Selby of Derwent, "nor
taste Nancy Grogson's grog, or her pretty daughter's lips, if
the fresh-water lads of Barnhourie surpass the salt-water lads
of Allanbay."

' "And for my part," said Charles Carson, "in answer to
my comrade's vow, may I be turned into a sheldrake, and
doomed to swim to doomsday in the lang black lake of Lough-
maben, if the powkpuds of Skiddaw surpass the cannie lads
of green Galloway." And both parties, matched in numbers,
in strength—of equal years, and of similar ability—stood with
looks askance on each other, ready to start, and willing to
win the bridal boast, and the bride or bridegroom's favour.

' "And now, my sweet bride," said Lord William, "shall I
help thee into thy barge?—Loth am I that thy kinsman's
vaunt causes a brief separation.—Now guide thy barge wisely
and warily," said he to her helmsman, "I would rather pay
the wine for thy mistress ten thousand fold, than one lock of
her raven hair should be put in jeopardy.—If thou bringest
her harmless into Allanbay, I will give a hundred pieces of
gold to thee and thy mates.—Shouldst thou peril her in thy
folly, come before my face no more."

' "Peril Beatrice Maxwell, Lord William!" said the Scottish
helmsman, with a look of proud scorn, "My fathers have
fought to the saddle laps in English blood for the men of the
house of Maxwell—and I would rather see all who own the
surname of Forster sinking in the Solway, without one to help
them, than be the cause of the fair maiden of Preston soiling
slipper or snood. I see ye dinna ken the Howatsons of Glenhowan."

' "I know nought of the Howatsons of Glenhowan," said
the bridegroom, "but what I am proud and pleased with—
therefore ply the oar, and manage the sail, for I have men
with me who will put you to your might in both."

'To this conciliating speech the maritime representative of the ancient Howatsons of Glenhowan returned no answer, but busying himself in his vocation, chanted, as was his wont on going upon any important mission, some fragments of an old ballad—made by one of the minstrels of the house of Maxwell, when its glory was at the fullest.

I.

'Give the sail to the south-wind, thou mariner bold,[118]
    Keep the vessel all stately and steady,
And sever the green grassy sward with her prow,
    Where yon lances gleam level and ready.'—
'An ominous star sits above the bright moon,
    And the vessel goes faster and faster;
And see the changed planet, so lovely ev'n now,
    Glows like blood, and betokens disaster.'

2.

'The moon, thou coward churl—lo! see the swift shafts
    All as fleet as the winter snow flying,
And hearken the war steed—he neighs in his strength,
    And tramples the dead and the dying.'
And the bark smote the ground, and ashore they all leapt
    With war-shout, and pipe-note, and clangor
Of two-handed claymore and hauberk—and soon
    Their foes they consumed in their anger.

3.

All on yon fair shore where the cowslips bloom thick,
    And the sea-waves so brightly are leaping,
The sun saw in gladness—the moon saw in death
    Three hundred proud Foresters sleeping:
And long shall the Cumberland damosels weep
    Where the sweet Ellenwater is flowan,
The hour the gay lads of Helvellyn were slain
    By Lord Maxwell and gallant Glenhowan.

'Ere the song had ceased, the bride proceeded to enter the barge, when she perceived at her feet a figure in a black mantle, and scarce refrained from shrieking. "Margery, what wouldst thou with me, Margery?" she said; "the cottage thou livest in I have given thee."

' "Worlds, wealth, and creature comforts, are no cares of mine," said the old domestic of the house of Maxwell. "I laid me down here, that ere Beatrice Maxwell departs with one of a doomed house she should step over my grey hairs. Have I not said—have I not prayed?"

' "Margery, Margery," said the bride, "be silent and be wise."

' "Are we to stand here, and listen to the idle words of a crazed menial?" said one of the house of Maxwell—"aboard, ye gallants, aboard!" and placing the bride on deck, the barges, urged by oar and sail, darted out of the bay of Preston, while the shout and song of clamouring multitudes followed us far into the ocean.

'The wind of the summer twilight, gentle and dewy, went curling the surface of the water; before us the green mountains of Cumberland rose; behind us we beheld the huge outline of the Scottish hills, while, a full stonecast asunder, the barges pursued their way, and the crews, silent and anxious, had each their hopes of conquering in the contest. As we went scudding away, I looked toward the hall of Helvellyn, and there I beheld on its summit the old lord, with his grey hair—his hands clasped, and his eyes turned intent on the barge which contained his son. I thought on the prophecy, and on the vision of the preceding evening, and looked towards the hills of Scotland, now fast diminishing in the distance. At first I thought I saw the waters agitated in the track we had pursued, and continuing to gaze, I observed the sea furrowed into a tremendous hollow, following the sinuous course of the barge. I now knew this to be a whirlwind, and dreading that it would fasten on our sails, I tacked northward—the whirlwind followed also. I tacked southward, and to the south veered the whirlwind, increasing in violence as it came. The last sight I beheld was the sea at our stern, whirling round in fearful undulations. The wind at once seized our sails, turned us thrice about, and down went the barge, headforemost, in the centre of Solway. I was stunned, and felt the cold brine bubbling in my ears, as, emerging from the flood I tried to swim—barge, bridegroom, and mariners were all gone. The bride's barge came in a moment to my side, and saved me, and standing for the coast of Cumberland, spread the tale of sorrow along the shore, where crowds had assembled to welcome us. The old Lord of Helvellyn remained on the castle top, after he had witnessed the loss of his son; and when his favourite servant ventured to approach, he was found seated in his chair, his hands clasped more in resignation than agony, his face turned to the Solway, and his eyes gazing with the deepest intensity, and stiff and dead. The morning tide threw the body of Lord William and those of his six mariners ashore: and when I walked down at day-dawn to the beach, I found them stretched in a row on the very spot where the vision had revealed their fate to me so darkly and so surely. Such a tale as this will be often told you among the sea-coast cottages of Cumberland—Young man, be wise, and weigh well the mysterious ways of Providence.'

JUDITH MACRONE, THE PROPHETESS

'But I am haunted by a fearful shape—[119]
Some hated thing which sharp fear forms of shadows;
Something which takes no known form, yet alarms
Me worse than my worst foeman arm'd in proof—
Something which haunts my slumbers—finds me out
In my deep dreams—in fiercest strife, when blood
Runs rife as rivulet water—in quiet peace
When rustic songs abound—in silent prayer,
For prayer, too, have I tried—still is it there—
Now—now—the dismal shadow stalks before me,
More visible than ever!'

The whole course of Annan-water, in Dumfriesshire, is beautiful; from where it arises among the upland pastures, in the
vicinity of the sources of the Clyde and the Tweed, and winding its way by old churchyard, decayed castle, Roman
encampment, and battle-field, through fine natural groves,
and well cultivated grounds, finally unites its waters with the
sea of Solway, after conferring its name on the pretty little
borough of Annan. The interior of the district, it is true,
presents a singular mixture of desolate nature and rich cultivation; but the immediate banks of the river itself are of a
varied and romantic character. At every turn we take, we
come to nooks of secluded and fairy beauty—groves of fine
ancient trees, coeval with the ruined towers they embosom—
clumps of the most beautiful holly, skirted with *rones*, or irregular rows of hazel, wild cherry, and wild plum, remains of
military or feudal greatness, dismantled keeps or peels, and
repeated vestiges of broad Roman roads and ample camps,
with many of those massive and squat structures, vaulted, and
secured with double iron doors, for the protection of cattle,
in former times, from reavers and forayers. The river itself has
attractions of its own: its inconsiderable waters are pure, and
the pebbles may be numbered in the deepest pools, save when
the stream is augmented by rains; and for the net, the liester,

and the fly-hook, it produces abundance of salmon, grilses, herlings, and trouts.

The peasantry are as varied in their character as the district they inhabit. Agriculture and pasturage claim an equal share in the pursuits of almost every individual; and they are distinguished from the people of many other lowland districts by superior strength, agility, and courage: the free mountain air, gentle labour, and variety of pursuits, give a health and activity which fit them for martial exercises; and they have, perhaps, more of a military air about them, than the inhabitants of any of the neighbouring vales. Many strange, romantic, and martial stories, linger among them; and those who have the good fortune to be admitted to their friendship, or their fireside, may have their condescension richly repaid by curious oral communications, in which history, true and fabulous, and poetry, and superstition, are strangely blended together. The tale of the spirit which for many generations has haunted the castle of Spedlans, will have its narrative of ordinary horror accompanied by fairy legends, and traditions more romantic in their origin, and more deeply steeped in the dews of superstition.

One fine September morning, for the combined purpose of angling, gathering nuts, and exploring the strong holds of the ancient heroes of Annandale—the Hallidays, the Jardines, the Carlyles, the Bells, and the Irvings,—I proceeded up the river bank, and employed my fish-rod with a success which drove me in despair to nut-gathering. It was past mid-day when I arrived at a fine bold sweep of the stream, where the shade of the bordering groves was invitingly cool, and the green sward fresh, soft, and untrodden. The sun was, to use the expression of a Scottish poet,—'wading 'mang the mist,'[120] or as a fastidious Englishman would say, 'struggling amid drizzly rain,' which abated the heat of the luminary, and rendered the grass blade cool and moist. A large oak tree or two, set down in the random beauty of nature, adorned the narrow holm, or bordering of green sward, between the wood and the water; while at the extremity of the walk, where the stream was limited by projecting rocks, stood the remains of one of those square peels, or towers of refuge, already alluded to. The building was roofless; and the walls had been lessened in their height by military violence; while from its interior ascended a thin blue smoke, which, curling away among the

straight stems of the trees, escaped into the free air through
the upper boughs of the grove. Between the tower and the
river lay many webs of fine linen, bleaching on the grass;
while from the ruin itself came the uninterrupted merriment
of some country maidens—a singular medley of open laughter,
fragments of song, and taunts about courtship, and sarcasms
on the lack of lovers.

'Lads!' said a shrill voice, 'I never saw such soulless
coofs—ane would think we had ne'er a tooth in our heads, or
a pair o' lips for the kissing.'

'Kissing, indeed!' said another; 'ane would think our lips
were made for nought save supping curds or croudy, and that
we were suspected of witchcraft,—here we have been daidling
in this den of woe and dool from blessed sun-rise, and deil a
creature with hair on its lip has mistaken its road, and come
near us. I think ancient spunk and glee be dead and gone
from merry Annan-water.'

'Ah, my bonnie lasses,' interrupted an old woman, half
choked with a church-yard cough, 'I mind weel in the
blessed year fifteen, we had a bonnie bleaching in this very
place—there was Jeany Bell, and Kate Bell, her cousin, who
had a misfortune at forty, and was made an honest woman
at fifty-eight; and there was Bell Irving and me,—lads! we
had the choice of the parish; ye might have heard the cares-
sing o' our lips as far as the Wyliehole; and what would ye
think—Pate Irving, now a douce man and a godly, was the
wantonest of all. All, my bonnie kimmers, that was a
night.'

This description of departed joys seemed to infuse its spirit
into the younger branches of the establishment; for while I
pondered how I might introduce myself to these water-
nymphs with discretion and humility, I observed a young rosy
face, ornamented with a profusion of glistering nut-brown
locks, projected past the porch, and reconnoitring me very
steadfastly. A forehead with dark eyes and raven hair instantly
assisted in the scrutiny; and presently the head of the ancient
dame herself appeared, obtruded beyond them both—like
Care looking out between Mirth and Joy, in a modern allegory. A tartan night-cap endeavoured in vain to restrain her
matted and withered hair, which the comb had not for a long
while sought to shed, or the scissors to abridge; her cheeks
were channeled; and a pair of spectacles perched on a nose

something of the colour and shape of a lobster's claw, assisted her in drawing conclusions from the appearance of a stranger.

I heard the tittering and whispering of the maidens; but the voice of the old woman aspired to something more elevated than a whisper, and mingled counsel and scolding in equal quantities.

'A fisher, indeed!' responded the sibyl to the queries of one of her greener companions—'and what's he come to fish? a snow-white web from the bottom of our cauldron?—Aye, aye, 'cause he has ae handsome leg, and something of a merry ee—mind ye, I say na twa—ye christen his calling honest. He's a long black fallow with a tinker look, and I'll warrant there's no his marrow from Longtown to Lochmaben, for robbing hen-roosts; and yet I shouldna wonder, Mysie Dinwoodie, if ye held tryst with that strange lad for a whole night, with no witness save the blessed moon.'

'Hout now, Prudence Caird,' said the fair-haired girl, 'ye are thinking on the mistake ye made with Pate Johnstone, of Dargavel—and how ye failed to mend it with Dick Bell o' Cowfloshan.'

The secret history of the old woman's unhappy loves was interrupted by the appearance of a very handsome girl, who, bearing refreshments for her menials, glided through the grove, with a foot so light and white—a look so sweet—a high white forehead, shaded with locks clustering over the temples—and with eyes so large, so bright, and blue,—that she seemed a personification of the shepherd maidens of Scottish song. Two fine moorland dogs accompanied her: they sat as she sat, stood as she stood, and moved as she moved. She withdrew from her companions, and approached where I stood, with a look at once so sweet and demure, that, trespasser as I imagined myself to be, I was emboldened to abide a rebuke, which I hoped would come softened from such sweet lips. Though apparently examining the progress of her linen towards perfect whiteness, and approaching me rather by a sidelong than a direct step, I observed, by a quick glance of her eye, that I was included in her calculations. I was saved the confusion which a bashful person feels in addressing a stranger, by a voice from the river bank, which, ascending from a small knoll of green willows, sang with singular wildness some snatches of an old ballad.

1.

O Annan runs smoothly atween its green banks,[121]
    The ear may scarce listen its flowing:
Ye may see 'tween the ranks of the lofty green trees
    The golden harvest glowing;
And hear the horn wound—see the husbandman's bands
Fall on with their sharp sickles bright in their hands.

2.

I have seen by thy deep and romantic stream
    The sword of the warrior flashing;
I have seen through thy deep and thy crystal stream
    The barbed war steeds dashing:
There grows not a green tree—there stands not a stone,
But the fall of the valiant and noble has known.

When the song ceased, I observed two hands shedding apart the thick willows, while an eye glanced for a moment through the aperture, on the young maiden and me. A song of a gentler nature instantly followed—and I could not help imagining that my companion felt a particular interest in the minstrel's story. The time and the place contributed to the charm of the sweet voice, and the rustic poetry.

BONNIE MARY HALLIDAY[122]

1.

Bonnie Mary Halliday,
    Turn again, I call you;
If you go to the dewy wood,
    Sorrow will befall you:
The ringdove from the dewy wood
    Is wailing sore, and calling;
And Annan-water, 'tween its banks,
    Is foaming far and falling.

2.

Gentle Mary Halliday,
    Come, my bonnie lady;
Upon the river's woody bank
    My steed is saddled ready;

And for thy haughty kinsmen's threats,
    My faith shall never falter;
The bridal banquet's ready made,
    The priest is at the altar.

3.

Gentle Mary Halliday,
    The towers of merry Preston
Have bridal candles gleaming bright,
    So busk thee, love, and hasten;
Come, busk thee, love, and bowne thee
    Through Tinwald and green Mouswal;
Come, be the grace and be the charm
    To the proud towers of Machusel.

4.

Bonnie Mary Halliday,
    Turn again, I tell you:
For wit, an' grace, an' loveliness,
    What maidens may excel you?
Though Annan has its beauteous dames,
    And Corrie many a fair one,
We canna want thee from our sight,
    Thou lovely and thou rare one.

5.

Bonnie Mary Halliday,
    When the cittern's sounding,
We'll miss thy lightsome lily foot,
    Amang the blythe lads bounding;
The summer sun shall freeze our veins,
    The winter moon shall warm us,
Ere the like of thee shall come again,
    To cheer us and to charm us.

During the song, I walked unconsciously down to the river
bank, and stood on a small promontory which projected into
the stream; it was bordered with willows and wild flowers,
and the summit, nibbled by some pet sheep, was as smooth as
the softest velvet. Here I obtained a full view of this singular
songstress. She was seated among the willows, on the indented
bank, with her bare feet in the stream: a slouched straw hat,

filled with withered flowers and black-cock and peacock feathers, lay at her side; and its removal allowed a fine fleece of hazel-coloured hair to fall down on all sides, till it curled on the grass. She wore a bodice of green tarnished silk; her lower garments were kilted in the thrifty fashion of the country maidens of Caledonia; and round her neck and arm she wore—as much, it is true, for a charm, as an ornament— several bracelets of the hard, round, and bitter berries of the mountain-ash, or witch-tree.

'It is poor Judith Macrone, Sir,' said the maiden, who with the privilege of a listener had come close to my side: 'she has found her bed in the wild woods for some weeks, living on nuts and plums: I wish the poor demented maiden would come and taste some of my curds and cream.'

Judith rose suddenly from her seat, and scattering some handfuls of wild flowers in the stream, exclaimed with something of a scream of recognition: 'Aha, bonnie Mary Halliday, lass, ye wear the snood of singleness yet, for a' yere gentle blood and yere weel-filled farms. But wha's this ye have got with ye? May I love to lie on wet straw wi' a cold sack above me if it is not Francis Forster, all the way from bonnie Derwentwater. Alake, my bonnie lass, for such a wooer! He could nae say seven words of saft, sappy, loving Scotch t'ye, did every word bring for its dower the bonnie lands of Lochwood, which your forefathers lost. No, no—Mary Halliday, take a bonnie Annan-water lad, and let the Southron gang.'

1.

There's bonnie lads on fairy Nith,[123]
    And cannie lads on Dee,
And stately lads on Kinnel side,
    And by Dalgonar tree;
The Nithsdale lads are frank and kind,
    But lack the bright blue ee
Of the bonnie Annan-water lads,
    The wale of lads for me.

2.

There's Willie Watson of Witchstone,
    Dick Irving of Gowktree,
Frank Forest of the Houlet-ha,
    Jock Bell of Lillylea;

But give to me a Halliday,
    The witty, bauld, and free,
The frackest lads of Annan-bank,
    The Hallidays for me.

3.

The Johnstone is a noble name,
    The Jardine is a free,
The Bells are bauld, the Irvings good,
    The Carlyles bear the gree,
Till the gallant Hallidays come in
    With minstrel, mirth, and glee,
Then hey! the lads of Annan-bank,
    The Hallidays for me.

This old rude rhyme was sung with considerable archness
and effect: the songstress then came towards the place where
we stood, not with a regular direct step, but a sidelong hop
and skip, waving, as she came, her bonnet and feathers from
side to side, accompanying every motion with a line of an old
song. Old Prudence Caird seemed scandalized at the extrava-
gant demeanour of the poor girl; and advancing towards her,
waving her hands to be gone, exclaimed,

'In the name of all aboon, what are ye skipping and skirling
there for, ye born gowk and sworn gomeral? Ye'll fall belly-
flaught, breadth and length, on the lily-white linen that has
cost such a cleansing. Away to the woods like another gowk—
away—else I'se kirsen ye with a cupful of scalding water—
my sooth shall I;' and partly suiting the action to the word,
she came forward with a cupful of water in her hand.

The singular person to whom these bitter words were
addressed, heard them with a loud laugh of utter contempt
and scorn; and with a thousand fantastic twirls and freaks, she
threaded, with great dexterity, the whole maze of linen webs,
and confronted old Prudence. She looked her full in the
face—she eyed her on one side, and eyed her on another,—she
stooped down, and she stood on tiptoe, examining her all the
while with an eye of simple, but crafty scrutiny.

'Protect us, Sirs!' said the wandering maiden, 'what wicked
liars these two blue een o' mine are—I'll ne'er credit them
again—and yet, believe me, but it's like her.—Hech be't,
she's sore changed since that merry time—it cannot be her.—

Harkee, my douce decent-looking dame, d'ye ken if Prudence
Caird be living yet?'

'And what hast thou to say to Prudence Caird?' said the
old woman, growing blacker with anger, and clutching, as she
spoke, the long sharp fingers of her right hand, portending
hostility to the blue eyes of Judith.

'Say to Prudence Caird?' said the maiden—'a bonnie question, indeed!—what advice could a poor bewildered creature
like me give to a douce person, who has had twice the benefit
of the counsel of the minister and kirk session?'

And, with unexpected agility, away Judith danced and
leaped, and laughed, eluding the indignation of her less active
antagonist.

I could not help feeling anxious to learn something of the
history of Judith; and while I was expressing this to Mary
Halliday, the poor girl approached and received a bowl of
curds and cream, which she acknowledged with abundance of
fantastic bows and becks.

'Look at her now,' said my companion, 'but say not a
word.'

Judith seated herself on the margin of the river; and throwing a spoonful of the curds into the stream, said, 'There, taste
that, thou sweet and gentle water,—and when I bathe my
burning brow in thy flood, or wade through thee, and through
thee, on the warm moon-light evenings of summer, mind
who fed yere bonnie mottled trouts, and yere lang silver eels,
and no drown me as ye did my bonnie sister Peggy, and her
young bridegroom.' In a small thicket beside her, a bird or
two, confiding in the harmlessness of a creature with whom
they were well acquainted, continued to pour forth their uninterrupted strain of song. 'Ye wee daft things,' said Judith,
changing from a tone of sadness to one of the most giddy
gaiety, 'What sit ye lilting there for, on the broad green
bough—wasting yere sweetest songs on a fool quean like
me,—but ye shall not go unrewarded.' So saying, she scattered a spoonful of curds beside her on the grass, and said,
with some abatement of her mirth—'Come, and peckle at my
hand, my poor feathered innocents—ilka bird of the forest,
save the raven and the hooded crow, is a sister to me.' A red-
breast, as she spoke, with an audacity which that lover of the
human face seldom displays, save when the snow is on the
ground, came boldly to her elbow, and began to obey her

invitation. 'Aha, Rabin, my red-bosomed lover, are ye there? Ye'll find me stiff and streekit under the greenwood bough some morning, and ye mauna stint to deck me out daintily with green leaves, my bonnie man:' and throwing the bird some more curds, she proceeded to sup the remainder herself, indulging between every mouthful in much bewildered talk.

The interest I took in the poor girl—a few handfuls of nuts,—and, above all, a few pleasant glances from one, who (though old, and bent, and withered now) was once twenty-one, had a handsome leg, and mirth in his eye,—obtained me the good graces of the nymphs of Annan-water. Our conversation turned upon poor Judith Macrone.

'She is a poor innocent,' said Mary Halliday, 'as wild and as harmless as the birds she is feeding. She was ever a singular girl, and wit and folly seem to keep alternate sway over her mind.'

'She an innocent!' said Prudence Caird; 'she's a cunning and a crafty quean, with a wicked memory, and a malicious tongue. It sets her weel to wag her fool tongue at me, and say a word that is nae to my credit.'

'Hoot, toot, woman,' said one of the fair-haired menials; 'we can scarce keep our balance with all the wit we have— what can ye expect o' such an addercap as crazy Jude? But of all the queans of Annan-bank, she is the quean for old-world stories. Set her on a sunny hill-side—give her her own will— and, wise or daft, who likes na that?—and she'll clatter ye into a dead sleep, with tales of spirits and apparitions, and the dead who have not peace in the grave, and walk the earth for a season. I heard douce John Stroudwater, the Cameronian elder, say that assuredly an evil spirit has filled her head with fool songs, and queer lang-sin-syne ballads, by and attour a foreknowledge of coming evil. It's well known that she fore-told the drowning of her sister and her bridegroom, in that black pool before us, where poor Jude now sits so sorrowful.'

'Troth and atweel, and that's too true,' said Prudence Caird, 'and I was unwise to grow cankered with such a kittle customer. She tried my patience sore, but I never heard of any one's luck who crossed her—that one never did good that she wished harm to yet,—I hope she'll wish no kittle wish to me.'

'I know not,' said Mary Halliday, with more than ordinary gravity, and in a tone something between hesitation and belief, 'I know not how Judith is informed of evil fortune; but her foreknowledge of human calamity, whether it comes from a good or an evil source, is of no use but to be wondered at, and, perhaps, sorrowed for. What is foredoomed will surely come to pass, and cannot be guarded against; and, therefore, I deem all warning of the event to be vain and useless. But touching her skill in minstrel lore—with her, each oak-tree has its tale, each loop of Annan-water its tradition, and every green knowe or holly-bush, its ballad of true love, or song of knightly bravery.'

'But the story of her sister's bridal,' said one of the menials, 'is the best of all the tales told of idle Jude—it is said to be sorrowful—ye may pick sorrow out of aught, as weel as ye may pick mirth; and some cry for what others laugh at—but I know this, that lang Tam Southeranairn, the tinker, told me, that save the drowning of the bride and bridegroom in the mirkest pool of Annan-water, shame fall of aught saw he to sorrow for; and he would not have such a duck again as he had that blessed night, for all the tup-horns of Dryfesdale, and the heads they grow upon.'

'I had better, without farther clipping and cutting of the bridal tale, relate it at once,' said Mary Halliday; 'it is a strange story, and soon told. The marriage of Margaret, the sister of Judith, happened in the very lap of winter—the snow lay deep on the ground—the ice was thick on the river, and the wheel of her father's mill had not turned round for full forty days. The bride was a sweet, and a kind-hearted, beautiful girl; and there was not a cleverer lad than her bridegroom, David Carlyle, from the head to the foot of Annan-water. I heard the minister of the parish say, after he had joined their hands together, that fifty years he had been a marrier of loving hearts, but he had never married a fairer pair. The bridegroom's mother was a proud dame, of the ancient house of Morison,—she took it sore to heart that her son should marry a miller's daughter; she forbade him, under pain of the mother's curse—and a woman's curse, they say, is a sore one—to bed with his bride under a churl's roof-tree; and as he wished to be happy, to bring her home to his father's house on the night of the wedding.

'Now, ye will consider that the house of the bride stood on one hill side, and the home of the bridegroom on another; while between them, in the bosom of the valley, lay no less a

water than the Annan, with its bank knee-deep in snow, and
its surface plated with ice. The mirk winter night and the
mother's scorn did not prevent one of the blythesomest bridals
from taking place that ever a piper played to, or a maiden
danced in. Ye have never seen, Sir, one of our inland merry-
makings, and seen the lads and the lasses moving merrily to
the sound of the fiddle and the harpstring, else ye might have
some notion of the mirth at Margaret's bridal. The young
were loudest in their joy, but the old were blyther at the
heart; and men forgot their white heads, and women that they
were grandames—and who so glad as they? An old man, one
of the frank-hearted Bells of Middlebee, wiped his brow, as
he sat down from a reel, and said, "Aweel, Mary, my bonnie
lass, there are just three things which intoxicate the heart of
man: first, there is strong drink; secondly, there is music; and
thirdly, there is the company of beautiful women, when they
move to the sound of dulcimer and flute: blest be the Maker,
for they are the most wonderful of all his works."

'But the merriest, as well as the fairest, was the bride herself; she danced with unequalled life and grace—her feet gave
the tone, rather than took it from the fiddle; and the old
men said, the melody of her feet, as they moved on the floor,
would do more mischief among men's hearts than her eyes,
and her eyes were wondrous bright ones. Many stayed from
dancing themselves, and stood in a circle round the place
where she danced. I listened to their remarks, which the catastrophe of the evening impressed on my memory.—"I think,"
said William Johnstone of Chapelknowe, "our bonnie bride's
possest—I never saw her look so sweet, or dance so delight-
fully—It's no sonsie to look so smiling on her wedding-night—
a grave bride's best—owre blythe a bride is seldom a blest
one."—"There's no a sweeter or more modest maid on
Annan-bank," said John Stroudwater, the Cameronian—
who, scorning to mingle in the dance himself, yet could
endure to be a witness of youthful folly where the liquor was
plenty—"she's a bonnie quean; yet I cannot say I like to see
the light which comes from her eyes, as if it were shed from
two stars; nor love I to hearken the vain and wanton sound
which she causeth the planed floor to utter, as she directeth
her steps to the strange outcry of that man's instrument of
wood—called by the profane a fiddle." Nor were the women
without their remarks on the bride's mirth on this unhappy

night. "I protest," said an old dame, in a black hood, "against all this profane minstrelsy and dancing—it is more sinful in its nature than strong drink—I wish good may come of it!" and she paused to moisten her lips with a cup of brandy, to which a piece of sugar, and a single tea-spoonful of water had communicated the lady-like name of cordial.—"I wish, I say, good may come of it—I have not danced these thirty years and three; but the bride is dancing as if this night was her last. I fear she is fey."

'If the bride and bridegroom were blythe, there was another sad enough—even poor Judith, who, retiring from the mirth and the dancing, went to her father's mill-door, and seating herself on a broken millstone, and loosing her locks from the comb, let them fall like a shroud around her, while she gazed intent and silent upon Annan-water, which lay still and clear in the setting light of the moon. I had an early regard for this unhappy maid—we were school-fellows, and play-fellows; and though her temper was wayward,—and her mind, equal to the hardest task one week, was unequal for any kind of learning another; yet, from the frequency of these remarkable fits of impulse and ability, she became one of the finest scholars in Annandale. So I went out into the open air, and found her sitting silent and melancholy, and looking with a fixed and undeviating gaze on the river, which glittered a good half mile distant. I stood beside her, and sought rather to learn what oppressed her spirit, from her actions and her looks, than by questioning her. It has been remarked, that on ordinary occasions, though she is talkative, and fond of singing snatches of songs, yet, when the secret of any coming calamity is communicated to her spirit, she becomes at once silent and gloomy, and seeks to acquaint mankind with the disaster awaiting them, by sensible signs and tokens—a kind of hieroglyphic mode of communication, which she has invented to avoid the misery, perhaps, of open speech. She seemed scarcely aware of my presence.

'At last she threw back her long hair from her face, that nothing might intercept her steady gaze at the river; and plucking a silver bodkin from her bosom, she proceeded to describe on the ground two small and coffin-shaped holes— one something longer than the other. I could not help shuddering while I looked on these symbols of certain fate; and my fears instantly connected what I saw with the wedding, and the bride and bridegroom. I seized her by the arm, and snatching the bodkin from her, said, "Judith, thou art an evil foreboder, and I shall cast this bodkin of thine, which has been made under no good influence, into the blackest pool of Annan-water."—At other times I was an overmatch for her in strength; but when the time of her sorrow came, she seemed to obtain supernatural strength in body as well as in mind; and on this occasion she proved it by leaping swiftly to her feet, and wresting the bodkin from me. She resumed her seat; and taking the bride and bridegroom's ribands from her bosom, she put the latter into the larger grave, and the former in the less, and wrung her hands, threw her hair wildly over her face, and wept and sobbed aloud.

'All this had not passed unobserved of others. "Mercy on us!" cried the Laird of Gooseplat, "but the young witch is casting cantraips, and making the figures of graves, and dooming to the bedral's spade, and the parish mortcloth, the quick instead of the dead. I'se tell thee what, my cannie lass, two red peats and a tar-barrel would make a warm conclusion to these unsonsie spells ye are casting—and may I be choked with a thimbleful of brandy, if ye should want a cross on the brow as deep as the bone, if I had my whittle."—Other spectators came to more charitable conclusions. "Red peats and sharp whittles!" muttered William Graeme of Cummerlair, "I'se tell ye what, laird, if ye lay a hand of harm on the poor demented lassie, I'se lend ye a Lockerby lick to take home with ye.—Eh, Sirs, but this be fearful to look upon—she is showing us by dumb looks, and sure nods, and sad signs, and awful symbols, the coming of wrath and woe. There are two graves, and the bridal ribands laid like corses in them—he that runs may read."

'While this passed out of doors, the dancing and bridal mirth abounded more than ever. It was now ten o'clock; and as the bridal chamber lay a mile distant, the bride and bridegroom prepared to depart, accompanied by a sure friend or two, to witness the conclusion of the marriage. "Let them go," said more voices than one; "we shall make the fiddle-strings chirp, and shake our legs, till the small hours of the morning. Come, Tom Macthairm, play us up something wily and wanton: who can leap rafter-high to a sorrowful psalm tune like that?" The fiddler complied, and wall and rafter quivered and shook to the reviving merriment. The young

couple now stood on the threshold, and looked towards their
future habitation, in which the lights of preparation were
shining.—"An' I were you, bridegroom," said one adviser, "I
would go by the bridge—I have heard oftener than once
to-night the soughing of the west wind, and the roaring of the
linns—the Annan is a fair water in summer-time, but I would
not trust such a bonnie lass as the bride on its fickle bosom
on a winter night."—"An' I were you, bridegroom," said
another counsellor, "I would lippen to the old proverb. The
nearest road to the bride's bed's the best; the bosom of the
Annan-water is bound in ice as hard and as firm as iron—ye
might drive Burnswark-hill over its deepest pools, providing it
had four feet. So dauner away down the edge of the wood,
and cross at the Deadman's-plump—and if ye give me a
shout, and the bride a kiss, when ye cross over't, it will give
pleasure to us both."

'The bride herself came forward, to bid farewell to her
sister, not unconscious that the time of sorrow had come over
her spirit, and that whispers of the import of her predictions
were circulated among the bridal guests. She stood before
Judith with a cheek flushed with dancing, and parting bene-
dictions from rustic lips, and her eyes gleaming with a wild
and unusual light—which has often since been noticed by the
tellers of her melancholy tale, as a light too unlike that of
earthly eyes to be given for her good. "Graves!" said the
bride, with a laugh, which had something of a shriek in it, "is
this all you have as an apology for your fear?—where's your
sight, if your senses be wandering?—My sister has only made
the bridal beds, and strewed them with bridal favours." She
turned round to depart—Judith uttered a piercing shriek, and
throwing her arms about her sister, clung to her, giving one
convulsive sob after another; and, finally, throwing herself
between her and the river, strove, but still strove in silence, to
impress her with a sense of danger. It was in vain: the bride
and bridegroom departed; while Judith, covering, or rather
shrouding herself in her mantle, and turning her face from the
river, sat as mute and as still as a statue; a slight convulsive
shudder was from time to time visible.

'The young pair reached the Annan, and attempted to pass
over the pool called the Deadman's-plump; the dancing and
merriment, which had sustained a brief remission, had recommenced, when, far above the din of the dance and the music,

one shriek, and then another, was heard in the direction of the river. "Hearken the shout!" said one rustic; "the bridegroom is fairly over the water now—then, hey, play up the runaway bride."—"Alas!" answered another peasant, "yon is not the cry of pleasure, but the shriek of agony—my kale-yard to the Johnstone's land, but they are fallen into the Deadman's-plump, and Judith's prophecy's true." The hall-door seemed much too narrow for the multitude who rushed to get out. The shrieks were repeated; and, mingling with the shrieks, and at last o'er-mastering them, was heard the downward dash of Annan-water, which, swollen suddenly with distant rains, descended from the hills with all its increase of waters, lifting the ice before it, and heaving it on the banks with a crash that resounded far and wide. The unhappy pair were seen struggling together against the overpowering element, which, encumbered with ice and trees, filled the channel from bank to bank, and rushed down six feet deep abreast. No effort could be made to save them; and when the river subsided in the morning, they were found in a distant eddy, the bridegroom's left hand round his bride's waist, and his right hand held out like one in the act of swimming. They lie buried together in the old kirk-yard of Dryfesdale. I have often seen Judith sitting weeping on their grave.'

THE GHOST WITH THE GOLDEN CASKET

'Is my soul tamed[124]
And baby-rid with the thought that flood or field
Can render back, to scare men and the moon,
The airy shapes of the corses they enwomb?
And what if 'tis so—shall I lose the crown
Of my most golden hope, 'cause its fair circle
Is haunted by a shadow?'

From the coast of Cumberland the beautiful old Castle of
Caerlaverock is seen standing on the point of a fine green promontory, bounded by the river Nith on one side, by the deep
sea on another, by the almost impassable morass of Solway
on a third; while, far beyond, you observe the three spires of
Dumfries, and the high green hills of Dalswinton and Keir. It
was formerly the residence of the almost princely names of
Douglas, Seaton, Kirkpatrick, and Maxwell: it is now the
dwelling-place of the hawk and the owl; its courts are a lair
for cattle; and its walls afford a midnight shelter to the passing
smuggler; or, like those of the city doomed in Scripture,[125]
are places for the fishermen to dry their nets. Between this fine
old ruin and the banks of the Nith, at the foot of a grove of
pines, and within a stone-cast of tide-mark, the remains of a
rude cottage are yet visible to the curious eye; the bramble
and the wild plum have in vain tried to triumph over the
huge, grey granite blocks, which composed the foundations of
its walls. The vestiges of a small garden may still be traced,
more particularly in summer, when roses and lilies, and other
relics of its former beauty, begin to open their bloom, clinging,
amid the neglect and desolation of the place, with something
like human affection, to the soil. This rustic ruin presents no
attractions to the eye of the profound antiquary, compared to
those of its more stately companion, Caerlaverock Castle; but
with this rude cottage and its garden tradition connects a tale
so wild and so moving, as to elevate it, in the contemplation

of the peasantry, above all the princely feasts and feudal atrocities of its neighbour.

It is now some fifty years since I visited the parish of Caerlaverock; but the memory of its people, its scenery, and the story of the Ghost with the Golden Casket, are as fresh with me as matters of yesterday. I had walked out to the river bank one sweet afternoon of July, when the fishermen were hastening to dip their nets in the coming tide, and the broad waters of the Solway sea were swelling and leaping against bank and cliff, as far as the eye could reach. It was studded over with boats, and its more unfrequented bays were white with water-fowl. I sat down on a small grassy mound between the cottage ruins and the old garden plat, and gazed, with all the hitherto untasted pleasure of a stranger, on the beautiful scene before me. On the right, and beyond the river, the mouldering relics of the ancient religion of Scotland ascended, in unassimilating beauty, above the humble kirk of New-Abbey and its squalid village; farther to the south rose the white sharp cliffs of Barnhourie,—while on the left stood the ancient keeps of Cumlongan, and Torthorald, and the Castle of Caerlaverock. Over the whole looked the stately green mountain of Criffel, confronting its more stately but less beautiful neighbour, Skiddaw; while between them flowed the deep wide sea of Solway, hemmed with cliff, and castle, and town.

As I sat looking on the increasing multitudes of waters, and watching the success of the fishermen, I became aware of the approach of an old man, leading, as one will conduct a dog in a string, a fine young milch cow, in a halter of twisted hair, which passing through the ends of two pieces of flat wood, fitted to the animal's cheek-bones, pressed her nose, and gave her great pain whenever she became disobedient. The cow seemed willing to enjoy the luxury of a browze on the rich pasture which surrounded the little ruined cottage; but in this humble wish she was not to be indulged, for the aged owner, coiling up the tether, and seizing her closely by the head, conducted her past the tempting herbage, towards a small and close-cropt hillock, a good stone-cast distant. In this piece of self-denial the animal seemed reluctant to sympathize—she snuffed the fresh green pasture, and plunged, and startled, and nearly broke away. What the old man's strength seemed nearly unequal to, was accomplished by speech:—

'Bonnie lady, bonnie lady,' said he, in a soothing tone, 'it canna be, it mauna be—hinnie! hinnie! what would become of my three bonnie grand-bairns, made fatherless and mitherless by that false flood afore us, if they supped milk, and tasted butter, that came from the greensward of this doomed and unblessed spot?'

The animal appeared to comprehend something in her own way from the speech of her owner: she abated her resistance; and indulging only in a passing glance at the rich deep herbage, passed on to her destined pasture.

I had often heard of the singular superstitions of the Scottish peasantry, and that every hillock had its song, every hill its ballad, and every valley its tale. I followed with my eye the old man and his cow; he went but a little way, till, seating himself on the ground, retaining still the tether in his hand, he said, 'Now, bonnie lady, feast thy fill on this good greensward—it is halesome and holy, compared to the sward at the doomed cottage of auld Gibbie Gyrape—leave that to smugglers' nags: Willie o'Brandyburn and Roaring Jock o'Kempstane will ca' the haunted ha' a hained bit—they are godless fearnoughts.' I looked at the person of the peasant: he was a stout hale old man, with a weather-beaten face, furrowed something by time, and, perhaps, by sorrow. Though summer was at its warmest, he wore a broad chequered mantle, fastened at the bosom with a skewer of steel,—a broad bonnet, from beneath the circumference of which straggled a few thin locks, as white as driven snow, shining like amber, and softer than the finest flax,—while his legs were warmly cased in blue-ribbed boot-hose. Having laid his charge to the grass, he looked leisurely around him, and espying me—a stranger, and dressed above the manner of the peasantry, he acknowledged my presence by touching his bonnet; and, as if willing to communicate something of importance, he struck the tether stake in the ground, and came to the old garden fence.

Wishing to know the peasant's reasons for avoiding the ruins, I thus addressed him:—'This is a pretty spot, my aged friend, and the herbage looks so fresh and abundant, that I would advise thee to bring thy charge hither; and while she continued to browze, I would gladly listen to the history of thy white locks, for they seem to have been bleached in many tempests.'

'Aye, aye,' said the peasant, shaking his white head with a

grave smile, 'they have braved sundry tempests between sixteen and sixty; but, touching this pasture, Sir, I know nobody who would like their cows to crop it,—the aged cattle shun the place,—the bushes bloom, but bear no fruit,—the birds never build in the branches,—the children never come near to play,—and the aged never choose it for a resting-place; but pointing it out, as they pass, to the young, tell them the story of its desolation. Sae ye see, Sir, having nae good will to such a spot of earth myself, I like little to see a stranger sitting in such an unblessed place; and I would as good as advise ye to come owre with me to the cowslip knoll,—there are reasons mony that an honest man should nae sit there.'

I arose at once, and seating myself beside the peasant, on the cowslip knoll, desired to know something of the history of the spot from which he had just warned me. The Caledonian looked on me with an air of embarrassment.

'I am just thinking,' said he, 'that as ye are an Englishman, I should nae acquaint ye with such a story. Ye'll make it, I'm doubting, a matter of reproach and vaunt, when ye gae hame, how Willie Borlan o' Caerlaverock told ye a tale of Scottish iniquity, that cowed all the stories in Southron book or history.'

This unexpected obstacle was soon removed. 'My sage and considerate friend,' I said, 'I have the blood in my bosom will keep me from revealing such a tale to the scoffer and scorner. I am something of a Caerlaverock man—the grandson of Marion Stobie of Dookdub.'

The peasant seized my hand—'Marion Stobie! bonnie Marion Stobie o' Dookdub—whom I wooed sae sair, and loved sae lang!—Man, I love ye for her sake; and well was it for her braw English bridegroom, that William Borlan—frail and faded now, but strong and in manhood then—was a thousand miles from Caerlaverock, rolling on the salt sea, when she was brided:—ye have the glance of her ee,—I could ken't yet amang ten thousand, grey as my head is. I will tell the grandson of bonnie Marion Stobie ony tale he likes to ask for; and the Story of the Ghost and the Gowd Casket shall be foremost.

'You may imagine, then,' said the old Caerlaverock peasant, rising at once with the commencement of his story from his native dialect into very passable English—'you may imagine these ruined walls raised again in their beauty—

whitened, and covered with a coating of green broom; that
garden, now desolate, filled with herbs in their season, and
with flowers, hemmed round with a fence of cherry and plum-
trees; and the whole possessed by a young fisherman, who
won a fair subsistence for his wife and children from the
waters of the Solway sea: you may imagine it, too, as far from
the present time as fifty years. There are only two persons
living now, who remember when the Bonne-Homme-Richard,
the first ship ever Richard Faulder commanded,[126] was
wrecked on the Pellock sand,—one of these persons now
addresses you—the other is the fisherman who once owned
that cottage,—whose name ought never to be named, and
whose life seems lengthened as a warning to the earth, how
fierce God's judgments are. Life changes—all breathing things
have their time and their season; but the Solway flows in the
same beauty—Criffel rises in the same majesty—the light of
morning comes, and the full moon arises now, as they did
then;—but this moralizing matters little. It was about the
middle of harvest—I remember the day well—it had been
sultry and suffocating, accompanied by rushings of wind, sudden convulsions of the water, and cloudings of the sun:—I
heard my father sigh, and say, "Dool—dool to them found on
the deep sea to-night—there will happen strong storm and
fearful tempest." The day closed, and the moon came over
Skiddaw: all was perfectly clear and still—frequent dashings
and whirling agitations of the sea were soon heard mingling
with the hasty clang of the water-fowls' wings, as they forsook
the waves, and sought shelter among the hollows of the rocks.
The storm was nigh. The sky darkened down at once—clap
after clap of thunder followed—and lightning flashed so
vividly, and so frequent, that the wide and agitated expanse of
Solway was visible from side to side—from St. Bees to Barnhourie. A very heavy rain, mingled with hail, succeeded; and
a wind accompanied it, so fierce, and so high, that the white
foam of the sea was showered as thick as snow on the summit
of Caerlaverock Castle.

'Through this perilous sea, and amid this darkness and
tempest, a bark was observed coming swiftly down the middle
of the sea; her sails rent, and her decks crowded with people.
The carry, as it is called, of the tempest, was direct from
St. Bees to Caerlaverock; and experienced swains could see
that the bark would be driven full on the fatal shoals of the

Scottish side; but the lightning was so fierce that few dared venture to look on the approaching vessel, or take measures for endeavouring to preserve the lives of the unfortunate mariners. My father stood on the threshold of his door, and beheld all that passed in the bosom of the sea. The bark approached fast—her canvas rent to threads, her masts nearly levelled with the deck, and the sea foaming over her so deep, and so strong, as to threaten to sweep the remains of her crew from the little refuge the broken masts and splintered beams still afforded them. She now seemed within half a mile of the shore, when a strong flash of lightning, that appeared to hang over the bark for a moment, showed the figure of a lady, richly dressed, clinging to a youth who was pressing her to his bosom. My father exclaimed, "Saddle me my black horse, and saddle me my grey, and bring them down to the Dead-man's bank,"—and, swift in action as he was in resolve, he hastened to the shore, his servants following with his horses. The shore of Solway presented then, as it does now, the same varying line of coast; and the house of my father stood in the bosom of a little bay, nearly a mile from where we sit. The remains of an old forest interposed between the bay at Dead-man's bank, and the bay at our feet; and mariners had learned to wish, that if it were their doom to be wrecked, it might be in the bay of douce William Borlan, rather than that of Gilbert Gyrape, the proprietor of that ruined cottage. But human wishes are vanities, wished either by sea or land. I have heard my father say he could never forget the cries of the mariners, as the bark smote on the Pellock-bank, and the flood rushed through the chasms made by the concussion; but he would far less forget the agony of a lady—the loveliest that could be looked upon, and the calm and affectionate courage of the young man who supported her, and endeavoured to save her from destruction. Richard Faulder, the only man who survived, has often sat at my fire-side, and sung me a very rude, but a very moving ballad, which he made on this young and unhappy pair; and the old mariner assured me he had only added rhymes, and a descriptive line or two, to the language in which Sir William Musgrave endeavoured to soothe and support his wife.'

It seemed a thing truly singular, that at this very moment two young fishermen, who sat on the margin of the sea below us, watching their halve-nets, should sing, and with much

sweetness, the very song the old man had described. They
warbled verse and verse alternately—and rock and bay
seemed to retain and then release the sound. Nothing is so
sweet as a song by the sea-side on a tranquil evening.

SIR WILLIAM MUSGRAVE[127]

First Fisherman

'O lady, lady, why do you weep?
Though the wind be loos'd on the raging deep,
Though the heaven be mirker than mirk may be,
And our frail bark ships a fearful sea,—
Yet thou art safe—as on that sweet night
When our bridal candles gleamed far and bright.'—
There came a shriek, and there came a sound,
And the Solway roar'd, and the ship spun round.

Second Fisherman

'O lady, lady, why do you cry?
Though the waves be flashing top-mast high,
Though our frail bark yields to the dashing brine,
And heaven and earth show no saving sign,
There is One who comes in the time of need,
And curbs the waves as we curb a steed.'—
The lightning came with the whirlwind blast,
And cleav'd the prow, and smote down the mast.

First Fisherman

'O lady, lady, weep not, nor wail,
Though the sea runs howe as Dalswinton vale,
Then flashes high as Barnhourie brave,
And yawns for thee, like the yearning grave—
Though 'twixt thee and the ravening flood
There is but my arm, and this splintering wood,
The fell quicksand, or the famish'd brine,
Can ne'er harm a face so fair as thine.'

Both

'O lady, lady, be bold and brave,
Spread thy white breast to the fearful wave,
And cling to me with that white right hand,
And I'll set thee safe on the good dry land.'—
A lightning flash on the shallop strook,
The Solway roar'd, and Caerlaverock shook;
From the sinking ship there were shriekings cast,
That were heard above the tempest's blast.

The young fishermen having concluded their song, my companion proceeded—'The lightning still flashed vivid and fast, and the storm raged with unabated fury; for between the ship and the shore the sea broke in frightful undulation, and leaped on the greensward several fathoms deep abreast. My father, mounted on one horse, and holding another in his hand, stood prepared to give all the aid that a brave man could to the unhappy mariners; but neither horse nor man could endure the onset of that tremendous surge. The bark bore for a time the fury of the element—but a strong eastern wind came suddenly upon her, and, crushing her between the wave and the freestone bank, drove her from the entrance of my father's little bay towards the dwelling of Gibbie Gyrape, and the thick forest intervening, she was out of sight in a moment. My father saw, for the last time, the lady and her husband looking shoreward from the side of the vessel, as she drifted along; and as he galloped round the head of the forest, he heard for the last time the outcry of some, and the wail and intercession of others. When he came before the fisherman's house, a fearful sight presented itself—the ship, dashed to atoms, covered the shore with its wreck, and with the bodies of the mariners—not a living soul escaped, save Richard Faulder, whom the fiend who guides the spectre-shallop of Solway had rendered proof to perils on the deep. The fisherman himself came suddenly from his cottage, all dripping and drenched, and my father addressed him:—"O, Gilbert, Gilbert, what a fearful sight is this!—has Heaven blessed thee with making thee the means of saving a human soul?" "Nor soul nor body have I saved," said the fisherman, doggedly: "I have done my best—the storm proved too stark, and the lightning too fierce for me—their boat alone came near with a lady and a

casket of gold—but she was swallowed up with the surge."
My father confessed afterwards that he was touched with the
tone in which these words were delivered, and made answer,
"If thou hast done thy best to save souls to-night, a bright
reward will be thine—if thou hast been fonder for gain than
for working the mariners' redemption, thou hast much to
answer for."—As he uttered these words, an immense wave
rolled landward as far as the place where they stood—it
almost left its foam on their faces, and suddenly receding,
deposited at their feet the dead body of the lady. As my father
lifted her in his arms, he observed that the jewels which had
adorned her hair, at that time worn long—had been forcibly
rent away—the diamonds and gold that enclosed her neck,
and ornamented the bosom of her rich satin dress, had been
torn off—the rings removed from her fingers—and on her
neck, lately so lily-white and pure, there appeared the marks
of hands—not laid there in love and gentleness, but with a
fierce and deadly grasp.

'The lady was buried with the body of her husband, side
by side, in Caerlaverock burial-ground. My father never
openly accused Gilbert the fisherman of having murdered the
lady for her riches as she reached the shore, preserved, as
was supposed, from sinking, by her long, wide, and stiff satin
robes—but from that hour till the hour of his death, my father
never broke bread with him—never shook him or his by the
hand, nor spoke with them in wrath or in love. The fisherman,
from that time, too, waxed rich and prosperous—and from
being the needy proprietor of a halve-net, and the tenant at
will of a rude cottage, he became, by purchase, lord of a
handsome inheritance, proceeded to build a bonny mansion,
and called it Gyrape-ha'; and became a leading man in a flock
of a purer kind of Presbyterians—and a precept and example
to the community.

'Though the portioner of Gyrape-ha' prospered wondrously,
his claims to parochial distinction, and the continuance of his
fortune, were treated with scorn by many, and with doubt
by all: though nothing open or direct was said—looks, more
cutting at times than the keenest speech, and actions still
more expressive, showed that the hearts of honest men were
alienated—the cause was left to his own interpretation. The
peasant scrupled to become his servant—sailors hesitated to
receive his grain on board, lest perils should find them on the

deep—the beggar ceased to solicit alms—the drover and
horse-couper, an unscrupling generation, found out a more
distant mode of concluding bargains than by shaking his
hand—his daughters, handsome and blue-eyed, were neither
wooed nor married—no maiden would hold tryste with his
sons—though maidens were then as little loth as they are now;
and the aged peasant, as he passed his new mansion, would
shake his head and say—"The voice of spilt blood will be
lifted up against thee—and a spirit shall come up from the
waters will make the corner-stone of thy habitation tremble
and quake."

'It happened, during the summer which succeeded this
unfortunate shipwreck, that I accompanied my father to the
Solway, to examine his nets. It was near midnight—the tide
was making, and I sat down by his side, and watched the
coming of the waters. The shore was glittering in starlight as
far as the eye could reach. Gilbert, the fisherman, had that
morning removed from his cottage to his new mansion—the
former was, therefore, untenanted; and the latter, from its
vantage ground on the crest of the hill, threw down to us the
sound of mirth, and music, and dancing, a revelry common
in Scotland on taking possession of a new house. As we lay
quietly looking on the swelling sea, and observing the water-
fowl swimming and ducking in the increasing waters, the
sound of the merriment became more audible. My father
listened to the mirth, looked to the sea, looked to the deserted
cottage, and then to the new mansion, and said:—"My son,
I have a counsel to give thee—treasure it in thy heart, and
practise it in thy life—the daughters of *him* of Gyrape-ha' are
fair, and have an eye that would wile away the wits of the
wisest—their father has wealth—I say nought of the way he
came by it—they will have golden portions doubtless. But I
would rather lay thy head aneath the gowans in Caerlaverock
kirkyard, and son have I none beside thee, than see thee lay
it on the bridal pillow with the begotten of that man, though
she had Nithsdale for her dowry. Let not my words be as seed
sown on the ocean—I may not now tell thee why this warning
is given. Before that fatal shipwreck, I would have said
Prudence Gyrape, in her kirtle, was a better bride than some
who have golden dowers. I have long thought some one would
see a sight—and often, while holding my halve-net in the
midnight tide, have I looked for something to appear—for

where blood is shed, there doth the spirit haunt for a time,
and give warning to man. May I be strengthened to endure
the sight!"

'I answered not—being accustomed to regard my father's
counsel as a matter not to be debated, as a solemn command:
we heard something like the rustling of wings on the water,
accompanied by a slight curling motion of the tide. "God
haud his right hand about us!" said my father, breathing thick
with emotion and awe, and looking on the sea with a gaze so
intense that his eyes seemed to dilate, and the hair of his forehead to project forward, and bristle into life. I looked, but
observed nothing, save a long line of thin and quivering light,
dancing along the surface of the sea: it ascended the bank,
on which it seemed to linger for a moment, and then entering
the fisherman's cottage, made roof and rafter gleam with a
sudden illumination. "I'll tell thee what, Gibbie Gyrape," said
my father, "I wouldna be the owner of thy heart, and the proprietor of thy right hand, for all the treasures in earth and
ocean."—A loud and piercing scream from the cottage made
us thrill with fear, and in a moment the figures of three
human beings rushed into the open air, and ran towards us
with a swiftness which supernatural dread alone could inspire.
We instantly knew them to be three noted smugglers, who
infested the country; and rallying when they found my father
maintain his ground, they thus mingled their fears and the
secrets of their trade—for terror fairly overpowered their habitual caution.

' "I vow by the night tide, and the crooked timber,"[128] said
Willie Weethause, "I never beheld sic a light as yon since
our distillation pipe took fire, and made a burnt, instead of a
drink-offering of our spirits; I'll uphold it comes for nae
good—a warning may be—sae ye may gang on, Wattie
Bouseaway, wi' yere wickedness; as for me, I'se gae hame
and repent."—"Saulless bodie!" said his companion, whose
natural hardihood was considerably supported by his communion with the brandy cup—"Saulless bodie, for a flaff o' fire
and a maiden's shadow would ye forswear the gallant trade?
Saul to gude! but auld Miller Morison shall turn yere thrapple
into a drain-pipe to wyse the waste water from his mill, if ye
turn back now, and help us nae through with as strong an
importation as ever cheered the throat, and cheeped in the
crapin. Confound the fizzenless bodie! he glowers as if this fine

starlight were something frae the warst side of the world,
and thae staring een o' his are busy shaping heaven's sweetest
and balmiest air into the figures of wraiths and goblins."—
"Robert Telfer," said my father, addressing the third smuggler, "tell me nought of the secrets of your perilous craft—but
tell me what you have seen, and why ye uttered that fearful
scream, that made the wood-doves start from Caerlaverock
pines."—"I'll tell ye what, goodman," said the mariner, "I
have seen the fires o' heaven running as thick along the sky,
and on the surface of the ocean, as ye ever saw the blaze on a
bowl o' punch at a merry-making, and neither quaked nor
screamed; but ye'll mind the light that came to that cottage
to-night was one for some fearful purport, which let the wise
expound; sae it lessened nae one's courage to quail for sic an
apparition. Od! if I thought living soul would ever make the
start I gied an upcast to me, I'll drill his breast-bane wi' my
dirk like a turnip lantern."

'My father mollified the wrath of this maritime desperado,
by assuring him he beheld the light go from the sea to the
cottage, and that he shook with terror, for it seemed no
common light. "Ou God! then," said hopeful Robin, "since it
was one o' our ain cannie sea apparitions, I care less about
it—I took it for some landward sprite! and now I think on't,
where were my een? did it no stand amang its ain light, with
its long hanks of hair dripping, and drenched; with a casket
of gold in ae hand, and the other guarding its throat? I'll be
bound it's the ghost o' some sonsie lass that has had her neck
nipped for her gold—and had she stayed till I emptied the
bicker o' brandy, I would have ask'd a cannie question or
twae." Willie Weethause had now fairly overcome his conster-
nation, and began to feel all his love for the gallant trade, as
his comrade called it, return. "The tide serves, lads! the tide
serves; let us slip our drap o' brandy into the bit bonnie boat,
and tottle away amang the sweet starlight as far as the King-
holm or the town quarry—ye ken we have to meet Bailie
Gardevine, and laird Soukaway o' Ladlemouth." They
returned, not without hesitation and fear, to the old cottage;
carried their brandy to the boat; and as my father and I went
home, we heard the dipping of their oars in the Nith, along
the banks of which they sold their liquor, and told their tale of
fear, magnifying its horror at every step, and introducing
abundance of variations.

'The story of the Ghost with the Golden Casket flew over the country side with all its variations, and with many comments: some said they saw her, and some thought they saw her—and those who had the hardihood to keep watch on the beach at midnight, had their tales to tell of terrible lights and strange visions. With one who delighted in the marvellous, the spectre was decked in attributes that made the circle of auditors tighten round the hearth; while others, who allowed to a ghost only a certain quantity of thin air to clothe itself in, reduced it in their description to a very unpoetic shadow, or a kind of better sort of will-o'-the-wisp, that could for its own amusement counterfeit the human shape. There were many who, like my father, beheld the singular illumination appear at midnight on the coast; saw also something sailing along with it in the form of a lady in bright garments, her hair long and wet, and shining in diamonds; and heard a struggle, and the shriek as of a creature drowning.

'The belief of the peasantry did not long confine the apparition to the sea coast; it was seen sometimes late at night far inland, and following Gilbert the Fisherman, like a human shadow—like a pure light—like a white garment—and often in the shape, and with the attributes, in which it disturbed the carousal of the smugglers. I heard douce Davie Haining—a God-fearing man, and an elder of the Burgher congregation, and on whose word I could well lippen, when drink was kept from his head,—I heard him say that as he rode home late from the Roodfair[129] of Dumfries—the night was dark, there lay a dusting of snow on the ground, and no one appeared on the road but himself—he was lilting and singing the cannie end of the auld sang, "There's a cuttie stool in our Kirk,"[130] which was made on some foolish quean's misfortune, when he heard the sound of horses' feet behind him at full gallop, and ere he could look round, who should flee past, urging his horse with whip and spur, but Gilbert the Fisherman! "Little wonder that he galloped," said the elder, "for a fearful form hovered around him, making many a clutch at him, and with every clutch uttering a shriek most piercing to hear." But why should I make a long story of a common tale? The curse of spilt blood fell on him, and on his children, and on all he possessed;—his sons and daughters died, his flocks perished, his grain grew, but never filled the ear; and fire came from heaven, or rose from hell, and consumed his house, and all that was therein. He is now a man of ninety years—a fugitive and a vagabond on the earth, without a house to put his white head in, with the unexpiated curse still clinging to him.'

While my companion was making this summary of human wretchedness, I observed the figure of a man, stooping to the earth with extreme age, gliding through among the bushes of the ruined cottage, and approaching the advancing tide. He wore a loose great coat, patched to the ground, and fastened round his waist by a belt and buckle,—the remains of stockings and shoes were on his feet; a kind of fisherman's cap surmounted some remaining white hairs, while a long peeled stick supported him as he went. My companion gave an involuntary shudder when he saw him—'Lo, and behold, now, here comes Gilbert the Fisherman! once every twenty-four hours doth he come, let the wind and the rain be as they will, to the nightly tide, to work o'er again, in imagination, his auld tragedy of unrighteousness. See how he waves his hand, as if he welcomed some one from sea—he raises his voice, too, as if something in the water required his counsel; and see how he dashes up to the middle, and grapples with the water as if he clutched a human being!'

I looked on the old man, and heard him call, in a hollow and broken voice, 'O hoy! the ship, O hoy,—turn your boat's head ashore!—and my bonnie lady, keep haud o' yere casket.—Hech be't! that wave would have sunk a three-decker, let be a slender boat—see—see an' she binna sailing aboon the water like a wild swan!'—and, wading deeper in the tide as he spoke, he seemed to clutch at something with both hands, and struggle with it in the water.

'Na! na! dinna haud your white hands to me—ye wear owre mickle gowd in your hair, and o'er many diamonds on your bosom, to 'scape drowning. There's as mickle gowd in this casket as would have sunk thee seventy fathom deep.' And he continued to hold his hands under the water, muttering all the while.

'She's half gane now—and I'll be a braw laird, and build a bonnie house, and gang crousely to kirk and market—now I may let the waves work their will—my work will be ta'en for theirs.'

He turned to wade to the shore, but a large and heavy wave came full dash on him, and bore him off his feet, and ere any assistance reached him, all human aid was too late; for nature was so exhausted with the fulness of years, and with his exertions, that a spoonful of water would have drowned him. The body of this miserable old man was interred, after some opposition from the peasantry, beneath the wall of the kirkyard; and from that time, the Ghost with the Golden Casket was seen no more, and only continued to haunt the evening tale of the hind and the farmer.

THE HAUNTED SHIPS

———————————'Though my mind's not[131]
Hoodwink'd with rustic marvels, I do think
There are more things in the grove, the air, the flood,
Yea, and the charnell'd earth, than what wise man,
Who walks so proud as if his form alone
Fill'd the wide temple of the universe,
Will let a frail mind say. I'd write i' the creed
O' the sagest head alive, that fearful forms,
Holy or reprobate, do page men's heels;
That shapes, too horrid for our gaze, stand o'er
The murderer's dust, and for revenge glare up,
Even till the stars weep fire for very pity.'

Along the sea of Solway, romantic on the Scottish side, with
its woodland, its bays, its cliffs, and headlands; and interesting
on the English side, with its many beautiful towns with their
shadows on the water, rich pastures, safe harbours, and
numerous ships; there still linger many traditional stories of a
maritime nature, most of them connected with superstitions
singularly wild and unusual. To the curious these tales afford
a rich fund of entertainment, from the many diversities of the
same story; some dry and barren, and stripped of all the
embellishments of poetry; others dressed out in all the riches
of a superstitious belief and haunted imagination. In this they
resemble the inland traditions of the peasants; but many of
the oral treasures of the Galwegian or the Cumbrian coast
have the stamp of the Dane and the Norseman upon them,
and claim but a remote or faint affinity with the legitimate
legends of Caledonia. Something like a rude prosaic outline of
several of the most noted of the northern ballads, the adventures and depredations of the old ocean kings, still lends life to
the evening tale; and, among others, the story of the Haunted
Ships is still popular among the maritime peasantry.

One fine harvest evening, I went on board the shallop of
Richard Faulder, of Allanbay;[132] and, committing ourselves
to the waters, we allowed a gentle wind from the east to waft
us at its pleasure towards the Scottish coast. We passed the

sharp promontory of Siddick; and skirting the land within a
stone-cast, glided along the shore till we came within sight of
the ruined Abbey of Sweetheart. The green mountain of
Criffel ascended beside us; and the bleat of the flocks from its
summit, together with the winding of the evening horn of the
reapers, came softened into something like music over land
and sea. We pushed our shallop into a deep and wooded bay,
and sat silently looking on the serene beauty of the place.
The moon glimmered in her rising through the tall shafts of
the pines of Caerlaverock; and the sky, with scarce a cloud,
showered down on wood, and headland, and bay, the twinkling beams of a thousand stars, rendering every object visible.
The tide, too, was coming with that swift and silent swell
observable when the wind is gentle; the woody curves along
the land were filling with the flood, till it touched the green
branches of the drooping trees; while in the centre current the
roll and the plunge of a thousand pellocks told to the experienced fisherman that salmon were abundant.

As we looked, we saw an old man emerging from a path
that winded to the shore through a grove of doddered hazel;
he carried a halve-net on his back, while behind him came a
girl, bearing a small harpoon with which the fishers are
remarkably dexterous in striking their prey. The senior seated
himself on a large grey stone, which overlooked the bay, laid
aside his bonnet, and submitted his bosom and neck to the
refreshing sea breeze; and taking his harpoon from his attendant, sat with the gravity and composure of a spirit of the
flood, with his ministering nymph behind him. We pushed our
shallop to the shore, and soon stood at their side.

'This is old Mark Macmoran, the mariner, with his grand-
daughter Barbara,' said Richard Faulder, in a whisper that
had something of fear in it; 'he knows every creek, and cavern,
and quicksand, in Solway,—has seen the Spectre Hound that
haunts the Isle of Man; has heard him bark, and at every bark
has seen a ship sink; and he has seen, too, the Haunted Ships
in full sail; and, if all tales be true, he has sailed in them
himself; he's an awful person.'

Though I perceived in the communication of my friend
something of the superstition of the sailor, I could not help
thinking that common rumour had made a happy choice in
singling out old Mark to maintain her intercourse with the
invisible world. His hair, which seemed to have refused all

intercourse with the comb, hung matted upon his shoulders; a kind of mantle, or rather blanket, pinned with a wooden skewer round his neck, fell mid-leg down, concealing all his nether garments as far as a pair of hose, darned with yarn of all conceivable colours, and a pair of shoes, patched and repaired till nothing of the original structure remained, and clasped on his feet with two massy silver buckles. If the dress of the old man was rude and sordid, that of his grand-daughter was gay, and even rich. She wore a bodice of fine wool, wrought round the bosom with alternate leaf and lily, and a kirtle of the same fabric, which, almost touching her white and delicate ankle, showed her snowy feet, so fairy-light and round that they scarcely seemed to touch the grass where she stood. Her hair, a natural ornament which woman seeks much to improve, was of bright glossy brown, and encumbered rather than adorned with a snood, set thick with marine productions, among which the small clear pearl found in the Solway was conspicuous. Nature had not trusted to a hand-some shape, and a sylph-like air, for young Barbara's influence over the heart of man; but had bestowed a pair of large bright blue eyes, swimming in liquid light, so full of love, and gentle-ness, and joy, that all the sailors from Annanwater to far Saint Bees acknowledged their power, and sung songs about the bonnie lass of Mark Macmoran. She stood holding a small gaff-hook of polished steel in her hand, and seemed not dis-satisfied with the glances I bestowed on her from time to time, and which I held more than requited by a single glance of those eyes which retained so many capricious hearts in sub-jection.

The tide, though rapidly augmenting, had not yet filled the bay at our feet. The moon now streamed fairly over the tops of Caerlaverock pines, and showed the expanse of ocean dimpling and swelling, on which sloops and shallops came dancing, and displaying at every turn their extent of white sail against the beam of the moon. I looked on old Mark the Mariner, who, seated motionless on his grey stone, kept his eye fixed on the increasing waters with a look of seriousness and sorrow in which I saw little of the calculating spirit of a mere fisherman. Though he looked on the coming tide, his eyes seemed to dwell particularly on the black and decayed hulls of two vessels, which, half immersed in the quicksand, still addressed to every heart a tale of shipwreck and desolation. The tide wheeled and foamed around them; and creeping inch by inch up the side, at last fairly threw its waters over the top, and a long and hollow eddy showed the resistance which the liquid element received.

The moment they were fairly buried in the water, the old man clasped his hands together, and said, 'Blessed be the tide that will break over and bury ye for ever! Sad to mariners, and sorrowful to maids and mothers, has the time been you have choked up this deep and bonnie bay. For evil were you sent, and for evil have you continued. Every season finds from you its song of sorrow and wail, its funeral processions, and its shrouded corses. Woe to the land where the wood grew that made ye! Cursed be the axe that hewed ye on the mountains, the hands that joined ye together, the bay that ye first swam in, and the wind that wafted ye here! Seven times have ye put my life in peril, three fair sons have ye swept from my side, and two bonnie grand-bairns; and now, even now, your waters foam and flash for my destruction, did I venture my infirm limbs in quest of food in your deadly bay. I see by that ripple and that foam, and hear by the sound and singing of your surge, that ye yearn for another victim; but it shall not be me nor mine.'

Even as the old mariner addressed himself to the wrecked ships, a young man appeared at the southern extremity of the bay, holding his halve-net in his hand, and hastening into the current. Mark rose, and shouted, and waved him back from a place which, to a person unacquainted with the dangers of the bay, real and superstitious, seemed sufficiently perilous: his grand-daughter, too, added her voice to his, and waved her white hands; but the more they strove, the faster advanced the peasant, till he stood to his middle in the water, while the tide increased every moment in depth and strength. 'Andrew, Andrew,' cried the young woman, in a voice quavering with emotion, 'turn, turn, I tell you: O the Ships, the Haunted Ships!' but the appearance of a fine run of fish had more influence with the peasant than the voice of bonnie Barbara, and forward he dashed, net in hand. In a moment he was borne off his feet, and mingled like foam with the water, and hurried towards the fatal eddies which whirled and roared round the sunken ships. But he was a powerful young man, and an expert swimmer: he seized on one of the projecting ribs of the nearest hulk, and clinging to it with the grasp of despair, uttered yell after yell, sustaining himself against the prodigious rush of the current.

From a shealing of turf and straw, within the pitch of a bar from the spot where we stood, came out an old woman bent with age, and leaning on a crutch. 'I heard the voice of that lad Andrew Lammie; can the chield be drowning, that he skirls sae uncannilie?' said the old woman, seating herself on the ground, and looking earnestly at the water. 'Ou aye,' she continued, 'he's doomed, he's doomed; heart and hand can never save him; boats, ropes, and man's strength and wit, all vain! vain! he's doomed, he's doomed!'

By this time I had thrown myself into the shallop, followed reluctantly by Richard Faulder, over whose courage and kindness of heart superstition had great power; and with one push from the shore, and some exertion in sculling, we came within a quoit-cast of the unfortunate fisherman. He staid not to profit by our aid; for when he perceived us near, he uttered a piercing shriek of joy, and bounded towards us through the agitated element the full length of an oar. I saw him for a second on the surface of the water; but the eddying current sucked him down; and all I ever beheld of him again was his hand held above the flood, and clutching in agony at some imaginary aid. I sat gazing in horror on the vacant sea before us: but a breathing time before, a human being, full of youth, and strength, and hope, was there: his cries were still ringing in my ears, and echoing in the woods; and now nothing was seen or heard save the turbulent expanse of water, and the sound of its chafing on the shores. We pushed back our shallop, and resumed our station on the cliff beside the old mariner and his descendant.

'Wherefore sought ye to peril your own lives fruitlessly?' said Mark, 'in attempting to save the doomed. Whoso touches those infernal ships, never survives to tell the tale. Woe to the man who is found nigh them at midnight when the tide has subsided, and they arise in their former beauty, with forecastle, and deck, and sail, and pennon, and shroud! Then is seen the streaming of lights along the water from their cabin windows, and then is heard the sound of mirth and the clamour of tongues, and the infernal whoop and halloo, and song, ringing far and wide. Woe to the man who comes nigh them!'

To all this my Allanbay companion listened with a breath-

less attention. I felt something touched with a superstition to
which I partly believed I had seen one victim offered up; and
I inquired of the old mariner, 'How and when came these
Haunted Ships there? To me they seem but the melancholy
relics of some unhappy voyagers, and much more likely to
warn people to shun destruction, than entice and delude them
to it.'

'And so,' said the old man with a smile, which had more
of sorrow in it than of mirth; 'and so, young man, these black
and shattered hulks seem to the eye of the multitude. But
things are not what they seem: that water, a kind and con-
venient servant to the wants of man, which seems so smooth,
and so dimpling, and so gentle, has swallowed up a human
soul even now; and the place which it covers, so fair and so
level, is a faithless quicksand, out of which none escape.
Things are otherwise than they seem. Had you lived as long
as I have had the sorrow to live; had you seen the storms, and
braved the perils, and endured the distresses which have
befallen me; had you sat gazing out on the dreary ocean at
midnight on a haunted coast; had you seen comrade after
comrade, brother after brother, and son after son, swept away
by the merciless ocean from your very side; had you seen the
shapes of friends, doomed to the wave and the quicksand,
appearing to you in the dreams and visions of the night; then
would your mind have been prepared for crediting the maritime legends of mariners; and the two haunted Danish ships
would have had their terrors for you, as they have for all who
sojourn on this coast.

'Of the time and the cause of their destruction,' continued
the old man, 'I know nothing certain: they have stood as you
have seen them for uncounted time; and while all other ships
wrecked on this unhappy coast have gone to pieces, and
rotted, and sunk away in a few years, these two haunted hulks
have neither sunk in the quicksand, nor has a single spar or
board been displaced. Maritime legend says, that two ships of
Denmark having had permission, for a time, to work deeds
of darkness and dolour on the deep, were at last condemned
to the whirlpool and the sunken rock, and were wrecked in
this bonnie bay, as a sign to seamen to be gentle and devout.
The night when they were lost was a harvest evening of
uncommon mildness and beauty: the sun had newly set; the
moon came brighter and brighter out; and the reapers, laying

their sickles at the root of the standing corn, stood on rock and bank, looking at the increasing magnitude of the waters, for sea and land were visible from Saint Bees to Barnhourie. The sails of two vessels were soon seen bent for the Scottish coast; and with a speed outrunning the swiftest ship, they approached the dangerous quicksands and headland of Borranpoint. On the deck of the foremost ship not a living soul was seen, or shape, unless something in darkness and form resembling a human shadow could be called a shape, which flitted from extremity to extremity of the ship, with the appearance of trimming the sails, and directing the vessel's course. But the decks of its companion were crowded with human shapes; the captain, and mate, and sailor, and cabin boy, all seemed there; and from them the sound of mirth and minstrelsy echoed over land and water. The coast which they skirted along was one of extreme danger; and the reapers shouted to warn them to beware of sand-bank and rock; but of this friendly counsel no notice was taken, except that a large and famished dog, which sat on the prow, answered every shout with a long, loud, and melancholy howl. The deep sand-bank of Carsethorn was expected to arrest the career of these desperate navigators; but they passed, with the celerity of waterfowl, over an obstruction which had wrecked many pretty ships.

'Old men shook their heads and departed, saying, "We have seen the fiend sailing in a bottomless ship; let us go home and pray:" but one young and wilful man said, "Fiend! I'll warrant it's nae fiend, but douce Janet Withershins, the witch, holding a carouse with some of her Cumberland cummers, and mickle red wine will be spilt atween them. Dod I would gladly have a toothfu'! I'll warrant it's nane o' your cauld sour slae-water like a bottle of Bailie Skrinkie's port, but right drap-o'-my-heart's-blood stuff, that would waken a body out of their last linen. I wonder where the cummers will anchor their craft?"—"And I'll vow," said another rustic, "the wine they quaff is none of your visionary drink, such as a drouthie body has dished out to his lips to a dream; nor is it shadowy and unsubstantial, like the vessels they sail in, which are made out of a cockle-shell or a cast-off-slipper, or the paring of a seaman's right thumb-nail. I once got a hansel out of a witch's quaigh myself,—auld Marion Mathers, of Dustiefoot, whom they tried to bury in the old kirk-yard of Dunscore, but the cummer raise as fast as they laid her down, and nae where else would she lie but in the bonnie green kirk-yard of Kier, among douce and sponsible fowk. So I'll vow that the wine of a witch's cup is as fell liquor as ever did a kindly turn to a poor man's heart; and be they fiends, or be they witches, if they have red wine asteer, I'll risk a drouket sark for ae glorious tout on't." "Silence, ye sinners," said the minister's son of a neighbouring parish, who united in his own person his father's lack of devotion with his mother's love of liquor. "Whisht!—speak as if ye had the fear of something holy before ye. Let the vessels run their own way to destruction: who can stay the eastern wind, and the current of the Solway sea? I can find ye Scripture warrant for that: so let them try their strength on Blawhooly rocks, and their might on the broad quicksand. There's a surf running there would knock the ribs together of a galley built by the imps of the pit, and commanded by the Prince of Darkness. Bonnilie and bravely they sail away there; but before the blast blows by they'll be wrecked; and red wine and strong brandy will be as rife as dyke-water, and we'll drink the health of bonnie Bell Blackness out of her left foot slipper."

'The speech of the young profligate was applauded by several of his companions, and away they flew to the bay of Blawhooly, from whence they never returned. The two vessels were observed all at once to stop in the bosom of the bay, on the spot where their hulls now appear: the mirth and the minstrelsy waxed louder than ever, and the forms of maidens, with instruments of music and wine-cups in their hands, thronged the decks. A boat was lowered; and the same shadowy pilot who conducted the ships made it start towards the shore with the rapidity of lightning, and its head knocked against the bank where the four young men stood, who longed for the unblest drink. They leaped in with a laugh, and with a laugh were they welcomed on deck; wine cups were given to each, and as they raised them to their lips the vessels melted away beneath their feet; and one loud shriek, mingled with laughter still louder, was heard over land and water for many miles. Nothing more was heard or seen till the morning, when the crowd who came to the beach saw with fear and wonder the two Haunted Ships, such as they now seem, masts and tackle gone; nor mark, nor sign, by which their name, country, or destination could be known, was left remaining.

Such is the tradition of the mariners; and its truth has been attested by many families whose sons and whose fathers have been drowned in the haunted bay of Blawhooly.'

'And trow ye,' said the old woman, who, attracted from her hut by the drowning cries of the young fisherman, had remained an auditor of the mariner's legend; 'And trow ye, Mark Macmoran, that the tale of the Haunted Ships is done? I can say no to that. Mickle have mine ears heard; but more mine eyes have witnessed since I came to dwell in this humble home by the side of the deep sea. I mind the night weel: it was on Hallowmass-eve: the nuts were cracked, and the apples were eaten, and spell and charm were tried at my fire-side; till, wearied with diving into the dark waves of futurity, the lads and lasses fairly took to the more visible blessings of kind words, tender clasps, and gentle courtship. Soft words in a maiden's ear, and a kindlie kiss o' her lip, were old world matters to me, Mark Macmoran; though I mean not to say that I have been free of the folly of daunering and daffin with a youth in my day, and keeping tryste with him in dark and lonely places. However, as I say, these times of enjoyment were passed and gone with me; the mair's the pity that pleasure should fly sae fast away,—and as I could nae make sport I thought I should not mar any; so out I sauntered into the fresh cold air, and sat down behind that old oak, and looked abroad on the wide sea. I had my ain sad thoughts, ye may think, at the time: it was in that very bay my blythe good-man perished, with seven more in his company, and on that very bank where ye see the waves leaping and foaming, I saw seven stately corses streeked, but the dearest was the eighth. It was a woeful sight to me, a widow, with four bonnie boys, with nought to support them but these twa hands, and God's blessing, and a cow's grass. I have never liked to live out of sight of this bay since that time; and mony's the moon-light night I sit looking on these watery mountains, and these waste shores; it does my heart good, whatever it may do to my head. So ye see it was Hallowmass night; and looking on sea and land sat I; and my heart wandering to other thoughts soon made me forget my youthful company at hame. It might be near the howe hour of the night: the tide was making, and its singing brought strange old world stories with it; and I thought on the dangers that sailors endure, the fates they meet with, and the fearful forms they see. My own blythe good-man had seen sights that made him grave enough at times, though he aye tried to laugh them away.

'Aweel, atween that very rock aneath us and the coming tide, I saw, or thought I saw, for the tale is so dream-like, that the whole might pass for a vision of the night, I saw the form of a man: his plaid was grey; his face was grey; and his hair, which hung low down till it nearly came to the middle of his back, was as white as the white sea-foam. He began to howk and dig under the bank; an' God be near me, thought I, this maun be the unblessed spirit of auld Adam Gowdgowpin, the miser, who is doomed to dig for shipwrecked treasure, and count how many millions are hidden for ever from man's enjoyment. The Form found something which in shape and hue seemed a left-foot slipper of brass; so down to the tide he marched, and placing it on the water, whirled it thrice round; and the infernal slipper dilated at every turn, till it became a bonnie barge with its sails bent, and on board leaped the Form, and scudded swiftly away. He came to one of the Haunted Ships; and striking it with his oar, a fair ship, with mast, and canvas, and mariners, started up: he touched the other Haunted Ship, and produced the like transformation; and away the three spectre ships bounded, leaving a track of fire behind them on the billows which was long unextinguished. Now was nae that a bonnie and a fearful sight to see beneath the light of the Hallowmass moon? But the tale is far frae finished; for mariners say that once a year, on a certain night, if ye stand on the Borranpoint, ye will see the infernal shallops coming snoring through the Solway: ye will hear the same laugh, and song, and mirth, and minstrelsy, which our ancestors heard; see them bound over the sand-banks and sunken rocks like sea-gulls, cast their anchor in Blawhooly-bay, while the shadowy figure lowers down the boat, and augments their numbers with the four unhappy mortals to whose memory a stone stands in the kirk-yard, with a sinking ship and a shoreless sea cut upon it. Then the spectre ships vanish, and the drowning shriek of mortals, and the rejoicing laugh of fiends are heard, and the old hulls are left as a memorial that the old spiritual kingdom has not departed from the earth. But I maun away, and trim my little cottage fire, and make it burn and blaze up bonnie, to warm the crickets, and my cold and crazy bones, that maun soon be laid aneath the green sod in the eerie kirk-yard.' And away the old dame tottered to her cottage, secured the door on the inside, and soon the hearth-flame was seen to glimmer and gleam through the key-hole and window.

'I'll tell ye what,' said the old mariner, in a subdued tone, and with a shrewd and suspicious glance of his eye after the old sibyl, 'it's a word that may not very well be uttered, but there are many mistakes made in evening stories if old Moll Moray there, where she lives, knows not mickle more than she is willing to tell of the Haunted Ships, and their unhallowed mariners. She lives cannilie and quietly; no one knows how she is fed or supported; but her dress is aye whole, her cottage ever smokes, and her table lacks neither of wine, white and red, nor of fowl and fish, and white bread and brown. It was a dear scoff to Jock Matheson, when he called old Moll the uncannie carline of Blawhooly: his boat ran round and round in the centre of the Solway,—every body said it was enchanted,—and down it went head foremost: and had nae Jock been a swimmer equal to a sheldrake, he would have fed the fish;—but I'll warrant it sobered the lad's speech; and he never reckoned himself safe till he made auld Moll the present of a new kirtle and a stone of cheese.'

'O father,' said his grand-daughter Barbara, 'ye surely wrong poor old Mary Moray: what use could it be to an old woman like her, who has no wrongs to redress, no malice to work out against mankind, and nothing to seek of enjoyment save a cannie hour and a quiet grave,—what use could the fellowship of fiends, and the communion of evil spirits be to her? I know Jenny Primrose puts rowan-tree above the door-head when she sees old Mary coming; I know the good wife of Kittlenaket wears rowan-berry leaves in the headband of her blue kirtle, and all for the sake of averting the unsonsie glance of Mary's right ee; and I know that the auld Laird of Burn-troutwater drives his seven cows to their pasture with a wand of witch tree, to keep Mary from milking them. But what has all that to do with haunted shallops, visionary mariners, and bottomless boats? I have heard myself as pleasant a tale about the Haunted Ships and their unworldly crews, as any one would wish to hear in a winter evening. It was told me by young Benjie Macharg, one summer night, sitting on Arbigland-bank: the lad intended a sort of love meeting; but all that he could talk of was about smearing sheep and shearing sheep, and of the wife which the Norway elves of the

Haunted Ships made for his uncle Sandie Macharg. And I
shall tell ye the tale as the honest lad told it to me.

'Alexander Macharg, besides being the laird of three acres
of peatmoss, two kale gardens, and the owner of seven good
milch cows, a pair of horses, and six pet sheep, was the husband of one of the handsomest women in seven parishes.
Many a lad sighed the day he was brided; and a Nithsdale
laird and two Annandale moorland farmers drank themselves
to their last linen, as well as their last shilling, through sorrow
for her loss. But married was the dame; and home she was carried, to bear rule over her home and her husband, as an honest woman should. Now ye maun ken that though the flesh
and blood lovers of Alexander's bonnie wife all ceased to love
and to sue her after she became another's, there were certain
admirers who did not consider their claim at all abated, or
their hopes lessened by the kirk's famous obstacle of matri-
mony. Ye have heard how the devout minister of Tinwald
had a fair son carried away, and bedded against his liking to
an unchristened bride, whom the elves and the fairies provided: ye have heard how the bonnie bride of the drunken
Laird of Soukitup was stolen by the fairies out at the back-
window of the bridal chamber, the time the bridegroom was
groping his way to the chamber-door; and ye have heard—
but why need I multiply cases? such things in the ancient days
were as common as candle-light. So ye'll no hinder certain
water elves and sea fairies, who sometimes keep festival and
summer mirth in these old haunted hulks, from falling in love
with the weel-faured wife of Laird Macharg; and to their plots
and contrivances they went how they might accomplish to
sunder man and wife; and sundering such a man and such a
wife was like sundering the green leaf from the summer, or the
fragrance from the flower.

'So it fell on a time that Laird Macharg took his halve-net
on his back, and his steel spear in his hand, and down to
Blawhooly-bay gade he, and into the water he went right
between the two haunted hulks, and placing his net awaited
the coming of the tide. The night, ye maun ken, was mirk,
and the wind lowne, and the singing of the increasing waters
among the shells and the peebles, was heard for sundry miles.
All at once light began to glance and twinkle on board the
two Haunted Ships from every hole and seam, and presently
the sound as of a hatchet employed in squaring timber echoed

far and wide. But if the toil of these unearthly workmen amazed the laird, how much more was his amazement increased when a sharp shrill voice called out, "Ho! brother, what are you doing now?" A voice still shriller responded from the other haunted ship, "I'm making a wife to Sandie Macharg!" and a loud quavering laugh running from ship to ship, and from bank to bank, told the joy they expected from their labour.

'Now the laird, besides being a devout and a God-fearing man, was shrewd and bold; and in plot, and contrivance, and skill in conducting his designs, was fairly an overmatch for any dozen land elves: but the water elves are far more subtle; besides, their haunts and their dwellings being in the great deep, pursuit and detection is hopeless if they succeed in carrying their prey to the waves. But ye shall hear. Home flew the laird,—collected his family around the hearth,—spoke of the signs and the sins of the times, and talked of mortification and prayer for averting calamity; and finally, taking his father's Bible, brass clasps, black print, and covered with calf-skin, from the shelf, he proceeded without let or stint to perform domestic worship. I should have told ye that he bolted and locked the door, shut up all inlet to the house, threw salt into the fire, and proceeded in every way like a man skilful in guarding against the plots of fairies and fiends. His wife looked on all this with wonder; but she saw something in her husband's looks that hindered her from intruding either question or advice, and a wise woman was she.

'Near the mid hour of the night the rush of a horse's feet was heard, and the sound of a rider leaping from its back, and a heavy knock came to the door, accompanied by a voice, saying, "The cummer drink's hot, and the knave bairn is expected at Laird Laurie's to-night; sae mount, good-wife, and come."

' "Preserve me!" said the wife of Sandie Macharg; "that's news indeed! who could have thought it? the Laird has been heirless for seventeen years! Now Sandie, my man, fetch me my skirt and hood."

'But he laid his arm round his wife's neck, and said, "If all the lairds in Galloway go heirless, over this door threshold shall you not stir to-night; and I have said, and I have sworn it: seek not to know why or wherefore—but, Lord, send us thy blessed mornlight." The wife looked for a moment in her husband's eyes, and desisted from further entreaty.

' "But let us send a civil message to the gossips, Sandy; and hadnae ye better say I am sair laid with a sudden sickness? though it's sinful-like to send the poor messenger a mile agate with a lie in his mouth without a glass of brandy."

' "To such a messenger, and to those who sent him, no apology is needed," said the austere Laird, "so let him depart." And the clatter of a horse's hoofs was heard, and the muttered imprecations of its rider on the churlish treatment he had experienced.

' "Now Sandie, my lad," said his wife, laying an arm particularly white and round about his neck as she spoke, "are you not a queer man and a stern? I have been your wedded wife now these three years; and, beside my dower, have brought you three as bonnie bairns as ever smiled aneath a summer sun. O man, you a douce man, and fitter to be an elder than even Willie Greer himself, I have the minister's ain word for't, to put on these hard-hearted looks, and gang waving your arms that way, as if ye said, 'I winna take the counsel of sic a hempie as you,' I'm your ain leal wife, and will and maun have an explanation."

'To all this Sandie Macharg replied, "It is written—'Wives, obey your husbands;' but we have been stayed in our devotion, so let us pray;" and down he knelt: his wife knelt also, for she was as devout as bonnie; and beside them knelt their household, and all lights were extinguished.

' "Now this beats a'," muttered his wife to herself; "however, I shall be obedient for a time; but if I dinna ken what all this is for before the morn by sunket-time, my tongue is nae langer a tongue, nor my hands worth wearing."

'The voice of her husband in prayer interrupted this mental soliloquy; and ardently did he beseech to be preserved from the wiles of the fiends, and the snares of Satan; "from witches, ghosts, goblins, elves, fairies, spunkies, and water-kelpies; from the spectre shallop of Solway; from spirits visible and invisible; from the Haunted Ships and their unearthly tenants; from maritime spirits that plotted against godly men, and fell in love with their wives—"

' "Nay, but his presence be near us!" said his wife in a low tone of dismay. "God guide my gudeman's wits: I never heard such a prayer from human lips before. But Sandie, my man, Lord's sake, rise: what fearful light is this?—barn, and byre, and stable, maun be in a blaze; and Hawkie and Hurley,—

Doddie, and Cherrie, and Damson-plum, will be smoored with reek, and scorched with flame."

'And a flood of light, but not so gross as a common fire, which ascended to heaven and filled all the court before the house, amply justified the good wife's suspicions. But to the terrors of fire, Sandie was as immovable as he was to the imaginary groans of the barren wife of Laird Laurie; and he held his wife, and threatened the weight of his right hand—and it was a heavy one—to all who ventured abroad, or even unbolted the door. The neighing and prancing of horses, and the bellowing of cows, augmented the horrors of the night; and to any one who only heard the din, it seemed that the whole onstead was in a blaze, and horses and cattle perishing in the flame. All wiles, common or extraordinary, were put in practice to entice or force the honest farmer and his wife to open the door; and when the like success attended every new stratagem, silence for a little while ensued, and a long, loud, and shrilling laugh, wound up the dramatic efforts of the night. In the morning, when Laird Macharg went to the door, he found standing against one of the pilasters a piece of black ship oak, rudely fashioned into something like human form, and which skilful people declared would have been clothed with seeming flesh and blood, and palmed upon him by elfin adroitness for his wife, had he admitted his visitants. A synod of wise men and women sat upon the woman of timber, and she was finally ordered to be devoured by fire, and that in the open air. A fire was soon made, and into it the elfin sculpture was tossed from the prongs of two pairs of pitchforks. The blaze that arose was awful to behold; and hissings, and burstings, and loud cracklings, and strange noises, were heard in the midst of the flame; and when the whole sank into ashes, a drinking cup of some precious metal was found; and this cup, fashioned no doubt by elfin skill, but rendered harmless by the purification with fire, the sons and daughters of Sandie Macharg and his wife drink out of to this very day. Bless all bold men, say I, and obedient wives!'

DEATH OF THE LAIRD
OF WARLSWORM

It happened on a fine harvest afternoon, that I found myself
at the entrance of one of the wild and romantic glens or vales
of Galloway; and as a Galwegian vale has a character of
its own, it would mutilate my story to leave it undescribed.
Imagine an expanse of brown moor-land extending as far as
sight can reach, threaded by innumerable burns or brooks,
and only tenanted in appearance by flocks of sheep, or by
coveys of red and black game. Here and there a shepherd was
seen with his dogs, or a bareheaded maiden with her pails of
milk, going homewards from the fold, and cheering her way
with one of those old tender traditional ballads which some
neglected spirit, like that of John Lowe,[133] has scattered so
largely among the pastoral glens of Galloway. A shepherd's
house, or his summer sheal, rising like the 'bonnie bower' of
the two heroines of Scottish song,[134] on a burn brae, and
covered thick with rushes, while it threw its long wavering line
of blue smoke into the clear sharp air, spoke of the presence
of the sons and daughters of man, or said, in the quaint and
homely language of the Galwegian proverb, 'where four cloots
go, man's twa feet maun follow.'

But this heath, barren and wild as it seemed, had other
attractions. At the distance of almost every little mile, numerous streams of smoke ascended from the brown moor; the
sound and the hum of man, busied with the flail, the hatchet,
or the hammer, was heard; the cry and the merriment of
children abounded; and here and there a green tree-top or a
chimney-head, a kirk-spire, or a ruined tower, projecting
above the horizon of blossomed heather, proclaimed to the
traveller that Caledonia, amid her deserts, has her well-peopled
glens, and her fruitful places.

On a summer sabbath morning the people of Galloway
are to be beheld in their glory; then every little deep-green
and populous vale pours forth its own sedate, and pious, and
well-dressed multitude. From the dame in the douce grey
mantle to the maiden in glittering silks and scarlets; from him

in the broad blue bonnet to her in the gallant cap and feather; from the trembling and careful step of age to the firm and heedless stride of youth; from her who dreams of bridal favours and bridegroom's vows, to him bent to the earth with age, musing on the burial procession and the gaping grave,—all are there, moving on staid and soberly to the house of God. Often have I stood and seen the scanty current of people issue out like the little brook of their native glen, join themselves to a fuller stream, and, increasing as they flowed on, become as a river ere they reached the entrance to the burial-ground, which, hallowed with their fathers' dust, encompassed their native kirk. I have heard the bell toll, and the melody of their psalms of praise and hymns of thanksgiving flow far and wide. I have thought, while these holy sounds arose, that the bleat of the flocks became softer, the cry of the plover less shrill, and that the divine melody subdued into music the rough brawling of the brook along which it was heard.

At the heathy entrance into one of these beautiful vales I accordingly stood and pursued the winding of a little stream, which, after leaping over two or three small crags, and forming several little bleaching grounds of greensward for the villagers' webs, gathered all its waters together, and concentrated all its might, to pour itself on a solitary mill-wheel at the farther end of the valley. On either side of the glen the shepherds and husbandmen had each constructed his homely abode, according to his own fancy; the houses were dropped here and there at random, facing east, and west, and south, each attached to its own little garden, the green flourishing of which was pleasant to the eye, while the fragrance of some sweet herbs, or a few simple flowers, escaped from the enclosure, and was wafted about me by the low and fitful wind. The whole glen was full of life, the sickles were moving beneath the ripe grain, the bandsmen were binding and stooking it, several low-wheeled cars were busied in depositing this rustic treasure in the farmer's stackyard; while the farmer himself moved about, surveyed the fulfilment of his wishes, and rubbed the full ears between his palms, and examined with a pleased and a curious eye the quality of his crop. At the doors of the cottages the old dames sat in groups to the sun, twirling their distaffs, and driving the story round of wonder or of scandal; while an unsummable progeny of barefooted bairns ran, and rolled, and leaped, and tumbled, and laughed, and screamed, till the whole glen remurmured with the din.

I sat down by the side of a flat grave-stone, bedded level with the grass; the ancient inscription, often renewed by the pious villagers, told that beneath it lay one of those enthusiastic, undaunted, and persecuted peasants, who combated for freedom of faith and body when the nobles of the land forgot the cause of God and their country. Presently the children desisted from their merriment, and gathered about and gazed on me, a man of an unknown glen, with a quiet and a curious eye. I ever loved the innocent scrutiny of youthful eyes; so I allowed them to descant at freedom on my southland garb, and wonder what could make me choose my seat by the martyr's tomb-stone, a place seldom visited, save by men in a devotional frame of mind. A venerable old dame, with a straggling tress or two of grey hair flowing from beneath her mutch or coif, laid aside her distaff, and advanced to free me from the intrusion of a dozen or more of her curly-headed descendants. The admonishing tone in which she said, 'Bairns, bairns!' with the rebuke of her eye, accomplished her wishes; the children vanished from my side, and retired to a little round green knowe or knoll, which rose on the rivulet bank in the middle of the village, and seemed appropriated for rustic games, pitching the bar, casting the stone, for leaping and for wrestling. 'A bonnie harvest afternoon, sir,' said the Galwegian matron, 'but ye would be wiser to come and rest ye in a comfortable house than sit on the cauld stane, though it lies aboon the dust of ane of the godly auld folk of the saintly days of Galloway, or may-be ye might like the change-house better to birl yere sixpence, and be behadden to none, and I cannot say that I can advise ye.'

I was prevented from replying by another of the village dames, who thus broke in on our parley.—'Birl his silver in the change-house!—wherefore should he? what can hinder him from slipping cannilie away up the brae to the gudeman of Warlsworm? he's either dead, or as good as dead; and if he's no departed, so much the better; he will leave the world with a perturbed spirit, for sore, sore, has he stuck to the earth, and loth will he be to leave his gowd and his gains, and his bonnie broad lairdships; and who kens but the sight of a stranger breaking his bread and drinking his milk may make him die through downright vexation for the unwonted waste? Andrew, my bonnie lad, take this strange man up to auld Warlsworm's hall door; I would gang myself, but I vowed never to cross his threshold or enter his land, since he cheated my ain cousin out of the green holms of Dee; black be his cast, and bitter his doom!'

A little boy came to my side, and put his hand in mine; and, willing to know more of a man of whom I had heard so much, away I walked with my barefooted guide, and soon came within sight of the mansion of Warlsworm.

It was a rough old house, built of undressed granite, and covered with a slating of coarse sandstone. The smoke, despairing to find its way through the windings of a chimney almost choked with sides of bacon and soot, sought its passage in many a curl and turn along the roof, and, finally descending, streamed out into the pure air through window and door. Groups of black cattle, after browzing on every green thing which the garden contained, and trying to digest the withered thatch which depended from the sides of the barn and stable, stood lowing knee-deep in a pool of muddy water before the mansion, and looking wistfully on the green hills and the golden harvest around them. The fowls, undismayed by foumart or fox, plundered the corn which hung drop-ripe and unreaped in the field; while a multitude of swine, breaking, in the desperation of hunger, from their pens, ran grunting through the standing grain, crushed the growing potatoes in unwieldy joy, and finally cooled their sides, and fulfilled the Scripture proverb,[135] by wallowing in the mire which encompassed as with a fosse this miserable mansion.

The door stood open. In summer, in the pastoral districts, few doors are closed; and, with the privilege which a stranger claims in a hospitable land, I entered the house. Wheeled towards the fire, and bedded thick with sheepskins and soft cushions, stood the lang settle, or rustic sofa; and on it lay a man bald and feeble with age; and kneeling by his side, I saw a fair-haired girl, her hands clasped, and her large blue eyes fixed with a moist and motionless gaze on his face. This was the owner of the mansion, the far-famed Laird of Warlsworm; and the maid was his niece, as remarkable for her gentleness and beauty, as her relative for his grasping and incessant greed. As my shadow darkened the floor, she looked up, and motioned me to silence and a seat. I accordingly sat down, and looked with an eye of deep interest on the touching scene before me. There lay Age, his face gross and covetous, his mind seeking communion with the riches of the earth, while his body was fast hasting to dust, and his soul to its final account; and there knelt Youth, glowing in health and ripe in beauty, her tresses bright, and flowing over her neck, like sunshine visiting a bank of lilies; her hands, white and shapely, and small, clasped over a white and a perturbed bosom; while from her long dark eye-lashes the tears of sorrow descended drop by drop. On both, a young man in a homely garb, but with a face comely and interesting, sat and looked, and looked too with a brow on which might be read more of love for the maid, than of sorrow for the man.

The old man uttered a groan, turned on his couch, half opened his eyes, and said, 'Bessie, my bairn, let me have hold of thy hand; my sight is not so good as it ought to be; and I think I see queer things, that should not be seen by a man when he lies down to die. But I have wronged no man; I took but what the law gave me; and if the law grips with an iron hand, it's the worse for them that made it. I thought I heard the footstep of the young portioner of Glaiketha; he'll be come to borrow gold and to wadset land. But Bessie, my lass, gold's scarce, and land abundant; no that I refuse the minted money when the interest will do thee good, and when the security's sicker; sae gang thy ways, my wean, to the old pose ahint the cathud, or hear ye me; there's a saddle bag of good red gold riding on the rannel-tree that has nae seen sun or wind these seven-and-twenty summers.'

'Oh! forget the cares of the world,' said the maiden, with a voice smothering with sorrow, 'and think of your health. This is not the young portioner of Glaiketha seeking for gold to cast away in eating, and drinking, and dancing, or in more evil pursuits; but a stranger youth come to repose him all night as strangers do, and recommence his journey in the morning.'

'Repose him!' re-echoed the old man, his voice deepening, and his faded eyes brightening, as he spoke. 'Have I wranged any of his kin, that he comes hither to riot on my substance? Have I ever darkened his father's door, that he should presume to darken mine? Alas! alas! the bonnie haughs of Orr, and the fair holms of Dee, will be wasted on loons and limmers, and I shall no find repose where all men find rest. Ay! ay! my hall will soon be a changed place; there will be fizzenless tea instead of weel buttered breakfast brose; a pudding with spices and raisins, for a gallant haggis dropping with fatness, and full of marrowy strength; and for the pleasant din of the spinning wheel there will be the sounding of fiddle-strings, and the leaping of wanton feet. Strangers will feast at my supper-board, where strangers never feasted before; and auld men will shake their heads and say, "Away fly the riches of honest Warlsworm." '

And putting his hands over his eyes, as if to hide the hideous picture of extravagance which his imagination had painted, and uttering groan succeeding groan, he stretched himself at full length on the lang settle.

His niece turned pale as she beheld him writhing under the infliction of the spirit which she mistook for a deadlier pang, and thus she addressed the young man, who seemed to remain there that he might gaze without intermission on her beauty. 'Oh, Willie, lad, if ye wish for wealth in this world, and weal in the ane to come—rise up, and run.'

The youth leaped to his feet, stood with his lips apart, his left foot forward, and his whole face beaming with joy at being commanded by so sweet a tongue.—'Oh run, William, run; fly over moor and moss, and seek and bring auld Haudthegrup, a man gifted in prayer and conversant with godly things; he will cheer my uncle's spirit. For oh, they're gladsome when they get thegither. I have seen them sit in the howe heart of winter, laying schemes for gripping and guiding wealth, when the snow was on the hill, and the icicle on the house-side, with less fire to thowe them than would warm a bairn's breakfast. Oh! run, William, run, tell him to hasten; for the sands of life are nearly out; and that my uncle talks of the gathered gold of faith, and the set siller of redemption; and that's nae symptom of health with him.'

The youth looked at her for a moment, then away he darted from the door, climbed the hill with the swiftness of a fowl in its flight, tarried for a second on its summit, to look back on the dwelling; nor were his glances unrewarded; he then vanished along the moor, to seek the home of auld Haudthegrup.

This devotional auxiliary soon made his appearance; he seemed a personification of penance and famine. He was tall and lean, with a frame of iron, a forehead villanous low, and eyes small, restless, and glimmering about in quest of gain,

like those of a cat seeking prey in the twilight. His nose was
sharp and thin, like the style of a sun-dial; while his lips,
though very broad, were too scanty to cover a seam of teeth
as rusty as the jaws of an unused fox-trap, and wholly unacquainted with the luxury of the pastoral district, the flesh of
lambs or ewes, unless when a friend's house had the scourge
of his company. He carried under his arm a mighty Bible,
garnished with massy clasps of iron; and entered the abode of
his dying friend with the satisfied look of a man proud of his
gifts, and conscious of the extensive influence of his interces-
sions.—'Peace be among you,' said the goodman of Haudthegrup, 'and may God claim his ain in his blessed time and
way; when the grain's ready let it go to the threshing floor,
and when the grapes are ripe, take them to the wine-press.'—
So saying, he made a stride or two, and, looking in the face
of his ancient friend, thus proceeded to comfort him.

'Bless me, Laird of Warlsworm! ye're no going to leave us;
leaving us, too, when golden days are at hand? Never was
there such an appearance of a harvest of gold, and the
precious things of the earth, all ripening and getting ready for
thy sickle and mine. Cheer up, man, ye'll hear the chink of
gold in yere left lug for mony a bonnie year yet. Would ye lie
there, and let the breath sough away frae atween your lips,
like a cow strangled with her tether in a field knee-deep of
clover? Look me in the face, I say; bankers are breaking, and
the credit of cattle-dealers is cracked—gold will be gold soon,
and the rate of interest will rise in Galloway. The crouse and
ringing frosts of winter will soon come to purify the air, and
make yere auld blood course boldly in yere veins. Then the
grass will grow green, the bushes will bud, and the primroses
will blow on the bonnie burn bank, and ye'll get yere feet
among the braw blooming gowans, that lie scattered o'er the
face of the earth, like as mony pieces of a spendthrift's gold.
Sae cheer up, man, ye would do wrong to die, and so many
blessings awaiting ye.'

The Laird of Warlsworm sat erect for a moment; the prospect of life, and the hopes of future gain, passed by him like a
bright pageant; his eyes sparkled with that unholy light by
which Mammon sums his treasure, and he stretched forth his
hand to clutch the visionary gold, which deceitful fancy
heaped up before him. But nature could not sustain the effort;
the light faded in his eyes, his hand sank, and his head declined,

and sinking on the cushions, he muttered, 'Na, na, it winna do; it winna do; I maun away to the worms, and my bits of bonnie gold will get a fearful scattering;' and fixing his looks on the old bag of coin, which was suspended in the chimney, he lay for a while in woeful rumination, and thus proceeded:—'Aye, aye, ye'll no hang lang in that cozie place now; the hand of the spoiler will come, and thy braw broad pieces which I gathered with care and with sorrow, and regarded as gods, will gang to the silk shop and the maker of golden gimcracks, glancing with polished stones for woman's neck and bosom.'—And shutting his eyes in despair, and clutching his hands in agony of spirit, he resigned himself to his fate.

Meanwhile the devout twin-brother of Mammon seated himself in an old chair, laid his Bible on his knees, uncovered his head, placed his long iron fingers on the clasps, and, with a prolonged preliminary cough, which hypocrisy had taught to imitate the listless and weary end of a dull sectarian sermon, he opened the volume. He glanced his eye around, to see if his auditors were composed, and commenced his search for a chapter befitting the perilous state of his friend. I was seated beside him, and thus I heard him converse with himself, as he turned over the leaves:—'A chapter fit for a sinner's state!—I mauna read about repentance, nor speak of the benefits of redemption. He'll never forgive me for directing his thoughts to such strange objects.'

The Laird uttered a low groan, and the devout man proceeded with his mutterings.—'He's going gear; he's going gear; he winna shoot over the coming midnight; he'll be a stretched-out corse, and Bessie Lamond, his niece there, a braw rich heiress before the morning light. She'll be a weel tochered lass, when auld Gripagain travels. Let me see,—there's Hurley-hawkie, a rich land and well watered; there's Auchenling, a dreary domain, it's true, but there's gallant shooting on't, though it bears little but cranberries; then there's Wyliehole, and the sixteen acre parks of Warlsworm; forbye bails and bonds, and gathered gold;—my sooth Bessie, my lass, many a gallant will cast his cap at thee.' And he glanced his sharp considerate eyes on the young maiden, to whose mind her uncle's danger seemed alone present.—'Aye, aye,' he resumed, 'she's a wellfavoured lass, and I'll warrant has a gift of knowing on't; de'il a doubt of that; but I am not so very auld,

and have been single for seven year, and, bating a sad cough,
which I can mend, when I like, for sixpence, and sundry grey
hairs, the lass may have sillier woosters than me. When I cock
my bonnet, and put on my crousest coat, and give my horse
a tasting of corn, and then a tasting of the spur, I think the
quean will no be a draps-blood to her uncle if she say me nay.
And the lassie, too, is modest of demeanour; she wears nae
silver in her shoon, nor frights the fowls with the feathers of
her cap; and weel I mind it was her thrifty mother's boast,
that she should never sit on a sark till she could spin ane. I'll
warrant her a gallant lassie, and a gude guider of gear. I
should like to lead her to a brankan bridal.' And, resuming
his search of a suitable chapter, he withdrew his looks from
the maid, who, with brimful eyes, a troubled brow, and
quivering hands, ministered to the sick man.

Her pure sincerity of heart won its way to auld Warlsworm's bosom, frozen as it seemed, and shut up resolutely
against the charities of nature.—'Ah, Bessie, lass,' he murmured, 'thy uncle maun leave the bonnie links of Orr, and the
gowany braesides of Dee. Many a tug, and many a toiled
brow, has it cost him to get them; but the strength of man
cannot endure like the hills, nor his spirit flow for ever, like a
running stream. And talking of running streams, that reminds
me that Miller Macmillan owes me a year's rent, past on
Tuesday; gar Jack Candlish gang and fetch it: the miller's a
sicker ane; he thinks my dam is nearly run, and that my wheel
of existence lacks the water of life, and sae he'll keep up the
rent till my head's happit, and then wheedle or swear thee out
on't. So that's settled, and my spirit's all the calmer for it.
And now for thee, lass, ye'll be a rich quean, Bessie, and the
lads will like ye nae the waur because he who lived before ye
had a gathering eye, and a sicker grip. But ye maun never
wear a towering bonnet with a long feather; for that is an
abomination in devout eyes, and a sad drain for the pocket;
and sair I slighted bonnie Jenny Duff for the pride of her
apparel: wear the snood of maiden singleness as lang as ye
can, lassie; and, if ye maun be a wife, wear a douce hood, or a
devout mutch; ye'll find ane of yere grandmother's treasured
by among my bonds; for I loved my ain mother better than
ever I loved gold; ye'll hardly credit that, Bessie; and I love
thee, too, my ain sweet sister's wean.'

He laid his arms around her neck, looked full in her face,

with a kind and a glistening eye, and the demon of lucre
spread his wings, to forsake the mansion where he had lived so
long. But it was otherwise ordered. The poor weeping girl
knelt over him, and wiped away from his face the tears which
flowed from her own eyes, for tears never flowed from his,
and hid her face in his bosom with many a bitter sob.

'Ah, ye waster hussey!' exclaimed the Laird, in a tone above
his strength, 'wherefore wipe ye my face with a damask
napkin, when a cloth three threads to the pound is too good
for a wadset about to be redeemed like me? And see, as I hope
to be saved, if ye are not consuming the good dry wood which
I kept for the cozie winter night; ground-elding (dried turf)
is good enough to warm such an old sapless bough as me,
which the feller's axe is fast lopping away from the green tree
of existence.'

This appearance of unwonted profusion smote sore on the
heart of the parsimonious old man, and in a tone of rebuke
and bitterness he continued his discourse.—'I may waste my
breath—and I ought to leave some for a scrap of prayer, it
may help me where I am going; I may waste my breath, Bess,
I say, in counselling ye how to choose a husband. When a
woman's eye is bright, her ear is deaf. Take not a man, Bess,
who counts kindred four generations back; he'll call his ancestor a gentleman, and spill the brimming cup of thy fortune
in justifying his descent. Nor yet marry a man who scorns his
ancestors; the man who mocks his forefathers, tramples on
their dust. I hold a father's fair name equal with hoarded
siller. Above all things wed not a lawyer, lass; ye should aye
strive to mend your fortune, and better your fame. Think not
of a sailor, for he thinks there is no Sunday in five fathoms of
water, and finds a love in every land. Shun, too, the soldier,
for shining scarlet, golden shoulder-knots, and a hat filled with
fowls' feathers, will consume thy gold, and fly away with thy
happiness; and, oh, what a gowk he maun be, who stands up
to be shot at for saxpence a day, Sunday included! But marry,
lass, for all women love to be married, were it only for the
sake of having somebody to scold at, and to bear the fault for
their folly,—wed, I say, a strong-handed chield, who can keep
the crown of the causeway, and make himself be obeyed at
his own fire-side. A cannie homely lad, who can clip seven
score of sheep while another clips six; kens the buttered frae
the bare side of the bread; loves nought so well as his own

wife, but the knotting of his own purse-strings; and who fears
the Lord, and can back five bushels of barley.'

This grave and worldly counsellor fairly exhausted himself,
and, laying his head on the cushion, and fixing his eye on his
bag of gold, which common fame calculated at a thousand
pieces, remained silent while that devout person, Haudthegrup, commenced family devotion. He had examined the
New Testament for a fitting and seemly text; but the divine
meekness, and charity, and self-denial, and scorn of all ter-
restrial grandeur, which inspire its pages, rejected all community of feeling, and obliged him to seek consolation under
the splendid and ostentatious dispensations of the Mosaic
law.

'Spoiling the Egyptians,' I heard him mutter, as he hastened along, 'the heathen Egyptians of their jewels of silver,
and jewels of gold, a meritorious deed;—making the molten
calf, a piece of dark idolatry, and a waste of precious metal;—
spoiling the Amalekite, a rich and a pagan people, a pleasant
act and an acceptable. The temple, aye, aye, the temple of
Solomon, the roof thereof was of fine cedar, the pillars of
ivory, the floor of pure silver, and the walls of beaten gold,—
this has often consoled me, and doubtless will console him. It
would be pleasant to die with a vision of this golden palace
before him.' Here he raised his head, and said audibly: 'Let us
begin the worship of Him on High, by reading in his praise
first Kings, chapter the sixth.' And, elevating his voice, he
chanted forth the history of the building of Solomon's temple,
adorning it with the prolonged tone and quavering grace-
notes of an ancient Cameronian professor. Nor did he fail to
express his own admiration at the profusion of precious metal,
by dwelling, with a delight that seemed unwilling to depart,
on the passages recording the overlayings of the wall with
gold, and the altar, and the floor. As he proceeded, the eye of
old Warlsworm looked on his own sooty rafters, and on his
coarse unhewn floor, and on the ark which contained his
meal; yet what were they, covered, as his imagination made
them, with beaten gold, compared to the immeasurable riches
of the Jewish temple! Devotion fell prostrate before the divinity of wealth, and the man who had not five hours to live,
leaped to his feet, smote his hands together, and exclaimed,
'Oh Lord, what, o' gowd! what, o' gowd!'

'Aye, lad, and pure gowd too,' responded Haudthegrup,

casting the Bible from him as he spoke, and pacing round the room with a proud look and an augmented stride.

At this lamentable conclusion to family worship and intercession for the soul of a departing sinner, the beauteous relation of Warlsworm seemed deeply affected and incensed. She caught the Laird in her arms, replaced him on his cushions, soothed down his worldly spirit, and wiped from his face the moisture which disease and excitement had brought to his brow, and that, too, with a cloth of a texture very unlike the fine twined linen and needle-work of Egypt which had contributed to this unseemly rapture. While this passed, I observed the shadow of a man, lengthened by the departing sun, moving on the hall-floor, and seeming to whirl round and round with the agility of a dancer. I looked about, and beheld a singular being, a man about the age of fifty, clad in coarse cloth, called by the shepherds hiplock plaiden, bare-foot, bare-legged, bare-necked, and bare-headed. About his shoulders hung a mass of withered and matted hair; and he carried in his hand a long straw, which he held up before his face, moving all the while round and round, and accompanying his gestures with wild and disjointed words.

'Alas, alas!' said the young maiden, 'what can have brought that poor demented simpleton here? He knows our doors were ever closed against him, and that our meal never augmented the little store which he obtained, more by the intercession of his own innocent face, than by the entreaty of his tongue, from the scrupulous charity of our neighbours. Ah, poor houseless, homeless, hapless creature! he is come to express the sorrow of his own harmless heart for the illness of the head of this house; and hame shall he not go without partaking of the mercies with which we have been so long blessed.' And with meat and drink in her hands forth she walked, and approached, not without hesitation, to the little green knoll on which the poor maniac had stationed himself, in order perhaps to give greater effect to the singular ceremony he was performing.

'East and west, and north and south,' he chanted in a tone of dissonance equal to the croak of the raven—'east, west, north, and south; not a cloud—not a breath of wind—a burning heat, and a scorching drouth—the grasshopper cannot sing for want of her evening dew.' He paused, and reversed the straw, and, holding it up before him, renewed his dancing and his chant. 'North, south, west, and east, the morning sun cannot ascend for the concourse of clouds—the little streams sing among their pebbles, for their banks will soon be overflowed, and the little flowers, bless their bonnie faces, hold up their parched heads, rejoicing in the descending shower. The rains fall, the winds blow, the rivulets swell, and the thunders roll, and rock the green hills. The wide and winding water—even the links of my bright and stately Orr—flows like a wild and a raging sea. I see it, I see it, I see it; man may not ride it; and the saddled steed neighs across the flood, which it trembles to take. Ah! I would not go to be buried in the old kirk-yard, beyond that roaring river, though ye were to make me a bed three ell deep, and lay the greenest turf in Galloway aboon me.'

'Gawain, Gawain,' said Bessie Lamond, in her sweetest tone, and with a smile of sympathy and kindness on her lips, 'Gawain—hinnie, have ye forgotten how many bowls of curds and cream, and pieces of bread and cheese, I have stolen from our penurious board to feed ye in the glen? Turn and speak to me, my bonnie man, and spae nae mair about uncannie things, and see nae mair unsonsie sights.'

But Gawain was possessed beyond the influence of the tongue and charms of the fair niece of the penurious Laird, and continued to elevate and dandle the straw with an increasing wildness of look and gesture. 'But who are those who ride mourning on their coal black steeds, two and two, and bear a coffined corse before them? I see some whom I shall not see long, and the owner of this house is among them; stretched full gay in his burial linen, and a velvet pall aboon him—the siller it costs would be a sore sight; it is well for him that his senses are shut, else the expense of the burial wine would break his heart. There is a deep grave dug, and the bedral leans on his spade, and looks to the burial train about to pass the river. Aha! Johnnie Feastheworm, ye're cheated, lad, ye're cheated,' shouted Gawain, changing the wild seriousness of his tone to that of laughter and merriment. 'Fill your kirk-yard hole again with the black mools, for auld Warlsworm's floating down the links of Orr, and his bonnie black coffin will frighten the seamen on Solway; and wha should float aside him but auld Haudthegrup? but he'll no float far, for twa pouchfuls of stolen gowd will tug the sinner down, and sink him to perdition: ye're cheated, Johnnie

Feastheworm, ye're cheated, sae fill yere kirk-yard hole with the fat mools again, my cannie man.'

These concluding words were too loud to escape notice, and out upon him sallied Haudthegrup, his face inflamed, his hand clenched, and burning anger on his tongue. 'What fiend hath possessed himself of this man, and utters this falseness through his foolish lips? Verily, I will cast him out; a sore buffeting shall the foul thief abide, that presumes to enter into the living image of the High One, and prophesy against righteous men. Lo! I will rebuke him with my right hand, and chasten him sorely with this rod of rowan tree, with which I once combated and overcame three witch-women in the wicked parish of Penpont.' And, advancing upon Gawain, as he spoke, he aimed a blow, which the maniac turned aside, exclaiming: 'Aha! auld greedy Haudthegrup, I have ye now, I have ye now; take that, man, for throwing a bone at me, at Joe Tamson's bridal, seven and thirty years syne come beltan.'[136] As he uttered these words, he dashed his opponent from him with such force, that he reeled several paces, and plunged into a miry hole, fairly under the verdant mantle with which the summer warmth had decked it. Gawain, having performed this feat, stalked perpendicularly into the hall—seated himself by the warm ashes on the hearth, and, looking on the sick man, said, 'Ye lie soft and braw on your bonnie white cushions there; and deed and trouth, an I was you, I wad nae die till the cauld frost and winter should come, when I care na to accompany ye to the kirk-yard hole mysel, and take my word for't, ye'll lie saftest and fealest on the Buittle side of the kirk; I aye think the gowans are bonnier, and the grass the fairer, and the blinks of the simmer sun sweeter on that side than the other: 'od, but lad, if ye hope to lie wi' me, ye maun lie quiet, and nae trouble ane with your weeping, and wailing, and gnashing of teeth—the cauld grave's a bad place to repent in.'

We were now rejoined by old Haudthegrup, purified by the fair hands of the maiden from the soil of the pond, and anxious to drown shame and mortification by a long and lamentable prayer. The sun was set, and a soft and balmy twilight had succeeded. The sound of the reaper's returning song, and the repeated call of the harvest-horn, were audible on all sides,—and in the hall of Warlsworm we had that silence which ushers in prayer, and that fitful and glimmering light afforded by the decaying beams of day, and the twinkling gleam of fading embers. As we knelt, I could not refrain from looking on the singular group thus strangely assembled.

Gawain, abasing himself in the ashes, and stooping his forehead quietly into the dust, accompanied with a chorusing groan the melancholy cough of the sick man; the maiden knelt by the couch, watching with a steady and uninterrupted gaze the changing looks of her uncle; while Haudthegrup himself clasped his hands, drew down his cheeks to a most hypocritical length, and, fixing his eyes on things above, namely, on the golden hoard which hung beyond reach in the chimney, proceeded with his prayer. The prayers of the righteous avail much, says the Fountain of Belief, but what avail the prayers of the hypocrite? Unwise would that man be who would give them a record and a sanctuary. A strong and a burning faith, a day of firm belief, and an hour of deathbed repentance, were pressed with many a mighty word and many a weary groan. He recommended the health of his friend to Him who sweetened the waters of Marah,[137] and his spirit to that Being who presided over angels and thrones, and the souls of just men made perfect. 'To thee,' said he, making a concluding address to the Fountain of all glory, 'to thee, who can make silver into gold, and the dust upon which we tread into precious gems, it can be little to mend a broken body and revive a contrite spirit. To thee, who made my lambs worth five half-crowns at the St. James's fair of Lanark, though when I supplicated thee they were worth but five and sixpence, the renovation of this frail and fainting man is but a breath from thy nostrils. But if it is thy will to glean this ripened ear, to snatch this brand from the fires of this sinful world, let him honour thee and serve thee, and leave a moiety of that worldly dross which men call gold, even unto him who thus wrestled with thee for his welfare and salvation.' Here the sick man moaned, and the glances of his gifted friend and him flashed towards the hidden gold like the hostile lights of two adverse planets. Haudthegrup concluded, 'and, leaving his red gold in thy servant's hand, let him dwell in that house not built with hands, eternal in the heavens.'

'A house not built with hands,' re-echoed Gawain in the tone of the prayer, and leaping to his feet, 'I never saw a house not built with hands except a magpie-nest in the foot

of my mother's garden.' With him, too, rose the Laird of
Warlsworm, the deadly paleness of rage and receding life in
his face; he fixed his eyes, shining with a light that seemed of
the world below, on Haudthegrup, and stretching his hands
towards him to pour forth his departing malediction, seemed
inspired by the fiend who presides over the last hours of evil
men. He opened his lips, the curse trembled on his tongue;
but words never came, for he was stricken speechless, and fell
back on the settle, his lips apart, his eyes fixed, and his hands
clenched. 'He'll never hound me frae his door mair,' said
Gawain, 'nor tell me that wet straw is owre good a bed for a
beggar bodie.'

'Let us carry him into the spence,' said Haudthegrup, 'his
spirit winna part in peace while his eye is fixed on that dross
called gold, and his worldly goods.' The dying man seized his
niece's hand, and pointed to several bags which hung among
hams and tongues in the chimney. 'Ah, he's making an edifying hinder end,' said his parsimonious friend, 'his hopes are
with things aboon, with the blessed, doubtless.' And away he
bore him amid some faint resistance to a little secluded
chamber, his hands still stretched towards the chimney, and
his lips moving with the rapidity of one who speaks to haste.
His dumb warnings were all in vain.

'Now, my bonnie young lady of Warlsworm,' said this
sanctified person in a whisper, 'watch over the last moments
of the righteous, and let these two youths and this simple innocent attend you; verily, they may profit by such an edifying
sight; I, even I, a man dead to the things of this earth, will go
and kneel down even where I lately knelt, and my intercession
shall arise and go upward for the welfare of the body, and
the glorification of the spirit.'

The maiden wept, and, half insensible with sorrow, bathed
her cheeks in tears, while away strode the comforter to the
hall, and presently his voice arose in vehement intercession—
the sick man groaned. In a little while, the sound of the
prayer seemed to ascend from the floor, the Laird made a convulsive effort to rise, the voice of Haudthegrup quavered and
hesitated, as the voice of a man will do when his hands are
busied, and then the sound as of gold falling was heard. At
this mishap, the tongue of the inteceder uttered a curse, and
the power of speech returning to the dying man, he smote his
hands together and exclaimed, 'He's herrying me, he's herry-

ing me, and I maun gang to the brimstone pit with no a
penny in my pocket,' and with these words he expired.

The singular prophecy of Gawain met with a remarkable
fulfilment. The day of the burial of the Laird was wild and
stormy, the place of interment was in an old church-yard on
the south side of the river Orr. The mourners were mounted,
and the coffin was borne on horses' necks, covered with a pall
of black velvet, the parochial mortcloth, which reached nigh
to the ground. Haudthegrup was chief mourner, and, to elude
the expense of a toll-bar, he proposed to ford the river, red
and swollen with rain. When he reached the middle of the
stream, his horse, unaccustomed to such processions, startled
and plunged, and fairly flung his rider over his ears. In his
fall, he seized the coffin of Warlsworm, and the quick and the
dead alike found a grave in the links of the Orr.

'Alas, for Haudthegrup!' said one of the mourners, 'watch
when he swims, and let us try to save him.'

'Swims!' rejoined another mourner, 'how think ye will he
swim, and seven hundred stolen pieces of Warlsworm's gold in
his pocket? I'll prophesy when his body's found he'll be
holding his hands on his breeches-pockets to preserve his
treasure.'

THE SEVEN FORESTERS OF CHATSWORTH: AN ANCIENT DERBYSHIRE BALLAD

In presenting this somewhat rude but curious ballad to the reader, it may be proper to observe, that those who profess to be charmed with truth only, and would wish one to swear to the certainty of a song, will learn with pleasure, perhaps, that tradition has recited, or sung, I know not which, this singular legend, for centuries, in the beautiful vale of Derwent, in Derbyshire. It is a tale current in the county. The projecting rock in Chatsworth wood, still bearing the name of the Shouter's Stone, is pointed out by the peasantry as the place on which this famous and successful Outlaw stood and shouted. It overhangs a wild and winding footpath in the Preserve, and in former times, before the wood became so luxuriant, commanded a fine view of the valley, in the midst of which stands Chatsworth-house, the favourite mansion of the ancient and noble family of Cavendish. In the house itself, this tale has sought sanctuary. There is a painting from no less a hand than that of Prince Nicolas, in which a portion of the tradition is sought to be embodied; but the illustrious artist has, with poetical license, put a gilded horn in the Outlaw's hand; and, with a departure from the story, which all lovers of oral literature will deplore, has given to the cavern below a couple of outlaws, who rouse and bestir themselves to the sound of their leader's horn. The ancient oaks of Chatsworth are to be found every where in the valley; and, perhaps, no oaks in England, except those in Sherwood Forest, can claim to be their coevals,—they are upwards of a thousand years old.

Chatsworth has many other attractions. The Flower Garden of the beautiful and unfortunate Queen of Scotland, a plat of earth elevated on a squat tower, and guarded with a foss, stands on the banks of the Derwent, within a stone's throw of the house. All around, the hills ascend and recede in woody or naked magnificence; and indeed the grandeur of nature is

such, that the beautiful mansion is diminished in the contemplation.

An attempt was made to abate the occasional provincialism
of the ballad, but the experiment threatened to ravel the
entire web, and it was not persisted in.

BALLAD

1.

The sun had risen above the mist,
    The boughs in dew were dreeping;
Seven foresters sat on Chatsworth bank,
    And sung while roes were leaping.

2.

Alas! sung one, for Chatsworth oaks,
    Their heads are bald and hoary,
They droop in fulness of honour and fame,
    They have had their time of glory.

3.

No stately tree in old merry England
    Can match their antique grandeur;
Tradition can tell of no time when they
    Tower'd not in pride and splendour.

4.

How fair they stand amid their green land,
    The sock or share ne'er pain'd them;
Not a bough or leaf have been shred from their strength,
    Nor the woodman's axe profaned them.

5.

Green, sung another, were they that hour
    When Scotland's loveliest woman,
And saddest queen, in the sweet twilight,
    Aneath their boughs was roamin'.

6.

And ever the Derwent lilies her tears
    In their silver tops were catching,
As she look'd to the cold and faithless north,
    Till her eyes wax'd dim with watching.

7.

Be mute now, the third forester said,
    The dame who fledged mine arrow
With the cygnet's wing, has a whiter hand
    Than the fairest maid on Yarrow.

8.

Loud laugh'd the forester fourth, and sung,
    Say not thy maid's the fair one;
On the banks of Dove there dwells my love,
    A beauteous and a rare one.

9.

Now cease your singing, the fifth one said,
    And choose of shafts the longest,
And seek the bucks on Chatsworth chase,
    Where the lady-bracken's strongest.

10.

Let every bow be strung, and smite
    The fattest and the fairest;
Lord Devonshire will taste our cheer,
    Of England's lords the rarest.

11.

String them with speed, the sixth man said,
    For low down in the forest
There runs a deer I long to smite,
    With bitter shafts the sorest.

12.

The bucks bound blythe on Chatsworth lea,
    Where brackens grow the greenest;
The pheasant's safe 'neath Chatsworth oaks,
    When the tempest sweeps the keenest.

13.

The fawn is fain as it sucks its dam,
    The bird is blythe when hatching;
Saint George! such game was never seen,
    With seven such fellows watching.

14.

In the wild wood of fair Dove dwells
    An Outlaw, young and handsome;
A sight of him on Chatsworth bank
    Were worth a prince's ransom.

15.

He slew the deer on Hardwick-hill,
    And left the keeper sleeping
The sleep of death; late—late yestreen
    I heard his widow weeping.

16.

Now bend your bows, and choose your shafts,—
    His string at his touch went sighing;
The Outlaw comes—now, now at his breast
    Let seven broad shafts be flying.

17.

The Outlaw came—with a song he came—
    Green was his gallant cleeding;*
A horn at his belt, in his hand the bow
    That set the roebucks bleeding.

18.

The Outlaw came—with a song he came—
    O'er a brow more brent and bonny
The pheasant plume ne'er danced and shone,
    In a summer morning sunny.

19.

The Outlaw came—at his belt, a blade
    Broad, short, and sharp was gleamin';
Free was his step as one who had ruled
    Among knights and lovely women.

---

* *Cleeding*, a word still used in the north of England; clothing, apparel. South of
  Germany, *kleidung*; Icelandic, *klaede*; Teutonic, *kleed.*

20.

See, by his shadow in the stream
    He loves to look and linger,
And wave his mantle richly flower'd
    By a white and witching finger.

21.

Now, shall I hit him where yon gay plume
    Of the Chatsworth pheasant's glancing;
Or shall I smite his shapely limbs
    That charm our maidens dancing?

22.

Hold! hold! a northern forester said,
    'Twill be told from Trent to Yarrow,
How the true-love song of a gentle Outlaw
    Was stay'd by a churl's arrow.

23.

It shall never be said, quoth the forester then,
    That the song of a red-deer reaver
Could charm the bow that my grandsire bent
    On the banks of Guadalquiver.[138]

24.

And a shaft he laid, as he spoke, to the string,
    When the Outlaw's song came falling
As sweet on his ear, as the wind when it comes
    Through the fragrant woodlands calling.

25.

There each man stood, with his good bow bent,
    And his shaft pluck'd from the quiver:
While thus then sung that gallant Outlaw,
    Till rung both rock and river:

26.

Oh! bonny Chatsworth, and fair Chatsworth,
    Thy bucks go merrily bounding;
Aneath your green oaks, as the herds flew past,
    How oft have my shafts been sounding!

27.

It is sweet to meet with the one we love,
     When the night is nigh the hoarest;
It is sweet to bend the bow as she bids,
     On the proud prey of the forest.

28.

One fair dame loves the cittern's sound,
     When the words of love are winging;
But my fair one's music's the Outlaw's horn,
     And his bow-string sharply singing.

29.

She waves her hand—her little white hand,
     'Tis a spell to each who sees her;
One glance of her eye—and I snatch my bow,
     And let fly my shafts to please her.

30.

I bring the lark from the morning cloud,
     When its song is at the sweetest;
I stay the deer upon Chatsworth lea,
     When its flight is at the fleetest.

31.

There's magic in the wave of her hand,
     And her dark eye rains those glances,
Which fill the best and the wisest hearts
     With love's sweet influences.

32.

Her locks are brown—bright berry brown,
     O'er her temples white descending;
And her neck is like the neck of the swan,
     As her way through heaven she's wending.

33.

How I have won my way to her heart
     Is past all men's discernin';
For she is lofty, and I am low,
     My lovely Julia Vernon.

34.

He turned him right and round about,
With a step both long and lordly;
When he was aware of those foresters bold,
And he bore him wondrous proudly.

35.

Good morrow, good fellows! all fearless he said,
Was your supper spread so sparely;
Or is to feast some sweet young dame,
That you bend your bows so early?

36.

The world is wide, and the world is broad,
There's fish in the smallest river;
Deer leap on the hill—fowls fly in the air,—
Was, is, and will be ever.

37.

And now I feast on the ptarmigan,
And then I taste the pheasant;
And my supper is of the Chatsworth fawn,
Which my love dresses pleasant.

38.

But tomorrow I feast on yon bonny roebuck;
'Tis time I stay'd his bounding;
He twang'd his string—like the swallow it sung,
All shrilly and sharply sounding.

39.

By my grandsire's bow, said a forester then,
By my shafts which fly so yarely,
And by all the skill of my strong right hand,
Good Outlaw, thou lords it rarely.

40.

Seest thou yon tree, yon lonely tree,
Whose bough the Derwent's laving?—
Upon its top, thou gallant Outlaw,
Thou'lt be hung to feed the raven.

41.

So short as the time this sharp shaft flies,
     And strikes yon golden pheasant—
There—thy time is meted, so bid farewell
     To these greenwoods wild and pleasant.

42.

The Outlaw laugh'd; Good fellow, he said,
     My sword's too sure a servant
To suffer that tree to bear such fruit,
     While it stands on the Derwent.

43.

She would scorn my might, my own true love,
     And the mother would weep that bore me,
If I stay'd my step for such strength as thine,
     Or seven such churls before me.

44.

I have made my way with this little brown sword,
     Where the war-steeds rush'd the throngest;
I have saved my breast with this little brown sword,
     When the strife was at the strongest.

45.

It guarded me well in bonny Scotland,
     When the Scotts and Graemes fought fervent;
And the steel that saved me by gentle Nith,
     May do the same by Derwent.

46.

Fair fall thee, Outlaw, for that word!
     Oh! Nith, thou gentle river,
When a bairn, I flew along thy banks,
     As an arrow from the quiver.

47.

The roebucks run upon thy braes
     Without a watch or warden;
And the tongue that calls thee a gentle stream
     Is dear to Geordie Gordon.

48.

The Outlaw smiled, 'Tis a soldier's saye
    That the Gordons, blythe and ready,
Ne'er stoop'd the plumes of their basnets bright
    Save to a lovesome lady.

49.

Now by Saint Allan, the forester said,
    And the Saint who slew the dragon;
And by this hand that wields the brand,
    As wight as it tooms the flagon;

50.

It shall never be told of the Gordons' name,
    Of a name so high and lordly,
That I took a gallant Outlaw in the toil,
    And hanged him base and cowardly.

51.

I'll give thee the law of Lord Nithisdale,
    A good lord of the border;
So take thy bow, thou gallant Outlaw,
    And set thy shafts in order.

52.

And we will go each one to his stance,
    With bows and arrows ready;
And thou shalt climb up Chatsworth bank,
    Where the wood is wild and shady.

53.

And thou shalt stand on yon rough red rock,
    With woodbine hung and bracken;
And shout three times o'er Derwent vale,
    Till all the echoes waken.

54.

Then loose thy shafts, and slay a buck,
    Fit for a monarch's larders;
And carry him free from Chatsworth park,
    In spite of seven warders.

55·

Do this and live, and I do vow
    By the white hand of my mother,
I'll smite him low who runs ere thou shout,
    Were he Saint Andrew's brother.

56.

The Outlaw smiled; Good Gordon, he said,
    I'll shout both high and gaily;
And smite a buck, and carry him off;
    'Tis the work I'm bowne to daily.

57·

The Outlaw stood upon Chatsworth rock,
    Like light his looks did gladden;
The sun was shining on Bakewell-Edge,
    And on the heights of Haddon.

58.

The Outlaw stood upon Chatsworth rock,
    He look'd to vale and mountain,
And gave a shout so shrill, the swans
    Sprung up from stream and fountain.

59·

The Outlaw stood upon Chatsworth rock,
    And shouted shrill and gaily;
Till the dun deer leap'd from brake and bower,
    Two miles down Derwent valley.

60.

The Outlaw stood upon Chatsworth rock,
    Looking o'er the vale so narrow;
And his voice flew fleet as away from the string
    Starts off the thirsty arrow.

61.

And loudly it rung in Haddon-wood,
    Where the deer in pairs were dernan:*
And loudly it rung in Haddon-hall,
    And up rose Julia Vernon.

62.

If ever I heard my true love's voice,
    'Tis now through my bowers ringing;
His voice is sweet as the wild bird's note,
    When the buds bloom to its singing.

63.

For well I know my true love's voice,
    It sounds so gay and clearly:
An angel's voice in a maiden's ear
    Would ne'er drop down so dearly.

64.

She took her green robe in a hand
    White as the opening lily,
And the morning sun and the lovely maid
    Look'd down on Chatsworth valley.

65.

Around the brow of the high green hill
    The sun's fair beams were twining,
And bend and fall of the Derwent stream
    In golden light were shining.

66.

The silver smoke from Chatsworth tower,
    Like a pennon broad went streaming,
And gush'd against the morning sky,
    And all the vale was gleaming.

---

* *Dernan*, concealing. 'Abusing and harming his Majesty's good subjects by
their darned (concealed) stouths.'—*Acts of James I. of England*. Anglo-Saxon,
dearn-an.

67.

She gave one look on the broad green land,
    And back her tresses sheddin',
With her snowy neck, and her bonnie blue eyes,
    Came down from the hill of Haddon.

68.

She saw the wild dove start from its bower,
    And heard the green boughs crashing;
And saw the wild deer leap from its lair,
    And heard the deep stream dashing.

69.

And then she saw her own true love
    Bound past by bush and hollow;
And after him seven armed men
    With many a shout and hollo.

70.

Oh! had I but thy bow, my love,
    And seven good arrows by me,
I'd make the fiercest of thy foes
    Bleed ere they could come nigh thee.

71.

Oh! had I but thy sword, my love,
    Thy sword so brown and ready,
I'd meet thy foes on Chatsworth bank,
    Among the woodlands shady.

72.

On high she held her white white hands
    In wild and deep devotion,
And locks and lips, and lith* and limb,
    Were shivering with emotion.

---

* *Lith*, joint. Anglo-Saxon, *lith*.

73.

Nay, stay the chase, said a forester then,
    For when the lion's roaring
The hound may hide:—May the raven catch
    The eagle in his soaring?

74.

Farewell, my bow, that could send a shaft,
    As the levin leaves the thunder!
A lady looks down from Haddon height
    Has snapt thy strength asunder.

75.

A lady looks down from Haddon height,
    O'er all men's hearts she's lordin';
Who harms a hair of her true love's head
    Makes a foe of Geordie Gordon.

76.

The bank was steep,—down the Outlaw sprung,
    The greenwood wide resounded;
The wall was high,—like a hunted hart
    O'er it he fleetly bounded.

77.

And when he saw his love, he sunk
    His dark glance in obeisance:
Comes my love forth to charm the morn,
    And bless it with her presence?

78.

How sweet is Haddon hill to me,
    Where silver streams are twining!
My love excels the morning star,
    And shines while the sun is shining.

79.

She and the sun, and all that's sweet,
    Smile when the grass is hoarest;
And here at her white feet I lay
    The proud buck of the forest.

80.

Now, farewell, Chatsworth's woodlands green,
    Where fallow-deer are dernan;
For dearer than the world to me
    Is my love, Julia Vernon!

THE END

TRADITIONAL LITERATURE.
NO. I

The rural faith sustain—[1]
These are the themes of simple sure effect.
Collins.

Much of the oral wisdom, and of the poetry of the early genius of our country, have long ceased to be as fugitives and vagabonds on the earth; the industry of man has treasured a large proportion of them in a secure sanctuary,—and it is pleasant to think that such treasures remain no longer liable to the vicissitudes which threaten things entrusted to human remembrance.—Yet, though they are thus gathered together, and adorned, and illustrated by the diligence and research of learning, something of their ancient influence continues to be felt amongst us; and it is in no disregard or derision of learning that we still cling with an affectionate remembrance to the unwritten reliques of our poetry, and the remains of our domestic and historical tales. Erudition has not yet achieved a full conquest over the ancient empire of oral literature. Reliques of the simpler times of traditional tale, and chivalrous ballad, are abundantly visible among the people of the northern provinces of England; and they at present communicate no small portion of true national beauty to the fixed splendours of written literature. While the genius of the scholar consented to accept the form and hue of its early labours from the poetic and historic achievements of ancient times, and filled Christian verse and prose with the dumb gods of the heathen,—there flourished a species of rustic, or national oral literature, in the shape of song, and ballad, and tale, which has certainly laid the foundations of our present literary originality and excellence.—In our provinces these primitive efforts of mind still linger—unwilling to depart:—they have been long since obliterated in the city, and, perhaps, among the good people of the town, they never secured more than a transient abode. The character of the city is not of that genuine original kind, which would incline its society to receive and retain those simple compositions that dwell in the minds and hearts of a pastoral and a rural people. While the latter retain much of that early singleness of disposition which belongs to an unmingled race, the former is so smoothed down and polished, in the outward and inner man, that the original English stamp is more than half effaced. The manners and refinements of a city, together with the ready facilities which recorded wit and written learning afford, abate attachments to the superstitious legends and rude ballads of shepherds and ploughmen. The oral wisdom, the historical and domestic traditions, and the rude, and sometimes ludicrous, lyric compositions, so common to all northern nations, cannot be supposed to live and flourish among the living martyrs of the day-book and ledger. A citizen is a being compounded out of our various commercial intercourses, and educated by mercantile usage;—and, although infinitely more lively, ready, and companionable than his ruder brethren of the plough-field and the sheep-fold, he is much less deeply imbued with the rough and original character of an Englishman. It was such considerations as these which probably extracted that querulous exclamation from the pious poet:—

God made the country, but man made the town.[2]

The language too of the people of the country differs from that of the city: it is of a more varied and original cast; abounds with poetical expressions, and contains a rich stock of practical and useful wisdom. It has a certain shrewd and proverbial cast, and an occasional elevation of thought, which show that the roller of artificial refinement has failed to crush the heights down to the hollows of the national character.

In old times, and until within the remembrance of living persons, certain gifted individuals wandered about the provinces, from house to house,—shunning the self-sufficient mechanics of the town, and associating only with farmers and portioners,—not only reciting traditional ballads, and singing traditional songs, but also relating portions of national and domestic history. By this they earned, like the ancient minstrel, 'their food and raiment, of which they were worthy.'[3]— Their narratives were related to audiences unsated as yet with literary productions, and who (unlike the multitudes who crowd our theatres,) assembled with the resolution of being pleased. The song and the tale resembled that fleeting litera-

ture 'which not even critics criticize;'[4] and the humble authors
had nothing to dread from the wit or the malice of men who
live by giving opinions on the productions of others. While
learning communicated with mankind through the tardy
medium of penmanship, the written wisdom of the sage was
literally a book shut and sealed to the bulk of mankind. At last
the art of printing multiplied the treasures of genius, and
transmitted them over the earth:—but still it was through the
expensive means of solid folios, with which the poverty of the
rustic part of the community prevented all intercourse.—Traditional literature still held up its head and prevailed, till the
fruits of the mind, becoming matters of merchandize, courted
the notice of the peasantry in an humbler form, and the historian and bard of the district found his occupation super-
seded by the rapid operation of machinery. The representative
of the minstrels was then compelled to make their ancient calling a kind of auxiliary to the city bookseller, whose manifold
productions he assisted in scattering over the land, which had
long been delighted with legend and song. In the progress of
printing a new swarm of literary labours arose, and gratified
by productions natural or unnatural, the desire of mankind
for amusement and instruction. During the period of manu-
script literature, men of vast genius alone could emerge from
the multitude, and surmount those obstructions which encompassed the seat of fame. But the art of printing let loose a
legion of inferior spirits, who, forsaking the primitive objects
of writing—truth and delight—began, as a surer and more
immediate way to profit and notice, to minister to the passions
and vanities of the people. The turbulence of party literature
appeared on the earth. Malice and destruction became the
hand-maids of the press,—and the impurities of politics
tainted the clear and healthy currents of literature. A few
master spirits, it is true, redeemed us from the entire influence
of this spotted plague, and criticism for a while, like the prophet's rod,[5] devoured the illegitimate progeny of letters. But
criticism soon profaned its strength, and forsook its high calling. Instead of continuing a judge it became a partizan, and,
swelled the clamour, and inflamed the rancour of party bitterness. It sought rather to crush and confound, than to direct
and reclaim; and for the sake of displaying the coxcomberies
of wit, and flourishing a smart saying, it rebuked and trod
down genius, and proclaimed war against all ascending talent.

No one can read the party animosities of our two popular
critical journals[6] without sorrow of heart and confusion of
face; nor see the mighty difference in their opinions on the
labours of the human mind, without feeling pain for the weak-
ness of those who propose to reform the literature of the age.

A kind of spurious and artificial literature has thus arisen,
which seeks the means of existence among the animosities of
mankind. It has no connection, or resemblance to the native
genius of the country; mental speculation has forsaken the
path of nature, and writers exclaim, with the member of the
Royal Academy, '*D—— Nature! she deserves to be kicked.*'[7] It will
be seen, however, on examining the labours of our present
most gifted spirits, that the beauties of their most celebrated
compositions bear a close resemblance to the oral national literature, and that their authors have drawn largely from the
sure and primitive sources of tradition. They have not
scrupled to embellish their conceptions with the poetic beliefs,
and singular and lofty superstitions, of the shepherd and the
husbandman. It is certainly amusing to hear accomplished
scholars brand, as low and vulgar, the pursuits of simple
times, and the beliefs of the peasant. It was once princely to
hold the plough; nor was it deemed unbecoming in a princess
to wash her bridal garments, nor in a hero to prepare his
own dinner. From rustic belief and superstition the poet supplies himself with the noblest materials of his high calling; the
machinery of a romantic tale is only a personification of
village creeds. These furnish dramatic sublimity to Shak-
speare, grandeur to Milton, and that supernatural light which
shines and lightens in the works of the illustrious *warlock* of
Caledonia.[8]

Yet, the decay of traditional literature, I cannot help con-
sidering as a loss: thousands are willing to listen to instruction,
for an hundred desirous to read it; and a multitude of people
might profit by oral communication, who will be too dull or
indolent to seek information, in seclusion, out of books. I
cannot help thinking that the English peasantry possessed as
much real literary knowledge an hundred years ago as they
do at present; and had among them as much practical
wisdom. The information obtained from the present popular
literature of the lower orders, can add little to the joy and
comfort of domestic life; and certain it is, that tradition
recorded more of lofty deeds, that embellish public annals,

than the regular historian. Froissart, the inimitable Froissart,[9] alone condescends to mingle the mighty events which convulse nations, with the exploits of single heroes, that adorn and illustrate humanity. Common history stoops not to acquaintance with those actions which brighten poetry, and gladden the heart. As an instance, it may be mentioned, that she has failed to adorn her page with the name of the French hero, so distinguished during Thurot's attack on Carrickfergus.[10]— Had traditional literature been then in its glory, a gentle and embalming light would have been shed around him. During the hottest of the battle between the French and English at Carrickfergus, a child came out to play, in the dangerous space between the combatants;—a French soldier laid down his musket, advanced, took up the child, removed it to a place of safety, returned, lifted up his arms, and resumed his duty. And this hero's name is forgotten! How Froissart would have rejoiced over this gentle and heroic spirit! History lost the name of the hero, because it was suddenly called to a speculation on the profits of raw hides, and the importation of hemp.

It is the wish of the writer of this brief and imperfect account of traditional literature, to endeavour still to redeem some of its remains. There are yet curious portions of tale and history, fragments of legendary lore, and whole or dismembered ballads and songs, thickly scattered about the northern provinces of England—the land of my maternal ancestors. To collect them is a labour, the thought of which I have cherished for many years, and to the fulfilment of which I come, not without thought and preparation. I have preserved in a memory particularly tenacious of such matters, sundry singular and interesting tales, and fragments of poems, and I am not without hope of reviving the tone of those old narratives, which gladdened the hours of my early life. To a person educated in a romantic and pastoral country, where the gift of song is felt, and the voice of the muse acknowledged, and where tradition is still full of the fame of her ancient chivalry, much of what is curious and interesting will be presented, and it has been the delight of a large portion of a long life to seek this kind of oral literature, where it is alone to be found. Of those who assisted me in such acts of redemption, and who willingly poured the streams of their own rich memories into the scanty rivulet which yet trickled, but did not flow, in the region of golden tradition, I will gladly give some account.

It was my particular good fortune to acquire, when at
school, the friendship and confidence of a man whose name
will be long remembered in Cumberland;—Richard Faulder,
mariner, of Allanbay.[11] His collection of native legends was
wondrously enriched with remarkable stories and superstitions, connected with a maritime life. He had gone down
when a boy, as the language of Scripture expresses it,—*to
witness the wonders of the Lord on the deep*, and had continued to
travel on the unstable element till far advanced in years. He
had brought legends from all quarters; from wherever the
wind had filled his sails; but it was in the dark and stormy
regions of Norway and Sweden that his spirit found the narratives most congenial to its disposition, and his tales and
ballads certainly savoured strongly of the superstitions and
beliefs of those nations of Teutons. In addition to the circumstances of his life, so highly favourable for fostering such a
taste, and adding to such knowledge as I have been describing, he had a strong but irregular poetic feeling, and
could draw down beautiful visions of departed glory to earth.
From every voyage he made, he returned to gladden mine
ear with strange occurrences, which had escaped the duller
observations of his less gifted fellow mariners. To the home of
Richard Faulder I always carried an observant spirit, and an
obedient ear; and neither the length of his tales—which the
sailors, in their maritime language, called Dickon Faulder's
long yarns,—nor the frequency of their repetition—nor the
variations which they submitted to, ever abated my attention,
or lessened my appetite for the marvels of the seafaring life.
His cottage was built on one of those white and romantic
cliffs, which hang over the sea of Solway, and it still remains
as a sea-mark to mariners, and is distinguished by the native
seamen with the name of Dickon Faulder's nest. It was to the
cottage nest of this cliff, that I climbed in my hours of summer
leisure, and during the long winter evenings, and I could not
fail to remark, that the seaman's narratives suited the com-
plexion and livery of the time of year. Those of summer were
joyous and amusing, full of fairy shapes and elfin whims, while
those of the winter were rough, and dark, and terrible, as
the tempestuous season itself. In summer he seated himself
at the door of his cottage, gazing constantly seaward, and
cheered by the approach of a ship—the music of the billows, and the gladsome 'hail' of passing mariners. In winter,

he retired to an interior chamber of his cottage, and covering himself with a large mantel of thick fur, basked himself before the fire:—then, while the waves rolled on in multitudes against the white cliffs, and the wind and sleet beat on his abode, adventures crowded thick upon his remembrance, and it was not without reason that I blessed a sudden squall, or a gentle tempest.

To the various and moving perils and adventures of my maritime friend, I was enabled to add many, equally curious, which occurred on land, by acquiring the friendship of Gilpin Macgowan, a Caledonian, whom the misfortunes of the rebellion of 1745[12] had driven to court the refuge of the interior mountains of Cumberland.—This, however, is only the suspicion of the peasantry, for the prudent Scotchman never committed himself by any confession to that extent; and, though he related many curious particulars of their incursion into England, and the perils which the Highland warriors personally encountered in private forays during the march, he avoided the vanity of connecting his own name with that ill-starred adventure. I found him a tender of flocks among a primitive race of men, who inhabit the Keswick mountains, and whose sheep and cattle roam over a vast extent of moorland pasture. He was accounted a skilful shepherd, was acquainted with the surgery of sheep, and even sometimes presumed to recommend medicines for the ailments of the human race. I once remarked to him, that, unacquainted as he seemed to be with the learned mysteries of physic, he was likely to introduce his patients to their 'last linnen.'—'And what if I should,' said the Caledonian, with a smile half serious and half comic, and confidential,—'it will be lang afore I can *avenge the slaughter at Clifton!*'[13]—I never had the fortune to chance upon such a singular mixture of human oddity. He had all the veneration of a Catholic antiquary for ruined abbeys, and the reliques of the old religion, and loved the deep pealing of the organ, as intensely and devoutly as he did the music of the Highland pipe. Then he was an admirer of, and, I am persuaded, once a communicant with, a certain wild sect of mountain worshippers, called Cameronians—and the joy of adoring heaven in the open air, and among the green pasture mountains, was often quoted against the Episcopalian propensities of the inhabitants of Cumberland. He was a fond admirer of civil and religious liberty, and delighted to quote the many triumphs of the 'sword' and the 'word' in Scotland. He admired still more the ancient names of the Douglas, and the Percy; and, in the cause of Prince Charles Stewart, I have been informed that he fought with great courage at Clifton—and escaped from the siege of Carlisle—a matter which few could boast of. His memory was stored with curious tales of pastoral and rural life, and his chief amusement, towards the close of his days, was to sit and sing fragments of ballads and songs, as motly and mixed as his opinions. Of these it may not be unacceptable to give a specimen now. The following was a ballad which he sang sometimes to the Cambrian maidens, as descriptive of the wooing of ancient times:—

MACMORAN'S MARY.[14]
A Scottish Ballad.

As I came down Dalgonar glen,
    'Mang woodlands wild, and waters many,
A bonnie maiden blessed my e'en,
    Her name was Miles Macmoran's Mary!

'O maid with foot so light and white,
    And clustering locks, as brown's a berry,—
And e'en mair bright than yon bright'ning star—
    Wilt thou come wi' me Macmoran's Mary?

'The doves moan amorous in my glen,
    On my green mountains bounds the fairy,
And a thousand swords are bare when I bid—
    Wilt thou come wi' me Macmoran's Mary?

'Now I would give me bonnie gray steed,
    My plaid, and blade, as brown's a berry,
Were I but fifteen miles from the north—
    And alang wi' me Macmoran's Mary!'

The maid blushed red, and the maid looked down,
    As the lily looks in lone Glenarie,
While I leaped down from my bonnie gray steed—
    'Oh come wi' me Macmoran's Mary!'

O out then spoke a silly old man—
    And O but he spoke wonderous saucy;—
'Ye may steal away my cows and my ewes,
    But steal nae away my ae sweet lassie!'

I mounted her on a milk white steed,
    And away it flew, as fleet's a fairy—
And I rode over hills and through grassy glens,
    Away and away wi' Macmoran's Mary.

And we passed swift floods, and spreading woods,
    Passed moorlands brown, and mountains many,
And came at length to a lonesome glen,
    Where a stream was simmering bright and bonnie:

Our bridal-bed was the grassy bank,
    Our covering was the breckans bonnie—
Our bridal light was the round flowing moon,
    Wi' ministering stars baith clear and monie.

'My mansion is this mountain dark,
    My sword's my kingdom, and I tarry
Amang Glengomar's bounding deer—
    Wilt thou be my queen, Macmoran's Mary?'

'In peril or joy I'll bide with thee,
    In glens and moors and mountains many,
For love is as true as yon lights aboon,—
    An' never dies'—quoth my bonnie Mary.

I wound my silver horn, and lo!
    Squire, page, and dame, came trooping ready—
'O these are mine, and I am thine,
    My kind and sweet and lovely lady!'

    I have made no attempt at softening the harshness of the
rhyme of this ancient ballad, or measuring its rude lines into
more equal quantities. In regard to all the more poetical communications of my friends, I imitated the scrupulous fidelity
of that prince of editors, honest Joseph Ritson,[15] and copied
them without even hazarding those occasional emendations so
usual with compilers. As it would be unfair to give a solitary

ballad as a specimen of the rich and varied rhymes, which I
have been instrumental in recovering, I shall transcribe another,
which I am not alone in thinking is the ancient ballad of
Bessie Bell and Mary Gray, modernized in its descent, by
means of oral communication, from the days of the luckless
heroines.

BESSIE BELL AND MARY GRAY.[16]
A Scottish Ballad.

O Bessie Bell, and Mary Gray,
    They are two bonnie lasses—
They have left their beds of driven-down
    To lie 'mang new mawn rashes;
And they have left the ruddie wine,
    To drink the crystal fountain,
And the song of love at gloamin' fa',
    For the plover's from the mountain!

Sweet Mary's breath came like the wind,
    Blowing o'er a bed of roses,
She sung like the lark to the morning star,
    When the shepherd's fold uncloses:
But Bessie's een were founts o' love,
    'Mang her lint-white ringlets willing,
And her looks came, like the May-morn sun,
    To set the world a smiling!

Where the moorland burn 'mang the yellow broom,
    Comes bright and gently pouring,
There I maun roam by the light o' the moon,
    Those lovely ones adoring:
And there one sits, and another sings,
    In a bower theeked o'er wi' rashes—
'O, kind love is a lightsome thing
    To two leal-hearted lasses!'

O can I e'er forget yon bower,
    With a' its fragrant blossom,
The smiling o' those lovesome een,
    And that white and heaving bosom!

For sweet's the joy o' kind sixteen,
   When the heart leaps warm and warmer,
At the first touch o' the lily hand
   Of a mild and beauteous charmer!

Nor to my garrulous Caledonian alone am I indebted for singular traditionary tales, and curious songs illustrative of departed days. From Eleanor Selby, an ancient dame, who resided in a cottage that resembled a hermitage, pertaining to the ducal castle of Naworth, I obtained much important information. She traced her descent from the second son of Sir Walter Seleby, who was slain in an incursion by the Scotch; and she detested that warlike and predatory people as much as she admired the Houses of Seleby, Dacre, and Howard. On every sabbath morn she made a pilgrimage to the old Abbey of Lanercost, in the romantic vale of Naworth, and, kneeling at the eastern entrance, offered up a prayer, which some supposed regarded the restoration of the priory to its ancient splendour, but which others, with more truth perhaps, believed to be an intercession for the repose of her ancestor's soul. The mountain ashes and wall-flowers, which flourished among the ruins, obtained more of her affection than the parish church, which stood, mean and squalid, in a lonely corner of the majestic pile. I won this aged dame's affection by a successful attempt to replace the mutilated font at the altar, and I have often blessed my instinctive love for ruined houses of worship.—Through this I became acquainted with many of those Cumbrian tales, which gladdened the winter evenings of the peasantry; and, by the kindness of Dame Selby, I shall be able to charm all lovers of true romance, with *the history of the spectre steeds and warriors*,[17] who, in 1743, coursed, visible to the eyes of Daniel Stricket, and John Wren, of Wilton-hall, up Soutra-fell—a mountain five and twenty hundred feet perpendicular!

Lammerlea, Cumberland.

Appendix B

THE TWELVE TALES OF LYDDALCROSS. INTRODUCTORY

Come turn your footsteps to wild Fancy's land,[1]
To haunted Lyddal, Solway's fairy strand;
To the charm'd ground where grey tradition tells
Of the dread lair where the old wizard dwells,
Who milk'd men's flocks, and drown'd the herds in Dryfe,
And coost seven witch-knots[2] on proud Willie's wife;
The blessed well where the sick pilgrim drinks,
The mermaid-water where the gay ship sinks,
The heath where flits the grisly ghost,—the glen
With spectres throng'd and fiery shapes of men.
We'll pull the ragwort on which witches prance,
Through the sick air, to quaff the wines of France;—
We'll dance upon the greensward upland, where
The elfin minstrels sooth'd the wintry air
To summer sweetness, while the dewy weet
Show'd the starr'd sparkling of ten thousand feet.
Of the fierce Kelpies, too, we'll talk—the lords
Of Lyddal's pools, and Dryfe's more deadly fords;—
Of spectre-lights which glimmer far and nigh,
Lights of the grave where all who live must lie;
Of elfin lights;—in all the lights which gleam
Down dim tradition we shall find a theme.
        On themes, too, sweeter shall we muse, and talk
With whispering maidens in the twilight walk;
With peasants revel; converse hold, and quaff
Ale berry-brown, and sing, and leap, and laugh;—
Paint the grave humour and the witty grace
Of Scotland's keen and England's honest face.
Pause 'mid our mirth, and sigh above the shroud
Where princely Percys lie and Musgraves proud;
The gallant Selbys wild of wit and will,
The Dacres hot, the Harclas hotter still:
Nor shall the Douglas be forgot,—the wight
And witty Gordons, Lindsays gay and light;
The Maxwell, too, whom Nithsdale matrons mourn,

Smote low and bleeding by the Dryfesdale thorn;
And Scott, a name which while the greenwood grows.
While Skiddaw towers, and silver Solway flows,
While eyes love light, and ladies lover-story,
Shall shine in martial might and minstrel glory;
And bold Kirkpatrick, Closeburn's fiery knight,
Dimm'd now and shining with diminish'd light.
And Halliday, what muse but thinks of thee,
The wight, the witty, friendly, frank, and free;
And ancient Lyddal, thou whose lineage long
Has cherish'd northern oral lore and song;
And all the names in olden tale renown'd,
Sung in romance on fancy's charmed ground;—
On these we'll muse, stretch'd on the sunward sod,
Ere while by mailed knight and fairy trod,
Swathed in the shepherd's maud—around, around,
Will gray tradition pour her fitful sound,
And charm us up old visions haught and high,
Reveal'd to none save ours, or the GREAT WIZARD's eye.[3]

The stream of Lyddal, in winding down the romantic border
vale on which it confers its name, partly encloses a small, round,
woody mount, or knoll, once occupied by a fortress or tower,
the residence of the ancient and warlike name of Lyddal. This
fortress, during the eventful times of the English and Scottish
wars, acknowledged for captains many of the martial names of
Cumberland and Dumfrieshire. If the winds of Lyddal fanned
the pennons of the Percys, the Musgraves, the Mordaunts, the
Selbys, the Dacres, and the Harclas; they also in succession
waved the banners of the Scotts, the Maxwells, the Johnstones,
the Hallidays, and the Lyddals. And tradition does not fail to
inform us, that the same breeze which blew on the loyal pennons
of these redoubted border chieftains, blew more than once with
equal gentleness on the banners of the marauding Grahames,
Armstrongs, and Jardines, fairly displayed on the summit of
Lyddal tower. Nay; to one of these temporary lords of Lyddal is
ascribed the famous war-cry in the onset at Ancram-moor,[4]
'Every man for his ain hand, and God for us a';' and a border
family still show a gold girdle, with an embossed sword, which
in that memorable day forsook the side of Sir Brian Latoun,
and attached itself to the side of Richard Armstrong, lord, for
the time, of the towers of Gillknockie and Lyddal.

But disuse, says the poet, will rust the brightest sword;[5] so time will sap the strength of the strongest wall. The castle of Lyddal was silently dismantled by the long peace which followed the first Stuart to the English throne; and though it held up its head for a season, during the great civil war, it gradually lost its martial appearance; and soon after the accession of the Hanoverian branch of the Stuarts, when the wars which filled our towns with fire, and flooded our hearths with blood, were carried to foreign lands, it reduced its exterior to the peaceful look of domestic repose, and national tranquillity. This quiet sustained a slight interruption by the march of the Highland host, in 1745, when the mutilated tower was occupied as a magazine by a retainer to the chief of the clan Macpherson. On the retreat of the rebels from England, orders were given to blow up the magazine, and this service was entrusted to a clansman, much better skilled in the virtues of sword-blades and dirks, than in the powers of twenty barrels of gunpowder. He made his way to the door, and throwing a blazing turf, which he plucked from a peasant's hearth, among the barrels, quietly awaited the result. The tower was shattered from turret to foundation-stone, and the astonished clansman thrown three acres broad from the spot where he stood. He started to his feet, much singed, and but little hurt, and shaking the fire from his kilt and plaid, exclaimed with a snort: 'Tamn ye! put ye're hasty elding' (fuel).

Walter Lyddal, to whom this tower pertained at the time of the highland incursion, was the last of the ancient and immediate race, and altogether a remarkable person. In his youth, he was renowned over the whole border for the beauty of his person, for his skill in all manly exercises, and for the undaunted bravery of his nature. He was in love with a young lady, of the ancient family of the Selbys, and won her affection from many opulent and noble rivals. They met and plighted their vows, and broke a ring between them at the foot of Lyddalcross, an ancient monument of stone held in superstitious veneration by the peasantry; but their affections were crossed by false friends, or by their own evil fortunes. He flew to a foreign land, and the loss of her lover, and the disasters which the fatal rebellion of 1715 brought on her family, conducted the lady to an untimely grave. Walter Lyddal returned to his native land, but he was no longer the gay and the fiery

youth, whose bravery kept the border-riders in awe, and influenced the hearts of many noble maidens. He abolished the
ancient state and splendour of his house—turned his deer-
herds to the mountains, permitted no one to call him lord,
and exchanged the mantle, and hat, and heron plume, worn
by many of the romantic youths of that period, for a lowland
bonnet, and a shepherd's maud. The sword and pistols, the
common badges of gentle birth, and which personal safety
often demanded, were exchanged for a simple staff; and for
the sound of the trumpet, and the marshalling of armed
men,—he had now the music of the shepherd's pipe, and the
management of numerous flocks, which he delighted to lead
out to pasture among the romantic hills of his native land.

This transformation was beheld with sorrow and pity by
the ancient dependants of the name of Lyddal; they had ever
been accustomed to associate the name with the sword, and
the spear, with chivalry and feats of arms, and sighed to see
the descendant of the heroes of their fathers' tales and songs
degenerate into a feeder of flocks. The rustic minstrels of the
north made ballads 'of scoff and of scorn' on this unhappy
degeneracy, but nothing would rouse him from his lethargy.
Even when the highland host took forcible possession of his
residence, and made it into a magazine, he offered resistance
neither in word nor deed, but seated himself on a little hill,
and looked unconcerned on the strange array of warriors as
they passed. When his home—the ancient dwelling of his race
was blown to the air, he was only observed to remove with
much anxiety the rubbish from the old stone cross which stood
beside the tower; and pulling an emblem or token from his
bosom, he walked round and round the ancient monument,
muttering words which sounded like a prayer, and of which
the name of Selby could alone be distinguished.

After the retreat of the Highlanders, the house was speedily
re-built, and the name was changed to Lyddalcross; a name
which the peasantry, out of love for the proprietor, allowed it
to retain. As he advanced in years, his attachment to a pastoral life became more and more decided; he sometimes admitted
visitors from among the gentle friends of his father's house;
but he heard of titles and rank conferred on names long in
rivalry with his own with perfect indifference, and drove out
his flocks to pasture, and consorted with peasants and shepherds, like one who had never aspired at distinction, or prayed

for ladies' love. But he was no churl, though churls were his companions; his heart was ever kind, and his hand was ever open. His hearth, during winter, blazed the brightest of all border hearths; his hall was crowded with the wretched and the indigent, and his tables loaded with the abundance which his extensive estates supplied. To a race of beings whom the sordid feelings of the present portioners of the earth have shut up in alms-houses and cells, 'the moping idiot, and the mad-man gay,'[6] his house was ever open, and his table ever spread. His large fire was commonly flanked by a couple of these wanderers,—to whose residence in a family, the merciful pro-verb of the north imputed half the good fortune that befel; nor did the incumbents think of removing, till perhaps the arrival of others, equally deranged, but more intractable than themselves, drove them from the chimney-cheek. The new occupants again in their turn were dispossessed, more by force than entreaty, by others of their brethren of the district.

To those fond of observing the revival of the rude hos-pitality of our ancestors,—a view of the evening fire-side of Lyddalcross would have given no small pleasure. The halt, the lame, and the blind; those who felt distress, or counter-feited misfortune; the young and the aged, the soldier from the wars, and the mariner from the waves, all were there. The soldier's wife, with her children, and her story of distress, and the last letter she received from one who would never more write again; the blue gown mendicant,[7] the privileged lifter of every door-latch, and the chronicle of the district; the strolling seller of ballads and tales, those wandering booksellers, whose traffic in abridged romances, legends, and songs, has been long cut up by the periodical venders of visionary reforms, and leading articles in the practice and morals contained in the impure pages of Paine;[8] and though last, not the least important, the pleasant packman, whose tact in selling snoods of silk, and kirtles of callimanco, had rendered him a standard favourite on the border; all considered Lyddalcross as a refuge and a home.

These various and discordant materials of fire-side felicity the proprietor knew well how to manage, and perhaps no person ever possessed equal skill in extracting information and amusement from such intractable matter. He entered into the peculiar habits and feelings, and singularities of each indi-vidual, and distributed little marks of attention and notice, with such a graceful, but yet frugal hand, that all felt pleased, went away satisfied, and returned with joy. He suited himself to the whimsical and capricious humours of the crazy and demented; and with the old mendicants, he entered deeply into the spirit and history of past times, and conversed on family feuds, domestic misfortunes, national quarrels, and stories steeped deep in popular belief and superstition. On those who possessed the gift of story-telling in the greatest perfection, the laird's favours not only dropt, but were absolutely showered; and, to tell the truth, to go to Lyddalcross, without some real or well-feigned story, was to expose the visitant, not to expulsion, but to the mortification of a seat distant from the fire, and cold cheer at the supper table.

Of all this the travelling people of the neighbouring districts were perfectly aware, and amply indulged the aged laird in this harmless propensity, so that the Tales of Lyddalcross became famous, like the minstrelsy of old, all over the north countrie. The shepherd maiden sang at bught and bridal the songs of Lyddalcross, and the mendicant tale-teller justified in remote parishes any departure which he made from the direct line of established narrative, by declaring 'such is the way at Lyddalcross;' so that this mansion became as famous for the cleverest versions of traditional story, as the Ballantyne press[9] is at present for the finest editions of popular books.

How I became acquainted with Walter Lyddal is a tale easily told, and to me, at this distant day, there is pleasure in relating it. In the early part of my life, I was pursuing my way along the border towards Carlisle, with the carelessness of one who had not learned to set value upon time, and to whom an hour of lingering by an old castle wall, or a couple of hours pondering around the circumference of a Danish or Roman entrenchment, were moments numbered by joy. It was nigh the close of harvest, and the sun had nearly an hour to shine, when, after pursuing the curves and freaks of a pure and beautiful brook, I came within sight of the house of Lyddalcross; I stood looking on the romantic scene before me, conjuring up as I gazed the forms of the heroes of old, whose names and deeds had rendered this valley famous in story. So deeply was I engaged among the imaginary heroes of the Round Table, the wizard Merlin, the enchanter Walter de Soulis, and, descending down the stream of traditional chivalry, among the English and Scottish knights and minstrels, who tilted and battled, and sang on the streamlet banks, that I scarcely observed the approach of two men, who seemed engaged in very earnest conversation.

They were travelling merchants or pedlars, one was old and bent, with a look of particular shrewdness and calculation; the other was young, but there was a forecast in his looks, and a spirit of consideration in his eye, which foreboded that he would become an accomplished person in his way. Of this his hoary companion seemed to be aware, from the particular pains which he took to school him in his craft or calling, and prepare him for making his 'first foot, or entrée,' at Lyddalcross, with honour and emolument. 'And now William,' said the old pedlar, 'having settled the mystery of merchandize, have ye got a tale to tell to the laird of Lyddalcross, to secure ye a cozie seat at the fire, and the choicest comfort at his supper-board? Let me tell ye, my man, never be wanting in your tale; better want an inch of your ellwand. Ye maun have a tale of love and witty courtship for the maidens, a tale of mirth for the young men, and a tale of devotion, weel larded with scripture warrant, and the death-bed saws of saints, for the old and devout. But for the Laird of Lyddalcross, ye maun have an auld-world tale of blood-spilling, and hership and spulziement; or something anent witches, and wizards may be. There was auld Marget Humlock, yere mother's nearest neighbour, as uncannie a cummer as a man may talk about; ye can readily spirit up some sinful story anent her, and may be, my lad, tell nae falsehoods for all that; she was a fearful woman: or a tale of fairy-rade and revelry-age; better than a', and more becoming for one of thy years.' 'Ah, Simon,' said he to the senior, 'let me alone for a cunning tale, and a grave face. I vow I have as rare a tale to tell as the ears of an old man may covet.' 'Hast thou indeed,' responded Simon, in a tone that seemed intended to reprove the presumption of the youth, 'it will be something notable gif it be brewed in thy own brain; let me have a tasting on't, my bairn; repeat me a bit, and repeat it deliverly.' 'Repeat to thee my tale; my chiefest of all tales,' answered Willie; 'my sooth man I'm nae sic simpleton; ye would tell't for your ain, and win the warm cheer, and the cozie seat frae the laird, and leave me a cauld and supperless seat, and a bed in the barn, under an ell-deep of damp sacks.' 'Aweel, aweel, keep it thyself,' said the senior, whose temper the insolence of the

youth seemed unable to ruffle. 'But what tempts thee to think
I would steal one of thy "quoth he" and "quoth I" stories;
and wi' sic a gallant collection of my own. I shall tell a tale
to-night, sic as has nae been heard in Lyddal tower since the
banner of Johnie Armstrong, the freebooter, floated oure its
rafters. But let us forward, else some daft and demented carlin
will catch the warmest nook before us; and ye maun ken, the
laird never moves the seat of a crazy bodie; no, for the fairest
tale ever invented and tauld. Ye need nae wonder at that; he
has a fellow-feeling, Willie, my man; he's tarred with the same
stick, as the corbie-crow said to the raven.' And forward the
two companions hastened, leaving me much interested in the
singular laird of Lyddalcross.

I had heard of Walter Lyddal, for the unhappy tale of his
youthful days had flown far and wide; and I had also heard of
his return to Scotland, of the remarkable style of rude hospitality in which he lived, and the curious characters which it
was his delight to assemble about him. As I recalled these
matters to my mind, two women, cloaked and hooded, with
long walking sticks in their hands, advanced along the road,
and the theme on which they turned the current of conversation was the same which at that time employed my own
thoughts. 'Aweel and aweel,' said one old cummer, showing
from below her hood, as she spoke, a long gray eyelash, and
lucken brows, 'aweel, it's a wonderous weel told tale; but it's
too common, Marion, it's too common; it looks too like yesterday to pass for a bairn of fern-year. A tale like that will never
win the notice of the laird, nor win a pound of hawslock wool
to make hose for your good man. I see ye're green at this gear;
sae hearken hinnie, and I will school thee. It is now some
sax and twenty years, come summer, since I began to feast on
the fat of Lyddalcross; mony's the good stone of gimmer-wool
I have gained by cannie management, and mony's the happy
and gladsome night I have spent at his fire-side. It was nae
sae in auld times, I have heard my douce good man say, low
as he now lies in Wamphray kirkyard, with the green grass
growing aboon one of the whitest and manliest brows the
sun ever shone on; it was nae sae, he said, when the hall of
Lyddalcross, instead of hanging full of the sides and spaulds of
sheep, and deer hams, and kippered salmon, and teats of wool,
and hanks of yarn, was gleaming from floor to rafter with
the swords and the bucklers of mighty men. The horn that

now blaws the shepherd to his sunkit on the hill side, had it been set to a Lyddal's lip, would have touted out two hundred helmets, with as mony bauld Lyddals and Hallidays, all on their barbed steeds, with their mail coats on, and their swords by their sides. But times, hinnie, are sadly altered now, and a man has to toil and sweat, and turn over dirty acres, from sun-rise to sun-set, for a handful of meal and a pint of skimmed milk. A man in the auld times would mount his horse at the gloaming, and clink into his wife's lap, sometime ere midnight, the golden gauds of some baron's lady; he lived, lass, by the bow and the spear, and reaped a richer and a readier harvest in ae night, than a farmer will reap now in seven years. But as I was saying, mony a happy night have I spent at the hearth of Lyddalcross; but for every night of howff and shelter have I rewarded him with some cannie auld-farrand tale. Sae all that ye have to do is to glide in at the gate like a ghaist, with a "peace be here," and "health t'ye laird of Lyddalcross;" and should ony ane say, "away ye strange quean, the laird disnae ken ye," ye maun make answer: "Eh, sirs, but that's the first unkindly word woman ever heard at Lyddalcross. The auld Lyddals had a frank hand, and a weel plenished board for their dependants; it's altered days indeed. I heard my grandsire say, that when the auld lords of Lyddal feasted the nobles and the princes, the venison smoked like Lyddal mount in a mist, and the wine ran as red as ever the Lyddal ran with English blood, mair by token three parishes feasted on the crumbs after the feast, and got drunk on the remnant wine." Say this, or something like this, and I'll be your warrant; only ye'll have yere tale to tell, or yere ballad to sing nevertheless:' and continuing this amusing admonition, the two cummers descended into the valley, and proceeded towards the house.

To resist the wish of visiting Walter Lyddal, after listening to these conversations, was impossible; so I descended into the valley, and approached the house, not without apprehension that I might fail in the curious trial of introduction to the warmest seat, and the choicest cheer. The door appeared to be guarded by a gray-headed domestic, who, on observing an utter stranger in the path, came forward to meet me: 'Ye'll be wanting to look at Lyddal mount, Sir, and the Saxon cross, whilk my master calls Lady Selby's cross,' said the retainer of the last lord of Lyddal; 'or ye may be wanting,' added he, in a lower tone, but of equal kindness, 'food and fire, and shelter.' I looked round the ancient mount, and the Saxon cross, and rewarding my conductor with a small gratuity for his trouble, prepared to pass the threshold; he whispered in a confidential tone, in which he perhaps wished me to think that my notice of him was not forgotten: 'Your food will be the richer, Sir, and your bed softer, and your welcome warmer, if ye can tell some brave auld-world tale to cheer the heart of my kind auld master; for, the saints help him! he kens of nae comfort now, save what comes frae strange lips.'

I entered, and found a large and roomy hall, already peopled with motley guests, while a huge fire in the middle of the floor shared the glory of illuminating the place with the last ray of the descending sun. Tale and ballad had already begun, for a wandering dealer in legends and songs endeavoured, as I advanced, to obtain a warmer seat, and augment his evening cheer, by singing the following song, of which he carried six dozen of printed copies, at the rate of seven songs for a penny.

THE AULD MAN.[10]

I.

Down Lyddal glen the stream leaps glad;
 The lily blooms on Lyddal lea;
The daisy glows on the sunny sod;
 The birds sing loud on tower and tree:
The earth laughs out, yet seems to say,
Thy blood is thin, and thy locks are gray.

2.

The minstrel trims his merriest string,
 And draws his best and boldest bow;
The maidens shake their white brow-locks,
 And go starting off with their necks of snow.
I smile, but my smiling seems to say,
Thy blood is thin, and thy locks are gray.

3.

The damsels dance; their beaming eyes
    Shower light and love, and joy about;
The glowing peasant answers glad,
    With a merry kiss, and mirthsome shout.
I leap to my legs, but well-a-day,
Their might is gone, and my locks are gray.

4.

A maiden said to me with a smile,
    Though past thy hour of bridal bliss,
With hoary years, and pains, and fears,
    A frozen pow, and a frosty kiss,
Come down the dance with me, I pray,
Though thy blood be thin, and thy locks be gray.

5.

Sweet one, thou smilest; but I have had,
    When my leaf was green, as fair as thee
Sigh for my coming, and high-born dames
    Have loved the glance of my merry ee;
But the brightest eye will lose its ray,
And the darkest locks will grow to gray.

6.

I've courted till the morning star
    Wax'd dim ere came our parting time;
I've walk'd with jewel'd locks, which shone
    I' the moon when past her evening prime;
And I've ta'en from rivals rich away
The dame of my heart, though my locks be gray.

The audience applauded the song, but I was too glad of
the opportunity which its singing gave me of contemplating
Walter Lyddal, to give that regard to the rhyme which probably it merited. The representative of this ancient border
name was seated on an antique settle, or couch of carved oak,
placed apart from the crowd, and cushioned deep with sheep
skins. He was muffled up to the chin in a dark gray cloak,
formed from the wool of his own flocks; his head was bare,
and sprinkled about the temples with long white hairs. His
form was perfectly erect, but the weight of sixty-five years,

many of them full of sorrow, had done much to pull down
a stately and powerful frame, and had given a palsied and
tremulous motion to the hands and head. He rested him over
a staff, and his large dark and inquisitive eyes roamed inces-
santly among the strange faces which thronged his hearth.
Dogs of the chase, and shepherds' curs, and curs of low degree,
lay stretched on the floor, while the beams and walls were
hung with dried flesh and fish, and all the preserved and
pickled dainties of a pastoral establishment.

At last the old man fixed his eyes on me, and making something like an effort to rise, said: 'You are welcome, Sir, to
Lyddalcross; welcome to such cheer as a frail old man can
give you. For the days are far away that were once here when
I had three fair sisters to make a stranger's seat soft, and
minister to his cheer. These days are all gone, Sir, so even
come and draw yere seat near me, and tell any strange tidings
ye may have heard; for I am one who hears nought, save what
the kindness of strangers gathers for my gratification.' Two
of his dogs, as he spoke, came and caressed me like an old
acquaintance; while one of the domestics, who evidently did
not confound me with the mendicants who thronged the floor,
placed a seat for my accommodation: so down I sat, without
farther ceremony; and thus I addressed the old man. 'I have
sought your hearth, and accept your welcome, and I doubt
not to find the truth of the ancient Dumfries-shire proverb,
"Aught's gude frae the hand of a Lyddal." ' 'And so ye're a
quoter of old proverbs,' said the laird to me; 'I like ye all the
better for that; the man who can apply a good old proverb
with discretion is no' a man to be met with under every blue
bonnet; and that's a proverb too. Halbert, bring hither the
drinking loom of Lyddalcross, the ancient fairy cup; and bring
it full of wine: keep your ale for the self-sufficient citizens of
cannie Carlisle; this is a lad of better mettle, his face reminds
me of old acquaintance and firm friendship, and we shall taste
wine together this night, were it only in honour of his looks.'

The old domestic advanced with the wine cup and the
flagon; and the laird, seizing the former by the two massy
ears, placed it beside him, poured it full of wine, and eyeing
me for a moment, renewed his discourse. 'I ken ye well, your
name is Halliday, descended from Thomas Halliday, the
sister's son of Sir William Wallace, the bauld and homely
Halliday; one of thy ancestors was Walter Halliday, marshal

of the English minstrels to Edward the Fourth; thy grandfather and I in the days of our youth were soothfast friends,
and the Lyddals and Hallidays have ridden side by side in
battle when Eden water ran red with blood; it's an old name
and a good,' and elevating the cup as he spoke, he drained the
wine at a draught. The cup was instantly replenished, and
placed in my hands; and even while I raised it to my lips, no
wise slow in doing honour to my entertainer, I could not help
admiring the exquisite beauty of the sculpture with which its
sides were adorned. The artist had represented a fairy procession, and the elfin people on horseback and foot moved along
to the sound of supernatural minstrelsy. The earth seemed
green under their feet, the sky sparkled with stars above them,
and the whole romantic scene seemed charmed into life and
beauty.

'It is a bonnie cup,' said my entertainer, 'and has belonged
to the name of Lyddal since the harrying of Holmecultrum-
house, when the strife was between Bruce and Baliol.[11] The
common people, who seldom err in traditionary matters, aver
it to be the work of elves, and call it the fairy cup of Lyddalcross. But I keep ye from your wine, Sir, and ye'll admire
the vessel not the less when ye have proved its contents.' I
obeyed, and emptied a cup of wine which was worthy of
wetting the lips of Queen Mab herself.[12] 'Laird of Lyddal,' I
said, 'if the cup be beautiful, the wine is delicious; and I much
question if more exquisite wine ever sparkled in the cup when
presented to the Princess of Fairy-land herself, by the hands
of ELPHIN IRVING, who was seven years cup-bearer to the
elves, in the vale of Corriewater.' 'Seven years cup-bearer,'
said Walter Lyddal, chaffing his huge hands together with
joy, 'seven years cup-bearer to the Queen of Elfland; I never
heard of the tale before. I'll warrant it's an odd one and a
wild:—Elphin Irving! I have never heard of the youth, so take
another tasting of wine, and tell me, and have the discretion
to speak out, for my hearing is less sharp than it should be.
But, first, let me tell ye the use and wont of Lyddalcross. I
dwell apart from mankind, and my main delight is in listening
to traditional stories; tales which are full of the failings and
the feelings, the beliefs, the superstitions, the sins, and the
actions of man: my hearth is crowded, as ye may see, with
curious old-world sort of people like myself, and many a well-
imagined story is related for my edification. Such is the use

and wont of my hall. If ye lacked invention and knowledge
in old matters, the name of Halliday should float ye over
family rules; yet, for the sake of old friendship, let me hear the
tale of ELPHIN IRVING, the FAIRIES' CUP-BEARER.'

Appendix C

ALLAN CUNNINGHAM'S CONTRIBUTIONS TO THE LONDON MAGAZINE

Abbreviations

Brooks   Elmer Leroy Brooks, *Studies in the London Magazine* (unpublished doctoral thesis, Harvard University, 1954).

Riga & Prance   Frank P. Riga and Claude A. Prance, *Index to the London Magazine* (New York and London: Garland, 1978).

v. 2, 12 (December 1820)

'Traditional Literature. No. I' (641–47).
Essay. Introduction to series, distinct from the Preface to the collected edition of *Traditional Tales*. Reproduced in this volume, 307–317. Signed 'Lammerlea, Cumberland'.

v. 3, 13 (January 1821)

'Traditional Literature. No. II. Richard Faulder of Allanbay' (26–32).
Tale. Appears as 'Richard Faulder, Mariner' in *Traditional Tales*. Signed 'Lammerlea, Cumberland'.

v. 3, 14 (February 1821)

'Traditional Literature. No. III. Rhyme Legend of Richard Faulder, Mariner. Voyage in the Spectre Shallop' (166–73).
Poem. This long ballad does not appear in *Traditional Tales*, but is reprinted in *Marmaduke Maxwell*. Signed 'Lammerlea, Cumberland'.

v. 3, 15 (March 1821)

'Traditional Literature. No. IV. Tale of Richard Faulder, Mariner' (255–63).
Tale. Appears as 'The Last Lord of Helvellyn' in *Traditional Tales*. Signed 'Lammerlea, Cumberland'.

v. 3, 16 (April 1821)

'Traditional Literature. No. V. Dame Eleanor Selby' (389–95).
Tale. Appears as 'Selbys of Cumberland. Part First' in *Traditional Tales*. Signed 'Lammerlea, Cumberland'.

v. 3, 18 (June 1821)

'Traditional Literature. No. VI. Eleanor Selby and the Spectre-Horseman of Soutra' (615–22).
Tale. Appears as 'Selbys of Cumberland. Part Second' in *Traditional Tales*. Signed 'Lammerlea, Cumberland'.

v. 4, 19 (July 1821)

'Traditional Literature. No. VII. The Death of Walter Selby' (19–28).
Tale. Appears as 'Selbys of Cumberland. Part Third' in *Traditional Tales*. Signed 'Lammerlea, Cumberland'.

'Fugitive Literature' (49–56).
Essay. Signed 'Lauchlin Galloway'. Tentatively attributed to Cunningham by Brooks.

v. 4, 20 (August 1821)

'Traditional Literature. No. VIII. The Ghost with the Golden Casket' (129–36).
Tale. Appears in *Traditional Tales*. Signed 'Lammerlea, Cumberland'.

v. 4, 21 (September 1821)

'Traditional Literature. No. IX. Judith Macrone the Prophetess' (237–46).
Tale. Appears in *Traditional Tales*. Signed 'Lammerlea, Cumberland'.

v. 4, 22 (October 1821)

'Traditional Literature. No. X. Placing a Scottish Minister' (401–11).
Tale. Appears in *Traditional Tales*. Signed 'Lammerlea, Cumberland'.

v. 4, 23 (November 1821)
'Traditional Literature. No. XI. The Haunted Ships' (499–507).
Tale. Appears in *Traditional Tales*. Signed 'Lammerlea, Cumberland'.

v. 4, 24 (December 1821)
'Traditional Literature. No. XII. Miles Colvine, the Cumberland Mariner' (594–603).
Tale. Appears in *Traditional Tales*. Signed 'Lammerlea, Cumberland'.

v. 5, 25 (January 1822)
'The Twelve Tales of Lyddalcross. Introductory' (5–13).
Essay. Unsigned. Reproduced in this volume, 319–332. 'Elphin Irving' follows on from this Introduction, as the first tale in the new series.

'The Twelve Tales of Lyddalcross. Tale the First. Elphin Irving, the Fairies' Cupbearer' (13–21).
Tale. Unsigned. Appears in *Traditional Tales*.

v. 5, 26 (February 1822)
'The Seven Foresters of Chatsworth, An Ancient Derbyshire Ballad' (129–36).
Poem. Unsigned. Appears in *Traditional Tales*.

'The Twelve Tales of Lyddalcross. Tale Second. Honest Man John Ochiltree' (142–52).
Tale. Unsigned. Appears in *Traditional Tales*.

v. 5, 27 (March 1822)
'The Twelve Tales of Lyddalcross. Tale Third. The King of the Peak, a Derbyshire Tale' (243–52).
Tale. Unsigned. Appears in *Traditional Tales*.

v. 5, 28 (April 1822)
'The Twelve Tales of Lyddalcross. Tale the Fourth. Allan-a-Maut' (321–30).
Tale. Unsigned. Appears in *Traditional Tales*.

v. 5, 29 (May 1822)
'As I Came down through Cannobie. An Old Jacobite Song'
(412).
Poem. Signed 'C'. Does not appear in *Traditional Tales*. Not
attributed to Cunningham by Brooks or Riga & Prance.

'The Twelve Tales of Lyddalcross. Tale the Fifth. The Mother's
Dream' (458–67).
Tale. Unsigned. Appears in *Traditional Tales*.

v. 5, 30 (June 1822)
'Lovely Woman. A Scottish Song' (524).
Poem. Signed 'C'. Does not appear in *Traditional Tales*. Not
attributed to Cunningham by Brooks or Riga & Prance.

'Tales of Lyddalcross. Tale Sixth. Death of the Laird of
Warlsworm' (539–49).
Tale. Unsigned. Appears in *Traditional Tales*. Note: Appears
under 'Tales of Lyddalcross', rather than 'The Twelve Tales
of Lyddalcross', perhaps signifying Cunningham's abandon-
ment of a set scope or plan for this series.

v. 6, 31 (July 1822)
'The Downfall of Dalzell' (27–29).
Poem. Appears in 'Ezra Peden', in *Traditional Tales*. Attri-
buted to Cunningham on contents page.

'The Haunted House' (63–71).
Tale. Unsigned. Subtitled 'a Tale of Lyddalcross' on contents-
page. Attributed to Cunningham by Brooks and Riga &
Prance.

Note: none of the contributions after this issue appear in
Traditional Tales.

v. 6, 32 (August 1822)
'The Mariner's Song' (132).
Poem. Better known as 'A Wet Sheet and a Flowing Sea'.
Subtitled 'By Allan Cunningham'.

'Narrative of Nathan Adamson, Student of Divinity' (152–
63).
Tale. Unsigned. Attributed to Cunningham by Brooks and
Riga & Prance.

'Halidon Hill, By Sir Walter Scott' (174–81).
Essay. Review of Scott's 'dramatic sketch'. Signed 'C'. Tentatively attributed to Cunningham by Brooks.

v. 6, 33 (September 1822)
'It's Hame and it's Hame' (220).
Poem. Note states: 'The following Song is noticed in the introduction to [Walter Scott's] The Fortunes of Nigel, and part of it is sung by Richie Moniplies. It is supposed to come from the lips of a Scottish Jacobite exile—the chorus is old' (220). Subtitled 'By Allan Cunningham'.

'King Bruce's Bowl, a Dramatic Legend of Galloway' (229–41).
Drama. Short play, in one scene. Unsigned. Attributed to Cunningham by Brooks and Riga & Prance.

v. 6, 34 (October 1822)
'Luke Lorance, the Cameronian' (309–21).
Tale. Signed 'Nalla'. This is first instance of this signature ('Allan' backwards). 'Nathan Adamson' and 'King Bruce's Bowl', are both unsigned, and the new signature seems to mark a fresh series, after 'Traditional Literature' and 'Tales of Lyddalcross'.

'Charlie Stuart, a Jacobite Song' (348).
Poem. Note states: 'A few lines of the following song have found a sanctuary among Hogg's Reliques of Jacobite Poetry; it has never before appeared in a perfect state' (348). Signed 'C'. The lines appear in *Jacobite Relics*, II (194).

v. 6, 35 (November 1822)
'The Tale of Allan Lorburne, Mariner' (421–36).
Tale. Signed 'Nalla'.

'Awake, My Love' (455–56).
Poem. Signed 'C'.

v. 6, 36 (December 1822)
'The Second Tale of Allan Lorburne, Mariner' (537–48).
Tale. Signed 'Nalla'.

'A Wish' (568).
Poem. Signed 'C'.

v. 7, n.s. (January 1823)
'On English Versification' (29–37).
Essay. Signed 'C'. Not attributed to Cunningham by Brooks
or Riga & Prance.

'Song: I'll Daut Nae Mair a Posie' (52).
Poem. Signed 'C'.

'Christina Swayne, an Icelandic Tale' (73–82).
Tale. Signed 'Nalla'.

v. 7, n.s. (February 1823)
'Corporal Colville, a Tale' (132–40).
Tale. Signed 'Nalla'.

'On English Versification. No. II' (173–80).
Essay. Signed 'C'. Not attributed to Cunningham by Brooks
or Riga & Prance.

'Meikle Sandie Gordon and Wee Sandie Gordon' (220).
Tale. Unsigned. Tentatively attributed to Cunningham by
Brooks.

v. 7, n.s. (March 1823)
'On English Versification. No. III' (273–82).
Essay. Signed 'C'. Not attributed to Cunningham by Brooks
or Riga & Prance.

'Riley Grave-Stones. A Derbyshire Story' (282–91).
Tale. Signed 'Nalla'.

v. 7, n.s. (April 1823)
'Kate of Windiewa's. A Tale' (410–20).
Tale. Signed 'Nalla'.

'On English Versification. No. IV' (429–36).
Essay. Signed 'C'. Not attributed to Cunningham by Brooks
or Riga & Prance.

v. 7, n.s. (May 1823)
'Lord William. A Scottish Song' (540).
Poem. Signed 'C'.

'The Land's End of Cornwall' (542–52).
Tale. Signed 'Nalla'.

v. 7, n.s. (June 1823)
'Bannocks of Barley' (643–44).
Poem. Note states: 'The following song was written to an old and popular air by Allan Cunningham, for the new edition of Thomson's Select Melodies of Scotland'.

'The Fairy Miller of Croga' (678–89).
Tale. Signed 'Nalla'.

v. 8, n.s. (July 1823)
'The Yorkshire Alehouse, a Tale' (69–77).
Tale. Signed 'Nalla'.

v. 8, n.s. (August 1823)
'Andrew Laurie's Return, a Tale' (193–205).
Tale. Signed 'Nalla'.

v. 8, n.s. (September 1823)
'The Nuns and Ale of Caverswell. A Sketch' (260–62).
Sketch. Unsigned. Attributed to Cunningham by Brooks and Riga & Prance.

'Sir Hugh Heron' (285–99).
Tale. Signed 'Nalla'.

v. 8, n.s. (October 1823)
'Lord Roland Cheyne, a Tale' (418–28).
Tale. Signed 'Nalla'.

v. 8, n.s. (November 1823)
'Old Corehead's Fireside' (513–16).
Poem. Signed 'Allan Cunningham'.

v. 8, n.s. (December 1823)
'The Curse of Coldengame: A Suffolk Tale' (621–34).
Tale. Signed 'Nalla'.

v. 9, n.s. (February 1824)
'Songs of the Maidens' (151–52).
Poem. Signed 'C'.

v. 9, n.s. (April 1824)
'Gordon of Brackley. An Ancient Scottish Ballad' (355–56).
Poem. Signed 'C'.

v. 9, n.s. (May 1824)
'The Two Ravens. An Old Scottish Ballad' (484).
Poem. Signed 'C'.

v. 9, n.s. (June 1824)
'The Pirate's Song' (598).
Poem. Signed 'C'.

v. 10, n.s. (July 1824)
'The Cuckoo. A Scottish Song' (36).
Poem. Signed 'C'.

v. 10, n.s. (August 1824)
'Ballad' (176–77).
Poem. Unsigned. Attributed to Cunningham by Brooks.

v. 10, n.s. (October 1824)
'Montgomery's Mistress. Modernized from the Poems of
Alexander Montgomery, Author of the Cherrie and the Slae'
(417).
Poem. Signed 'C'.

v. 10, n.s. (December 1824)
'Fair Annie of Lochroyan. A Traditional Version of the
Ancient Romantic Ballad' (607–08).
Poem. Signed 'C'.

Appendix D

EMENDATION LIST

page.line   emended text / previous text

The Selbys of Cumberland. Part Second
44.13   proprietor of Wilton-hall / proprietor of Wilton hall
53.25   only earls' coronets / only earl's coronets

The Selbys of Cumberland. Part Third
57.25   more about separation," / more about separation,

Placing a Scottish Minster
Several passages in this story have been silently emended, to give consistency to the use of single and double speech marks.

The King of the Peak
Several passages in this story have been silently emended, to give consistency to the use of single and double speech marks.
98.23   true love be. / true love be;
103.37   the summit of Haddon Hall / the summit of Haddon hall

The Mother's Dream
127.19   existence prolonged? / existence prolonged.

Miles Colvine, the Cumberland Mariner
159.23   one who recalls / one who recals

Honest Man John Ochiltree
Several passages in this story have been silently emended, to give consistency to the use of single and double speech marks.

Elphin Irving, the Fairies' Cupbearer
199.4   the laird of Johnstone bank / the laird of John-stonebank
199.17   said the laird of Johnstone bank / said the laird of Johnstonebank

Richard Faulder, Mariner

212.4   sat high on Saint Bees's-head / sat high on Saint
             Bees's head

The Last Lord of Helvellyn

218.4   twin hillocks of Preston-bay / twin hillocks of
             Preston bay
220.21   common spirits dread / common spiritsd read
222.27   gates of Preston-Hall / gates of Preston Hall

Judith Macrone, the Prophetess

230.12   whole course of Annan-water / whole course of
             Annanwater
236.33   the bonnie Annan-water lads / the bonnie Annan-
             water lads
237.3   frackest lads of Annan-bank / frackest lads of
             Annanbank
237.11   hey! the lads of Annan-bank / hey! the lads of
             Annanbank
243.4   the blackest pool of Annan-water / the blackest
             pool of Annanwater
244.10   bosom of the Annan-water / bosom of the
             Annanwater

Traditional Literature. No. I

313.20   tender of flocks / tendor of flocks
314.27   come wi' me / come with me
316.22   'Mang her lint-white ringlets / Mang her lint-
             white ringlets
316.35   those lovesome een / those lovesome e'en
317.31   coursed, visible to the eyes / coarsed, visible to the
             eyes

The Twelve Tales of Lyddalcross. Introductory

325.33   responded Simon / responded Symon
326.25   it's a wonderous weel told tale; but it's too
             common, Marion, it's too common / its a won-
             derous weel told tale; but its too common,
             Marion, its too common

Appendix E

GLOSSARY

a': all, every
aboon: above
addercap: spider; ill-natured person
ae: one
affeir: appearance, manner
afore: before
agate: on the way or road (literally, a-going)
agen: again
ahint: behind
aiblen: perhaps
airn: iron
ain: own
amang: among
amaist: almost
ane: an
aneath: beneath
anent: before, against, about, concerning
asteer: astir, up and about
attour: see *by and attour*
atweel: assuredly, certainly
aught: anything
auld: old
aver: swear, assure
awa': away
aweel: well (introductory remark)
awmous-powk: a beggar's slow, plodding gait (literally, alms-walk)
aye: yes; always, ever
bairn: child
bairntime: offspring; child-bearing years; pregnancy
baith: both
bandsman: harvester who binds the sheaves
bane: bone
basnet: helmet
bating: subtracting; not counting
bauld: bold
bear: variety of barley

bedral: beadle
bee-byke: beehive
beeves: beef
behadden: beholden
belly-flaught: flat on the ground
ben: inside, through
bensel: strength, vigour (e.g. of a storm)
bicker: drinking vessel, usually wooden
bigg: variety of barley
bink: cooking hob
birks: birch; aquatic plant, belonging to the willow family
birkie: lively or smart person; conceited; sharp-tongued
birl: to carouse; to spend money; to spin (especially a coin)
bit: small piece or portion
blaw: blow
blink: glance, look; gleam
bodie: body; person, human
bodle: small copper coin
bonspiel: tournament (especially curling)
bootikin: torture implement (wood and iron boot used to
    crush the foot)
bousing: immoderate drinking (of alcohol)
bowne/boune: to make ready, prepare; bind, bound
brae: hill, slope
brake: break, broke
brand: sword
brankan: finely dressed
braw: brave; worthy, excellent
breckan: bracken, fern
bree: brow
brent: smooth, unwrinkled
brittling: cutting up of game (especially deer or boar)
broil: brawl, violent argument
brose: oatmeal porridge
bught: gathering of people
burgh: borough, town
burn: stream, brook
busk: adorn, dress up; adornments
by and attour: in addition to, over and above
ca': call
calf-love: young or immature love, unlikely to last
cannie: careful, cautious; pleasant, kind; lucky

cantie: comfortable, pleasant
cantraip: mischievous trick
carabine: carbine (firearm, between a pistol and musket in size)
carle/carlin: man; peasant; churlish old man
carline: woman (especially an old woman); crone
cathud: large stone at the back of a fireplace
cauld: cold
cauld steerie: mixture of sour milk and oats
chaffer: buy and sell, engage in trade
chambering: lewd or licentious behaviour
change-house: small inn
cheeped: speak softly, whisper; squeak, creak
chield: child
cittern: guitar-type musical instrument
clangor: clang, loud metallic clash
claymore: Scottish broadsword
cloot: cloth, material; hoof, foot
clout: mend, patch
cog: wooden vessel made of hooped staves
coif: woman's cloth cap or hood (see *mutch*)
coldrife: lukewarm
collops: slices of meat
conjunct: connected, united
coof: fool, simpleton; coward
coost: cast off, shed
cope: coping; top section of a wall
cope-stone: top or head stone of a building
corbal: beam or projection supporting a wall
corse: corpse, human body
corslet: a section of body armour
couper: dealer
coupit: upset, overturn
coz: cousin
crapin: crop, craw, throat
craw: crow (like a cock)
crazy: infirm, frail
crock: old ewe, or one that has ceased bearing
croudy: cold mixture of oatmeal and water
crouse: bold, confident, pert
crowdie: see *croudy*
culverin: hand-gun or small cannon

cummer: witch, gossip; midwife; woman, wife; girl, lass

daffin: foolish or licentious behaviour

daimen: rare, occasional

dainty: pleasant, handsome

dandle: bounce on one's knee; pet, fondle playfully

dauner: stroll

daw: jackdaw

deed: indeed; upon my word

deil/de'il: devil

deliverly: lightly, nimbly, smartly

dinman: dinmont; a wether between the first and second shearing (see *wether*)

dinnelled: shook, rattled

dirk: dagger (especially of a Highlander)

disnae: does not

distaff: cleft staff used for spinning wool

dod: an exclamation (deformation of God: see *od*)

doited: confused, crazed

dool: woe, grief

douce: quiet, sober, steady

dowie: sad, dismal

drap: drop

dree: endure, undergo; fear, dread

dreeping: dripping

drouket/droukit: drenched

drouth(ie): thirst, thirsty; drunk, drunkard

dub: pool or puddle of water

dule: see *dool*

ee: eye

een/e'en: eyes

e'en: even; evening

elding: fuel, flammable material

ell: Scottish measurement, approximating the length of an arm (about 37 inches)

ellwand: stick used for measuring an ell

en: end

fa': fall

fain: glad, happy

fairy-rade: fairy procession

farrand: having a specified appearance, -looking; handsome, comely

fash: fuss, bother, annoyance

faured: favoured
faut: lack, want (of something); fault, flaw, misdemeanour
feal: firm, constant, faithful
feg: faith, goodness (exclamation of surprise)
fer: for
fern-year: last year
fey: fated to die; unlucky, doomed; displaying supernatural or
    fairylike qualities
fillet: slice, section (of cloth)
fizzenless: lacking in mettle, spirit
flaff: flap, puff, gust
forbye: besides
forfairn: ruined, destitute, forlorn
fore-night: evening, interval between twilight and bedtime
foss/fosse: ditch, moat
fou: full
foumart: polecat, ferret, weasel
fowk: folk, people
frack: bold, eager, impetuous
frae: from
froward: perverse, forward
fu': full
fule: fool, foolish
gae/gane: go/gone
gang: go, get along
gar: make, cause to
gaud: trick, prank; showy ornament or clothing, gewgaw
gauger: exciseman, customs officer
gauging sticks: gauger's instruments, for measuring capacity or
    contents
gear: property, wealth; equipped, kitted out; stuff in general
ghaist: guest
gied: give, given
gif: if, whether
gilpie: lively, mischievous youth
gimmer: young ewe
glaive: weapon (variously a lance, sword or halberd)
glede: kite (bird)
gleg: keen, sharp
going gear: going into decline, going to wreck
gomeral: fool, idiot
gorget: collar

gowans: daisies
gowd: gold
gowk: cuckoo; fool, idiot
gree: eminence, rank, status; favour, goodwill
griens: longs, yearns
gude: good, goodness; substitute for God (e.g. gude-send)
ha': hall
hained: held, saved, hoarded
hallan: inner wall, partition; innermost reaches
halser: hawser; sailing rope or cable
halt: crippled, lame
hame: home
hansel: gift, present; first instalment
happit: wrapped, covered up
harquebuss: early type of portable firearm; musket
haspen: young boy, stripling
hassoc: clump or tuft of vegetation, sometimes used as a seat
hauberk: armour, chain-mail
haud: hold
haugh: low-lying land near a river (see *holm*)
haurl: haul, drag
haver: oats
hawslock wool: fine wool from a sheep's neck
hech: an exclamation (of surprise, sorrow, fatigue)
hempie: rogue, villain; mischievous person
heritor: landowner, proprietor; one liable for the upkeep of a
    parish
herrie: harry, harass
hership: plundering, pillage
hie: hasten
Hielandman: Highlander
hinnie: honey (term of endearment)
holm: low-lying land near a river (see *haugh*)
hooly: gently, softly, cautiously; tardily
hough: thigh
hout: exclamation expressing dissent or impatience
howe: hollow, depression; lowest point
howff: enclosed place; courtyard
howk: dig
hummel: polled, hornless (of farm animals)
i': in
ilka: each, every

kane: payment in kind
kelpie: water-horse (spirit or demon haunting rivers)
ken/kenned: know/knew
kilt: tie or tuck up (clothes)
kimmer: see *cummer*
kirk: church (usually Presbyterian)
kirking: attending church
kirn: butter churn; mess, confusion
kirsen: christen
kirtle: woman's gown
kittle: anger; stimulate, tickle; touchy, sensitive; tricky, capricious
knowe: knoll
lair: bed, couch
lane: alone
lang: long
lang-sin-syne: long ago, long since
lamiter: lame person
lath: narrow strip of wood, used in roofing
laving: washing
leal: loyal, true
leaping-illness: disease in sheep (also known as louping ill), so-called because of the leaping motion it induces
letts: restraints, hindrances, impediments
levin: lightning
liefer: rather
liester: pronged fishing spear
limmer: rascal, villain
linn: steep gorge; waterfall
linsey-woolsey: cloth made of mixed wool and linen
lippen: rely, trust
lowe: love, praise, honour, glory
lowne: calm, quiet
louping-on-stone: horse-block (block of stone used to help mount a horse)
lour: frown
lucken: drawn together, knitted
lyart: streaked with grey
lyke-wake: the watch kept at night over a dead body
mair: more
malison: a curse
marrow: match, equal

maud: checked plaid or cloak of a shepherd

maun/mauna: must/must not

maut: malt

mawks: maggots, grubs

mawn: mown

meat: food

mends: compensation, amends

meikle: see *mickle*

mete: fit, appropriate, apt, well suited

mickle: much, great, numerous

mim: prim, proper

mirk: dark

monie/mony: many

mools: mounds; lumps of earth (especially from a grave)

moorill: disease seen in livestock grazing on moorland
    (literally, moor-ill)

moudie-tammocks: molehills

mug ewe: breed of sheep with a woolly face

mutch: woman's cap or hood (see *coif*)

mutchkin: liquid measure (about three-quarters of a pint)

nae: no

nane: none

od: an exclamation (deformation of God: see *dod*)

onstead: farmstead, farm buildings

ony: any

owre/oure: over

pearlin: lace, used for trimming garments

peebles: semi-precious stones, usually found in rivers (e.g.
    agate)

peels: stockades, fortifications; small towers

pelf: goods, money; junk, fluff

pellock: porpoise, dolphin

plaid/plaidy/plaiden: woollen blanket-like garment, usually with
    a checked pattern, worn as a mantle or shawl; the material
    to make a plaid; checked, tartan

plat: plot (of land)

portioner: proprietor of a small estate; joint tenant or owner

pose: hoard, cache

pow: head (especially the crown)

powkpud: poke-pudding (derogatory term for an Englishman)

pu'ing: pulling, plucking

quaigh: two-handled drinking cup

quean: queen; young woman, lass
quoit-cast: the distance a curling-stone may be thrown
rannel-tree: rafter, beam
rashes: rushes (plant)
ratton: rat
reavers: thieves, pillagers
rede: advise, counsel
reek: smoke
reel: traditional, whirling dance
rid-handed: red-handed; one who rescues (especially from fire)
rones: thickets, patches of woodland
rood: staff, rod; cross (Christian symbol)
rowed: folded, wrapped (in cloth)
sae: so
saft: soft, weak; calm
sair: sore
sang: song
sappy: moist, juicy
sark: shirt
saul: soul, spirit; mettle, courage
saut: salt
sawney: Scotsman; young man; yokel (diminutive of Alexander)
sax: six
scale: scatter, disperse, break up
scone-bonnet: broad lowland cap
sea-maw: seamew; gull
several: divide, break up into separate parts
sheal: grazing pasture
shealing: shepherd's hut
shedlands: dividing point of a road, crossroads
sheen: shine, gleam
shock: clash together
shoon: shoes
sib: similar, related, alike, kindred
sic: such
sicker: certain, sure; hard (of bargain)
siller: silver
simmer: summer
skirl: scream
slae: sloe
slaw: slow
sleekie: smooth, glossy; sly, sneaky

smoored: smothered, suffocated

snaw: snow

snood: ribbon worn tied round the head (specifically by unmarried women)

snoring: moving at speed, with a rushing sound (especially a ship)

sock and share: ploughshare

sodded: covered in turf

sonsie: friendly, pleasant; lucky; honest; plump

soothfast: true, loyal, firm

sough: sigh

Southron: southern, southerner; English, Englishman

spae: prophesy, foretell, predict, tell

spauld: shoulder

spence: inner room; spare room; storage room

sponsible: responsible, reliable

spool-bane: shoulder-blade; joints, limbs

spulziement: despoliation, plunder, pillage

spunkie: will-o-the-wisp; sprite

stark: strong, robust

stane: stone

stave: walking stick, staff

steeve: firm, sturdy, resolute; stiff, rigid

stent: type of tax

stooking: placing (corn) into sheaves

stoup: flagon, jug

strake: strip of iron, attached to the left side of a plough

streek: stretch

stride-legs: astride

strook: struck

styme: small amount, particle

sunket/sunkit: something (especially something to eat); provisions, tit-bit

sunket-time: meal-time

sward: grass, turf

syne: directly, then, afterwards

targe: be strict with, scold; light shield or buckler

target: shield (see *targe*)

tass: cup, goblet (especially for spirits)

tauld: told

teat: tuft

ted: scatter, spread out (in either orderly or disorderly way) *tent*: care, heed

thairm: gut, intestine; fiddle string (made from cat-gut)

theeked: roofed, covered over

thegither: together

thowe: thaw

thrapple: throat, windpipe; throttle

throstle: song-thrush

through-stone: stone laid horizontally over a grave or tomb

tocher: dowry

toom: empty, drain

tottle: tipple (drink alcohol); walk unsteadily, totter; ripple, babble (as running water)

tout: drink (the whole contents of a vessel)

tow: rope, cable

treddle: wooden lever, operated by the foot as part of a loom

troth/trouth: truth, good faith, honesty

trow: trust, believe, give credence to

tup-horn: ram's horn

twa/twae: two

uncannie: supernatural, unnatural, weird, strange (see *cannie*)

unsonsie: ill-omened, evil, weird, strange (see *sonsie*)

untaken-down: undiluted; full strength (of alcohol)

upcast: upwards glance; reproach, taunt, accusation

wad/wadnae: would/would not

wadset: mortgage

wae: woe

wale: choose, select; choice, pick

wame: stomach, belly

wark: work

waur/warse/warst: worse/worse/worst

weal: well-being, happiness, prosperity; wealth, riches

wean: child, little one (contraction of wee-un)

web: piece of woven cloth

wee: little

weel: well

weet: wet

wether: ram (specifically, a castrated male sheep: see *dinman*)

wha: who

whig: yokel, country bumpkin; Presbyterian

whilk: which

whin-stone: hard rock; solid, inflexible

whisht: hush, be quiet

white: silver (when applied to money: e.g. white half-crown)
whittle: knife
whomel/whomble: capsize, overturn, collapse
wight: brave; strong; swift
winna: will not
wooster: wooer, suitor
woot: would
wonned: lived, dwelled
wot: know
wranged: wronged
wud: wild, fierce, violent
wyse: direct (oneself); contrive, make
yarely: quickly, nimbly
yestreen: yesterday evening
yett: gate

NOTES

Abbreviations

Traditional Tales	Allan Cunningham, *Traditional Tales of the English and Scottish Peasantry*, 2 vols (London: Taylor and Hessey, 1822).
Marmaduke Maxwell	Allan Cunningham, *Sir Marmaduke Maxwell: A Dramatic Poem, The Mermaid of Galloway, The Legend of Richard Faulder, and Twenty Scottish Songs* (London: Taylor and Hessey, 1822).
Songs of Scotland	Allan Cunningham (ed.), *The Songs of Scotland, Ancient and Modern*, 4 vols (London: John Taylor, 1825).
Poems and Songs	Allan Cunningham, *Poems and Songs. With an Introduction, Glossary, and Notes by Peter Cunningham* (London: John Murray, 1847).
Remains	R. H. Cromek (ed.), *Remains of Nithsdale and Galloway Song* (London: Cadell and Davies, 1810).
Life of Cunningham	David Hogg, *The Life of Allan Cunningham: With Selections from his Works and Correspondence* (Dumfries: John Anderson, 1875).
Jacobite Relics	James Hogg, *The Jacobite Relics of Scotland*, ed. Murray G. H. Pittock, 2 vols (Edinburgh: Edinburgh University Press, 2002–03).
Child	Francis James Child. *The English and Scottish Popular Ballads*, 5 Vols (1892–98; Mineola, NY: Dover, 2003). References are to the number in Child's ballad sequence.

All biblical quotations are from the Authorised King James Version.

Introduction

[1] Cunningham had a fascination with the Ossian poems—a literary hoax perpetrated in the 1760s by James Macpherson, who presented his own poetry as translations from an ancient Gaelic bard. From the outset, the origin of the poems was disputed, and the argument raged across the eighteenth and nineteenth centuries, with parties on both sides producing elaborate scholarly defences of their positions. For further discussion of the ongoing controversy, see Fiona Stafford and Howard Gaskill (eds), *From Gaelic to Romantic: Ossianic Translations* (Amsterdam: Rodopi, 1998), and Thomas M. Curley, *Samuel Johnson, the Ossian Fraud and the Celtic Revival in Great Britain and Ireland* (Cambridge: Cambridge University Press, 2009).

[2] James Hogg, *Reminiscences of Former Days*, in *Altrive Tales*, ed. Gillian Hughes (Edinburgh: Edinburgh University Press, 2005), 70. Hogg describes the events as taking place 'some three-and-twenty years ago'. His *Reminiscences* were first published in the *Edinburgh Literary Journal* in 1829, suggesting that the meeting occurred around 1806.

[3] For a detailed discussion of the publication of the *Remains*, see Dennis M. Read, 'Cromek, Cunningham, and *Remains of Nithsdale and Galloway Song*: A Case of Literary Duplicity', *Studies in Bibliography*, 40 (1987), 175–87, as well as Read's recent biography, *R. H. Cromek, Engraver, Editor, and Entrepreneur* (Farnham: Ashgate, 2011).

[4] Letter to James Cunningham, 8 September, 1810. Cited in David Hogg, *The Life of Allan Cunningham: With Selections from his Works and Correspondence* (Dumfries: John Anderson, 1875), 79.

[5] Sigurd Bernhard Hustvedt, *Ballad Books and Ballad Men* (Cambridge, MS: Harvard University Press, 1930), 64.

[6] Sources: Hogg, *Life of Cunningham*; Oxford Dictionary of National Biography; Allan Cunningham, *Poems and Songs. With an Introduction, Glossary, and Notes by Peter Cunningham* (John Murray: London, 1847); *The Modern Scottish Minstrel*, ed. Charles Rogers, 6 vols (Edinburgh: Adam and Charles Black, 1855–57); *The Times* (31 October 1842); 'Literary Retrospect (No. V): Allan Cunningham', *Bentley's Miscellany*, 17 (January 1845), 557–64.

[7] In July 1822, the *London Magazine* announced a forthcoming publication: *The Adventures of Mark Macrabin, the Cameronian. By Allan Cunningham. In two Volumes* (53). However, I have not been able to find any trace of the publication of this work.

[8] The sources of Cunningham's songs and ballads, where identified, are given in the notes to the text. My heartfelt thanks to folk musicians Geordie McIntyre and Alison McMorland, who kindly assisted with the attribution of Cunningham's verse.

[9] Letter to James Cunningham, undated. Cited in *Life of Cunningham*, 229.

[10] A full account of the publication of Hogg's work can be found in Ian Duncan's detailed introduction to the Stirling/South Carolina edition of *Winter Evening Tales* (Edinburgh: Edinburgh University Press, 2002).

[11] J. G. Lockhart, *Memoirs of Sir Walter Scott*, 5 vols (1837–38; London and New York: Macmillan, 1900), V, 70. Entry for 14 November, 1826.

[12] Hogg, *Reminiscences of Former Days*, 71.

[13] Thomas De Quincey, 'Sketches of Life and Manners', *Tait's Magazine*, 7 (December 1840), 765–76, 772.

[14] *Literary Gazette*, 287 (20 July 1822), 447–50, 447.

[15] *Monthly Review*, 99 (November 1822), 246–52, 247.

[16] De Quincey, 'Sketches of Life and Manners', 772.

[17] Allan Cunningham, 'Progress of Genius', *Literary Recreations*, 3, 17 (November 1807), 339–40, 339.

[18] Letter to James Cunningham, 8 September, 1810. Cited in Hogg, *Life of Cunningham*, 80.

[19] 'Memoirs of the Life and Writing of Sir John Suckling', *London Magazine*, 1, 4 (April, 1820), 369–79, 369.

[20] Richard M. Dorson, *History of British Folklore*, 3 vols (1968; London and New York: Routledge, 1999), I, 122.

[21] K. M. Briggs, *The Fairies in English Tradition and Literature* (Chicago: University of Chicago Press, 1967), 189.

[22] Preface to *Traditional Tales*, see this volume, 3.

[23] Penny Fielding, *Writing and Orality: Nationality, Culture, and Nineteenth-Century Scottish Fiction* (Oxford: Clarendon Press, 1996), 41–42.

[24] Cited in Hogg, *Life of Cunningham*, 204.

Preface

This Preface was composed for the collected edition of *Traditional Tales*, and does not appear in the *London Magazine*. Cunningham's introduction to the *London Magazine* series was published in December 1820, titled 'Traditional Literature. No. I'. This essay is reproduced as an Appendix (307–317).

[1] *won their food and their raiment, of which they were worthy*: possibly a reference to Blind Harry, a medieval minstrel famous for the *Wallace*, an epic poem composed in the late fifteenth century that celebrates the life of William Wallace. Cunningham's phrase echoes a description of Harry in John Major (Mair)'s 1521 *History of Greater Britain*: 'by the recitation of [his poems] in the presence of men of the highest rank, he procured, as he indeed deserved, food and raiment'.

[2] *Colonel David Stewart*: the quotation is an abbreviated passage from Stewart's chapter on Highland traditions in *Sketches of the Character, Manners, and Present State of the Highlanders of Scotland* (1822).

Ezra Peden

This story was first published in the collected edition of *Traditional Tales*, and did not appear in the *London Magazine*.

[3] *motto*: probably by Cunningham.

[4] *the reign of king Saul*: the first biblical King of Israel, Saul's reign was associated with driving out witchcraft from his country: 'And Saul had put away those that had familiar spirits, and the wizards, out of the land' (1 Samuel 28. 3).

[5] *a watcher of old on the towers of Judah*: watch-towers were built in the forests of Judah to guard against attack by other tribes. See 2 Chronicles 27.

[6] *auld Mahoun*: the Devil, or any false god.

[7] *a broad road*: 'wide is the gate, and broad is the way, that leadeth to destruction' (Matthew 7. 13).

[8] *Tophet*: or Topheth; a valley near Jerusalem where child sacrifices were supposed to have been conducted. The term was also invoked as a symbolic manifestation of Hell. See Jeremiah 19. 1–6.

[9] *Covenanter*: the Covenanters were a Scottish Presbyterian sect (also called Cameronians, after their leader Richard Cameron). The name derives from the adherence of the sects' members to a series of 'covenants' (legal proclamations), which asserted Presbyterianism as the true religion of Scotland. The Covenanters' campaigns for religious freedom brought them into opposition with the ruling Stuart monarchs during the late seventeenth and early eighteenth centuries, and their various uprisings were violently repressed through a policy of persecution that became known as the 'killing time'.

[10] *The Downfal of Dalzell*: published as a stand-alone piece, attributed to Cunningham, in the *London Magazine* for July 1822 (27–29). Also appears in *Songs of Scotland*, IV (264–68). 'Dalzell' is possibly a reference to General Thomas Dalziel (1615–1685), a loyalist soldier, charged with the suppression of the Covenanters.

[11] *When Grierson fled, and Maxwell fail'd, / And Gordon stood aghast, / And Graeme, saved by thy sword, raged fierce*: the poem is delivered by a Covenanter, who curses Bonshaw for his part in the persecution of his sect. Grierson, Maxwell and Gordon are the names of Covenanter soldiers. Graeme may be a reference to John Graham of Claverhouse (1648–1689), who led the violent suppression of the Covenanters and was known colloquially as 'Bluidy Clavers'.

[12] *Sarah's bosom [...] Abraham's*: Heaven, or more specifically the place where the shades of the righteous dead await Judgement Day: 'And it came to pass, that the beggar died, and was carried by the angels into Abraham's bosom' (Luke 16. 22).

[13] *General Turner*: Sir James Turner (1615–1686), one of the leaders of the persecution of the Covenanters.

[14] *kirk repentance-stool*: also called a cutty-stool, or cuttie-stool: a raised seat placed near the altar, on which a person receiving punishment (usually for lapses in chastity) would sit during the service for three consecutive Sundays. An essay by Cunningham on the excessive severity of the repentance-seat as a punishment is included as an appendix to *Remains*.

[15] *banished their native princes, and sold their country to an alien*: after the Glorious Revolution of 1689, Scotland held a Convention of the Estates, at which the nation accepted the Hanoverian monarchs, William and Mary. The Stuart prince, James Francis Edward (son of James II and VII, and known as the Old Pretender), was forced into exile in France.

The Selbys of Cumberland. Part First

First published as 'Traditional Literature. No. V. Dame Eleanor Selby', *London Magazine*, 3, 16 (April 1821), 389–95. Signed 'Lammerlea, Cumberland'.

[16] *motto*: probably by Cunningham.

[17] *Lady Selby*: attributed to Cunningham in *Life of Cunningham*.

[18] *instead of practising with the bow, or that still more fatal weapon the gun*: the magazine version of this line reads: 'instead of practising with the cross-bow, or that still more fatal weapon the hand-bow' (392).

[19] *throwing the bar*: tossing the caber.

[20] *Sir Roland Graeme*: this ballad appears with an attribution to Cunningham in several Victorian anthologies.

The Selbys of Cumberland. Part Second

First published as 'Traditional Literature. No. VI. Eleanor Selby and the Spectre-Horseman of Soutra', *London Magazine*, 3, 18 (June 1821), 615–22. Signed 'Lammerlea, Cumberland'.

[21] *motto*: slightly misquoted from James Hogg's 'Willie Wilkin', published in *The Mountain Bard* (1807).

[22] *the exiled branch of the house of Stuart*: this story is set during the 1715 Jacobite Rebellion, and deals with the Battle of Preston, at which the Jacobite forces were defeated by armies loyal to the Hanoverian government. The Jacobites' aim was to reinstate a Stuart monarch—at this period James Edward, the Old Pretender, son of James VII of Scotland (James II of England).

[23] *the hostile banners of the lion and the bonnie white rose*: the Hanoverian flag incorporated lions rampant and passant, while the white rose was the symbol of the Jacobites.

[24] *sectarians*: adherents of the sectarian party (also called Independents by the Presbyterians) and opposed to any state-sanctioned church.

[25] *The Cuckoo is a Gentle Bird*: variant of a Jacobite song, probably by Cunningham, which uses allegory to mask the discussion of political themes (the cuckoo stands for the Old Pretender). James Hogg included a song called 'The Cuckoo' in the first series of his *Jacobite Relics* (1819), which differs from Cunningham's, but has the similar refrain 'the cuckoo's a bonny bird', and also refers to him chasing other birds away from the throne, see *Jacobite Relics*, I (111–12).

[26] *The Pedlar's Ballad*: Jacobite song, probably by Cunningham, which incorporates the names of famous Jacobite families. The first three verses of this poem were set to music by Walter Turnbull and published as a score: *It is Pleasant to Sit on Green Saddleback's Top, A Favorite Glee, For Three Voices, The Words Selected from Baldwin's London Magazine* (London: G. Walker). The score is undated, but was probably published in the early 1820s. *Baldwin's Magazine* refers to the *London Magazine*, which was published by Baldwin, Cradock, and Joy. Setting popular poems to music was common in the early nineteenth century, and Cunningham would perhaps have been pleased that his songs were being circulated in this way.

[27] The *London Magazine* version includes the following footnote, appended to the last line of the story:

* The attested account of this extraordinary vision, as we find it in the pages of several travellers, differs little from the narrative of Eleanor Selby; it is signed by two peasants, Daniel Stricket and William Lancaster, who with about twenty-four other persons witnessed this spectral procession for several hours. Several learned men have written many wise pages, to prove that all this was either real or imaginary—a conclusion to which many will probably be able to come to without the aid of learning.

The Selbys of Cumberland. Part Third

First published as 'Traditional Literature. No. VII. The Death of Walter Selby', *London Magazine*, 4, 19 (July 1821), 19–28. Signed 'Lammerlea, Cumberland'.

[28] *motto*: probably by Cunningham.

[29] *Oh! Preston, Proud Preston*: Jacobite song, probably by Cunningham.

[30] *I rede ye, my lady*: see motto (above).

[31] *Kenmore's on and awa, Willie*: version of a traditional Jacobite ballad (specifically the first and second verses). A variant by Burns is the best known. Cunningham included the ballad in *Songs of Scotland*, III (180–82).

[32] *Lament for Walter Selby*: probably by Cunningham. The *London Magazine* version ends with this ballad. The final section and the song 'Carlisle Yetts' were added for the collected edition.

[33] *Carlisle Yetts*: appears in *Songs of Scotland*, III (214–15). Cunningham presents the poem as a traditional Jacobite ballad, but James Hogg, who included a version of the song in the second series of his *Jacobite Relics* (1821), comments that 'It is from Cromek [i.e. *Remains*]; and if it is not Allan Cunninghame's [*sic*], is very like his style', *Jacobite Relics*, II (371).

Placing a Scottish Minister

First published as 'Traditional Literature. No. X. Placing a Scottish Minister', *London Magazine*, 4, 22 (October 1821), 401–11. Signed 'Lammerlea, Cumberland'.

[34] *motto*: from Burns, 'The Ordination' (1786). In Burns's poem, and throughout Cunningham's story, 'patronage' refers to the ecclesiastical right to place a member of the clergy in a particular church or living.

[35] *the Prophecies of Peden*: Alexander Peden (1626–1686) was a Scottish Covenanter and preacher, revered for his supposed gifts of prophecy. Tracts which detailed Peden's predictions were popular during the eighteenth century. The other works carried by the packman have typical tract-style titles.

[36] *an Erastian field among the Egyptian stubble*: Thomas Erastus (1524–1583) argued that the state held supremacy over the church in some ecclesiastical matters, and Erastianism came to broadly denote a doctrine subordinating ecclesiastical to secular powers. 'Egyptian stubble' may refer to Pharaoh's increase of the Israelites' burden by forcing them to gather their own straw for bricks without decreasing their output (see Exodus 5. 6–19). The comment perhaps indicates the old dame's shaky grasp of theology and implies her understanding of the religious issues is haphazard, rather than comprehensive.

[37] *The preaching man of Belial, with his red dragons*: Belial is a biblical demon, though the term can also refer to the Devil, to Hell, or to the wicked or idolatrous in general. Cunningham's phrase echoes 2 Samuel 16. 7: 'And thus said Shimei when he cursed, Come out, come out, thou bloody man, and thou man of Belial'. The 'red dragons' is presumably a reference to the red-coated Dragoons.

[38] *the lady of Babylon*: the Catholic Church.

[39] *old Mahoun*: see 'Ezra Peden' (10n).

[40] *seceders of all denominations*: members of various Presbyterian sects, which had split from the Church of Scotland for reasons of dogma.

[41] *Let Dagon defend Dagon*: Philistine god. See 1 Samuel 5.

[42] *I shall kiss thee with kisses of my mouth*: 'Let him kiss me with the kisses of his mouth: for thy love is better than wine' (Song of Solomon 1. 2).

[43] *Placing the Parson*: probably by Cunningham.

[44] *Rimmon*: one of the 'uttermost cities' in Judah, described in Joshua 15. 21–32.

[45] *kirk's cuttie stool*: see 'Ezra Peden' (22n).

[46] *Down with the men of Moab*: a kingdom bordering Israel, whose people had close connections with the Israelites, and with whom relations fluctuated between hostile and friendly.

[47] *bender of the bicker*: a drinker (a bicker is wooden drinking vessel, often used for alcohol).

[48] *the Shimeis of the land*: Shimei is one of David's tormentors during his flight from Absalom. See 2 Samuel 16. 5–7.

[49] *sleepy Samuel*: as a child, Samuel was called by God while he was asleep, and mistook the voice of the Lord for that of his father, Eli. See 1 Samuel 3.

[50] *choice Geneva*: spirit flavoured with juniper, also called Hollands.

[51] *sectarian*: see 'The Selbys of Cumberland. Part Second' (43n).

[52] *Mirk-Monday*: Monday 24 March, 1652. Literally 'dark Monday', so-called because of a solar eclipse on that date.

The King of the Peak

First published as 'The Twelve Tales of Lyddalcross. Tale Third. The King of the Peak, a Derbyshire Tale', *London Magazine*, 5, 27 (March 1822), 243–52. Unsigned.

[53] *motto*: probably by Cunningham, although the legend of the elopement of Dora Vernon and John Manners from Haddon Hall did inspire a variety of poems and tales. The *London Magazine* version gives the source as 'Old Derbyshire Rhyme of Dora Vernon'.

[54] The first three paragraphs of this tale do not appear in the *London Magazine* version, which opens with a similar theme of after-dinner storytelling, but connects more closely to the 'Twelve Tales of Lyddalcross' framing narrative that Cunningham had established in the magazine (the introduction to this series is reproduced as an Appendix, 319–332).

[55] *Dora Vernon*: probably by Cunningham.

[56] *Come, burn your incense, ye god-like graces*: untraced—probably by Cunningham.

[57] *for the selvage of the web [...] is aye the coarsest cloth*: the people from the furthest reaches of the country or region (i.e. the Borderers) will be the least civilised.

[58] *some bright particular star and think to wed it*: *All's Well That Ends Well*, I. i. Presumably, the 'wild wizard of Warwick' is a reference to Shakespeare's birthplace of Stratford-upon-Avon, in Warwickshire.

[59] *gold Harry*: gold coin, bearing the head of Henry VI, VII or VIII.

[60] 'The Minstrel's Song': attributed to Cunningham as 'Last night a proud page came to me' in *Songs of Scotland*, IV (270–71).

[61] *Cavendo tutus!*: 'Safety through Caution'—the motto of the Dukes of Devonshire, whose seat is Chatsworth House in Derbyshire. The Lord of Haddon is speaking to Sir Ralph Cavendish, Duke of Devonshire.

[62] *Let seas between us swell and sound*: from 'The Minstrel's Song' (above).

The Mother's Dream

First published as 'The Twelve Tales of Lyddalcross. Tale the Fifth. The Mother's Dream', *London Magazine*, 5, 29 (May 1822), 458–67. Unsigned.

[63] *motto*: a version of this poem titled 'The Maiden's Dream', attributed to Cunningham and substantially reworked, was published in *The Athenaeum*, 219 (7 Jan, 1832), 17.

[64] *Song of Benjie Spedlands*: probably by Cunningham.

[65] *the wind bloweth as it listeth*: John 3. 8.

[66] *death-lights*: also known as death-fires—luminous fire or glow that supposedly appears over the location of a dead body.

Allan-a-Maut

First published as 'The Twelve Tales of Lyddalcross. Tale the Fourth. Allan-a-Maut', *London Magazine*, 5, 29 (April 1822), 321–30. Unsigned.

[67] *motto*: attributed to Cunningham in *Songs of Scotland*, IV (287) and in *Poems and Songs* (139).'Maut' is malt, and Allan-a-Maut is invoked as a personification of alcohol (specifically whisky).

[68] *Turner, or Callcott, or Dewint*: J. M. W. Turner (1775–1851), Sir Augustus Wall Callcott (1779–1844), and Peter De Wint (1784–1849)—painters of the late eighteenth and early nineteenth centuries renowned for their depictions of landscapes.

[69] *the metal worm through which my precious drink dribbles*: long coiled pipe attached to a whisky still, in which the alcohol steam condenses.

[70] *Sanquhar rug*: town in Dumfriesshire, noted for its textiles.

[71] *Mungo Macubin's Song*: attributed to Cunningham as 'Come, Toom the Stoup' in *Songs of Scotland*, IV (307–08).

[72] *John Mackleg's Song*: probably by Cunningham.

[73] *My Mind to me a Kingdom is*: there is a well-known sixteenth-century poem of the same title, by Sir Edward Dyer. Cunningham's version is more downbeat, but retains an early-modern style through its use of rhyming couplets.

[74] *surely one vessel is made for honour, and another for dishonour*: 'Hath not the potter power over the clay, of the same lump to make one vessel unto honour, and another unto dishonour?' (Romans 9. 21).

Miles Colvine, The Cumberland Mariner

First published as 'Traditional Literature. No. XII. Miles Colvine, the Cumberland Mariner', *London Magazine*, 4, 24 (December 1821), 142–52. Signed 'Lammerlea, Cumberland'.

[75] *motto*: fragment of a popular eighteenth-century broadside ballad, usually called 'William Glen' or 'Captain Glen'. The term Barbary refers to the North African coast.

[76] *O Mariner, O Mariner*: attributed to Cunningham as 'Miles Colvine' in *Songs of Scotland*, IV (258–60).

Honest Man John Ochiltree

First published as 'The Twelve Tales of Lyddalcross. Tale Second. Honest Man John Ochiltree', *London Magazine*, 5, 26 (February 1822), 142–52. Unsigned.

[77] *motto*: this fragment is based largely on the traditional song 'The Brisk Young Lad', which appears in David Herd's 1769 anthology *Ancient and Modern Scots Songs*.

[78] *bad eminence*: 'Satan exalted sat, by merit rais'd / To that bad eminence', *Paradise Lost*, Book II.

[79] *the mystery of thairms*: presumably a reference to the power and charm of a musician, or of music in general (thairms are fiddle strings, made from dried cat-gut).

[80] *the laws of the Medes*: laws of the Persian kings, which were unalterable. See Daniel 6. 15.

[81] *quoting the Song of Solomon*: a book of the Old Testament, also known as *Song of Songs* or *Canticles*. The book describes a courtship and eventual consummation of the relationship (usually read as an allegory of the relationship between God and his subjects). It's possible that the couple are literally quoting from the book, but the Song opens with 'Let him kiss me with the kisses of his mouth', suggesting that 'quoting the Song of Solomon' may be slang for kissing.

[82] *the tempest which 'roared and rustled'* : 'Outside, the storm might roar and rustle, / Tam did not mind the storm a whistle', Burns, 'Tam O'Shanter' (1790).

[83] *Jock Gomeral*: a gomeral is a fool or an idiot.

[84] *the time of the Scottish persecution*: the late seventeenth century, the so-called 'killing time' at the height of the persecution of the Covenanters. See 'Ezra Peden' (11n).

[85] *laird of no-town-brae; lord of windy-wa's*: without means or property.

[86] *the cheese-siller, and the siller for the udder-locks*: 'siller' is silver, and the terms refer to the money earned from selling cheese and the 'udder-locks' (the wool pulled from around the sheep's teats, to allow easier access for lambs).

[87] *Beltane [...] Hallowmass*: Beltane is a Scottish quarter-day festival held in early May. The term is also sometimes used as a synonym for May-Day. Hallowmass is All-Saint's Day (the day after Halloween).

[88] *Ten came east, and ten came west*: from 'Tibby Fowler o' the Glen', a traditional Border ballad. Cunningham included the ballad in *Songs of Scotland*, III (21–22).

[89] *the heroine of Tintock-top*: Tibby Fowler, of the above ballad.

[90] *O, have ye not heard of John Ochiltree?*: probably by Cunningham. A different, traditional ballad titled 'John Ochiltree' appears in *Songs of Scotland*, II (308–09), which Cunningham reprinted from Allan Ramsay's *Tea-Table Miscellany* (1724).

[91] *the idly feigned poetic pains*: from Burns, 'The Lament' (1786).

[92] *far kenned and noted is thy name, as the rhyme-maker said of Satan*: 'Great is thy pow'r an' great thy fame; / Far ken'd an' noted is thy name', Burns, 'Address To The Deil' (1786).

Elphin Irving, the Fairies' Cupbearer

First published as 'The Twelve Tales of Lyddalcross. Tale the First. Elphin Irving, the Fairies' Cupbearer', *London Magazine*, 5, 25 (January 1822), 13–21. Unsigned.

[93] *motto*: these verses are from a version of the Tam Lin/Tamlane traditional Scottish ballad (Child 39). In the story, a mortal is rescued from fairy enchantment by the strength of a woman's love. Cunningham's tale borrows some of the motifs of the Tam Lin legend.

[94] *a follower of the camp*: civilians who form part of the entourage of an army, supplying the soldiers with goods or services. The 'interruption' here derives from 'The Twelve Tales of Lyddalcross' framing narrative that precedes the *London Magazine* version of this tale.

[95] *Fair Phemie Irving*: attributed to Cunningham in *Songs of Scotland*, IV (291–92) and *Poems and Songs* (103–04).

[96] *in maiden meditation fancy free*: A Midsummer Night's Dream, I. ii.

[97] *The Fairy Oak of Corriewater*: attributed to Cunningham in *Life of Cunningham*. The ballad draws on the Tam Lin legend, but the protagonists are changed to brother and sister to fit Cunningham's tale.

[98] *palmer's poke*: the bag or bundle carried by a traveller or pilgrim (the term is derived from the practice of carrying a palm from the Holy Land).

Richard Faulder, Mariner

First published as 'Traditional Literature. No. II. Richard Faulder of Allanbay', *London Magazine*, 3, 13 (January 1821), 26–32. Signed 'Lammerlea, Cumberland'.

[99] *motto*: attributed to Cunningham as 'The Mariner' in *Songs of Scotland*, IV (271).

[100] *the Scottish gate of Carlisle*: see 'The Death of Walter Selby' (72–73) for a description of the practice of placing the heads of traitors above Carlisle gate.

[101] *The Song of Richard Faulder*: attributed to Cunningham in *Songs of Scotland*, IV (312–13).

[102] *Contented wi' little and cantie wi' mair*: from the song of the same name by Burns (1794). Cunningham included the poem in *Songs of Scotland*, IV (93–94).

[103] *Sir Richard's Voyage*: probably by Cunningham. Both of the poems from this story were reprinted in Elizabeth Scott's anthology *Specimens of British Poetry* (1823). Scott includes a footnote which repeats the assertion of Cunningham's narrator that the second poem is 'the fragment of an old maritime ballad, part of which is still current among the seamen of Solway'.

[104] *the battle and the breeze*: from Thomas Campbell, 'Ye Mariners of England'. Cunningham included this poem in *Songs of Scotland*, IV (351–52).

[105] The *London Magazine* version omits the final sentence, and instead reads 'Now lend an ear to his romantic adventures'. This tale was the first to be published in the *London Magazine*, and was followed in the next two issues by 'Traditional Literature. No. III. Rhyme Legend of Richard Faulder, Mariner. Voyage in the Spectre Shallop' (a long ballad, not included in the collected edition) and 'Traditional Literature. No. IV. Tale of Richard Faulder, Mariner' (retitled 'The Last Lord of Helvellyn' for the collected edition). The focus on Faulder in the early magazine pieces reflects his prominence in the introduction to the series, and presents him as a recurring narrator (see Introduction, vii–xxv, and 'Traditional Literature. No. I', 307–317). In the collected version of *Traditional Tales*, Faulder has a much less prominent position, only appearing in the middle of the second volume.

The Last Lord of Helvellyn

First published as 'Traditional Literature. No. IV. Tale of Richard Faulder, Mariner', *London Magazine*, 3, 15 (March 1821), 255–63. Signed 'Lammerlea, Cumberland'.

[106] *motto*: probably by Cunningham. The *London Magazine* gives the source for this line as *'Old Ballad'*.

[107] *the shape of a barge, with a shroud for a sail*: this line is italicised in the *London Magazine* version.

[108] *Richard Faulder, arise […] without Richard Faulder!*: this passage is italicised in the *London Magazine* version.

[109] *Let the Lord of Helvellyn look long on the sea*: probably by Cunningham.

[110] *a wizard, whose name has not yet ceased to work marvels*: this passage is italicised in the *London Magazine* version. The wizard is perhaps Sir Michael Scott, the medieval Scottish magician who appears in Walter Scott's *The Lay of the Last Minstrel* (1805). Cunningham went on to write a novel, *Sir Michael Scott* (1828), in which he mentions the legend of the wizard cleaving the Eildon Hills into three.

[111] *The Maidens' Song*: probably by Cunningham.

[112] *What wouldest thou, William Forster […] valiant name of Forster*: this passage is italicised in the *London Magazine* version.

[113] *False and fathomless sea […] dainty morsel is at hand*: this passage is italicised in the *London Magazine* version.

[114] *Sam Dacre of Skiddawbeck*: appears as 'Sam Selby' in the *London Magazine* version. Cunningham presumably changed the name to avoid confusion with the Selbys of Cumberland trio of tales, which were published in later issues of the magazine.

[115] *them that will to Couper will to Couper*: what will be, will be. The saying refers to the town of Coupar, in Angus.

[116] *Michael Halmer's Song*: attributed to Cunningham as 'The Bride of Allanbay' in *Songs of Scotland*, IV (281–83).

[117] *Sir Marmaduke Maxwell*: eponymous hero of Cunningham's 1822 play.

[118] *Give the sail to the south-wind, thou mariner bold*: probably by Cunningham.

Judith Macrone, the Prophetess

First published as 'Traditional Literature. No. IX. Judith Macrone the Prophetess', *London Magazine*, 4, 21 (September 1821), 237–46. Signed 'Lammerlea, Cumberland'.

[119] *motto*: from *Marmaduke Maxwell*, V. v. The *London Magazine* version gives the source as 'Old Play'.

[120] *wading 'mang the mist*: 'For yet the sun was wading thro' the mist', from Allan Ramsay's play *The Gentle Shepherd*, I. i (1725).

[121] *O Annan runs smoothly atween its green banks*: probably by Cunningham.

[122] *Bonnie Mary Halliday*: this poem appears with an attribution to Cunningham in several Victorian anthologies. A variant titled 'Mary Halliday' is also included in *Poems and Songs* (120–21).

[123] *There's bonnie lads on fairy Nith*: probably by Cunningham.

The Ghost with the Golden Casket

First published as 'Traditional Literature. No. VIII. The Ghost with the Golden Casket', *London Magazine*, 4, 20 (August 1821), 129–36. Signed 'Lammerlea, Cumberland'.

[124] *motto*: from *Marmaduke Maxwell*, II. i. The *London Magazine* version gives the source as 'Old Play'.

[125] *the city doomed in Scripture*: in the Biblical prophecy of the destruction of the city of Tyrus (or Tyre) its ruined walls are used to dry fishing nets. See Ezekiel 26. 3–5.

[126] *the first ship ever Richard Faulder commanded*: see 'Richard Faulder, Mariner' (213n) for a discussion of the role of Faulder in Cunningham's tales.

[127] *Sir William Musgrave*: probably by Cunningham.

[128] *crooked timber*: nautical term describing curved pieces of wood used in the construction of ships. The phrase was also used by Kant: 'Out of the crooked timber of humanity, no straight thing was ever made', from *Idea for a Universal History with a Cosmopolitan Purpose* (1784).

[129] *Roodfair*: biannual festival held in May and September. 'Rood' refers to the symbol of the cross in Christian worship.

[130] *There's a cuttie stool in our Kirk*: seat of repentance in a church, often used to punish lapses in chastity (see 'Ezra Peden', 22n). References to the stool appear in a number of poems, including Robert Fergusson's 'The Farmer's Ingle' and Burns's 'The Fornicator'.

The Haunted Ships

First published as 'Traditional Literature. No. XI. The Haunted Ships', *London Magazine*, 4, 23 (November 1821), 499–507. Signed 'Lammerlea, Cumberland'. An abridged version of the story of the elves and Sandy Macharg, which forms part of this tale, is included in *Remains* (305–06).

[131] *motto*: from *Marmaduke Maxwell*, III. iv.

[132] *Richard Faulder, of Allanbay*: see 'Richard Faulder, Mariner' (201–213).

Death of the Laird of Warlsworm

First published as 'Tales of Lyddalcross. Tale Sixth. Death of the Laird of Warlsworm', *London Magazine*, 5, 30 (June 1822), 539–49. Unsigned.

[133] *John Lowe*: Scottish poet (1750–1798), most famous for 'Mary's Dream'. Cunningham wrote a pseudo-legendary version of the poem which he presented to Cromek, who printed both versions in *Remains* (362–65), comparing Cunningham's 'fake' favourably with Lowe's. In *Songs of Scotland*, Cunningham reprints both versions and adds a note in which he passionately defends the legitimacy of producing variations on popular songs, see *Songs of Scotland*, III (305–09).

[134] *the 'bonnie bower' of the two heroines of Scottish song*: a reference to the traditional ballad of Bessie Bell and Mary Gray. In an associated legend, the two girls die of the plague and have a bower erected over their grave. Cunningham incorporated a version of the poem into his essay 'Traditional Literature. No. I'

(see 307–317), and included two variants of the ballad in *Songs of Scotland*, III (58–61).

[135] *scriptural proverb*: 'But it is happened unto them according to the true proverb, The dog is turned to his own vomit again; and the sow that was washed to her wallowing in the mire' (2 Peter 2. 22).

[136] *beltan*: Beltane—see 'Honest Man John Ochiltree' (178n).

[137] *Him who sweetened the waters of Marah*: see Exodus 15. 23–26.

The Seven Foresters of Chatsworth

First published as 'The Seven Foresters of Chatsworth, An Ancient Derbyshire Ballad', *London Magazine*, 5, 26 (February 1822), 129–36. Unsigned. The ballad is probably predominantly of Cunningham's own composition, but has some thematic similarities to 'Johnie of Breadislee' (Child 114), which appears in *Songs of Scotland*, I (314–17). In this traditional ballad, the hero (also called Johnie Cock, Johnie O'Cox, or Johnie of Cockielaw in other variants), is chased by foresters through a deer-park. The poem also has a connection to 'The King of the Peak', in its device of an aristocratic Derbyshire lady (called Julia Vernon in this poem, and Dora Vernon in the earlier tale) who elopes with her lover.

[138] *Guadalquiver*: river in southern Spain.

Appendix A—Traditional Literature No. I

First published in *London Magazine*, 2, 12 (December 1820), 641–47. This essay was Cunningham's inaugural contribution to the *London Magazine*, and introduces the first set of stories that would go on to make up *Traditional Tales*.

[1] *motto*: from William Collins, 'Ode on the Popular Superstitions of the Highlands of Scotland'. Collins's poem was written between 1749 and 1750, and published posthumously in 1788.

[2] *God made the country, but man made the town*: from William Cowper, *The Task* (1785), Book I. Cunningham slightly misquotes the line, which reads 'God made the country, and man made the town'.

[3] *their food and raiment, of which they were worthy*: see Preface to *Traditional Tales* (111). This whole passage was reworked by Cunningham, and incorporated into his introduction to the collected edition.

[4] *that fleeting literature 'which not even critics criticize'*: i.e. newspapers—from Cowper, *The Task*, Book IV.

[5] *the prophet's rod*: the rods of Moses and Aaron were credited with miraculous powers before and during the Israelite Exodus.

[6] *our two popular critical journals*: the *Edinburgh Review* and the *Quarterly Review*. The *Edinburgh* was established in 1802, edited by Francis Jeffrey. The *Quarterly* was set up in London by John Murray in 1809, as a Tory counterpoint to the Whig *Edinburgh*.

[7] *D—— Nature! she deserves to be kicked*: possibly a corruption of the famous abnegation of naturalism delivered by the artist, Henry Fuseli: 'Damn Nature! she always puts me out'.

[8] *the illustrious warlock of Caledonia*: Walter Scott, known colloquially as the Wizard of the North.

[9] *the inimitable Froissart*: Jean Froissart (c.1337–c.1405)—medieval French historian.

[10] *Thurot's attack on Carrickfergus*: the Battle of Carrickfergus (1760) took place in Ireland during the Seven Years War. A small French force, under the command of François Thurot, captured the town from the British.

[11] *Richard Faulder, mariner, of Allanbay*: see Cunningham's story, 'Richard Faulder, Mariner' (201–213).

[12] *the rebellion of 1745*: the Jacobite rising of 1745 (often called the Forty-Five), was an attempt by Charles Edward Stuart (the Young Pretender) to regain the British throne.

[13] *the slaughter at Clifton*: the battle, or skirmish, at Clifton Moor in Cumbria was fought during the rising of 1745.

[14] *Macmoran's Mary*: a substantial reworking by Cunningham of the traditional song 'Glasgow Peggy' (Child 228).

[15] *honest Joseph Ritson*: Ritson (1752–1803) was a ballad collector who advocated editorial accuracy and minimal intervention in the treatment of traditional material.

[16] *Bessie Bell and Mary Gray*: Cunningham uses the first four lines of the traditional ballad (Child 201) as a starting point for his own more ornate version. This song is referred to in 'Death of the Laird of Warlsworm' (276) and Cunningham included two versions of the ballad in *Songs of Scotland*, v. 3 (58–61).

[17] *the history of the spectre steeds and warriors*: a description of this event is included in 'The Selbys of Cumberland. Part Second' (41–54).

Appendix B—The Twelve Tales of Lyddalcross. Introductory

First published in *London Magazine*, 5, 25 (January 1822), 5–13. This essay introduces the second set of stories that would go on to make up *Traditional Tales*. In the magazine version, the introductory essay immediately precedes the tale of 'Elphin Irving'.

[1] *motto*: probably by Cunningham.

[2] *witch-knots*: tangled knots of hair, supposedly made by witches and used in spells.

[3] *great wizard's eye*: Walter Scott. Cunningham makes a similar genuflection to Scott in the first of his essays, 'Traditional Literature. No. I' (307–317).

[4] *Ancram-moor*: The battle of Ancrum Moor (1545), fought during the Anglo-Scottish War of the Rough Wooing.

[5] *disuse, says the poet, will rust the brightest sword*: 'Keep up your bright swords, for the dew will rust them', *Othello*, I. ii.

[6] *the moping idiot, and the madman gay*: from George Crabbe, *The Village* (1783), Book I.

[7] *the blue gown mendicant*: a mendicant is a beggar or almsman, and the blue gown signified that the wearer was a King's Bedesman. Scott describes the order in the Introduction to the Magnum Opus edition of *The Antiquary* (1829): 'These Bedesmen are an order of paupers to whom the Kings of Scotland were in the custom of distributing a certain alms, in conformity with the

ordinances of the Catholic Church, and who where expected in return to pray for the royal welfare and that of the state'.

[8] *the impure pages of Paine*: Thomas Paine (1736–1809)—radical philosopher, pamphleteer and author of *The Rights of Man* (1791).

[9] *the Ballantyne press*: the Scottish printer James Ballantyne was a friend and business partner of Walter Scott. Ballantyne was involved in the printing, editing and publication of Scott's poetry and fiction, usually in partnership with other publishers.

[10] *The Auld Man*: probably by Cunningham.

[11] *the strife was between Bruce and Baliol*: Robert the Bruce and John Balliol contested the throne of Scotland in the late thirteenth century.

[12] *Queen Mab herself*: fairy queen, associated with dreams and the fulfilment of wishes. See *Romeo and Juliet*, I. iv.